BATTLEGROUND

Also by Terry A. Adams:

THE D'NEERAN FACTOR
(*Sentience | The Master of Chaos*)

BATTLEGROUND

BATTLEGROUND

TERRY A. ADAMS

DAW BOOKS, INC.

DONALD A. WOLLHEIM, FOUNDER

375 Hudson Street, New York, NY 10014

ELIZABETH R. WOLLHEIM
SHEILA E. GILBERT
PUBLISHERS

www.dawbooks.com

First Printing, October 2013

1 2 3 4 5 6 7 8 9

DAW TRADEMARK REGISTERED
U.S. PAT. AND TM. OFF. AND FOREIGN COUNTRIES
—MARCA REGISTRADA
HECHO EN U.S.A.

PRINTED IN THE U.S.A.

*Dedicated
with gratitude
to Patricia*

PART ONE

NEW EARTH

Chapter I

ON OLD EARTH, a man and a woman sat on a terrace in the first mild evening of not-quite-spring. Between them, on the flagstones at their feet, a baby slept in a cradle. The woman rocked it with her foot.

The woman had once been Lady H'ana ril-Koroth of D'neera. She now used only the offworld form of her first name—Hanna—and her birth name, Bassanio, as surname. She was well known, even infamous, by either name. She sometimes forgot she was D'neeran, but inescapably, she was; she was a telepath, and D'neera was the telepaths' world.

The man's name was Starr Jameson, and he had never seen any reason to use another. He had once been a great planet's representative to the Coordinating Commission of the Interworld Polity, and he missed it. He was now director of the Polity's Department of Alien Relations and Contact, answering to a commissioner himself. A commissioner had as much power as anyone could get in the societies of billions occupying human space. A director had none, except in that director's own department. Jameson still felt the change acutely. He had always liked power.

They were an unexpected couple, people said: the big light-skinned man with the face all angles; the woman dark, rather small, blue-eyed. It was said he was a little old for her, although that meant less than it would have at any other time in history; two hundred years was not, now, an especially long span of life.

The two were perceived, as a couple, to be somewhat reserved. They lived together, along with the baby, but in public appeared to be edgy colleagues rather than anything more.

In private, they made love often, with a passion that surprised them both.

They were not getting along particularly well, otherwise. Jameson had recently compared Hanna—to her face—to something that might finally stop itching if you scratched it just one more time.

The child was her son. Jameson was not its father. The baby's father had died violently, before Hanna's eyes and, worse, in the full presence of her thought. She still mourned.

Jameson was growing accustomed (without liking it) to the flow of her emotions, when she chose to project them. She was doing so now. A balance was moving, he thought. There was a sense of tenuous peace slowly supplanting deep grief, which was as good as it got with Hanna; but there was also a new restlessness.

It was not a welcome thought. Not long ago she had turned her back on everything she had achieved and gone outlaw for a time, seduced to it by the man now dead.

Jameson looked up from the reader he had been studying and said, "What is it, Hanna?"

"I don't quite know . . ."

Her son woke and began to fuss. She leaned over and picked him up. Her hands—small hands, experienced in imposing sudden death—caressed the baby's soft cheeks.

"I think," she said, "it's just that there is nothing new . . ."

On New Earth, where a human colony had been misplaced and recently rediscovered, the Polity's Colonial Oversight and Protection Service had been busy for some months. The New Earth Task Force's historian had recently turned her attention to the colony's archives. Today she skimmed a document like nothing she had ever seen before—here or anywhere. She asked the native archivist about it: yes, he knew the document she meant. No, there was nothing else like it in the files. He had been curious when he ran across it himself. He had looked.

Later, when there was time, the historian showed the report to her commanding officer. The older woman read it and said, "I think Alien Relations and Contact should see this, don't you?"

"Of course. I've never made a report to them, though. Do you know what the channels are?"

"Oh, never mind channels," the officer said. "I know Starr Jameson slightly. I'll see that it goes straight to him."

On Battleground, which its inhabitants called by a name that meant "the World," there was war.

Chapter II

SOME WEEKS LATER, when it was really spring, Hanna went to Contact's primary suite in Polity Admin's central tower. Jameson had told her the night before (late, very late) that he had something interesting to show her. "No hurry, though," he had said.

She had taken him at his word. He was the most self-contained human being she had ever known, and not just outwardly; only rarely could she sense a thought or an emotion naturally projected, and he knew her telepathic touch too well for her to skim his thoughts undetected. Like most ordinary humans, he disliked telepathy intensely, perceiving it as a threat and an invasion. And anyway, at the time, there had seemed to be plenty of night left. He had pulled her to him again, and she had turned her attention willingly to other demands.

Now one of his aides, the dark woman Zanté, smiled at Hanna and said, "Conference. He's almost done, though. Do you have time to wait?"

Here Jameson was Hanna's superior just as he was Zanté's.

"A little," she answered, and sat down.

The offices of Alien Relations and Contact were on the fortieth floor of this cloud-piercing tower. An ancient river lapped at its foundations. From where Hanna waited, the far edge of the river — gray under an early April sky — ended at low bluffs and hills, heavily populated but blurred in the haze from just-ended rain. Hanna had been here so often that she looked at the clouded scene with the appreciation of one contemplating an artist's vision of home.

Presently Jameson came to the inner door and said, "Nothing better to do?"

"I have a Level One class starting in half an hour. Nothing until then. You spoke of something I should see?"

They went in and sat on opposite sides of Jameson's desk, acknowledging their respective positions. Hanna was never quite comfortable in this daunting room, where beautiful, irreplaceable old furnishings hid batteries of data displays that tracked relations with sentient nonhuman species almost minute by minute. Here, she was always aware that Jameson had once been used to having almost absolute power, he was determined to have it again, and he carried himself as if it were a certainty. In the abstract, she could resent that. In his presence, always, she was seduced by his strength—body, mind, will—and by her knowledge of qualities he preferred to hide. He did not give much of himself away, even to Hanna, but at times when grief and loneliness had seemed all that was left for her, when sobs like seizures shook her body and burst out in inhuman sounds, he had comforted her without reservation. She had loved him deeply once—years ago. She did not mean to love him again.

". . . a rather strange report," he was saying. "A possible opening for a first contact. I want to know what you make of it."

"Something that might require a telepath?" she said "But you would have told me sooner if you thought it important."

"That's because if the incident happened at all, it was two Standard centuries ago."

"And?"

Hanna folded her hands in her lap and waited. Over time she had come to appreciate Jameson's style of analyzing and presenting fact and theory. Whatever he had to say would be worth the exercise of some patience.

"We are back to Lost Worlds," he said.

"I am sick of Lost Worlds," she muttered.

"I know . . ."

Jameson had plenty to do on the Alien Relations side of his job, but lately he had been fighting for Contact's life. During a period that extended from seven to five hundred years before the present, human beings had fled Earth for the stars in such numbers that the era was now called the Explosion. Many expeditions had vanished from history, their ends unknown. But two lost human colonies were now certainly known to exist to the present day, and Contact's tiny exploration fleet was in danger of being redirected completely to search for signs of human habitation.

He shrugged; he even seemed rather pleased. "I've just gotten agreement for the *Endeavor* fleet to place equal emphasis on Contact and the search for colonies," he said. "That's better than it might have been. How much can I argue when the issue is one of rescuing human beings? And really, Hanna, we would not now be building *Endeavor Three* if it were not for the outcry over colonies. *One's* refit is nearly finished; soon all three will be in space. Meanwhile we're left with—what we have. And what we have is an old, but very clear, sighting from New Earth."

"I haven't paid much attention to New Earth," she said. "It prospered, I understand."

"Very much so. That was one of the best-run and best-documented of the settlement ventures. It was mounted near the end of the Explosion, and the organizers had studied their predecessors' mistakes. Their equipment and supplies were of the very highest quality. The settlers were of mixed social classes, but the aim was egalitarian, and they did not start out with, nor develop, the rigid class division you found on Gadrah, and which proved so disastrous there. A friend in Oversight told me last week, by the way, that there is little hope for Gadrah."

Hanna had been thinking of a return to Gadrah—only to see it once more, never to stay—since the baby's birth. Her son's father had been a native of Gadrah, had returned and died there; the child's aunt was there. So was a grave on a mountainside. But going there would not get her back the part of her heart that was in that grave. Best not to think of that—

She said, "So New Earth should never have become a Lost World."

"No. Except New Earth isn't New Earth."

She looked at him in exasperation. "You are being deliberately obscure again—"

"The New Earth settlers never got to their original destination," he said. "When they stumbled across the world that is now New Earth, they didn't plan on staying there. The planet had been missed by the independent explorers, and the expedition stopped long enough to document it carefully. There was no relay system in place then, not that far out. The Polity was in its youth, the Interworld Fleet not yet under a central command. Without relays they could not report the find—"

He paused and looked at her doubtfully. He could not understand her lack of interest in history, and was often uncertain of what she knew.

Well, so was Hanna.

"I did know that," she said. "So they documented it and went on. And?"

"Their Inspace systems began to fail. First-rate equipment, as I said, but not as capable of self-diagnosis and self-repair as today's. Their technicians were good, but even now a failure of the kind they had requires assistance and resources from outside. And they could get none. There was no way to call for help."

"So they turned back?"

"And returned to the planet now called New Earth. They were lucky to make it there.

"They didn't give up their original plan at first, all the same. They established a temporary, provisional settlement while they continued to attempt repairs. Finally they acknowledged there was no choice. They brought down the remaining settlers, the breeding stock and seeds—everything flourished there, not at all the way it was on Gadrah—"

(*The rats did well there,* Hanna thought, remembering sounds in broken walls.)

"—the dwellings, the factories for basic needs, and all the rest—and left their mothership in orbit. It's still there; the mayday it transmits is the signal *Endeavor Two* picked up. And *Two* found a self-sustaining colony—agrarian, of course, but doing very nicely.

"When Colonial Oversight arrived—in a hurry, I assure you—"

—*and with what delight you can imagine,* said his thought—

"—their historian found remarkably good archives. New Earth has had fine data storage from the start. Unfortunately from our point of view, it's heavily biased toward public records, crop reports, legal proceedings, that sort of thing. Understandable. But there's very little in the way of personal memoirs, or reference back to a larger society with which, of course, they had no contact.

"And Oversight found a report, nearly two hundred years old, which states clearly that New Earth was visited by nonhumans. I've had it transmitted to your office."

He paused, and she said, "Tell me more . . ."

"You're out of time. You have a class, I think?"

She shook her head at him, not even bothering to swear, and went to class.

———

In fact, she taught all the classes in Alien Relations' new Contact Education Division, and all three met today. In the intervals she slipped back to her rooms, skimmed the report Jameson had sent her, and spent some time editing it to essentials and resolving some ambiguities in language. The colonists had left Earth before the newborn Polity mandated Standard as the language throughout human space. The colonists' language of choice had been English, however. It had not been the native tongue for all of them, but all of them spoke it. English—a rich and flexible tool with the largest vocabulary of any language Earth had ever produced—had also been the foundation for Standard. Jameson could have told her in detail how it got that way—conquest and assimilation, mostly—but the salient point was that New Earth and Colonial Oversight had communicated readily from the first, and translation programs for the written word were already good. But not perfect.

———

She meant, at the end of the day, to study the report intensively, but was interrupted by a student so distressed that his hands were shaking.

"Can I talk to you?" he asked—meaning more than talk, because like her he was D'neeran, a telepath.

Of the fifteen men and women who had actually finished Hanna's recently established program, only four were D'neeran, all of those except Bella Qu'e'n now attached to Contact's *Endeavor* vessels. Hanna kept closely in touch with all four.

"Come in, Hal," she said gently. "What happened?"

He showed her an image of himself on Admin's concourse, enjoying the view of the river between rain showers. And an image of the couple who passed by and the man glancing his way. Hal did not know the man, but evidently at some time Hal had been pointed out to him as a—

D'neeran! spat the man's thought—*filthy, snooping telepath!*

I know, Hanna answered.

H'ana, I couldn't help it, I know you tell us not to react but I couldn't help it, I looked at him, that's all, just looked at him, and H'ana, he wanted to kill me!

I know, she said again; took him into the embrace of her thought and soothed him, showing him again what she had gone through in her own first immersion in true-human society, not as long ago as it seemed. Things were even a little better now.

Routine teaching duties, she thought after he left.

She had gone through this with all her D'neeran students. A dozen more had started it, besides the successful four. But most could not endure what true-humans thought of them even with all the solace she could give them, and relinquished their hopes and fled home. She did not think Hal would finish the course.

She had not let him see that, though. In theory, she should not have been able to hide it from him. But she was a telepathic Adept, one of a rare class even on her own world. And in some part of her brain forever subtly, materially changed, she had acquired an immense power from the group mind of the alien People of Zeig-Daru—the power to block as much of her thought as she wished from any human telepath.

No one except Starr Jameson knew this, and there was another thing she had not told even him (though he must suspect). While she taught her students how to keep from slipping into true-humans' thoughts uninvited—difficult for a D'nceran—and how, in the interests of harmony, they should never, ever attempt to probe those thoughts, she had long since dispensed with her own scruples. If true-humans wanted to lie to her explicitly or by omission, she had decided, they were fair game.

———

The document was headed simply:

"Report to Archives.

"I'm writing this because our grandchildren might want to know about it someday.

"*This place, the town of Dwar on New Earth, has been visited by nonhumans.*

"*There were only a few of them and they only stayed a few days. They didn't show any sign of hostility but they didn't respond to friendly overtures, either. Mostly they just walked around and looked at things. They seemed to prefer to sit under trees and talk to each other most of the time. Maybe this was some kind of rest stop for them. I said there were only a few, but that could mean we only saw a few at a time, not necessarily the same ones every time. They looked so strange to us that they would have had to stay longer for us to learn to tell them apart. And they were here, or some were here, two or three times a day, with gaps in between, so maybe they were on some kind of rotation. We assume they were using a shuttle, unless there's some way to build a starship small enough to land on a planet. Earth couldn't, when our ancestors left, but they said it wouldn't be long, so why couldn't somebody else?*

"*Anyway, they came down in the meadowland out past Li Chen's farm. Nobody saw the first landing, but once we knew what to look for we could see their craft coming and going from there, and after they left we went over to look, and that was obviously the place they used for landing.*

"*We talked about them a lot while they were here, and we've talked about them since. This is a consensus report, so I'm including everything that everybody saw.*

"*It doesn't seem like much now. A lot of us tried as best we could, with gestures and single words, to start some kind of language exchange, but they just flapped their ears at us and walked away. Same thing when we tried drawing pictures. Same thing when we offered them food. We have no idea what it meant when they flapped those ears, which they did with each other, too. Maybe it meant they were laughing.*

"*I don't know how far we could have gotten in a language exchange anyway, because I don't think we could make the same sounds they do. Maybe because of the way their mouths are made, a lot of the language we heard when they were talking to each other consisted of whistling. They use clicks, too, almost as much as the whistling. They do use words (we assume they were words) along with that, though. It's really kind of a musical language to listen to, but I don't think a human being could ever speak it.*

"I guess the best thing I can do is explain what they looked like. We're agreed on that.

"They're shaped like human beings, but slender and taller than we are, at least these were all taller than any of us, by maybe thirty centimeters on the average. Arms and legs proportionate by our standards to the human head and torso, but there seem to be extra joints, or more versatile ones than we have, judging by the way they walk and point at things. It makes them look graceful and it made us wonder what kind of dances they have. They have a head covering similar to human hair in different shades of brown, but it's thin, sparse. You wouldn't think it would give much protection from the weather, but nobody ever saw one wear a hat. Of course, it was summer, and we didn't have much rain while they were here.

"Under the forehead there are what look like two bony plates most of the time, but a few responsible, truthful people saw the plates slide up and roll back one time, in one individual, and there were eyes under them, although they must not use that pair often. Maybe when they want to get a really good look at something.

"Under that there's a pair of regular eyes. They come in different colors, but they're all on the light side, gray or yellowish. They don't seem to have pupils, so we don't have any idea what the mechanism is for seeing. There isn't any equivalent of a human nose on the face, which is all eyes and mouth. Their mouths seem to be perfectly round. Several people got a glimpse of teeth, not white like ours but black or dark gray, and they have flexible tongues, the impression being that those are longer and thinner than ours.

"Their ears are where you'd expect them to be, but stretched out they're huge—as I said, flapping them seems to be part of the way they communicate. Most of the time, though, they keep them folded toward the backs of their heads. The ears move around a lot, but they're only completely unfolded for that flapping. All the individuals we saw, by the way, had shades of grayish-brown skin. None of them were anywhere near as dark as some of our people.

"But their noses! If I may interject a personal comment, their noses—I have to call them that, they obviously function for breathing—were the most surprising thing of all to me. They've got one on each side of the neck, finger-shaped but short, sort of curved to fit the neck and attached there like tubes, *and the tips are flexible too, though nothing like the ears—the tubes just seem to expand and contract with the breath, and they each have three openings at the front. They might connect directly to lungs, bypassing the gullet, but there's no way to know, and no way to know what they use for a larynx or how air gets to it or how it works.*

"Their hands look surprisingly like ours—four fingers, although proportionately longer and with an extra joint, opposable thumbs, ditto. Nobody ever saw their feet. That I know of.

"The rest of this report is not consensus. I want to make that clear.

"I heard a rumor that one of the nonhumans, just one, had been seen coming out of the woods with Mi-o Roland, who is about twelve in Earth years, so I went to ask her about it. That did happen—it was her mother who saw them. If I didn't know better, I would suspect they had been having some kind of sex. Mi-o is said to be somewhat advanced for her age in that respect. Anyway, Mi-o's mother was there, and Mi-o wouldn't answer any questions with a yes or no, unless a giggle means one thing or the other. I wish I had recorded that conversation! Mi-o did seem to be implying that that's exactly what they had been doing. But she wouldn't come out and admit it, so even if she knows what's under those creatures' boots and baggy coveralls, the rest of us might never find out.

"Maybe she said more to her mother, though, because when Ms. Roland walked me outside, she asked if I thought a nonhuman could get a human pregnant. I told her it was genetically impossible.

"Respectfully submitted by Maya Selig. Sworn statements from forty-seven citizens attached."

Hanna sat back and muttered, "Thank you very much for nothing, Maya Selig."

On reflection, though, the people of Dwar had done the best they could with damn little to start with. In fact, they had done an excellent job.

It was late. Hanna made a quick meal in her office and went home.

———

There were three people in Jameson's study when she went in, one of them Jameson. The second was three months old going on four; he lay on his stomach on the floor, pushing at it to get his head up in the air so he could look around in a wobbly way, his eyes huge with pleasure and surprise. The third was Thera August. She loved lecturing adults on the minutiae of infant development, and since Hanna was not much interested, and Jameson was, he would do.

Thera was arguably the best child companion in human space. She had lived in the homes of the rich and powerful for a hundred and twenty years, and had been on the point of comfortable retirement when she agreed to come to Jameson for reasons lost in an obscure skein of family and political relationships. In her long career she had heard more secrets than an entire espionage network could have gathered, and she had never divulged one of them. She was not a friend and she was not a servant. Although paid (well), she was not exactly an employee, either. She was an independent, completely liberated planet. She was not the tribe of relatives and neighbors who would have helped care for a baby on Hanna's homeworld, but she was not (the option Hanna had violently rejected) a perfectly programmed, humanlike servo, either. She was one of the rewards that came with the kind of old wealth Jameson had inherited with the family estate on Heartworld, and Hanna had been in no position to turn this favor down.

She went straight to the baby and dropped to the floor and picked him up. He chuckled and reached for her face, and she covered his with kisses. He smelled sweet and fresh and it was some time before she paid attention to the adults in the room.

"I can take him with me tomorrow," she said to Thera, "for the morning at least. There's a holo conference with F'thal in the afternoon. Not that he'd be disruptive. Just distracting—last time they started bragging about their own young and we never got back to the agenda."

"I doubt he'll ever be deliberately disruptive," Thera said. "You can tell a lot about personality by this stage. This one is going to be sunlight."

Like his father, Hanna thought.

She kissed her son again and looked at him, determined to focus only on his own, individual face. How unfair it would be to seek resemblances! He was not Michael Kristofik all over again; he was Michael Bassanio, unique, himself, and Hanna would not even call him by his formal name. He was Mickey: the future, not the past.

Hanna held herself to this standard by an effort of will because the past was still close as her breath. Mickey's father had died a little more than twelve Standard months ago, though the anniversary itself, blessedly, had meant nothing to her. A year of twelve Standard months was not a year on her native world; it certainly was not a year on Gadrah, where seasons stretched through far more days than in other places where humans lived. The preceding fall in this hemisphere on Earth had been harder, because it had been autumn in the place where Michael had left her. He had not meant to die, it was true. But sometimes that did not seem to make a difference.

Perhaps, she still thought sometimes, *I will take Mickey and flee always ahead of fall, spend my life in springs and summers.*

But it would be wrong to do that to him. I must give him a lasting home, if I can.

She looked at her son's happy face and thought that Michael must have been an infant like this. She knew his childhood had been secure and safe, full of work but full of love. Until he was about ten.

Then came the rest of it.

She whispered, "That will never happen to you, Mickey."

Because she would kill for her son. She did not think: die for him—because she simply wouldn't die. She would go on killing and killing, until everybody who might hurt this child as his father had been hurt was just—gone.

Chapter III

*O*N BATTLEGROUND, *there was war. There had always been war. There would always be war. There had never been anything else and there never would be.*

The being the humans would call Kwoort did not entertain a thought that it might be otherwise. Kakrekt might, but she did not tell anyone. Especially not the enemy and its Demon High Commander, Kwoort.

On Old Earth, Starr Jameson requested further information from New Earth. Knowing bureaucrats well, he was specific about what kinds of information he wanted and how to go about finding it.

Sometimes, when Hanna wasn't looking, he rocked Mickey's cradle himself. Wondering, as he did, why he discouraged Hanna's suggestions that it was time she and Mickey made a home of their own. Wondering if the quiet of his house would one day be empty instead of restful, without Hanna's voice, without Mickey.

But certain political currents were shifting, and soon he would be too busy to notice that they were gone.

Of course he would.

On New Earth, the archivist ran the specified searches. They were without result. He reported the fact with some relief. He had too much work already without legendary Earth sticking its nose in farther than it already was.

And on Old Earth, Hanna Bassanio said grimly, "I'm going to have to go out there."

Chapter IV

HANNA HAD HUNTED (and been hunted) in a variety of modes, but this one was new.

The first part of it was simple enough, if frustrating. To begin with, there were restrictions on her movements, a reminder that officially, thanks to her foray outside Polity law, she was an accused felon, however leniently treated and however silken her prison's walls. At this time she was allowed to leave Earth only on demonstrably official business for Alien Relations and Contact; she had not even been allowed to go home to D'neera for Mickey's birth. Jameson managed to get permission for her to go to New Earth, though, with no more than routine bureaucratic delay. But permission for Mickey to accompany her was denied, as assurance that she would return.

Then, having no access to a vessel she could pilot herself—Jameson did not even bother trying to get someone to loan her one—she had to wait a month until an Oversight transport going to New Earth could take her there. In the interval she sometimes thought wistfully of the years when Jameson was Heartworld's representative to the Coordinating Commission of the Interworld Polity, one of the most important beings in human space. He could certainly get things done quickly then!

"I'm somewhat more limited now," he said when she complained. He was smiling, she noticed. He had almost never smiled in those days.

"What, no more government-funded star-going yachts at your disposal?"

"I miss the yacht," he admitted.

Since he might still be a commissioner if it had not been for Hanna (leaving aside the fact that she had, at a crucial moment, blown up the yacht) this was a sore point for her. *He* put it down to routine political upheaval, a minor swirl in the currents of history. Either way, she didn't bring it up again.

In any case, it meant she had time to get Bella Qu'e'n, her prize pupil and a D'neeran, detached from Bella's current job and trained to replace Hanna for the uncertain duration. The detaching was easy—graduates of Hanna's program were understood to be on call for Contact, and Bella now headed a similar program of studies that Hanna herself had initiated, several years before, on their native world. Harder was convincing Bella, who had a thicker (mental) skin than most of her kind, that she would have to resign herself to holding some students' hands.

Eventually Hanna was taken aboard the Colonial Oversight ship for the three-week flight to New Earth, and immediately found herself at odds with reality.

This spacecraft was much larger than Michael Kristofik's *Golden Girl* had been. But the isolation and confinement of all spaceships was fundamentally the same. You were as dependent on the functioning of a complex artifact as a fetus on the womb it inhabited; however clean the air you knew it subtly as re-breathed, and there were literal limits to how far you could walk in any direction. The transport therefore *felt* like Michael's *GeeGee,* and much of Hanna's time with Michael had been lived in space. Now, often, it seemed he must be just out of sight, that she could go into the corridor and he would be standing there, face alight at seeing her, arms open as she went to him. She found herself weeping again; the uncontrollable bursts of tears had stopped for a while. She did not know how long it would be before they stopped altogether, or if they ever would.

She had experienced other deaths firsthand, but that one—the sudden death of the man she loved wholly, while she was fully engaged with his mind and emotions—had been destructive beyond belief. The detachment of the Adept trance had been the only thing, probably, that saved her from dying when Michael did. Afterward there had been nothing to shield her from her own sorrow and anger—even when she was taken back to Earth, not quite in chains, and took shelter with Starr Jameson.

Temporarily, she had said, but she was still there, and so was the unexpected rage at Michael for abandoning her in death. She tried not to redirect it at Jameson, usually succeeded, occasionally failed. He appeared not to notice her fury, but he had to when she threw things at him. He ducked, and remained calm. Her anger did not move him and he would not pity her.

Over the course of some ten years he had been—at one time or another or simultaneously—her lover, superior, colleague, nemesis, mentor, protector, friend. Hanna had never gotten anywhere trying to pin down what he was to her and had given up trying.

It did not help that he could stir her sexually with one calculated touch.

She talked to him often during the flight. She made sure no tears were visible, and she didn't tell him reality was shaky. When he was at home for these conversations he brought Mickey to the viewer, and held up the baby's tiny fist and made waving motions with it, and did all the stupid things adults did on such occasions. He didn't say anything stupid, though. Hanna thought he had probably never said a stupid thing in his life.

This occupied very little of the three weeks. It took much less time to get to more remote destinations in space, the space-time laws governing Inspace transit having an entirely counterintuitive relation to those directing three dimensions. A shorter way to New Earth—meaning a shorter interval in time—might be found someday, but now Hanna, trying to anchor herself in what was instead of what had been, had too much time on her hands.

Work helped. She had learned that when, without much choice about it, she had taken over Contact Education—

(She had hardly spoken in weeks. Her voice sounded rusty.

"Contact—education? I can't."

"You can. Let me give you the reasons why you will. Bodily assault on an operative of Intelligence and Security. Conspiring and aiding in holding him against his will. Conspiring and aiding in setting him adrift in deep space with no life support but a spacesuit—"

"He was not adrift! He was securely fastened to a relay structure and I gave Fleet his exact location within minutes!"

"The charge will not mention that. You will also be charged as accessory to everything Michael Kristofik would have been charged with if he had lived. I won't recite the list. It was too long to memorize. Ask yourself why you are here instead of in a cell."

"You. You are using your influence to protect me. Again."

"Nobody has that much influence! No human individual. The full Commission might—if someone influences them."

Silence.

"Ask me who can do that, Hanna."

She said grudgingly, "Who."

It was better than the night before, when he had remarked that Michael Kristofik had not been unambiguously heterosexual. She had said, "He was not ambiguous with me*," and savagely hurled a teacup at his head.*

"Relations with the nations of Uskos are of paramount importance to the Commission. At the moment Norsa of Ell is one of the most important beings on Uskos. He is therefore extremely important to the Commission. It would make Norsa unhappy to see you imprisoned—"

"You cannot imprison me. I was made a citizen of the nation of Ell."

"Norsa has made that clear. There is Personality Adjustment, however."

Silence. And fear.

"Whereas it would make Norsa happy, and would therefore make all the Commissioners happy, to see you heading the new division. Think about it, Hanna."

Silence. But the sullen blue glare was an answer.)

—so Hanna worked. She had begun studying New Earth's language before leaving Old Earth, a minimal challenge for someone who had had to become fluent in three alien tongues, and now she practiced it, and added a study of Oversight's files on New Earth. She was not going to be welcomed there, at least not by Oversight. She was going as a functionary of another government department, one now locked in a power struggle with Oversight over resources: search for aliens, or search for lost colonies? She knew she could not make them forget that, but at least she could demonstrate respect for their work by demonstrating knowledge of it. Besides, the knowledge might come in handy when she got there.

When she did, though, Oversight wasn't the problem.

The Oversight historian was friendly, in fact. She was Amir Almond, a native of Earth, a slight Asian woman, a little hesitant at first. She said they needed to talk before Hanna went to meet with the archivist.

They sat outdoors in a warm shower of sunlight, in front of the building where Almond had her office. This was an interim outpost, not designed to be permanent, but the buildings that housed offices, laboratories, and dwellings did not look flimsy.

"The New Earth population pays attention to its towns," Almond said when Hanna commented. "We didn't want to put up something ugly. Functional, yes. Grotesque, no."

"Thoughtful ... Have the people been pleased about getting back in contact with Earth? I know their historical knowledge of Earth ended pre-Polity."

"They have a lot of catching up to do, but they're very pleased. On the whole." Amir sighed. "Of course, the very first thing we had to do was tell them about the Plague Years and say, by the way, Plague's still around, so here's your vaccine, now drink it down like good little colonists ... !"

Hanna laughed, but without humor. "I saw what Plague did to Gadrah. Although I knew it as Dawkins' Fever."

"Yes, that's its other name. The original name. You ... ?" Amir looked at her curiously. Comprehension came into her eyes.

"Oh!" she said. "That was you!"

"Yes, I was there."

"Some of my colleagues haven't forgiven you yet for getting there before us ... !"

Amir's lips curved, but Hanna said, "There were five of us." *On the run.* "We were only trying to survive. One of us didn't make it. But not because of Plague."

Amir seemed not to have noticed her change in mood.

"Did you know you're a case study?" she asked.

"What, the five of us on Gadrah? An Oversight how-not-to-do-it study, or something?"

"No, no! You personally. In a medical text. It came up when I was talking to a physician friend once about cross-infection from alien species. He said there was only one known case. You got a knife cut on Zeig-Daru and it became infected, am I correct?"

It had happened on a Zeigan spacecraft in a knife fight to the death.

"Close enough."

"Topical infection of subject's right arm. Something like that."

"Amir, they had to take my arm apart and regenerate out from the bone! Does that sound like a topical infection to you?"

Amir thought something like, *Oops!*

Hanna sighed. "Amir, I'm sorry. These things we've been talking about—I have some bad memories. Can we talk about something else? What did you want to see me about before I go to the archives?"

"The archivist," Amir said. She almost patted the bench beside her, a subliminal soothing motion. Hanna had gotten up at some point, at one of the painful jabs to memory, without being aware of it. She went back and sat down again.

Amir said, "He's really a nice man—one of those big-bear types. Loves his archives. And his tea—oh, my, how he loves his tea! He made the jump to Standard right away, and the translation programs for the archives got done twice as fast as they would have without his help. He's been grumbling a little lately. Sort of growling! I don't think," she laughed, "he was used to working quite so hard, especially over such a sustained period. He wasn't really pleased when your department's request came in. 'What!' " Amir tried to growl. " 'On top of all this other extra work I have to do these days?' You know the attitude I mean?"

"I certainly do. I've felt that way myself from time to time."

"I guess we all have. Anyway, he wasn't thrilled about your coming here, but he was prepared to be helpful. Until last night."

Amir was suddenly wary. Something in Hanna twitched. She said, "What exactly happened last night?"

"Someone dropped a remark—well, it was me, actually.

Just in passing. I said, oh, by the way, the woman who's coming is D'neeran. And he said, what's that? So I explained about D'neera."

"And he hates me," Hanna said.

"Well, yes."

Even though she was forewarned, Chain Charpentier's hostility hit Hanna like a fist. She stammered for the first time in years, and she was only trying to introduce herself.

"I know who you are," he said. He thought: *I know what you are, too.*

"Mr. Charpentier," she said, "what do you think I am?"

"That!" he said triumphantly. A stubby forefinger poked at the air in her direction. "You read my mind just now. Didn't you?"

"Mr. Charpentier," she said, "I could hardly help it. Do you know how strongly you're projecting? Would you kindly stop projecting? And may I have a cup of tea?"

"I'm doing *what?*" he said, and added, "I'm not working with you. And no tea!"

The tea-making apparatus was in a corner of the archivist's office. Hanna went to it, calculating dates in her head. The ancestors of these people, otherwise apparently free of prejudice, had left Earth at a time when hostility to telepaths had become vicious. And nothing had happened to their descendants here, in their isolation, to add to their knowledge or change their minds.

Hanna started to make tea. Charpentier, stunned by the effrontery, did not protest because he was briefly speechless. Hanna decided to take advantage of his silence. She did know some history: her own.

"Mr. Charpentier," she said, "I would like to tell you a story. I ask only that you listen."

Without turning to look at him, or waiting for a response, she began.

"My many-times-great grandmother was named Constanzia Bassanio. She was born on Earth, and she was a member of the first completely telepathic generation. Whatever plans the governments of Earth had for telepaths when they started the so-called New-Human Genetic Project had been dropped. They were already afraid of what they saw in people like Constanzia's mother and father. They were terrified of children like Constanzia. And that fear seeped into the population of Earth like poison."

He wasn't interrupting, at least.

"By the time Constanzia was six, no one identified as a telepath was safe anywhere on Earth. Many were murdered. So were others who were not telepaths; it was enough to point a finger and shout 'New-human!' and a mob would form.

"The governments of Earth built an enclave—a sanctuary, they called it—and moved the entire population of the New-Human Project into it. There were fifty to sixty thousand people there, all telepaths. Except the guards. They had to be true-human, because it's hard for telepaths to learn to fight. We feel other people's pain. And that first generation had not learned to block, even when it meant the difference between surviving and—not."

Charpentier had not moved. The tea was ready. Hanna filled two mugs and set them on the small table nearby. She still did not look at Charpentier, and she didn't stop talking either.

"Constanzia spent her entire childhood and adolescence in that enclave. Conditions were humane, but if she wanted to go out, she had to have an armed true-human escort. In time, people stopped asking to go out. At some point the guards had begun to feel that they were not guarding the telepaths from true-humans, but the other way around."

Hanna sat down and sipped tea.

"All this guarding was getting expensive. So the governments of Earth built another enclave, this one on Earth's airless moon, where there was no population to guard against—or to guard. Earth's satellite keeps one face always to the planet, a spectacular sight. I've seen it. But the enclave was built deep inside. The people in it never saw the home they had been torn from, and they never saw the sun.

"This enclave was segregated by gender. The governments of Earth were afraid to kill some sixty thousand people outright. There would have been a terrible outcry, even with the endemic hatred of telepaths. But this way the problem would, so to speak, die out. No more telepathic children, no more problem. And meanwhile the entire population was well away from Earth.

"The governments of Earth were so used to guarding, however, that they kept it up. It couldn't have been easy for the guards, either. A telepath doesn't just tell you he's in pain; he makes you feel it with him. But by then the character of the true-humans chosen to be guards had by necessity changed. They were selected, so to speak, to be impervious to the suffering of others. At least that. I will not say they were chosen specifically to enjoy it. But many of them, it appears, did.

"The first weeks were terrible. The guards could not stand the bombardment of emotion. They urgently needed to force the captives to stop projecting their fear and grief, their loneliness at being separated from spouses and lovers and children, and they turned to violence. Many people were beaten, including Constanzia. It's said she was badly scarred.

"It's hard to keep beating innocent people if you see them as people, so steps were taken to make the people seem less human. They cut off Constanzia's lovely hair and shaved her scalp. The family story says her hair was much like mine, black as space, and that she wore it long, as I do. The story says she even looked like me—and perhaps she did, but no images from those days survive.

"That phase didn't last long. The governments of Earth found a solution: the telepaths' water supply was infused with strong sedatives.

"And that was supposed to be the end of it—all the telepaths half-awake, half-asleep, until the last of them died."

Chain Charpentier suddenly came to the table and sat down. He said, "This must have been just after my ancestors left. How did yours get out?"

"With the help of good people," Hanna said. "And they were true-humans.

"They were wealthy, but not wealthy enough to fund a settlement ship. It wasn't a settlement ship that went to D'neera, but a strung-out fleet, one ship at a time, as the rescuers scrambled for the money to buy them. Worse than that: fertile, Earth-like planets were in high demand. In return for giving up such a lovely piece of real estate, the governments of Earth, or corrupt officials, required payment for each and every refugee allowed to leave, even the smallest infant, even the unborn child Constanzia was carrying. There was a price on each of my ancestors' heads, Mr. Charpentier.

"Not all the ships made it to D'neera. There was no one in the Lunar enclave experienced in spaceflight, and there was time only for hasty, last-minute training. Desperation training. There was a time limit, you see. An amnesty period, the governments of Earth called it . . .

"Not everyone on Luna got off, either. Some of them died there, after many years, drugged and alone," she said, and saw Charpentier shudder.

"The order of departure was fixed by lottery. Constanzia was one of the last to make it out. But—would you like to hear a happy ending to one story, Mr. Charpentier? Constanzia and the man she loved had conceived a child just before the removal to Luna. On the very night before it began, it's said. She was pregnant all those months in the deeps of the moon. And her lover found her on the last ship, and he was there when the next of my line, their daughter Melisande, was born. They went on to have two more children, both sons, and they were together until they died.

"And that's the end of my story," Hanna said.

Charpentier finally drank his cold tea. He set the mug down with a thump. He said, "Well, do you want to get some work done or not?"

It was still grudging, but it was consent.

It was late afternoon when they had their tea, and they did not start work until the next morning. Hanna had only gone back to the module assigned her in the Oversight complex. She looked around at Dwar with enjoyment as she returned to the Archives office at Town Center next day. There were deciduous trees in the region of Dwar and they were in full leaf; it was summer here, and a hydra-headed fountain splashed vigorously in the town's main square. The day was warm, the square quiet, and Hanna stood for a while by the fountain, admiring the bursting joy of the water and feeling fresh wind on her face. She was accustomed to the confinement of spacecraft, but journeys in space always reminded her that a simple variable of terrestrial worlds—changing weather—was a treasure. Dwar too was a jewel in its gentle way. Its builders had used warm brown native stone for most structures, and laid roadways of crushed white rock. It made for a pleasing contrast, and Hanna, surrounded by the fantastic architecture of Admin's city for too long, took her time getting to Archives.

Chain had petitioned Amir Almond for all the data he could get about D'neera, and about Hanna, and absorbed as much as he could while he waited. Hanna sensed that, but he did not say anything about it at first, so neither did she.

"We start where?" he asked.

"Well, let's re-run the searches Starr asked for, just as a check, and go on from there."

"Starr? Jameson?"

"Contact," she said absently, eyes on the text on a screen.

"That wouldn't be the one who used to run the Polity, would it?"

It appeared that Chain had not thoroughly absorbed several hundred years of history in a few months' time. He could hardly be blamed for that—especially by Hanna.

"No one commissioner 'runs' the Polity," she said patiently. "And their powers are limited. To some degree. It's complicated, Chain."

"So he used to be *one* of the people running the Polity?"

"In a manner of speaking," said Hanna, trying not to laugh.

"And he's your boss?"

"Technically."

"What does that mean, technically?"

She thought, to herself, *It means we sleep together.* Out loud she said with equal truth, "He wouldn't try to make a first contact himself. I wouldn't dream of trying to administer something like the department he heads."

"These first contacts. You've done two of them?"

"And I'm here looking for a starting point for a third. Yes, Chain. That's what I do. That's what we'll be doing together, you and I."

As they started the searches she heard him think: *Just wait till I tell people who this is!*

She was getting used to being a legend.

They had a second keyword list ready before the first, predictably fruitless, search was done: anything and any combination they could think of having to do with aliens, nonhumans, starflight, spacecraft, and on and on. Chain threw in "strange beings" for good measure. Nothing, except for many alerts on "landings"; but those dealt with maintenance flights to the mothership.

"That's right, she's still up there," Hanna said with interest. "And you still send people up?"

"On a regular basis. If the orbit starts decaying into the atmosphere, we're going to push her out toward space and wave good-bye."

"Chain, why didn't your people do that long ago? It wouldn't have affected your mayday beacon, and you wouldn't have to worry about debris coming down on your heads. The thing's huge. It would break up coming down through atmosphere, but it could do a lot of damage. Why's it still there?"

"Sentimental attachment?" He shrugged. "I guess someplace inside we still like to think we're space travelers."

Hanna nodded. It made sense to her. She said, "Let's see if Mi-o Roland ever put anything on record."

She had not. In fact, except for a birth record for Mi-o Roland consistent with the chronology, there was no evidence the girl had ever existed, apart from the *Report to Archives*.

"Could she have changed her name?" Hanna said. "I forget—do women here customarily take their husbands' names?"

"Not usually," he said, "but it's not consistent. It's an unusual first name, though. Let's try—"

Nothing.

"Could she have changed that too? It's a little awkward to pronounce. If she had wanted to change it to something easier, would it be a matter of public—well, no. That first search would have given us that."

Chain said, "This is a land of small towns, Hanna. We've spread over one continent, no more, and we're spread thin at that. In a small town everybody knows your business anyway, so if you get around to reporting it to some central office—that's me, for now—fine. If you don't, nobody's going to fine you or whatever they do where you come from. *All* reporting is voluntary."

He wore glasses; Hanna, who had never seen spectacles

before, had examined them thoroughly. He took them off and laid them on the console where they worked. He looked sad. He said, "I've spent a lot of time with the Oversight historian. The kinds of questions she asked started me wondering. I've asked questions of my own, and Oversight's free with its library. It's different out there. With your people, I mean."

He meant the five worlds of the Interworld Polity and the others within its sphere of influence. He had ceased to see Hanna as D'neeran.

He said, "We have a family named N'goto who make the finest porcelain you people have ever seen. Something about the clay on the riverbanks where they farm. The family developed the art of making it, oh, four hundred years ago? The rest of us buy it, sure. We ask for it a year in advance, usually a tea set for a marriage gift, and we pay the price the N'gotos ask, and it's a high one, and it's fair. We know how precious it is better than you Oversight people do." (Hanna did not correct him. Oversight or Contact, it was all the Polity to him.) "The N'gotos don't have much time to spare from the land, and this is their art, and it's beautiful. Cherished.

"Now Oversight is talking about markets in the Polity, and the family's in an uproar.

"I see things coming, Hanna. I see things I don't like. They even say we have to stop calling this world New Earth, they say every colony ever settled wanted to call itself that and they all had to pick something else, and we'll have to do that too. Not everybody sees everything I've been thinking about, but we're *all* mad about that."

"Understandably," said Hanna, but she was thinking of the alternatives to change. Stagnation, for one. A turning in, a narrowing of vision, knowledge trickling away. Helplessness in the face of new threats. She thought of Plague, and Gadrah.

"Well, let's get back to work," he said.

"Nothing," Hanna said later to Jameson, light-years away. It was late night in Dwar; Hanna had stayed up to reach Admin in Jameson's morning. "I was reminded of the mothership, though. At the time of the incident, it was exactly where it is now—in orbit around New Earth. Surely the aliens would have boarded it. It's clearly a starship, at least, to any beings with experience with starships. If they were here for R&R—a reasonable hypothesis, based on the accounts—they would have checked it for threats. Do you think they might have left traces?"

She watched him think about it. She had always liked watching him think. The results were often surprising—and sometimes were direct hits on a target no one else had even seen.

"I wouldn't expect to find physical traces," he said. "Not after generations of colonists making inspection trips. Presumably they would have noticed any damage or anything out of place—"

"—like alien picnic leavings—"

He gave her a startled look but said, "If they were curious about it, they might have tried to access the computers."

"I don't know if I could recognize that if they had. Especially since these systems are obsolete. Do you think it's worth my persuading someone here to take me up for a look? If there's anything to find, finding it is probably beyond me."

He didn't answer directly. "That would be beyond Oversight's capabilities, too," he said. "I will contact Fleet, though. It's worth a look from them."

He would get results; and if anything substantial came of the examination of New Earth's mothership, anything to make the whistling beings more real than one old report made them, Hanna might not be waiting around for transport the next time she needed it.

The next morning Chain said he couldn't think of anything else to try. Hanna put her feet up and stared at uninformative displays. *We're too dependent on databanks,* she thought. *We think if something's not in there, the something doesn't exist.*

"Chain," she said, "do you know anything about—oh, what is it?"

She was dredging deep in her memory now. Some casual conversation Jameson had had with a dinner guest one evening, something that interested him; he seemed to be interested in everything.

Often, Hanna listened to those conversations, even—once she was speaking—participated, but that night her hearing had felt muffled. That night she had only been waiting for the last guest to leave.

Michael Kristofik had been dead four months. With every part of herself, with a completeness she had never known before, she had loved every part of him—the sunlight, and all the rest of that fractured personality, parts dark or damaged, haunted or lost. She had been deep in the trance of the Adept with him when he died, and all the light she had ever known went out in the moment of his death, and she had been insane with loss. Until she returned to Earth—was returned, like a package no one cared about—to Jameson.

She still loved Michael, but he had rekindled an almost forgotten flame in her body, and it had not gone out with his death. She was used to being touched, used to being loved; her skin was starved, crying out with need. Desire was back. She desired Jameson with all the heat of their first coupling years before, and she knew she was desired in turn. She knew he thought her beautiful even in the pregnancy that was just becoming visible; she knew it every night when they went to their separate beds.

There were scarcely any words. They were not necessary; she had hardly taken her eyes from Jameson all evening, and he had known it.

He came back from saying the last good night and stood in front of her. She began to speak, and he lifted a hand in a slight gesture she knew: *Don't talk.* He said, "I intend to make you forget him for a while."

She would have laughed at anyone else who said that. She did not laugh that night. And, for a while, she forgot.

Chain was looking at her strangely.

She got her brain going again.

"Folklore?" she said. "Oral histories?"

"Amir asked me about that," Chain said. "Sure, every family's got stories. Mostly lies, though."

"Are there still Rolands around?"

"Lots of Rolands," he said. "Some moved out to other towns, but there's plenty around here still. Why?"

"I want memories," she said. "Things that never made it to the computers. Can you give me a roster of the Rolands who live near Dwar? I'm going to talk to them personally. And, Chain?"

"Yes?"

"Can you transmit an appeal for help from anyone who might have heard about Mi-o from old stories? And anybody who might have an artifact from her time? What I wouldn't give for one little, insignificant alien artifact from her time!"

During the afternoon, mindful of farm families' crowded days, she only went to see Amir, who said, "I'd love to see them collect the family stories. Before they're lost."

"But why would they lose them, Amir?"

"Because they're stories people tell in limited societies," Amir said. "Societies—small ones—where gossip is a primary medium, and people say, 'Do you remember old so-and-so?' and other people laugh because they do. When that stops, oral history stops. And it doesn't make it into official records: old so-and-so probably *was* an old so-and-so, and the family's going to talk about it, but they won't be eager to put it in a database. So it stops. It stops when the society reaches a critical limit—in size, in mobility and resulting dispersion, or as a result of outside pressures like invasion or the influence of a larger culture."

"And that's going to happen here?"

"Well, the stressor here will be the last I mentioned—assimilation as a subculture into the Polity. It's inevitable, I think. Unless they tell us to go away. They can, you know. And if they tell us to do that, we will."

All the same, Hanna thought as she walked away in the summer afternoon, maybe the name should be modified. To Colonial Oversight and Destruction Service, perhaps.

She knocked on the first Roland door that evening between dinner and bedtime. She got no new information, but Odele Roland made some calls, and assured Hanna that if she showed up at George Selos and Mindy Roland's farm the next evening, there would be more Rolands to greet her.

She took Chain with her. Forewarned, he came prepared to record. He retrieved half a dozen stories of interest (to Rolands—and to Amir, as it later turned out). Nothing on Mi-o.

The next day, she had said, she would—

"But why tomorrow?" several Rolands said. Mindy had been making and getting calls and messages all evening. "Why not a couple weeks from now? We're past due for a family reunion—we'll never have a better excuse!"

———

A fully equipped Interworld Fleet starship arrived and took up orbit around New Earth. This caused some excitement among the colonists, but only mild surprise among Oversight personnel, once it was explained that the old mothership was an object of interest to a famous specialist in the history of early expansion and settlement.

Fleet sent incredibly expensive vessels here and there for sillier reasons, they said.

———

The day before the Roland family reunion, early in Dwar's morning, Hanna got an urgent call from Jameson. She was at the Archives Office with Chain, and her heart jumped hard in her chest when she saw the priority code.

Jameson took one look at her face and said hastily, "Nothing wrong with Mickey. Nor anybody else as far as I know."

"Then what—Starr, you scared me half to death!"

"I'm sorry. I'm expecting a certain level of security restrictions on communication to go into effect momentarily, and I wanted to talk to you privately while I can. It seems the aliens did access the mothership computers, and in the eyes of Fleet that makes Earth a target."

It was two hundred years ago!

"Well, they are going to be minimal restrictions." He appeared to think it was funny. Hanna had never thought "Fleet" and "funny" belonged in the same sentence. But then, when Jameson was a commissioner, the Interworld Fleet in its entirety had answered directly to him and his colleagues. Clearly, this gave him a different perspective.

"Is there any information that might suggest where to look for them?" she asked.

"Surprisingly, yes—but not enough. The human race hasn't explored very far from Earth, and these beings could have come from anywhere in this galaxy—or another, I suppose, in theory. There's just too much space out there, unless we find something to narrow it down. I expect sooner or later the Fleet people will be able to work back to more definitive information. What we do have appears to be there because the aliens did some very preliminary modeling with an idea of taking the mothership home with them."

"I wonder why?"

"A souvenir? Scrap? Well, you're the expert on alien motivation."

"My expertise is failing me just now. Not armaments— the settlement ships weren't warships. Technology— obsolete even at the time of this contact. Information—anyway they would only have needed the data, not the ship. And they didn't seem to be interested in getting information from the colonists at all."

He shrugged. "The Fleet people will get more—but probably not soon, and not about motivation. We'll have to communicate with them to find out what that was." He hesitated. "Do you think you'll be there much longer?" he said. There was an odd inflection to the question, puzzling Hanna.

"Probably not," she said. "Why?"

He frowned. He said as if surprised, "I miss you."

"Ah . . ." said Hanna, and could not think of what to say next. She could not bring herself to say *I miss you too,* though she missed his hands and his mouth and the hard body that could make her feel fragile, which she was not. That might be worth going back for—if only she had not *had* to go back.

She said slowly, "I don't suppose I can talk to every Roland on the planet—this is nothing like Gadrah, human fertility is *not* depressed here—but I'll have a chance to talk to a lot of them tomorrow. I'll evaluate the need for staying longer after that."

"Keep me informed," he said, as if that strange moment had not happened, and it was not until she had closed the call that Hanna thought: *Maybe I do miss him. But I think I am less myself when I am with him. And I do not miss the way that feels at all.*

———

Rolands, Hanna decided, knew how to throw a party.

There were tents and tables and chairs and people spread out all over the lawns and a nearby field at the biggest Roland farm in Roland (of course) County. Two family bands took turns performing. People here did not eat much meat, but there were a hundred different kinds of fruits and vegetables and cheeses, legumes and nuts and breads. Hanna was glad she had worn loose clothing.

And there were races! She had not ridden a horse since introducing the species to Awnlee of Ell, but she remembered how to think to the surprised animal between her knees. They didn't win, but they didn't come in last, either. Which had seemed to be the colt's preference.

One of the family bands put away its instruments and took out others. New Earth's society was not innovative, but had held true to the best elements of Old Earth's arts, music first of all. Michael Kristofik had taught Hanna about the music he most loved: the plangent harmonies of western Earth's Renaissance. Starr Jameson had taught her more. So when she realized what was coming, Hanna moved closer to the stage.

A young violinist came to the edge of the platform, not separable from the instrument she carried. She did not look at the crowd, which was quieting now. Her eyes were on the first, exquisite notes of the *Violin Concerto in D Major.*

After the concerto, after the silence, after the applause, the band started playing again.

Back to earth! cried the guitars. *Enough of heaven! Time to rock and roll!*

———

Hanna got to talk to all the Rolands she wanted. She gave them copies of the *Report to Archives,* too, and asked Rolands to pass them on. Chain and Amir were busy, capturing stories from group after group.

If this doesn't turn something up, Hanna thought, there's nothing to turn up.

She relaxed and ate and danced and ate some more. The reading she had done on this society paid off; she felt comfortable and accepted. Nobody mentioned telepathy (at least not to her—there were some wary glances), and nobody treated her like a legend.

Toward dusk she settled on the grass in front of the big stone farmhouse to digest her most recent meal. New Earth's sun was easing down into a bank of red cloud, and the cooling air was infused with herbal smells that made her dizzy. Minutes of pure contentment like this were rare, and she treasured them. Carrie Roland and her husband, she remembered, were the householders. In a minute she would get up and go thank Carrie for her hospitality.

On the porch behind her Carrie Roland said suddenly, "Oh, for God's sake!"

"Carrie, what?" said another woman.

"This thing from the archives! That's got to be old Mia Ferguson they're talking about!"

"*That* woman!"

Voices coming quick now, stories coming to mind.

"But she was notorious!"

"Honey, she still *is*!"

"Well, there's nobody alive who knew her, naturally—"

"But, dear, does her memory live on!"

"—married Grant Ferguson for that farm and everybody knew it—"

"—changed her name, but her daughters took it back—"

"—daughters by who, sweetie? Nobody ever knew!"

"They say old Grant never seemed to care—"

"—she must have been something—"

"—had young men warming her bed when she was eighty—"

"—oh, my, *that* woman—!"

The women were rocking with laughter. So was Hanna.

They quieted, wiping their eyes. Into the quiet a young voice said, "You know those holos Destiny has?"

"What holos, honey?"

"Oh, you know. The alien. And that one of the starfield."

"What–oh, those! Haven't thought about them since I was your age!"

Hanna, who had been sprawled on the grass with laughing, sat up very slowly.

The young voice said, "Do you think they could have come down from old Mia?"

Chapter V

*O*N NEW EARTH, *Hanna Bassanio left Chain Charpentier with a public kiss of gratitude so passionate it made* him *a legend.*

She left behind family histories still pouring in, and a mountain of artifacts, none of them alien.

New Earth was about to get its first museum.

On Old Earth, Thera informed Starr Jameson that she planned to make alterations to his formerly immaculate home. Mickey was crawling. Very fast, at times. Soon he would walk. And soon after, he would run.

On Battleground, at a border, armed Soldiers of the Holy Man fired on Soldiers of the Demon. The Demon's Soldiers here were a tattered band, and they charged throwing stones. They dropped at once, dead as the stones.

Or perhaps armed Soldiers of the Demon fired on stonethrowing Soldiers of the Holy Man. It all depended on your point of view.

Chapter VI

HANNA RETURNED TO EARTH IN OCTOBER, unsure how long she would be there. Her work with Contact Education tapered off; her role now was to shut the division down, pending her return to Earth from an as yet hypothetical location "somewhere west of Orion," Jameson said, uncharacteristically vague. Fleet's scientists had pounced enthusiastically on the second holo owned by young Destiny Roland, an alien's gift to the precocious Mia, which illustrated a patch of stars that had had some meaning to a whistling nonhuman observed one time two hundred years ago. It didn't seem like much—it might still prove a dead end—but the hypothesis that it included the star of the aliens' homeworld, combined with traces left in the mothership's data banks, might be enough.

Hanna had been away less than three months, but she found changes. Mickey was mobile, looking around at a welcoming world with eager interest, and trying to get hold of (and put in his mouth) anything that would hold still for it. Hanna held him and nuzzled him and got her hair pulled and thought with a hand clutching at her heart that she would be away much longer than three months next time. It was mixed comfort to see that Jameson had acquired a habit of casually picking the baby up and addressing comments to him that he could not possibly understand but that got a happy response. On one level, she was not surprised at Jameson's ease with Mickey; she knew that he rather liked what he called "the species human child," and that relatives, friends, acquaintances, and complete strangers often inflicted their offspring on him in the course of his public life. But there had been a subtle restraint before, and it had vanished in her absence. Jameson behaved, in the terminology of her own culture, like one of her kinship group, as if there were some tie of love or blood to all of them, though the faraway persons who composed her actual kinship group were convinced that he was bad for Hanna in every way. His assumption that he stood in such a relation to Mickey would have horrified them. He must have known it, too, but it did not seem to affect him.

And it was clear that he *had* missed her, though he did not say so. He touched her more often and more openly, drawing surprised glances from people previously convinced that whatever he was getting from her presence in his home had little to do with affection—and Hanna could not decide if she liked it. She knew precisely how to respond to his touch when it was meant to arouse her—with the willing certainty of what he was going to make her feel. Now that he seemed ready to consider the possibility of loving her—*finally,* she thought—she also thought she probably did not want to wait another ten years or so for him to make up his mind. It seemed a long time to wait for the satisfaction of rejecting him.

Equally surprising, and more troubling, was the dramatic increase in the number of social gatherings at Jameson's home. Formerly these had been rare and Hanna had joined them with a minimum of discomfort, even, often, with enjoyment, because the guests were interesting. Now there were not only more of them; now the people invited were usually not companions she would have chosen. Many were from Heartworld, where Hanna was especially unpopular. She resolutely shut her mind to their frequently demeaning thoughts about her, and minded her manners. She was Jameson's guest herself, in the final analysis, so she owed the others courtesy, at least.

But at last she said to him: "What are you up to?"

She asked the question in his study after an especially boring evening, purposely avoiding the intimacy of the bedroom. This could turn out to be the kind of conversation you wanted to have with clothes on.

"In what way, exactly?" he said, which was his fairly predictable reply to such a global question.

"Fifty of the last sixty-five people you have had to this house have been from Heartworld, and most of those have close ties to its council," said Hanna, who had expected the demand for precision.

"Groundwork," he told her.

"For?"

"I don't intend to be exiled from the Coordinating Commission for the rest of my life."

"No one ever thought you did. What does that have to do with the people I have to put up with lately?"

Her tone was amiable enough, if the question was not, and his was too.

"I've been hearing rumors of some weaknesses of Edward's for some time, and it seems likely that they're true. I've been informed, in the usual roundabout ways, that the administration in Arrenswood might be ready to forgive me. Apparently I've begun to look better to them again, compared to Edward." He meant Edward Vickery, who had succeeded him on the Commission and took great pleasure in such mastery as he had over Jameson.

"To forgive you for me, among other things . . . ?"

They were standing nearly on opposite sides of the room. A cool wind blew in through the doors from the gardens outside. The smell of autumn came with it, the wealth of fallen leaves. Hanna was wearing something dark blue and long and beaded; the fabric was warm enough, but her arms were bare, and she shivered. But the breeze had nothing to do with the chill that touched her. She had known Jameson only briefly as a commissioner, and he had been different then: harder, colder.

"It seems to me that you would be wiser to keep me out of sight," she said.

"Do you think I'm ashamed of you?"

She said slowly, "No. But . . . you know as well as I that people—some people, your people—think you ought to be. So wouldn't it be politic to give the impression that you are?"

"I made that mistake once before, and you left because of it."

"This is not supposed to be permanent!"—it had already gone on longer than either of them had expected, and the unyielding strength that had comforted Hanna now felt, sometimes, like a weight.

"I don't suppose it will be. But when we decide to end it,

other people's opinions will not be the reason. Many of them will never accept you. That is a fact. But they are damned well going to have to accept a fact themselves—that you and I will be together for as long as we choose and on whatever terms we choose."

She looked at him in silence for a moment. She had pointed out on other occasions that he had a good deal more to say about the terms than she did; she might also have pointed out that insisting on the right to run his private life as he liked had nothing to do with her personally, and in the long run might do him little disservice in the society that would decide whether he returned to the Commission or not. Undoubtedly there were worse things than being viewed as a strong man's weakness, but she could think of better ones.

She started to turn around and walk away. She thought she had, but somehow she was drifting across the room, as if drawn by gravity. *I really must end this,* she thought, but somehow a kiss intervened, deep and sensuous, and somehow the gown was slipping from her shoulders, and *really, I really must,* and then the costly beading was hard under her back and she did not think of endings any more; not then.

Chapter VII

HANNA BEGAN TO ASSEMBLE her Contact team. There was no reason to gather them physically together in these early days. The entire team would finally meet on the new *Endeavor Three* when the time came. But she contacted them individually and they conferred as best they could, given that they were scattered across human space, and those not actually in space lived in wildly divergent local times.

Bella Qu'e'n, now home on D'neera, would be part of the team. So would the other three D'neerans who had completed Hanna's program and adjusted to living with true-humans. Hanna chose Dema Gunnar simply because Dema, when she studied at Contact Education, had been a serene presence, soothing to the overexcitable. Dema also had returned temporarily to their homeworld; she was attached to *Endeavor One*, and had been awaiting completion of its refit. Joseph Luomobutu, the most likely candidate to become overexcited, was already on the new *Endeavor Three*. He had studied with Hanna before on D'neera and later performed superbly in Contact Education studies. Besides, Hanna was fond of him. She did not know Arch Harm as well, but he was at ease with true-humans and generally could charm them into forgetting that there was anything different about him. He would be missed when he left *Endeavor Two*. Especially, as he observed to Hanna, by the women of the crew.

Hanna advised all of them to apply for home leave while they could get it.

She picked two true-humans, too—the ones whose minds she thought most fluid and flexible, and who had been most at ease with their D'neeran counterparts. They were younger than the D'neerans, perhaps too young, but more tolerant than even slightly older true-humans. Hanna hoped that would make up for their youth.

She told them to start tying up the loose ends in their lives.

There were some she needed to tie up too, but they were acutely painful, and she did nothing until winter was nearly on them, when Jameson gave her no choice.

She was home early, but it was dark on the terrace behind Jameson's house. The November day had been unseasonably warm, but the rising wind was cold enough to cut through the terrace's minimal climate control. The major autumn storms were late and there were still leaves on the surrounding trees, yellow and brown, barely illuminated from a hidden source so that they glowed faintly. Enough were gone to make Admin's varied spires visible, looking farther away than they were. The towers were studded with the lights of men and women working through the night to keep civilization safe from ruin.

Jameson said, hardly raising his voice, "Thera. This child is drooling on my knee."

Thera materialized. She had her own quantum-dimension capabilities. An independent planet would, of course.

"He does that," Thera said. "Are you wet enough?"

"I think so."

Hanna lifted her son and held him close for a moment. He laughed—he laughed often—and bubbled spit in her face. She gave him to Thera, who bore him protesting away. Mickey could manage a few steps on his own now, and did not like to be carried until he got tired of falling down and scrambling up again. There was a brief wail of "Mama!" and then laughter again, as he fixed his ready glee on something else. Hanna stored the laughter in her memory. The search for the unknown aliens' stellar system was narrowing, and Mickey's first birthday would fall just before she expected to join *Endeavor Three*.

She said, "I wish I knew how long I will be gone. However long it is, I will miss so much of him!"

Jameson felt, and did not resist, her longing to take her

son with her. He knew she was resigned to the fact that she could not possibly take him into potential danger.

She picked up *danger* from a thought—not as a specific threat, but as something that would be an intrinsic part of her mission, at least at the beginning.

He said, "Hanna, I have been thinking about Mickey's future if something should happen to you."

"I see that you have," she answered.

"There is a reasonable solution, if it's acceptable to you."

She thought—to herself—*There is no "reasonable solution" to Mickey's growing up without me!*

He said, "I hope you will formally arrange for my guardianship of Mickey in the event of your death or disappearance."

Hanna slowly turned her head. No one had to tell her what that could mean for Mickey. She had no reservations about leaving him here while she was gone; she had simply assumed that he would stay where he was in Thera's care. Since her journey to New Earth, knowing the likelihood that she would have to leave again, she had not even thought of removing Mickey from this house. But the responsibility Jameson now proposed taking on was something different. It was vast.

"You would do that?" she said.

"What did I just say?"

"Yes, then," she said at once. Strong and clear. No hesitation. The people of her kinship group would love the child completely, but he was not a telepath. He could never be D'neeran.

She said, "I'm very grateful, Starr."

"There is something else," he said. Now he was beginning to pick his way very carefully.

"Gadrah," she murmured, catching another thought, put on alert by something behind it.

"I know you want to go back there."

"When I can; when I can go where I want."

She saw, with dread, something in him rising to speech.

"Hanna," he said softly, "Oversight is nearly finished with Gadrah. There were fewer than three thousand people left on the entire planet. They are all leaving. When the last of them has gone there will be no one, and all flights will cease. It will be an uninhabited world."

"No . . ." The grief for Michael Kristofik was not gone but she had thought it retreating. She felt it swell, and swell again to monstrous size in a breath, so fast there was no time to put up a defense. "No!" she cried, and the tears came and she doubled over, out of control, gasping for breath; there was no point even attempting control when it was like this. She hardly felt Jameson's hand on her back. There was nothing else he could do for her yet.

Finally she could speak, between fresh bursts of tears, and it was all anguish.

"I can't bear it—I can't bear it!—to think of him all alone on an empty world—nothing but the wind—not even a friend at his side—that loving, that dearly loved man—no, no, that is just not acceptable! Oh, love of my life!" she cried.

Jameson could not quite be still at that last outburst. Astonishingly, it hurt.

He thought: *What did Kristofik ever do for her except nearly get her killed? What did he ever do except get himself killed, and leave her alone to grieve?*

But he had had his own chance, and knew it, and he also thought: *What was he to her that I cannot be?—I have never asked. But . . .*

If I had not been so intransigent, seven years ago . . .

If she had not been so proud . . .

Seven years ago, though, others—not all of them human—had already been moving on paths that would intersect Hanna's. She would have met Michael Kristofik, inevitably.

When he thought she could listen he said—because it was best to do this quickly—"I thought you would feel that way. Hanna, I'm going to have his remains removed from Gadrah. You don't have to decide until you're ready where you want him finally buried. Nearby, perhaps, so you can take Mickey there when it's time. But I'm going to make arrangements immediately, while there is still substantial traffic."

Done.

He closed his eyes in relief.

"Thank you," she whispered, and after a silence in which she projected nothing of her thought, did not even look at him, said wearily, "I think I'll go to bed now. I'm so cold."

He watched the exhausted woman go into the house. Her rational mind knew as well as his that there was nothing left of Michael Kristofik but bones and scraps of tattered skin, but the man would be more than bones to Hanna for a long time still.

Jameson was on his way to join her and hold her—tonight, only hold her—when he remembered something he had said himself, something unplanned: "Nearby, perhaps, so you can take Mickey there when it's time."

It seemed he expected both of them to stay—nearby. Near himself.

PART TWO

ENDEAVOR THREE

Chapter I

ENDEAVOR-CLASS STARSHIPS WERE designed expressly for the purpose of seeking contact with star-traveling alien species. Since the philosophical basis of the search was peaceful, the *Endeavor*s went unarmed. For the same reason, so they would not seem threatening through sheer size, they were small. The original *Endeavor* had carried (and still did, as *Endeavor One*) a full ship's complement of only three hundred fifty. *Endeavor Three* was not much larger, having a capacity of three hundred sixty-five.

On the other hand, there was a warship at her back.

Just in case.

"We covered this in class," Hanna said patiently.

Anticipation was high. *Endeavor* had pinpointed the star system that was home to the beings who had visited New Earth.

Carl Ruck, the last of the team to join *Endeavor*, said stubbornly, "We're supposed to be coming in peace. They've been peaceful so far. Mostly. That was one of your own basic postulates in *Sentience*."

He meant the work that had won Hanna her first award from the Goodhaven Academy for the Study of Xenopsychology. The second was for *Shaping Reality*, about Zeig-Daru. The third was for *A Preliminary Study of Uskos,* a work she had written while actually on Uskos, leaving it behind in an Ellsian data bank when she left that world for the forgotten colony of Gadrah, following a man who was finally going home.

There had been some question about whether the *Study* should even be considered for the award, since Hanna had been a fugitive at the time of its submission (made on her behalf by Norsa of Ell). Then the Academy, one eye on

Norsa, had said the hell with it and just given her the prize. In absentia, and good riddance.

She said, "I know you read *Sentience*, Carl. It was our basic text, after all. But do you *remember* the book? Or didn't you notice I was wrong in some respects?"

He looked at her uncertainly. He was true-human and remained more comfortable with words than with thought, but he was not always comfortable with Hanna's.

"Girritt's not even interested in technology, much less war," he said. "Uskos never wanted war, F'thal never did. You said yourself, I remember from class. The capacity's there, knowing you might have to defend yourselves, but peace is better. Peace is prosperous. The Zeigans didn't really want war either. Zeig-Daru was a special case."

Endeavor was deep in space now, the target certain though still far off, and the team was meeting as a whole for the first time. Hanna had taught all of them. She felt like saying, *Class, repeat after me: They are ALL special cases!*

She said, "If we ever, ever get even a *hint* that there is anything else out here like Zeig-Daru, I'm going back to New Earth and taking up farming. Carl, the *Admiral Wu* is a day's transit behind us, and it will never show itself unless we scream for it. Mission protocol. No argument."

She looked around the conference room. Joseph had told her no one relaxed on this ship, or at least was not allowed to appear anything but completely alert, but there was no stiffness here: Joseph perched on the table, Glory Bosman curled exquisitely in her seat, Bella lounged.

"Communications is pulling in a steady stream of data, randomly sampling radio and video transmissions," Hanna said. "None of it was ever meant for destinations in space. They're working on teasing out audio components, so we'll have a grasp of a dominant language before direct contact. They'll have something for us to start working on in a few days, so get oriented here while you have the chance.

"Are any of you . . . D'neerans, I mean now . . . picking up anything you can identify as alien? That you suspect is alien?"

"No," said Dema Gunnar. "And if you're not either . . ."

"Not yet—"

The telepaths caught a hesitation the true-humans missed. Arch Harm said, "Have you tried?"

No.

"No? Oh, that's interesting!" He said it out loud, a courtesy to Glory and Carl. They might have heard the subtle mockery behind it; Hanna knew her face had changed.

"It's not going to be easy, you know! They're not telepaths, like the Zeigans. They're still so far away . . ."

Truth, but not all of it. She had never forgotten the wild fear of her first telepathic contacts with the People of Zeig-Daru, before anyone knew anything about them and even her perception of their existence was questioned. It still haunted her, however much she tried to bury it, and to bury a further fear that burst into consciousness now and then, which made her look for distraction immediately: had too much fear, too much loss, damaged her beyond repair? The doubts slipped into her mind again; she felt herself sink into quicksand. *Once I was whole but it was long ago and I will not be whole again. Whole in body, yes, but in spirit? I think not . . .*

They all stared at her; the telepaths had felt it, seen what lay behind the calm mask, and even the true-humans saw something strange in her face.

"I'll try," she said, "when we're closer," and this time hid the following thought. She was not sure how hard she *could* try; and she knew she didn't want to.

Shakedown time, she thought a little later, burying her reservations in practicalities. *Endeavor Three* had had its shakedown cruise while Hanna was still on Earth and was operating at one hundred percent efficiency, but her own team had some adjusting to do—to *Endeavor*, and to each other. The D'neerans had known each other at home because they were members of its small community of interest in nonhumans, but they did not know each other well, except for Arch and Joseph, who were related in complicated ways. D'neerans were as subject to personal frictions as anyone else, and the close quarters of *Endeavor* made a customary remedy—getting the hell out of each other's hair for a while, often by taking vacations on opposite sides of the world—impossible. Hanna had talked to them about this, emphatically, across space. It was not part of her usual Contact curriculum and she made a note to herself to include it in the future for D'neeran students. *Practice blocking,* she told them. *Review everything you were ever taught about tolerance and if you hadn't already integrated it—all of it—do it now. You won't be able to avoid each other.*

She was not seriously worried about them; they were stable and good-humored men and women, or she would not have accepted them for her program in the first place, and she reminded them of that (in case they needed reminding). She let them know too that their presence was a luxury for her personally. It felt good to relax into the natural habits of a born telepath, to know she was hearing the truth, that no one was crunching away at hidden grievances. She had been painfully homesick for exactly that for a long time, and had been homesick for something else without knowing it: her fellow D'neerans knew her for herself. True-humans were inclined to see a hero or a criminal or, in some cases, a piece in a political game or even merely, dismissively, as Starr Jameson's inexplicable and no doubt temporary sexual partner. D'neerans only saw H'ana ril-Koroth (though even they could not get into the habit of thinking of her by her original name). Hanna was satisfied with them.

She thought Carl Ruck would be satisfactory, too. Her only concern about him was that he had proved himself, while he was at Contact Education, over-earnest. He liked statistics and concrete facts; he had had difficulty understanding that Uskosians, for example, could be as devious as true-humans if they thought their motives good. Norsa had known exactly what he was doing when he invoked his stature on Uskos to help Hanna, and he had not done it because of an interest in justice, but from affection for Hanna. Carl, when Hanna told him this, had been appalled.

"They're no better than human beings?" he had said.

"So far nobody is," she had assured him, and at the conclusion of his studies at Admin arranged for him to do fieldwork on F'thal, where innuendo was the primary political tool and operated with a speed and complexity that made true-humans look naïve. She was pleased to see that Carl had made some progress. Living with a group of D'neerans who did not hide their motives, even those that did them no credit, would further the eye-opening process.

Glory Bosman was not quite as satisfactory. She was extraordinarily pretty, and accustomed to using her bright curls and flower-face for the kind of manipulation many true-humans thought Hanna practiced. Hanna had thought of making Glory do *her* fieldwork on D'neera, where manipulation was virtually impossible. She had decided regretfully, however, that she could not really pass her own people off as alien. So Glory had gone to Uskos, where she looked like just another human, and there weren't any secondary sexual behaviors for her to absorb and mimic, because there weren't any sexual behaviors at all. Her appreciation of the intrinsic differences between humans and nonhumans was genuine, though, and she never minded for long when a D'neeran poked at her ego. That ego was too healthy to be permanently damaged; it might sustain a minor dent, but would repair itself quickly.

Which left Hanna, who had not even started to do her job.

She knew quite well why she had postponed trying to get a sense of the whistling beings. A fear that could not be vanquished in twelve years' time had deep roots. Time was kinked. There was a ghost at her shoulder.

She reported to the team. Team members could not keep secrets about things like ghosts. A ghost that could keep you from acting needed to be made visible. You did not want it slipping up on you and paralyzing you at the wrong time.

Team protocol. No argument.

"The ghost is me," she told her team. "I'm thirty-six now, in Standard years. The ghost is still twenty-four. She hasn't figured out true-humans yet, and she's the only one of her kind among them. This is *Endeavor Three*, but she still thinks she's on the first *Endeavor*. She's expecting to breathe and sense unrelieved hostility from almost everyone around her. No one on that ship invited her. They didn't want her. She was forced on them.

"We're looking for beings we've designated Species Y.

That sounds too much like what the ghost was looking for; it was called Species X, then. Now we call them Zeigans. And she knows what Species X did to her when she found them."

She watched them think it through. Dema had tears in her eyes. They all knew what had happened to the ghost, the wraith of a Hanna who had been almost destroyed in body and in mind.

Bella Qu'e'en said quietly, "H'ana, as long as you know the ghost is there, you should be all right. And with a little time, so will she."

Hanna nodded.

"Just don't forget she's there," Hanna said. "You don't want her commanding this team. She's far too young."

――――――

Communications put together an audiovisual loop, at first an hour long but extended constantly, starting with the oldest electromagnetic traces from Species Y that *Endeavor* could detect. It would be updated as *Endeavor* moved in. Hanna watched perhaps two minutes of it, and then went to Communications and with absolute sincerity told the men and women there that she honored them for their skill and dedication.

Then she called her team together and they went to the auditorium and stayed there for days, watching the ever-lengthening loop.

――――――

Their faces are small, she thought. *It was not so apparent in that old holo.* The beings' heads altogether were proportionately small, mounted above slender necks, and the breathing tubes were covered with an insulating layer of downy hair or fur. The mouth, the eyes, and the bony plates that hid other eyes crowded faces that looked like afterthoughts.

Someone appeared at the corner of Hanna's own tired eye and she glanced up. Cork or Cock? She had been on *Endeavor* long enough to pick up the crew's nicknames for Officers Corcoran and Cochran. One or both of them accompanied Captain Hope Metra everywhere.

"Captain wants to see you, ma'am," this one said. Corcoran.

Finally, Hanna thought, but she got up without saying anything. Her attempt to report to the captain on boarding had been diverted to Cochran, a later attempt at a courtesy call to Corcoran.

Jameson had gotten some information about Metra from official and unofficial sources. *First major command. Strict disciplinarian. No combat experience. Old Heartworld family, not top-tier but connected by marriage to Edward Vickery's.* He hadn't liked the appointment but had no power to veto it.

Hanna walked into Metra's private office in Command and stopped dead at the sight of her.

The captain was huge. She was the tallest woman Hanna had ever seen, her frame was heavy, and Hanna thought everything under that green uniform might be muscle. Metra was standing and Hanna did not think the reason was politeness. She widened her perception: yes. Metra meant to have exactly this impact. She was used to intimidating people —with rank, with ultimate power aboard ship, with sheer size. Her skin was very dark; it was like standing in front of a granite mountain.

Corcoran moved up on Hanna's right. Cochran stood behind Metra. All three of them looked first at her right hand, and only then at her face.

Telling her what they thought she was.

Hanna wore a ring. The setting was simple, the stone at first glance unremarkable except for being the same deep blue as her eyes. Appearances lied. The gem was a scarce commodity from Zeig-Daru. It was incredibly rare, wildly valuable, and possibly, in some sense, alive. At infrequent and unpredictable intervals it pulsed with blue light generated, apparently, from within, but by no discernible mechanism. Not even the People of Zeig-Daru knew how that light was made. The jewels were too precious for one to be taken apart to find out. Jameson had given the ring to her; his reasons seemed as confused and ambiguous as her reasons for accepting it. They knew it acknowledged a bond, but could not describe the bond and could not find the words to discuss it. Others had been less economical with comments about the costly gift. It was evident that Metra had heard some of them.

The ring chose this moment to emit a flash of extraordinary light, as if flaunting itself. It was there and gone so quickly that Hanna might have imagined it. But Metra blinked.

No courtesies were exchanged. Metra said, "It has come to my attention that you have not responded to Officer Cochran's directive to assign members of your team to regular watches."

"I apologize for not responding," Hanna said slowly—but she thought fast. Arguments that favored flexibility would not find an audience here. *Draw the line now,* she thought (and almost heard Jameson saying it). "We are not Interworld Fleet personnel. We are civilians and the Contact team is an independent unit."

Metra said, "There are detailed protocols addressing the respective roles of crew and civilian scientists under transport on Fleet vessels. If you haven't bothered to develop rotas, you probably haven't read the protocols either."

"No," Hanna said. "I am relying on personal assurances from members of the Coordinating Commission." She wasn't—yet; but she would talk to Jameson and he would get them before the day was out.

Metra said, "Your department reports to Commissioner Vickery. I think you'll find that in this regard he is a strict constructionist. You won't find him as—flexible—as his predecessor." Her eyes slid to Hanna's hand and away again. Her expression did not change, but what Hanna felt in her was contempt: *Sex buys you nothing here.*

It was not the time to mention Vickery's well-founded fear that Jameson would get that Commission seat back again, and how close the change might be.

Hanna said pleasantly, "I believe you'll find the Commission as a whole will support Director Jameson in this. But I'll read the protocols at my earliest opportunity."

"Read them now," Metra suggested.

"I'll read them now," Hanna lied.

She was not escorted back to the auditorium, she was quite alone in the corridor outside it, but she heard a whisper, and even turned around before she heard it again, and this time knew who it was.

i told you this was just like Endeavor One
The ghost.

———

Hanna won her round with Metra, or Jameson won it for her, and there was no duty roster for the team. You took a break or you had a meal or you got some sleep, and you went back to the auditorium. Fascinated members of the ship's crew came and went as their duties permitted, but they had other responsibilities. Hanna's team did not. Even Joseph Luomobutu had been released from his routine assignment in Communications.

The Y beings looked and spoke exactly as Maya Selig had described. But Joseph said Maya had been wrong about the human inability to make analogous sounds.

"I've studied the part of Earth my ancestors migrated from," he told the team. "It's written in my DNA, and I know exactly where that was. A people lived there even in historic times who spoke a language unique on Earth, and the oldest records describe it as using whistles and clicks. But it's dead."

"Was it swallowed up by Standard?" Hanna asked.

"No, exterminated long before interstellar spaceflight began. H'ana, you can't imagine what Africa endured. Someday when there's time I'll teach you some history."

History again. Hanna smiled for the first time in several days.

———

They started paying closer attention to the content of the transmissions. Arch was the first to say, "It's all the same. I don't see any variety. No evolution. And there should be. We're moving from early to present-day transmissions. We ought to see change. How could a civilization this static develop starflight?"

"There's some movement," Hanna said. "Communications says there are changes in the vocalizations, changes in what they wear—look, those 'baggy coveralls' Maya Selig wrote about must have come later." They were looking at a crowd, and the loop switched to a series of stills of individuals dressed in identical multipart uniforms.

"No fashion sense," Dema said. Hanna lifted an eyebrow. It was a comment she might have expected from Glory, not from the dignified Dema, whose garments were uniformly black and white (to save the bother of matching colors). Dema added, "There seems to be a lot of war."

"And a lot of speeches," said Bella. "War and speeches and public assemblies, I guess you'd call them. And war. Is Communications doing some kind of selecting? This can't be all there is."

Hanna went to Communications. She reported back, "There are huge gaps in the transmissions. Times when there weren't any, or just a few, and weak ones at that. Or our instruments aren't good enough to pick them up. But the only selection criterion is clarity. What Communications is leaving out is just more of the same — war, speeches, and public assemblies. And more war."

"Why the gaps?" Carl said.

"War," said Glory. "Everybody's capability destroyed at times."

Arch said, "The place is just one big battleground, isn't it?"

A D'neeran Adept did not have to fear ghosts. In trance, in fact, you didn't have to fear much of anything — depending on how much humanity you were willing to give up.

On Hanna's first attempt to "listen" to Species Y, her humanity tripped her up. She detached herself from *Endeavor* steadily and remorselessly, and then, in trance or not, could not resist reaching straight out for one little human boy. Telepathy was not supposed to be possible over such immense distances, but telepathy, notoriously and unpredictably, could shatter boundaries when love was involved. Love, it seemed, did not recognize distance.

Oh, what a happy little boy he was! He knew a surprising number of words but did not think in them consistently; instead there was straight, shining clarity of experience, vivid as a glowing dream. Bath time: splashing water, delight. A woman's love as certain and surrounding as Hanna's womb had been, love like shafts of sunlight binding woman and child.

But the woman was Thera. Not Hanna.

She slipped out of trance. The emotions trance did not permit crashed in on her. She wept.

She reported to the team. They had to know each other's vulnerabilities if they were to strengthen their bond.

Team protocol. No argument.

She kept trying, and felt only the people on *Endeavor.* Once there was a surprise, a trace of wildness that seemed not quite human—but it was. There was, Hanna concluded the first time it happened, something strange about at least one person on *Endeavor,* but her business was aliens, and after that she ignored it. She did not touch Mickey again, but she could not move toward Species Y either. Mickey appeared to be the telepathic equivalent of a black hole for Hanna, and she could not break orbit.

She reported to the team.

"You should have brought him along," Glory said.

Hanna blinked at her, picked up an image: some hybrid warrior queen/earth mother, baby in one hand, sword in the other.

Hanna reminded herself that youth sometimes masquerades as insanity.

"I'm sure you left him in good hands," Glory said sweetly. "Our director has him, I heard." Glory had met Jameson and liked him very well. Women did. That hooded gaze suggested (accurately) that he had applied his formidable intelligence to the art of pleasuring as thoroughly as any other subject he wished to master.

And our director is how you got this choice assignment, too. The stab of jealousy, professional and sexual, seemed to flash out of nowhere.

Hanna wanted to slap her.

Instead she said, "Someone here thinks this could be genuinely dangerous."

"That's me," said Dema Gunnar. "You're our only Adept. We don't know yet what abilities we're going to need, or how we'll need to use them. But we might need you as a fully functioning Adept."

"I'll work on it," said Hanna. "May I have a word with you, Glory?"

Later the others found out that Hanna had showed the

girl the full horror of that first contact with Zeig-Daru. If Glory had needed credentials, she got more than she wanted. What Hanna had gone through left even people who disliked her in awe of her.

They were only surprised that Glory voluntarily remained on the team. She spoke to Hanna with a new respect, and she never said the words "our director" again. *That* was no surprise.

They had to be able to trust each other.

Team protocol. No argument.

The linguists had identified a dominant language, indeed the only language—the absence of variation arguing a long history of worldwide communication—and begun to work on translation programs. A computer could learn to reproduce the sounds the Y beings made much faster than humans could educate their own vocal equipment. The body resists too much novelty. Novelty is work.

Hanna tired of watching the repetitive loop. She wanted to know what the beings were saying. She wanted to talk to the chief linguist, but when she went to see him, a harried-looking woman intercepted her and said Mister Mortan was busy and by order of Captain Metra was not to be disturbed. Getting five real live D'neerans aboard an *Endeavor* explorer was a first—in certain circles on D'neera it had been cause for celebration—but not everybody thought telepaths were important people even at first contacts. Hanna turned then to Communications' chief, with whom she already had, so to speak, some credit, and got an audience with her without difficulty.

"They won't talk to you because they're having fits," said Kaida Aneer.

"About—?"

"They don't talk to me any more than they have to, either. Of course," Aneer said with satisfaction, "I'm in charge, so that's more than they'd like."

"What's the problem?"

"Not enough variety in the sources. They thought they could analyze language use across different contexts and work the matches from one context to another, but there aren't enough contexts."

"Ah," said Hanna. "War, speeches, and public assemblies?"

"You got it."

Time passed. Kaida Aneer hinted that Linguistics had made progress. There were visuals of texts from some periods, there were audiovisuals of Species Y individuals reading texts aloud, there were correlations being made. Maybe there would be translators soon. Everyone on the team had spent time on Girritt, F'thal, or Uskos, and they knew how to use translators. But when they began to discuss it Hanna said they ought to try to understand as much of the language as possible, even if they did not learn to speak it.

"Suppose they take your translator away, and you need to know what they're going to do to you," she said. "You might need to escape. Or attack." The last two words might have sounded doubtful. Hanna had not chosen her team for aggressiveness.

Everybody nodded and turned back to the AV loop. Somebody's surface navy was taking a beating.

Carl Ruck said suddenly, "Wait a minute. What just happened? What just happened to our peaceful mission?"

Hanna muted the loop's audio. The sounds of explosions stopped, along with the soft accompaniment of clicks and whistles and spoken syllables that might be commentary. Carl looked stunned. Hanna felt stunned.

She said at last, "We've started thinking we're going into a war zone. But for all we know most of the planet is at peace. Or maybe it wasn't at the time of these transmissions but it is now."

Dema said, "H'ana, ludicrous as it is, I once saw a transmission on four hundred and sixty-two ways to prepare the F'thalian sqwiddit. For breakfast alone, and not counting taxidermy. Have you seen *anything* like that on this loop?"

"You know there isn't anything like that . . . Of course, we don't know what they're saying yet in those speeches and public assemblies."

Dema said, "H'ana. Look a little closer at those public assemblies. They do a lot of marching."

"I haven't seen any marching forma—"

"They march in place. It's subtle, but that's what they're

doing. If you listen hard you can hear the rhythm. They *march*, H'ana. All of them."

After a silence Hanna said, "Well, Communications has the translators programmed to recognize and project the right sounds, anyway. I'd better find out how Linguistics is doing on meaning."

This time she got to see Kit Mortan and he said they were doing just fine. Of course, so far everything seemed to be about some religious war, but they'd only just gotten started.

Chapter II

*O*N ALTA, *a colony world that had never been lost and was not in the least important, Brother Gabriel Guyup considered the possibility that divine intervention was responsible for his remaining comfortably dry in spite of the rain pouring onto his abbey and its grounds.*

The material reason for this was that the walkways between buildings had been roofed over not long before Gabriel, himself once an orphan rescued by the monks, had finished the offworld part of his education and returned to join the faculty of the abbey school. He had vivid memories of getting soaked to the skin as he ran from class to class in earlier years.

The divine intervention, one might reason, had taken the form of inspiring a donor to contribute a large sum of money to the school, some of which had been used for this improvement. Gabriel wondered if the donor had been a student here, and had his own memories (rather fond ones, years later, when one was dry) of getting soaked in the damp climate where the abbey had been built.

The likelihood of that was high, Gabriel thought, and what—aside from divine inspiration—might have motivated the giver? Gratitude for the haven the abbey had been to a child who had no one to love, as it had been for Gabriel? Or, possibly, the guilty conscience of one who had strayed far from its teachings?

Gabriel sat down on a convenient stone bench without looking. It had a puddle on it, as he noticed too late. It was not worth getting up. He deserved to have his backside soaked for that last cynical thought. But he no longer tried to cut off the thoughts when they came. They had been battering him for so long that he had given up.

I do not like this, he thought, I do not like what I am becoming.

He looked out at the silver curtain of rain. The other frequent, unwelcome thought followed naturally. Perhaps he did not belong here any more. Perhaps he ought to leave. As he could, without recrimination. Almost all the other brothers had come here midway through worldly lives. Perhaps he was even expected to leave; certainly it seemed his superiors had hinted at it in the last year, assuring him God would understand such a need, and that they would welcome him back if the time came to return.

It was not doubt of God that ate at him. Doubt could be accommodated; the long history of his church was full of doubters, and some had even made it to sainthood. Disillusionment with humankind was harder, and he did not know where it had come from; it had crept into his heart unnoticed until it was firmly in place and he felt it burning like unshed tears? Had he seen one traumatized child too many, perhaps?

So far it had not affected his behavior. He remained a steady, reliable brother, father, teacher, and friend to boys whose ages ranged from five to eighteen Standard years. His fellows saw what they had always seen and expected to see: a man who dried the youngest children's tears, won the older boys' admiration as an athlete, and spoke convincingly of perfect peace and love at the heart of creation. But there was seldom peace in his heart these days.

Presently he got up and went on, knowing he only waited for the day to be over, knowing that meant there was something wrong with the way he lived his days. The night would be his own, and there would be something to take him away from gnawing introspection: a new paper by a Contact Education student who had spent several months on Uskos.

Some of his colleagues thought he should drop this freakish interest in aliens. Speculation on the children of other stars had dimmed the Star of Bethlehem considerably ever since Neal Girritt, six hundred years ago, had stumbled across the planet named for him and found it occupied by indisputably intelligent nonhumans who had no Savior and had no idea they needed one. The contact with F'thal fifty years later had not helped. But the faith of Gabriel's fathers had muddled along, if in slow retreat, and the last decade's *contacts with Zeig-Daru and Uskos did not seem to have speeded (or reversed) its decline.*

And there are going to be more contacts, Gabriel thought. For the first time humanity was systematically and consistently seeking them, and this new Gabriel wondered if the Department of Alien Relations and Contact might eventually accomplish what all of humankind's holy wars had not, and put an end to an ancient, dwindling faith.

On Old Earth, Thera produced holo after exquisite holo of Mickey walking (sort of), trying out words, and exhibiting an early draft of his father's sweet temper. Thera was sure he would also develop his mother's not-easily-classified intellect. He had to have gotten something from her, and it certainly wasn't the sweetness.

Starr Jameson, meanwhile, found himself not unpleasurably pursued by interested women. It was not a new phenomenon, but had been in abeyance while Hanna lived with him; her absence apparently signaled open season. He might have responded warmly to some of the overtures, but—there was Hanna, who had foreseen this. "Do as you wish," she had said, but he did not like the complications of dealing with more than one woman at a time, and he was emphatically still dealing with Hanna, emotionally if not (regrettably) physically. He preferred to entertain lovers at his home, too—"Because here you are in complete control," Hanna had said—but how would Mickey, interrupting an intimate breakfast, react when the woman he found there was a stranger?

So Jameson allowed himself to be pursued but not caught. He was too busy for an affair anyway.

And he wasn't lonely.

Certainly not.

Chapter III

HANNA HAD A SMALL holo of Mickey in her cabin. There was none of Starr Jameson, because it would not be appropriate. Any other lover, yes. Just not the Director of Alien Relations and Contact.

There were no holos of any kind in the small conference room where she waited for now-daily voice contact to be established. It would have been an appropriate place for an image of the director, and Hanna was relieved there was none there. She would want to take it down every time she saw it. Or put it up again.

"Good morning, Hanna."

She warmed to his voice in spite of herself.

"Good morning."

"Status, please."

"Temporary hold."

"Why is that?"

Because it's not working the way it's supposed to, that's why.

"As you know, Communications and its Linguistics division have completed preliminary collection and analysis of available data and are producing prototype translators. The mission plan calls, at this point, for sociological and other specialist interpretation of the data while Contact team telepaths assimilate their findings prior to actual contact. However—"

She stumbled. When had she gotten so good at spouting this nonsense?

"However, data produced by Species Y societies appear to be, by a process of self-selection within those societies, restricted within narrow, narrow—"

You're laughing at me. I just know you are.

"—parameters, leaving," she said abruptly, "the specialists with little data to interpret. Unless we reverse the sequence. Come up with something new, some less quantifiable information. Prior to contact. From out here. Telepathically."

"I see."

Silence. He had ghosts of his own.

(*"There is a new sensor in operation,"* he had said early in the search for Species X. *"The telepath, the D'neeran child. She said perhaps she can come up with more, if she is alone."*

And someone had answered, "You sound as if you're putting her out to be a sort of gauge of what there might be to fear . . .")

"Starr? Are you there?"

"Yes. Have you made a deliberate attempt yet? To carry out telepathic observation?"

"A few tentative tries, with no result."

"You haven't reported that."

"I haven't tried very hard. It didn't seem important until the scarcity of information available from monitoring became apparent. I believe it's time to make a serious effort at telepathic observation, but I wanted first to advise you that that is my recommendation. As the team's only Adept, I would be lead in this effort. With your approval, we'll proceed."

After another, rather long silence, he said, "I suspect that 'lead' in this context means 'solo.'"

"Not necessarily. In theory."

"But in practice?"

"In practice, Bella, at least, might be able to connect with a distant consciousness. But she does not have Adept skills; she cannot use the altered state of the *satya* trance. Any contact she made might be more easily perceptible to the subject."

More silence. Finally: "Approved. Is there anything else?"

"No."

"Until tomorrow, then. Endit."

The voice sounded normal. Almost casual. Not quite.

Jameson looked at the river forty stories below. It was nearly a year since he had gotten the first tantalizing infor-

mation about Species Y from New Earth. Winter was near
its end; it had come to Admin late but hard. There was un-
seasonable ice on the river, and a clear blue sky that did not
hint at the merciless, knife-edged wind.

It was Jameson who had forced the original *Endeavor* to
accept Hanna, and it was he, personally, who had sent her
alone in search of Species X. He had seen exactly what they
had made of her: a thing mutilated and unrecognizable.
Even in these last months, though years had passed, there
were nights when he had waked and called for light so that
he could see the triumph of regeneration he held in his
arms, and sleepy blue eyes opening without fear.

She's not alone this time, he reminded himself.

He kept telling himself that all day.

Hanna found a way to stay clear of the gravity well that was
Mickey. Simple visualization and imagery, after all. But she
needed help to do it.

From their quarters, from the team's conference room,
wherever the D'neerans could isolate themselves from true-
humans, they guided her through a dream.

The baby sleeps, with love his watch and ward.

It's safe to move away. The baby sleeps.

Look back without fear. There's no danger to be seen.
He's safe.

Turn away, turn to your work. He's safe.

It's all right to move away. It's safe to move away. The
baby sleeps.

Endeavor Three was quieter than usual. Nobody seemed to
know why. People were awake as usual, alert as usual. It was
just —

Funny, I remember when my daughter was young, a man
found himself thinking. *Nothing could wake that one once*
she fell asleep, but I used to tiptoe, all the same.

She floats.

She has not been so deep in trance for many months.

Before, twice, she was holding hard to life.

*First, her own. Succeeded because help was near and she
held on long enough.*

*The second time, Michael's. Failed. Because no help could
ever have been enough.*

*No emotion in trance. There, but distanced. Return when
you choose.*

*She has searched in space for alien minds before, but not
as an Adept, and those she found, the People of Zeig-Daru,
were powerful telepaths, far more powerful than any
D'neeran, and they were searching for her, too. That's not
how it is this time.*

*But this will work, if she has the will to do it. In trance,
emotionless, she has the will.*

She knows how they appear in one another's eyes.

So . . .

*Visualize those strange heads, the great ears, multiple eyes.
Seek a match, look for images, slip behind the eyes that see
other faces. Eyes that look into another's.*

Feel something like an ocean, a susurration of thought.

Slip into it, float in it, let it surround—

*Ah, a coalescence, closer, deeper, see the separate threads.
Pick one. Follow. Look. Feel . . .*

Look away from those other eyes to see a strip of beach.

Danger. But only alertness, no feeling of fear.

*Expecting attack. Not from her. From everywhere, all the
time.*

A wily one, this one. Old.

Old! So old!

That was a shock.

No emotion in trance.

*There's a place behind, some distance behind, out of sight.
Underground.*

Defend it.

*Nothing ahead but hot sand, ocean to the left, dense foli-
age to the right. Orders. Break for cover as soon as Demon
Soldiers appear.*

A subliminal pulse of drumbeats.

*Suppose in this skirmish they have guns? Because we only
have spears. But maybe they only have knives, like the skirmish near the place where missiles are made. Then we were
the ones with knives. But I survived, like the time before that
and the year of the summer before that.*

Who makes the decisions, about knives and guns and spears? The High Commander? The Holy Man? They have so many summers, their decisions must be right.

But I have many summers now, I wonder why I have a spear when some in some battles have weapons that spit fire or deform the hearts in the chest.

Why do I ask such questions, this year of this summer? The two hundred forty-sixth. But the Commanders have many more so they must be right, and the Holy Man has even more than the Commanders.

But two hundred and forty-six summers is something. It is something! All my crèchemates ceased surviving long ago but I survive. Maybe I will be a Commander one day—

"H'ana!" someone calls. The D'neeran form of her name. "Time's up. You agreed."

Hanna opened her eyes, felt her metabolism speed up like a smooth machine. She was in her cabin. Carl and Glory watched her drink to ease her dry throat. Then she told them what she had learned.

They didn't believe her at first. The telepaths did.

———

"Status, please."

"An important fact."

"And that is?"

"They can live for hundreds of years. Standard centuries. Unless they die in war. Nearly all of them do. Maybe all."

There was a silence. When the deep voice spoke again, it was as calm as ever. No shock.

"How sure are you that your perception of time correlates one-to-one with theirs?"

"Positive."

"What else?"

"This war appears to be religious, as our linguists thought. As you know, they tentatively assigned the words 'holy man' and 'demon' to certain terms—there's some confusion about which side is which. What I sensed confirms the working definitions. The subject also thought of a wide range of variation in weaponry. There'll be details in my full report."

"And what else?"

"I'm not sure . . . I pushed the subject a little, questioning some underlying assumptions, but—they weren't quite new questions. He seemed to have been asking himself a few. The—oh, how can I explain it, the track, the trail, the connections, the circuits—the *pattern* of the thoughts I saw—they were already there—recent and faint, but that's why I went that way—they're questions he's never asked before, maybe doubt— "

Explaining this kind of intimate contact to true-humans was nearly impossible. She did as she always had, explained as best she could.

"All right. And what else?"

"Nothing else, I think. Not from this one contact."

"Can you draw any conclusions about their society from it?"

"Only one. This contact was real-time, not a transmission from the past. It supports the hypothesis that war is ongoing. I don't know how they tell one side from the other, by the way. Insignia, facial appearance, racial characteristics—I had no impression of anything that would distinguish enemy from ally."

"What is your recommended next step?"

"I'll do it again." *And again, and again.*

For once, the breath of a sigh. For once, the other voice. The one that says: *thou.*

"I thought you would say that."

"Until tomorrow?"

"Until tomorrow. Endit."

After that it was easier.

This one—much younger. Reading something on a—screen? No, a bound book—that—she?— I think it's she—holds in her hand. Surroundings a gray blur, underground, aboveground? A building? A—tent?

"Status?"

"The linguists have seen no literature as we know it because there is none."

"There are treatises on warfare, I understand. And religious texts."

"I have found no trace of admiration for their form, nor contemplation of the art of making them."

"Poetry?"

"No trace in any text extracted from the data. No trace in any mind that I have touched."

She spent so much time in trance that it bled over into daily life. What she got in trance ground her down, outside it, with frustration. That first contact proved exceptional, a suggestion of riches that came to nothing. Nearly everyone on the planet, it seemed, walked through life without question or analysis. She learned rote details of an infinity of tasks, laid over equally rote consciousness of a distant, god-like authority; she drifted in an undercurrent that reminded her of rote prayer, borrowed ears to hear the hiss of rhythms that reminded her of drums, borrowed eyes that in the spaces between tasks fastened on video projections of war, speeches, and public assemblies.

Eventually she met with something different; and when she came out of trance, hated it.

"Status, please."

"We have seen no transmissions of domestic life because there is none."

"You told the social scientists there is a child-rearing structure."

"I've seen it now. It's a structure for producing Soldiers for the Holy Man. There is no evidence of childhood or parenthood as we know it."

"Explain, please."

"Wait. A moment."

Jameson waited patiently through a silence that was longer than a moment. He wished he could see Hanna's face, but he was not yet willing to push the restrictions on voice-only, limited-data communications. When she spoke again the odd, remote quality of trance was gone, but she was choosing words thoughtfully, carefully.

"In this contact, I observed a dialogue between a male and a female. They are—filling a certain role in the life of the society of which they are a part. It is . . . in another society it would be a parental role, but the emotions we associate with that role are absent. The adults view themselves only as breeders. The structure is not familial, and is directed only toward physical survival of the young to maturity. There is no parallel in my experience. Except, perhaps, breeders of animal stock . . ."

She paused. Jameson was used to these pauses. He did not try to rush her.

She said at last, "The only Standard words that work here are 'nursery,' or 'crèche.' The male and female I was with are caretakers; they are two of many in this one place. The females primarily suckle multiple infants. The males see to supplying the females' enormous nutritional needs, and to feeding older children and keeping the complex organized. I don't know if this pair are the biological parents of any of the children there. It seems possible, in context with some of the things they thought about, but it doesn't seem to matter. My impression is that whatever connection there was, even to the female's identification of her own young, is weakening, and soon will be gone."

Another pause. When it had gone on for a long time he said, "I was beginning to think some kind of personal parent-child relationship was universal among sentient species."

"Evidently not," Hanna said. "We thought two genders were standard for optimal evolution, too, until we came into contact with Uskos. Now we know that one will work, under certain conditions. Reproduction here might require three."

"What?" he said, but she went on without answering.

"The dialogue was about crèche issues. I will give staff sociologists the details I have. But mostly I watched for other things they thought about, in the intervals when they weren't talking.

"The female is changing roles. She is—" Hanna was choosing words even more carefully now. "She has been in a nurturing mode . . . nurturing, in this context, meaning no more than nursing. She is moving toward a, a warrior role, a fighting mode. It feels instinctual, cyclical, but still there is the sense of a, a—a structure of some sort, directed from outside—military? Governmental? I don't know."

"What about—"

"The male has filled a military role too, and will do it again, but he's at—the center of the reproductive cycle? While she's emerging from it?"

"You are asking me?"

"Just thinking. Of the best way to describe it. He's immersed in caretaking and mating. They think about mating a *lot*. There's an enormous reward there, I think."

This time the pause was very long. Finally he said, "Go on. Is there more?"

"There's something there that scares me," she said unexpectedly. "When they think about mating, it's not about a particular mate. It's only about intense pleasure and an impersonal drive. It's compulsive."

"Sounds like sex to me," he said dryly.

"No, no. Stop thinking like a human male. I think," she said slowly, "I think there is an actual third party involved. When they think of mating there is another presence in their thoughts."

"Who?"

"I can't see it. It's like they *don't* see it. Their perception of it, the sense they have of it, is purely tactile. Physically—physically, it might be quite small. And it might—" Her voice wavered. "I think it might not look like the ones I've been calling the male and the female at all."

They were both silent, thinking about it. Jameson felt an unaccustomed prickle in his spine. Something that could scare Hanna? Something about, of all things, sex, that could scare Hanna?

He said suddenly, "What inhibitions do you have, Hanna?"

He half expected her to say *None, as you very well know,* but there had to be something.

After a while she said slowly, "I'm biased against impersonal sex. Even putting aside you and Michael, going back all the way to the first boy I made love with—I remember every boy, every man, I took to bed. Well, maybe not . . . do you remember every woman you've been with? Of course not. I can't give you a list with the names of every man who's pleasured me, either. But you'd recognize your lovers again. You'd know them. And you would have emotions along with the memories. 'This one was good company': a memory with pleasant connotations. 'That one lied': lingering anger, perhaps. 'This one wanted to use me. That one genuinely liked me.' That's human thinking, for both male and female. It comes naturally to us; there's some of that lasting personal connection to our sexual partners in all except the sickest individuals among us. No, even in them, twisted though it is."

She knew what she was talking about. She had known one of those human-seeming horrors. She had been present when Michael Kristofik put a monster to death.

He said, "We designate those individuals as evil—"

"They *are* evil."

"Is that what you sense?"

"No . . . No. There's no sense of malice where a human spirit should be. This element—" her voice was going dreamy now—"this element is part of a coherent gestalt. It's integral to what these beings are. Oh . . ." Her voice changed again, hardened. "I see now. The impersonality touched something in me that is still sensitized. I just wish I could have killed them slowly," Hanna said.

It sounded like a non sequitur, but it was not. Hanna had personally killed two men who had raped her, and one of Michael Kristofik's companions had killed the other two. Hanna had seemed to regard it as the appropriate penalty for what they had done. Apparently she now thought it had been too lenient.

He gave her more time, finally prompted her: "And?"

"Nothing else," she said, suddenly sounding tired. "Nothing I can pull out as a viable thread."

"Well, what you have is substantial. This is going to be interesting," he added, half to himself.

"What? The crèches? How they mate?"

"All of it. F'thal, Girritt, Zeig-Daru, Uskos—we knew nothing whatsoever about those populations prior to actual contact. For the first time we're assembling a body of knowledge *before* we talk to them for the first time."

She murmured something; he did not think he could have heard her correctly. She could not have said, *I don't like them,* not Hanna, and he said, "What was that, please?" and she said more loudly, "I don't like them."

It was so unexpected that he could not respond immediately, and she went on. "It isn't just the compulsive nature of their mating, the absence of emotion toward another individual. It's that same impersonal attitude toward the young. Every single sentient species we've encountered has one thing in common: the deep, loving attachment to their children. Adults will even sacrifice themselves for other adults' children, simply because they are children. I don't think," she said, her voice becoming very quiet, "anyone on that whole world feels love."

He took a deep breath. He could not tell how deeply she was disturbed by the idea; he could not even ask so intimate a question when everything they said was laid out in transcripts seen by many other eyes. He had to be as impersonal in his response as the creatures of Species Y.

"Very well," he said. "We'll treat it as a hypothesis for now. We may find evidence to overturn it. Until tomorrow?"

"Tomorrow," she said.

"Endit, then."

———

Here was another difference. The scholars said, puzzled, that the religious and military texts picked up from old transmissions were curiously one-dimensional. There seemed to be no cultural layering. Even allowing for the limited subject matter, they said, the chief characteristic was repetition.

In contrast, they brought up titles from Earth's civilization, where cultures were layered richly one on another. The *Gallic Wars*. The *Holy Bible*.

———

"Status, please."

"The culture appears to lack layering because there is none. Past is assumed to resemble present. Future, it is assumed, will mirror past."

"With all the years they have at their disposal . . ."

A sigh. Was that melancholy in the deep voice? But probably only Hanna would hear it.

Jameson was one of a handful of humans whose immune systems were fundamentally incompatible with anti-senescence techniques, the prospect of their turning deadly always present. It was not the only reason he continued to resist his enduring attraction to Hanna, but it was an important one. Chronologically, he was no more than thirty years her senior. In terms of life span, there could be no estimate. It depended on whether the next attempt killed him or not.

Hanna was one of the few people who knew it. She could imagine what he thought of squandered centuries.

Expect the unexpected, she had told her Contact Education students. *Better yet, dispense with expectations.* She was pretty good at that, she thought. Even allowing for the possibility that she was starting to believe her own legend, she thought she was pretty good at that.

Until she detached from the mind of a Battleground child and found herself, with no apparent gap in time, screaming at someone in Communications to get her through to Earth *now*, she had to see her son's face *right now—!*

That ended, and she woke up seconds (it seemed) later in a darkened room. She was in sickbay. She knew she was sedated; had been forcibly sedated.

"Coming around," someone said.

"Hanna?" said Jameson's voice. "Can you hear me?"

"Starr . . ." A whisper.

She sat up slowly. She was sore all over, especially her jaw, which felt like it had taken an efficient left cross. She picked up an image from one of the shadowed figures around her—picked it up from the man's nervousness at her movement. There had been some kind of fight, she had been at the center of it, had started it, had beaten up somebody in Communications, had finally been overpowered.

She uttered a soft expletive. The people around her stirred.

"What happened?" Jameson said, almost casually.

She turned her head and he was standing there. It was holo, of course. He held Mickey's hand.

Something leaped in her chest. Longing shook her; she drank in the sight of her child. She must have made a move to get up and go to him, because Jameson put out a warning hand. She felt, then, the distrust that surrounded her. People were afraid of her. She made herself hold still.

"Mommy!" said the little boy, laughing with joy, but he didn't try to run to her either. He knew the difference between reality and holography. Children learned that early.

"Mickey . . ." Her voice was unsteady. She calmed herself, a tremendous effort. Never mind the people around her. She would do nothing that might frighten Mickey.

"I'm sorry," she said. "Did I hurt anyone?"

Jameson answered. "Not seriously."

The tension in the room began to ease. She could not take her eyes off Mickey. Her arms ached for him.

She said slowly, "There was a child, a boy. Only it was like touching the consciousness of an insect. Not even a mammal. More intelligent than an insect, but confined, limited, like being in a box—" She shuddered. "I got it mixed up with Mickey. I had to make sure nobody'd done that to *him*."

"As you see . . ."

Mickey bounced up and down, steady enough on his feet with a hand to hold. He was happy, his eyes bright. They were not his father's eyes; they were the eyes of his paternal grandmother, almost black. *Hers were dark*, Michael had said, *she hid things in them*.

"Mommy home?" Mickey asked, the words astonishingly clear. "Mommy someday?"

"Someday . . ." she said, and pain filled her. He was talking and she was not there to hear him; she had not even known it.

She found that she was pushing at her hair, a habit almost abandoned. It had been a habit of the ghost.

Jameson said, "I'm curious as to why this happened. I believe there's often a kind of emotional backlash when you break from the trance state, yes? But you appeared to be—I've seen Communications' visual log—in some sort of fugue. That's not usual, unless I've misunderstood the process."

"You didn't misunderstand. It's never happened to me before and I've never heard of its happening to another Adept."

"A new factor, then. Not just the contact with an alien mind. That's not new; even these aliens are no longer new to you."

He looked down at Mickey, who was watching something outside the holo field; who suddenly laughed, pulled away from Jameson's hand, and wobbled off toward whatever fine thing beckoned.

Come back! she wanted to cry out; she leaned toward the image, and felt all the eyes that watched her. She could see Mickey's nursery suite dimly, like a ghost of itself, and a glow that suggested it was bright with sunshine. Jameson must have gone straight home and commandeered the child as soon as he was notified of Hanna's outbreak.

"A new factor. Having a child?" Hanna said.

"Maybe. That's about as primal as instinct gets."

"I must have thought—oh, that something had been *done* to the child. Because I know—" Her voice wavered. "Because I know a little boy and he's not limited at all. He never will be. I won't let it happen."

"Nor will I." Jameson looked away from her, in the direction Mickey had gone. There was a sudden flurry of unexpected noise: sharp yaps, a shout of laughter from Mickey.

"You got him a *Pup*?" Hanna said.

"Of course not. He's got a young Dog," Jameson said, meaning an animal that had not been genetically tailored to remain cuddly all its life. He added, "It's a Mutt."

"Mutts are imports! They cost a fortune!"

"There is also a Cat."

"But you detest Kits—"

"An infant Cat. An Alley Cat."

"Oh, God," Hanna said.

———

Hope Metra issued an order that prohibited Hanna from attempting further telepathic contact with the beings of Battleground. Hanna told Jameson about the order, and waited with interest to see how long it would take her director to trump Metra's commissioner.

Not "if." Just how long.

Jameson had regained the prestige he had lost when he was forced to leave the Coordinating Commission. Alien Relations and Contact had been elevated to department status in the first place because Jameson's former Commission colleagues did not want him wasted on Heartworld. Under Jameson, the department had gone from being the object of horrified fascination to an object of fascinated respect; it had become a force. Hanna thought negotiations on a compromise might take a day or two, but she was still contemplating her bruises when Jameson contacted her.

Back to voice only: apparently she was not to see him (or her son) unless she became violent again. It was tempting.

He told her she was to resume doing what she had been doing. "But with a condition attached," he added.

"That being?"

"Guards. Armed only with stunners, and they'll be outside the room. No ship's personnel inside with you, but you can have people from your own team monitoring you, as usual."

"I guess the captain doesn't care if I attack *them*."

Jameson ignored that. "There is some concern about your stability."

"When has there not been?"

"I've shared it, from time to time. This could be one of those times."

"It was a fluke—I think. There are a great many—I can't think of them as children, call them the beings' young—but they're . . . undifferentiated. A recognizable stratum. It won't be hard to stay away from them."

"Good. How much choice do you exercise in which subjects to observe, by the way?"

"I've been drifting," she admitted. "Sampling. I don't know what else to do at this stage."

"Can you return to an individual? Do you learn enough about any single personality, know it well enough, to do that? You can do it with human beings you're familiar with, I know."

Hanna thought about it. She was not in a conference room but in her own cabin, lying on her back, waiting for the bruise-absorption compounds to do their job, along with something she had been given to restore a strained muscle or two. She put her arms behind her head and looked up at the plain white ceiling. In the bedchamber she shared with Jameson the ceiling bore a tranquil design in glossy wood. She did not know when she would see it again, feel the downy pillows under her head—feel, above all, those big hands, strength barely restrained, moving slowly across her skin.

"Could you repeat that?" she said.

"Aren't you listening?"

"I was distracted. Just say again, please."

He did. She thought about the questions.

"I don't know. They're individuals, but most don't have sharp personality profiles," she said. "Why?"

"You said you did a certain amount of guidance with one of the subjects—pushed him, I think you said. How far can you go with that?"

"I don't know what you mean."

"Use one individual to direct you to another. Leapfrog, so to speak. Do that until you connect with a pre-selected target. A high-ranking official, perhaps."

"I don't know if they have any 'high-ranking officials' as we understand the term. Military authorities, maybe. Religious figures."

"Same thing. Can you do that?"

"I don't think so."

"How do you know? Have you tried?"

He was at his most didactic. All thoughts of eroticism vanished. She said dubiously, "All right. I'll try."

Akkt scans monitors all through the long day, a long day indeed, much longer than a Standard day. He looks for anomalies, sometimes corrects errors. At least one other worker has scanned the same data, made some corrections, missed mistakes that Akkt finds. Akkt misses some too; still other workers will scan the data until all the errors are gone. Akkt misses them because he often falls—

"H'ana?"

"Um?"

"What happened? It seemed like you just went to sleep."

"Oh. I did. That was the most incredibly boring experience I've ever had."

Twek and Kwrr and the facilitators are mating—

Hanna broke out of trance quickly, but not quite quickly enough. She looked at Joseph and Bella, the monitors today. She knew what her expression must be. It had been described to her. *Smoldering* was one word for it. She knew what she was projecting, too, and saw its effect, but she could not seem to stop.

She smiled at Joseph. He smiled back.

She smiled at Bella. Bella smiled back.

Hanna preferred men, unlike Bella. But she had been known to make exceptions.

Oh, yes! Bella said.

Hanna thought: *Backlash.*

Then she thought: *NO.*

There were few absolute prohibitions in the free-floating cloud of D'neeran sexual mores, but *NO* was unassailable. Joseph's mouth was nearly on hers, Bella's fingers reached to caress her hair; both wrenched away abruptly. Their hurt and confusion washed over her. She picked a question from the tangle. She said, "I don't *know* why! Just *because!*"

Bella, immediately accepting, eyed Joseph; Bella occasionally made exceptions, too. But Joseph's attention was still fixed on Hanna. He said, "It's not like you have a vowed bond with that man. What could you have with a true-human anyway?"

"It's not because of him," Hanna answered. She got to her feet. Her legs shook. "But it wasn't—it didn't come from me. It's *not* me. That's sufficient. Leave it."

They left it, left her; left the room holding hands. She thought for a moment about Michael Kristofik and about Starr Jameson. She said to the silent room, "Those two spoiled me, I think. Spoiled me for uncomplicated pleasures."

She let it go and thought about the backlash effect. Something in that brief contact was outside her experience—and there was no one as experienced with aliens as Hanna to go to. She was on her own.

Almost.

new, said the ghost. *what do we know about instinct?*

oh you're *back. eat, breathe, breed—*

fight, said the ghost, remembering alien blood.

fear, Hanna said, remembering terrors the ghost had known.

universal? the ghost wondered.

so far. here, too, I think. though not fear so far

but could there, said the ghost, *be something else . . . ?*

Hanna was at the door. Her moving hand stopped in the air, but the door opened anyway.

She said slowly, aloud: "If a nonhuman has a drive that does not parallel any of mine, how in heaven's name will I know it for what it is?"

"Are you asking me?" said a flustered voice; she had forgotten the guards, who had not left yet. She didn't respond, listening to a different voice.

it's not what they have. it's what they don't, said the ghost. It was said with a lot of conviction, for a ghost.

is that it

the mate is not a person. the child is not
i don't like these beings
they won't care. they can't

Woort takes inventory.
One case of vegetable-based protein food. One case of
vegetable-based protein food. One case of vegetable-based
protein food. One case of electronic wrenches—what is that
doing here? One case of vegetable-based protein food—
"H'ana?"
"Mmmm?"
"You fell asleep again."

INCOMING, INCOMING! IN

"Status, please." The voice sounded tight.
"I'm not having any luck with—"
"I understand one of the beings died while you were in
contact."
"Oh. That."
A silence.
"Hanna?"
"Yes. What do you want to know about it?"
"I want to know"— (with careful patience) —"if the
event affected you emotionally."
"No."
Silence. She didn't break it because she had nothing to
say. When he did, the voice was so controlled as to be ex-
pressionless.
"I'm told your heartbeat spiked and you lost conscious-
ness."
"Yes." She resigned herself; he wasn't going to give up. "I
was out for less than half a minute. The being—I don't even
know if it was male or female—was in a combat situation
and under attack. I had barely touched its mind when it
died. It did not even have time to know it was going to die.
A consciousness was there and then it just . . . wasn't. Don't
worry. All right?"
"If you say so."

"I say so. And I wouldn't put the mission at risk by lying about my ability to continue."

"My apologies for interrupting. You were saying?"

"I've had no luck re-establishing contact with a previous subject. I don't know any individual I've touched well enough to do it easily, and we're still a long way out. You know distance is a factor in telepathy, although no one knows why. We're so far from our own space now, from human space, that I couldn't even touch your mind—"

She thought: *Or could I? Don't I know you well enough by now?*

And heard, as distinctly as if he had been in the room: *I hoped you did not!*

Such a long silence this time. How strange this transcript would look!

Hanna was too shaken to speak. She did not reach out again; she had not meant to do what she had done, and if she was shaken, he must be reeling. It was one thing to put up with occasional invasion when you lived with a telepath, but how he must hate it from five hundred light-years away!

She tried to remember what she had been saying. He remembered before she did.

"You think the effort to find a known individual is a waste of time, then?"

Hardly anyone except Hanna would have heard the strain in his voice.

It was a few seconds before she could respond, but when she did, she thought she sounded normal, too.

"I do think so. I'll continue trolling, hoping for a useful contact. Unless you want to abandon this line of inquiry altogether."

"No, not yet. You are aware that *Endeavor's* initial target position is a point approximately five light-days from Battleground?"

"Yes. I've lost track of our ETA, though." *Endeavor,* mapping as she went, might cover light-years with one Jump, but working out calculations for the first transit into unknown space took days, sometimes weeks. Where they would end up if the calculations went wrong was unknown, although one of the other universes—known to exist but inaccessible—was most likely. No probe that disappeared had ever been found or heard from again.

"You might as well continue until *Endeavor* reaches the target. The probability curve suggests a period of two to eight weeks. Of course, that could change."

It could change drastically after the next Jump, depending on calculations based on the new position. Hanna shrugged. She imagined him doing the same.

"Until tomorrow?" she said.

"Until tomorrow. Endit."

No possibility of asking, even if she dared, about the undercurrent to the words that had formed in his mind in that fleeting contact—the surprise that bordered, contrary to anything she might have expected, on pleasure.

She couldn't have picked a worse time.

Jameson closed the call, saw the blip of light that meant the transcript was being routed to the dozen people who monitored Hanna's daily oral reports and theoretically read her written reports as well. He doubted that most of them did all that—*he* did—and this report would get submerged in all the rest. Even if others thought something was odd about it, no one else could know that she had touched his thoughts, his mind, his *self*, from that inconceivable distance. Mickey, yes—the child who had grown inside her body, was formed from her flesh. That would surprise no one. With great effort she could, probably, communicate with her own mother, or with another beloved telepath like Iledra, the Lady of Koroth on D'neera. But she should not be able to do it with him, a true-human not of her blood and with virtually no natural bent for telepathy.

I'm glad she has survived as long as she has so that when she gets back I can kill her, he thought—thought as he went into a meeting with the Commissioners of the Interworld Polity with no time to spare. It was an informal meeting, too, in Peter Struzik's chambers instead of the elaborate formal hall, so there were no busy aides to provide distraction, no technicians monitoring recordings. And the only two commissioners present in the flesh were his closest friends.

Andrella Murphy shot him a look as soon as he sank into one of Struzik's comfortable chairs. Struzik, president of the Commission for almost as long as Murphy had been the commissioner from Willow, saw it and looked narrowly at Jameson too.

"Don't ask," he said.

The three who only appeared to be present barely looked at him at first; the meeting had been going on for half an hour, and earlier agenda items still occupied them. But Muammed al-Nimeury did take a second look. Jameson nodded to al-Nimeury, so old an enemy that he was almost a friend. Al-Nimeury was far away on Co-op; Jameson wondered where the other two were in reality. Karin Weisz supposedly was on her homeworld, Colony One, and Abel Chu, like Struzik a native of Earth, officially was at least on the same planet as Polity Admin. He was probably, in fact, with Karin, wherever they were, while maintaining the polite fiction that they were professional colleagues only.

At least, thought Jameson, I never made the mistake of trying to hide an affair, though acknowledging Hanna cost me dearly. This liaison will come back to haunt Karin and Abel one day.

He had thought the same thing when he first learned that greed had diverted Edward Vickery into paths incompatible with public trust, and the knowledge had delighted him. It was the opportunity he needed, and Heartworld's Commission seat was nearly in his grasp again. Vickery was not present either materially or virtually; he was on Heartworld, too busy fending off official censure to attend this casual session. Which was why Jameson was here to run through a routine briefing on the Battleground mission.

Routine was what they were going to get. He wasn't going to tell them about that contact with Hanna, the underlying sadness, the loneliness embedded in the question ... *Don't I know you well enough by now?* He had endured enough intrusive questions about his personal relationship with Hanna in years past. It was almost accepted now, and tolerated (barely) even on his homeworld, and he would not do anything to revive old controversies.

Chapter IV

HANNA WAS GETTING TIRED. She was seriously tired of her own compatriots, for one thing, and what they were doing to the true-humans around them. Her inadvertent arousal of Joseph and Bella had repercussions that complicated everyone's lives. Bella, having enjoyed Joseph, had sent him away and told him not to come back. Joseph sulked, declined to be consoled by Glory (which hurt her feelings), but allowed a broadminded *Endeavor* crewwoman to cheer him up. Bella became interested in the same woman, who enjoyed the attention, decided she was undecided about her own preferences, and teased both her suitors until they realized she was engaging in the kind of game D'neerans did not play. Arch, comforting Glory for her rejection by Joseph, ended up assuaging her curiosity about what it was like to have sex with a D'neeran.

"No wonder you people do it so much!" she said to Hanna, who did not want to hear about it.

But Arch reported to Hanna, "She wasn't with me, not all of her; she was *comparing*. Why do those people do it so much? How can you do it with them?"

Hanna wanted to hear that even less, but she answered.

"It was educational, when I first came into close contact with true-humans," she told Arch, not entirely in words. "And I had fun, too, of course."

"But later? Those other two?" he said, but she was not going to expose Michael or Starr so intimately in order to satisfy Arch's inquisitiveness.

"Starr is an exceptional man, and so was Michael," she said.

He wanted to know more, but she blocked his probe easily; she was practiced in Adept skills and did not have to fall back on the greater power she held secret.

"I guess I'll have to keep trying until I figure it out for myself," Arch said. He would, too, and happily; making love was Arch's avocation. Rejection (which he had experienced from Hanna early on) did not trouble him. There were women everywhere, he said cheerfully, and he liked all of them, and many of them liked him right back. Now he added, not unkindly, "You're hiding what you feel. That's what true-humans do. Have you gotten so exceptional yourself that you've turned into one?"

"I sometimes think that has happened," she said.

It was not a new thought. She let him feel her sadness about it, but did not show him how deep it went. She was neither one nor the other, neither D'neeran nor wholly true-human, and there was not another like her. Nor would there be, because an alien race also had engraved some pathways in the substance of her brain that no other human being of any origin possessed.

She was tired of the Battleground beings, too. And just plain tired.

"Status, please."

"I'm getting nowhere." No preamble. "I've surveyed a machinist, some kind of computer technician, another nursing female, a—a—just a minute. I'm looking for the list."

"I have one. An instructor of marksmanship—at a firing range, or some analogous place, apparently. A heavy vehicle operator, and someone preparing meals. Hanna?"

"Yes?"

"Did you get any sleep in the intervals between these contacts?"

"What?"

Jameson leaned back and looked out across the river. Finally spring, but the day was cool, the sky cloudy. It was time to get a medical report on Hanna, he thought.

"How much sleep did you get in the last twenty-four hours?"

She was silent, probably trying to remember. Finally she said, "I don't think I've slept for a while."

"Why? What are you trying to do?"

"We need a breakthrough," she said. "I need to find one of their authorities. What we've been calling the Holy Man, or the Demon."

"It's not working. You're randomly sampling an enormous population for a few individuals. The odds of finding an 'authority' this way are poor."

"What, then? What do you think I should do?"

"Just a moment."

He found the report he wanted in seconds; he had gone back to it several times since first reading.

"Remember the fighter who was part of an effort to take a section of beach?"

"Yes, of course. That was the first one I touched. It was when I found out how long-lived they are."

"Even longer-lived than you thought, probably. Have you seen the reports on the planet's orbital statistics?"

"Yes, but I haven't studied them."

"You do know the year is longer than a Standard year?"

"Not by much. Something over a couple of months?"

"It adds up. Your fighter, with his two hundred and forty-six summers, is almost three hundred Standard years old. And he thought of the commanders and the Holy Man as being much older than that."

After a moment she said, "I don't see why you've brought this up."

"I don't either, exactly. It's incidental; I was just thinking about that fighter . . ." He found himself tapping the screen with the end of a stylus. "Forget about trying to find a particular individual. You've been taking a wide view; suppose you go deeper instead. The fighter was . . . contemplating a possible future. There was an aspiration involved, remember? A personal motivation. He thought he might become a Commander. That's what's lacking," he said abruptly. "You're skimming surface thoughts, goal-oriented. There's more than that to some of them, at least. This fighter had — would you call it hope? Is that the only emotion you've been able to pick up?"

"Well . . . not quite. The nursing female, the first one, I mean" — there were so many she had lost count — "was getting impatient, you know. Ready to be done with it and go on to another role. And the male doing inventory was a little, oh, aggrieved when he found something in the stores that shouldn't be there. So they do have emotions. I just haven't looked at emotion closely. Trance is not really compatible with experiencing it. I can *observe* what others feel, and sometimes it hits me later—I've done that—"

Her voice faltered and stopped.

Damn it, if I could only see her face!

"What instance are you thinking of, Hanna?"

"That . . . last . . ." The words dragged out one by one into silence. But he could guess what she had not said.

Last hour or last minute or last second. And then Michael Kristofik's death. She had never been able to speak directly of those moments, from which she had emerged half-sane, or worse.

He said her name softly. If she could talk of it now he would listen in spite of all those other ears. But she only said, "Never mind—" and he heard the effort in it.

"I'm sorry," he said gently, and meant it, though he could not have known what his questions would trigger and could not have anticipated this.

Because she was healing, and on the night before she left to join *Endeavor* she had murmured sleepily, smiling, sated, "You are in danger of making me fall in love with you again . . ."

She said, "Can we talk about this another time?"

"Of course. But . . . try to go deeper, Hanna. As best you can."

———

Some hours later, secured in her cabin with Arch as monitor, she tried something new.

———

A mirror, a face. So young. The (past-eyes) hardly indentations. My mouth is too small and my ears are too big. What can I do to make him look at me?

Wistfulness.

I know it will not matter but I wish my fellow-Soldier would look at me more. My hair will not grow longer. I think the color is pleasant, I wish he would look at my hair.

Thin four-jointed fingers. Both hands moving, fingers in hair.

A braided rope is pleasant to look at. I looked at Kwee's hair when she braided it. I wonder if my fellow-Soldier would look at mine.

A narrow plait, another, and another.

Pleasant to see! They sway when my head moves! And my ears do not look so big. Maybe he will look at my hair. Although I know it will not matter when the time comes and the facilitators come. When the time comes it will be any Soldier whose time has also come. That is the power of Abundant God.

I wish I could think of a way to make my mouth bigger. I wish my fellow-Soldier's time could come when mine does and I could be with him when the facilitators come, but it won't happen.

But if my mouth was bigger, maybe he would look at me more.

"Time. H'ana? It's time."

Hanna came slowly out of trance. Her cheeks were immediately wet with tears.

"Why are you crying?"

"She wants to look nice for her friend," Hanna said. "She wants to look pretty."

There was a mirror in the room, which Hanna occasionally consulted to make sure her face was not dirty. She rose and went to it now and looked at herself. She had lost a little weight, not enough to matter, and not unusual when she was under a strain. She looked past the image in the mirror to what it meant. D'neerans did not much prize appearances, and she had not realized until she began to go among true-humans that by the standards of their dominant culture, she was beautiful. On the rare occasions when she took pains about what she wore, even Jameson's eyes widened, and he was not easily impressed. There were elements of true-human culture that she had often observed but had been slow to internalize. So it had only recently occurred to her that how she looked might be turned to her advantage in certain situations; or maybe it was not recognition of the fact, but the first wedge of willingness to use it.

She was not shielding her thoughts, and Arch caught the last one and came up behind her. His hand closed on her shoulder. He said, "Does the word 'corruption' mean anything to you?"

She said, "I think about it, from time to time."

"You think you're not using your face, your body, to your

advantage now? You think that true-human man would take such good care of you if you were ugly?"

"He would take care of me because I'm useful," she said. "That's how it started in the first place. Alien Relations and Contact would not be what it is without me. He would take care of me no matter what I looked like. But he would not make love to me, if I were ugly."

Arch took his hand away and said, "He hasn't been able to keep the whole legal apparatus of the Polity from threatening you. You're selling yourself pretty cheap."

She said slowly, "The cost to him has been very high. You have no idea."

———

Looking for emotion now, consciously.

He and she and their facilitators are mating—

A violent stop. Dema and Joseph were saying *What what what is wrong?*

"I'm not doing that again!" she said.

———

She has memorized all of it, it is never difficult, there are only so many variations on the text. Almost time to speak. Beyond the folding doors they wait, a whole marching field of them. Exhort them to obey, exhort them to sacrifice! For the Holy Man.

Fill myself with strength. Fill myself with certitude! Fill myself! Such good cakes. Time for one more. Maybe two more. It is almost time, time to go through the doors, this uniform is too tight, why didn't they get me one that fits. Maybe there is time for one more cake—

Joseph said apprehensively, "You were in there a long time this time."

"It was sort of compulsive," Hanna said. She looked around, not sure what she was looking for. Glory started to hand her a flask of water.

"No," Hanna said, "I'm not thirsty. I'm hungry. God, am I hungry."

———

He is looking at a vehicle. It runs on treads; what fuels it is obscure, although if his thought were guided that way, it would be clear, because he knows. There are things he is supposed to know, but—

It fell off. Again. I thought I had. The screws just right. I must have done it right. Part right. The assembly held. Together. In my hands. It felt solid when I lifted it. But then the bolts and the first nut and I tightened the second nut and why did it fall off? I cannot do anything right, and the officer will come and she will flap her ears at me and say everything I do is incompetent it is always this way—

"H'ana? You're crying again."

She wiped her eyes. She said, "God damn him."

"Who? Your subject?" Joseph put out a hand to comfort her.

"No. Starr. I swear, when I get back I'll prowl through *his* emotions and feed them back to him. See how he likes it!"

"Does he have any?"

She said the same thing she had said to Arch: "You have no idea."

———

Skimming again. Impatient. *Endeavor*, they told her, was nearly at the end of its journey. Her communications with Jameson were strained. She refused to open herself to the emotions of the Battleground beings again, told him trance was no use if she could not use its detachment. She knew (and knew that he did too) the truth was that she had had enough of tears—her own—and declined to cry someone else's. He stopped short of ordering her to do exactly that.

Somewhere between dragonfly landings in alien thoughts, the ghost surfaced.

we always did what he wanted us to do and it always worked. even when we didn't want to do it—

you always did what he wanted you to do. i resigned from his control one day on Michael's GeeGee. you must have missed that

you tried but. what are we doing at contact education

surviving. you must know what personality adjustment would mean. there would be only a white shadow left of me. you would be the ghost of a ghost

The ghost subsided, unhappy. Hanna went on sampling

surface thoughts. Surface thoughts would do just fine. Surface thoughts would tell them all they had to know.

"Status?"

"Their theology appears to lack moral implications because it has none."

"Elaborate, please."

"They go each moment with the consciousness of a godhead. It is a universal, it is, so to speak, the default, when they do not concentrate on a task or attack or defense. I have met perhaps two humans whose minds go that way. I thought them psychotic. Here it is the norm, and the norm cannot, by definition, be psychotic."

"But moral implications?"

"In this consciousness there is no place for the importance of others' lives. They do not matter. Only what will come after, and they imagine the afterlife ecstasy is akin to what they feel in mating. Killing is encouraged. Death in battle is their expected end. I have seen no sign of conscious personal cruelty, such as human beings sometimes inflict on one another. But I have sensed no concept of universal brotherhood, either, or of spontaneous kindness."

"How," said the voice—always calm, but this time with a kind of astonishment—"can they possibly live?"

"I don't know. Yet."

Gabriel Guyup stumbled through old stone corridors, half-asleep and full of apprehension. He was waked occasionally to comfort a sick child, or one prone to chronic nightmare, but this time the night-duty brother had said: "Father Abbot wants you."

"Wha—?" said Gabriel, half a syllable all he could produce.

"Father—Abbot—wants—you."

Oh, dear God, if a child has died . . .

He rounded the last corner and the door was before him, spilling light into the dim hallway. He slowed down when he reached it, but sick fear went before him, and the abbot took one look at his face and winced.

"What's wrong?" said the abbot, which ought to have

been Gabriel's question, and Gabriel found a mug of coffee thrust into his hand. He had an accurate reputation as a heavy sleeper.

"You called for me—"

"Yes, but there's nothing to be afraid of. I know you're not afraid of me!"

"It's ..." He looked at the chronometer on Father Abbot's wall. Alta stubbornly insisted on dividing its days into twenty-four hours, though they were not Standard hours. At the abbey it was just past two o'clock in the morning.

"It's daytime at Polity Admin, apparently. Sit down."

Gabriel sat and sipped. His fear eased. Admin—this would have something to do with Colonial Oversight, then; though they were usually good about calling in daylight, local time.

"Are they bringing a child?" he asked.

"Who?"

"Oversight?"

"This isn't about Oversight. Definitely not."

The abbot sat at his desk. He said, "This hobby of yours. Sentient nonhuman species."

Gabriel drank more coffee. Maybe the conversation would make sense if he was fully awake.

"What about it, Father?"

"Maybe I should have paid more attention to it."

"Why?" asked Gabriel, diverted. "My spiritual advisor is fully aware of my activities. I know some of my brothers disapprove, but Father Tomas believes faith is not incompatible with intellectual inquiry. So do you."

"I do. No, I don't find anything to object to. I just don't think we realized how *good* you are at it."

Thank you, God, for coffee, Gabriel thought, and said, "Father, I'm completely lost."

"Yes, no wonder. I'm sorry, I'm a little in shock. I've just been talking to the Director of Alien Relations and Contact."

"What? Starr Jameson?"

"I suppose you know all about him. I barely recognized his name. I looked him up afterward. Have you ever talked to a stranger who was being very, very polite and charming because he knew he could squash you like a bug and knew you didn't know it? That describes our conversation."

Gabriel, who knew exactly who Jameson was and his importance in the Polity, said, "That must have been interesting."

"Yes. He said you've had some correspondence with his department. With Hanna ril-Koroth. I know who she is, of course—"

Because Michael Kristofik had once been a student at the abbey; because some older brothers had known him, and a few years ago had been given reason to remember.

"The director said you sent the department a schematic of core beliefs among sentient species and suggested further study is warranted."

Gabriel forgot the hour and the oddity of the summons. He could talk aliens all night if someone was willing to listen.

"Lady Hanna didn't agree. I never actually talked to her; it wasn't a debate. She just replied that with one exception there *weren't* any substantial core beliefs, where I think belief is there but not explicit, possibly unconscious. But she didn't seem to consider the proposition valid, so I didn't try again."

"Yes, Director Jameson told me. He wants to recruit you to join a Contact team. I wonder how he knew it was proper to start with getting my permission?"

"*Contact* wants me?" This was too much information to process. Gabriel tried—and failed; he nearly dropped the coffee. Deep fear was gone, now he was transported to high excitement, and only ingrained discipline allowed him to say something practical. "I guess I could do distance teaming, if you do allow it and I can make time for it. Or would I have to spend some time in the Polity?"

"Not the Polity. Deep space. *Endeavor Three*?" said the abbot, as if he was not sure he remembered the correct name. "I remember an *Endeavor.* I'm sure you do too. For some reason my predecessor thought it needed blessing. Do you know what *Endeavor Three* is?"

"*Endeavor Three* is a Contact vessel," Gabriel said slowly. "According to the publicly available information, it's searching for a suspected alien presence in the direction of Orion. However, Lady Hanna is aboard. I thought, when I read she was there, that the 'alien presence' might be more than suspected. Confirmed, in fact."

"Really? Well, that's where they want you. I said we could spare you if you want to go."

"But I can't just—" It would take a week to decide if he even wanted to go—but of course he couldn't, some of his charges were fragile—but if he meant to leave the abbey altogether, or maybe a leave of absence—but he hadn't even thought seriously of that, not yet—

But what came out of his mouth was: "When do they want me to start?"

"Why do you think I sent for you at this ridiculous hour?" the abbot said. "They want you yesterday. If you're going, go and pack."

Chapter V

HE IS ORDERING A COMPANY into battle. He will lose nearly every fighter and will not take the objective; the balance of weaponry is decisive. If a few escape it will be by God's will. So they say. Perhaps a future Commander will be among them. The Holy Man has so ordered—

"H'ana? It's time."

Wait.

Mark this one. Mark him well. Feel the texture of his thought, burrow deep—run the risk with this one that he might feel my presence, he is that important. Where is he? Narrow it down. Guide a visualization, not hard to do, the topography is not far from his conscious thought. A simple surface map, good enough. A continent that covers almost a hemisphere, and he is near the center. Who is he? A Commander. But what is he, so different from the rest? A High Commander.

"H'ana!"

She felt, as if from a distance, someone shake her: Carl. Bella called to her in thought: *Return.*

Wait. Only wait.

———

Bella said, "She won't come out."

Carl looked at the still figure, cross-legged on the floor, back straight, eyes closed. Hanna's hands rested, curved, in her lap. She didn't look like she was breathing, but she was; he knew he would see a shallow respiration if he watched long enough. Not a fold moved in her loose white tunic and trousers, nor a strand of the rather unkempt hair that streamed down her back. There had been no alarm from the remote monitor that registered her heartbeat—the faint chirps seemed shockingly far apart, but the monitor recognized them as normal for Hanna in trance.

Still, he said to Bella, "There's nothing wrong, is there?" and knew that he sounded uncertain.

"There was something, just for a second, that was different—different, but wrong? I don't know," said Bella. He recognized the sudden sense of bewilderment as something she was projecting to him; he was well used to telepaths by now. His own mind came up with the image of a wall, something from Bella transmuted in him.

"That's not a bad referent," Bella said. "She told us to wait—did you get that?"

"No. I don't think so. What do you mean, she said to wait? What's she doing?"

"I can't tell. That bothers me."

They were on the floor too. Bella got up and paced as well as the small space would allow. Hanna, maybe because she was famous or maybe because of Starr Jameson, had been offered an officer's suite and refused it, giving no reason except that she did not need it. There was a bare-bones bed and an all-purpose information-communications terminal with a shelf and chair in front of it. There had been a minimalist couch, which Hanna had had taken out to provide floor space for exactly what she was doing now.

Bella said, "I did not see a single thing that she was thinking or observing. I once communicated with an Adept in trance, and it wasn't like that with him. And I never heard an Adept say they could do this. Maybe it just didn't come up . . . I talked with a Master not long ago about doing the training myself, and he said exactly how far you can go depends on the individual as much as on the training. I've heard H'ana is very good. But I never heard of a block like this. I should be able to sense *something* from her besides that order to wait."

Carl looked from Bella's restless figure to Hanna's still one. He said, "What should we do?"

"Wait," Bella said. "I guess."

They waited a long time.

He uses no weapons himself. Gives orders. Observes a battle-field; observes a massacre. The one he ordered. He ordered it because the Holy Man ordered him, but I think it was his idea first. There are reasons such orders are given—

Edward Vickery was back on Earth, but not for long, and when he left again there would be no returning. He did not even know why he had come to Admin. He could have watched his position slip away from anywhere.

It was full night. He stood at the edge of his private office and looked out on the river, at water going by like an extension of the floor, apparently—though only apparently—without artifice. He did not like its proximity; he never had. He had taken over the suite just because it had been Jameson's previous domain. Somehow he had never been able to take over the respect Jameson commanded.

Someone came unheralded into the room behind him. Vickery knew who it had to be. Nobody else would walk in unannounced.

He said, "What do you want this time?"

"Video," Starr Jameson said. He added unnecessarily, "With *Endeavor.*"

"What for?"

Vickery expected the usual detailed but succinct summary of well-considered reasons. The subtext, of course, was always the same, whatever the request: If Jameson didn't get what he wanted from his nominal superior, he would drop a word in Andrella Murphy's ear, or Peter Struzik's, and pretty soon all of them, Chu, Weisz and even al-Nimeury, would be looking at Vickery with those puzzled expressions that said *Don't you think you're being petty, Edward?*

But Jameson just said, "I want to see Hanna's face when I talk to her."

"No unnecessary risk of data spill," Vickery said. "No special privileges." He was pleased; the others would back him up on that!

"I don't like the way she sounds," Jameson said. "I got a medical report on her. It says she's within normal parameters on all the standard scales, just stressed. 'Stressed,' for Hanna, means she's forgetting to eat and sleep. We're ready to enter the system, and she has to be at optimum; if she's not, I need to know. If I ask her how bad it is, voice only, she probably won't admit it. I want her to be looking at me when I ask. Andrella knows Hanna very well; she'd understand what I mean. Mission-critical request, Edward. I won't accept a no."

Vickery finally turned around, no longer pleased.

"Since when do D'neerans lie?" he said.

"They can't, telepathically. But they can do it with words as well as the rest of us, once they learn how."

"Are you telling me she'd lie to *you?*"

"She won't if I'm looking in her eyes."

"You hope," Vickery said. "She probably got good at it when she was with what's-his-name, Kristofik, all that time."

He felt quite happy again. The insult was multilayered and ought to hurt.

But all he saw was a subtle smile around Jameson's eyes.

"She was already good at it," Jameson said. "Who do you think taught her in the first place? Video, Edward."

"All right," Vickery said unwillingly.

Jameson turned and walked out with the same sure stride he had used coming in, as if the place already belonged to him again. Out of the corner of his eye Vickery saw a light blink red. It was a personal circuit and the light meant more bad news.

He looked at it for a long time, knowing what he would hear if he responded to it, and in the end he left without answering.

———

Almost lost him. What is he seeing? *This looks layered, almost. Two fields of vision, another battlefield—and another and another, how does he see them all at once? The other pair of eyes, but still! Someone thought of them. Thought of them as past-eyes. Who . . . ?*

Casualty report. So many dead. He is saying, is saying—
The wounded—
His orders, his expectation—
End them? Finish them? Execute them?

On *Endeavor*, Hanna's heartbeat speeded up. Bella was anxious; she let the anxiety flow out to Carl as naturally as she would to another D'neeran.

"The last time that happened, the subject died," he said.

"The pulse isn't spiking, though. It's just faster."

"You still can't tell what she's—?"

He fumbled for a word. Seeing? Sensing?

"Nothing. It really is a wall."

"Maybe one of the others—?"

"If I can't get past it, they can't."

Done with orders. It's done. Returning to base. Something in his hand, puts it in his ear. Someone naming him—would I hear it as Kwoort? Talking to, ah, he is talking to the Holy Man! Something about balance, another battlefield, a crèche, a city underground—

Here is a, oh, what is it in Standard? A train? Gets on it. Rests. He thinks he will—

No, not sleep, I won't let him sleep. He might dream, I've seen a few dreams, they tell me nothing. Suggest. That he think of where he is—

———

At the edge of the system now, mapping details of two discrete asteroid belts, the surface of the star, the satellites of gassy giants, Battleground itself. The world's three moons, too, spying for secondary settlements; there were none. *Endeavor* shut down Inspace mode and traveled by conventional means, though moving fast. A comet had penetrated the system near the remotest planet's orbital apogee. If any eyes were turned outward, they were likely to be focused on that comet, as an object of current interest. *Endeavor* therefore entered at perigee.

Hope Metra read the D'neerans' reports again. Given the emerging picture, the human beings—true-humans and D'neerans alike—had become very interested in Battleground's military capabilities, especially in space. (They all called it Battleground now.) Time to talk to Lady Hanna, Metra thought. Then she remembered that Hanna had severed her official connection with D'neera's governing magistrates, and revised the name, with satisfaction, to plain Bassanio.

Metra knew her own prejudices, which were many and long-lived. She was neither blind nor ill-intentioned, and over many years had modified, even eliminated, some of them. Others she retained; she thought them reasonable. Quite a few were in play now, and she knew exactly which ones they were.

Beauty angered her, in women or in men, because beautiful people did not have to work as hard as the not-beautiful at gaining the good opinion of others.

Women who were rich men's possessions angered her because they settled for a fantasy that pandered to the worst in men (and in the women, for that matter).

D'neerans angered her on general principles, all the more because the few she had met, until now, seemed skittish around true-humans, like wary animals that would bolt at a sudden move. Admittedly, this group did not fit that pattern, with its implication of shiftiness; they had a sureness about them Metra had not previously associated with D'neerans. That angered her, too—so Hanna Bassanio, who appeared to be confidence distilled, angered her most of all.

Metra reviewed those attitudes one by one, consciously, and consciously set them aside. When she thought she was in a neutral frame of mind, she summoned Bassanio, and was told Bassanio could not come, and got furious all over again.

Endeavor moved in, toward Battleground.

———

Kwoort, a being on a train. A fine specimen of his kind, large and strong.

There are windows on the train. Kwoort, seated, looks out one of them.

He is uneasy and does not know why. The fight was routine. The units he commanded were destroyed. That was expected. Fifty survivors, they will be promoted, that is good, one or two may survive to become Commanders. They fought well. They were not injured. That is how it was with Kwoort, long ago.

The train goes through agricultural country. This locality was spared by the storms last summer, surely God's work, because little is grown beneath the land of this region, construction lags and surface crops must suffice. For now the fields on either side show green with the hope of new growth. But maybe the storms will spare nothing, this summer. Ahead, in the direction the train is going, as best Kwoort can see from this perspective, black weather is moving in.

The train moves rapidly. A figure stands far off to the right, alone in a field. No vehicle is in sight, it is impossible to say how this worker (undoubtedly it is someone who works these fields) got to this position. The figure also looks toward the black sky. The train flashes by and the figure is left behind. Does the worker wonder, as Kwoort does, when it was that Abundant God inspired a Holy Man to grow foodstuffs underground? Kwoort has wondered a long time, asked the question long ago.

There was no answer; there were no records. The Holy Book says Abundant God prohibits records, that nothing matters but obedience in the day. Consequently, God sees to the destruction of the past.

Kwoort sees suddenly, without warning, a void behind him, yawning backward from his own time. There's no telling how far it extends. He has never had such a vision before, he stands up quickly, he is dizzy, is this thought, this sensation, this thing that seems imposed, almost, from outside, a sign of incipient madness? Does this happen to others on the crux, so near the final ascension?

He moves quickly along the aisle, which is close to the windows and the wall of the train, but there is nowhere, really, to go—

Interworld Fleet regulations permitted varying degrees of luxury in officers' quarters, proportionate to rank. Some captains' private quarters were downright sybaritic. Hope Metra's were Spartan.

There were hours to go before the first attempt at contact, and Metra had ordered a rest period for command personnel. She was asleep when the communication roused her, then awake in a split second.

"We triggered something." Kaida Aneer's voice, excited, apprehensive. Probably more apprehensive about disturbing Metra than about whatever the something was; Aneer's second would have waked her without hesitation.

"Details," Metra said immediately, confirming the crew's belief that the captain never slept. She was already out of bed, reaching for a uniform.

"We've been hit by a composite electromagnetic beam, can't tell yet if it's sophisticated enough to recognize *Endeavor* as an artifact. No other data yet. We're working on it."

"Source?"

"Got that right away. A quarter of a million klicks off at two o'clock. Can't tell yet if it's an orbital or a ship."

"Any information coded in the signal? Any attempt to communicate?"

"No sign of that. Designed for detection, as far as we can tell."

"Then it's transmitting something to somebody. Traced the destination yet?"

"We're on it."

"I'm joining you. Get one of the damn telepaths up there too. Bassanio, if she's not still out in la-la land."

"Ma'am?"

"Out," Metra said.

—stands at the window, how long has he been there? The black is overhead now, shot through with lightning, it hangs low over a shallow basin in the land. A crèche was there once, now the basin is filled with shadows. The Holy Man recently ordered a crèche moved aboveground. A big one, its capacity tens of thousands, a primary target.

Balance.

From inside the train he does not hear, but sees, wind bending grasses and trees. Wind broke a train like this once and whirled the pieces away. When?

And when underground, his own command center, it can't be far—

If this was not precisely a Commission emergency, the situation certainly called for a Commission alert. Metra had not imagined how hard sounding it would be.

Mission protocol called for bypassing Fleet if she judged it advisable, communicating directly with the commissioner in charge. She spent a frustrating hour intermittently contacting Edward Vickery's night staff before she finally got them, through sheer force of will, to admit that they could not get a response to any effort to reach him, not even signals to the implant in his ear, which was supposed to make him accessible every minute of every day. The implant could be deactivated, but its user was on oath to keep it active unless it developed a malfunction that threatened to scramble the brain. Metra hoped Vickery's brain had gotten fried.

She gave up on his bewildered staff and tried to detour through Starr Jameson's offices. No response. There was no night staff at Contact; a director rated one, but Jameson had dispensed with it, moving the allotted funds to expand Contact Education and arguing privately, Metra had heard, that anything worth waking him for was worth waking Vickery first. Reluctantly, she tried his home. Oh-three-hundred hours on *Endeavor* was three o'clock in the morning at Admin, the standard for Standard time, and the house politely informed her that she was not on the list of people authorized to disturb the director in the middle of the night. "Who is?" she demanded, and the obliging house recited a list that began with Hanna Bassanio. That would do a lot of good! Edward Vickery—that too, under the circumstances. Mickey Bassanio, for God's sake, he was a baby! Portia Jameson, a relative, who Metra knew rarely left Heartworld. Commissioner Andrella Murphy. And Thera August, who, the house said, actually lived in it and actually could be disturbed at any hour.

So it was Thera August who went to get Jameson out of bed, and Metra was prepared for the worst. Vickery had warned her that at one time Jameson had habitually used psychotropics, and might do so still. He might be spaced—or he might be with someone he wouldn't want Bassanio to know about. She activated video; Bassanio had been authorized to use it just hours ago, and Metra appropriated the privilege.

But Jameson, though somewhat disheveled, looked fully alert and only worried, not angry or defensive. He said, "What's going on?"

Metra started her report and saw him relax at once. Had he expected Bassanio to go psychotic again?

Metra's people had learned a little more in that frustrating hour. Now that they knew what to look for, they had found satellites studding the system, sentinel beams crisscrossing it. One satellite was transmitting information to Battleground's surface, had probably started at the same time *Endeavor* registered the first hit from the beams.

"Is the transmission Inspace, or conventional?" Jameson asked.

"Electromagnetic only, like the sensor beam. Two-point-three hours, now, before it's received on the surface. I ordered diminished speed at once; *Endeavor's* almost at rest."

"Good. The medium is interesting. I wonder if they've lost their Inspace capabilities? There was no reference to interstellar exploration in the datastream, and Hanna hasn't picked up anything about it. What does Commissioner Vickery think?"

"He is unavailable," Metra said.

"I see," Jameson said, but he looked puzzled. "Let me talk to Hanna, please."

"She is also unavailable. She's been in that trance the Adepts use for hours. The others say as far as they know she's in no danger, and there's no way to force her out of it. If they're telling the truth," Metra added. "Do you know anything about it?"

Jameson did not look alarmed. He said, "This time? No. I know she spent a couple of days in it once, but it was an extreme situation. Are her vital signs normal for trance?"

"They're fine."

"Have the others tried to communicate with her?"

"They say she's blocking them. They say she told them to wait, and since then trying to reach her is like walking into a wall."

"Then she's got a good reason," he said, but abstractedly, as if he were thinking something over. "She might have connected with someone important. Good . . . What do you recommend next, Captain?"

Metra said, "Start transmitting a greeting now. Communication's worked on it for weeks; we can get it going right away. Give them some information about us before they have time to get worried and maybe mount an attack. These are not peaceful people."

"I agree, on the whole—with the reservation that they seem to be so busy fighting each other that it'd take them a while to plan an attack. We haven't seen any evidence of fighting in space, remember; they could be ineffective there. And I'd like to give Hanna more time. But you need to be reporting to a commissioner, don't you? Sorry . . . I forgot I'm not one."

Metra almost heard the unspoken *yet*. But Jameson smiled, the amusement at himself so clearly genuine that

Metra wondered for the first time if Bassanio saw more in this man than the obvious advantages to herself. None of her business, but she said, "Could you get Bassanio to respond to you?"

"Possibly. Or not, depending on her estimate of the importance of what she's learning. Let her stay as she is for the moment. I'm going to sign off, but stand by, please. I want to contact Commissioner Murphy."

"Can you reach her at this hour?"

"I'm on her most-personal list." He looked away, touched something out of sight. "You are on mine, as of now."

The rain begins without preliminary drops, driving down, blotting out the flat, battered fields. Thunder cracks audibly even through thick windows and the darkness is like night between attacks of lightning, or maybe there would be a little light, but the lightning blinds him and the intervals for recovery are short. Soon his own rooms, what's left of an image once painted on a wall, that place that was quiet and green and no work of Abundant God—

Dema was with Hanna and Carl now that Bella had gone to Communications at the captain's command. She started to rise, stopped on one knee. "I thought she was coming out of it—"

"I thought I saw her move."

"I thought I saw her *think*. Something important, but I couldn't quite catch..." After barely a pause, Dema said, "Bella didn't feel anything."

Carl said crossly, "Ordering a telepath to Communications seems like a waste of energy. What about Joseph and Arch?"

"Joseph's asleep. Sensible, that's Joseph. Arch is in bed with somebody. Not asleep."

"Who?" said Carl, diverted.

"Does it matter? Arch is *always* with somebody."

Dema settled down again. They waited some more.

—stumbling through corridors to his own rooms, the halls seem disconnected, it is like careening through a gray space

made of cubes. At least there is no lightning, no rain, no wind, no hail—

Words in his ear, Prookt Commander's voice, a small object detected in space, outer limit of the system, potentially deadly asteroid they thought at first but no, manufactured and under power, the Demon has taken to space again—unless the not-Soldiers, thinks Kwoort, but he does not say so to Prookt, who knows nothing of not-Soldiers—

Hanna moved at last, convulsively.

They know we are here.

Carl blinked; he knew what Hanna's thought felt like and this was Hanna, and her eyes were open now, but he wasn't much good at separating sense from affect—not when the medium was thought—and the package was an overload: urgency, thirst, weariness, all blurred the content for him.

Not for Dema. She said, "This is not news. You'll have to do better than that, H'ana, or you'll never hear the end of it!"

"Well," Hanna said, dry throat making her hoarse, "they think we're the enemy. I mean, whatever side this one I was watching is on, they think we're on the other side. Is that better?"

"Back me up," Jameson said to Andrella Murphy and she said, "Just who is the commissioner here?" but there was no question she would do it. After that he made a fast (but not fast enough) contact with Iledra, Lady Koroth, on D'neera. Talking to Iledra was at rock-bottom of the list of things he liked to do, but he did it—a waste of time, because Iledra could offer nothing more than agreement that Hanna probably was not in danger, and probably remained in trance because she had fastened on something important.

It was worse than a waste of time—but Jameson had expected it to be worse—because Iledra then informed him that it was all his fault that D'neera, specifically Koroth, had lost Hanna—but he had expected that, too; she always harangued him about it when he talked to her.

"She's not necessarily gone forever," he said reasonably, but Iledra was not reasonable on this subject.

"For the foreseeable future, at least," she said. "The Polity has her, Contact has her. *You* have her."

"Mickey has her," he said. "You can hardly blame me for her true-human child."

Not this one, anyway, he thought, a thought so unbidden and amazing that he simply sat where he was and stared at nothing, thinking *Where the hell did that come from?* — while Lady Koroth scolded on, unheard.

Lavatory first, urgently, and as long as she is here get the water on, make it cold, stand under it, wash off the staleness — there is the eerie trace of a connection with the being called Kwoort, although she has broken the conscious link. Overly sensitized, too open, now that the block is gone, to every thought, every thought of every human being near her

Carl afraid, afterimage of Hanna stumbling with muscle cramps, banging into a wall

Dema repeating her name and with it an old image, she'd once been thought of as Wildfire

Make the water colder, make it icy, freeze the racing thoughts

Fix on Dema, calling aloud just outside the fall of water: *H'ana, you need to see the captain, Bella says it is urgent*

Focus on the captain, oh, she is talking to Starr, I want to

A memory, *The worst mistake I ever made was touching you the very first time* but oh, you loved it, only forgot why you did it, I'd seen into your heart and you hate it but you need it

Dema, starting to worry, *This is no time to think of love affairs*

Bella! It was a scream in thought for Bella, the strongest

Calm down, Dema again, *calm now, breathe, breathe, like the start of the trance*

So she breathed, focus on the breath, the breath. The breath.

After a long time the cacophony faded.

"It was only a few minutes," Dema said. Hanna was curled on the bed now, warm in a wrap of blankets, Dema gently brushing tangles from her wet hair.

"Drink," said Carl, handing her water; he watched her drink, took the tumbler from her hand, refilled it and gave it back.

"Drink some more," he said. Hanna obeyed.

"I'm sorry you were frightened," she said.

"I wasn't."

"You were."

"Wasn't." He grinned.

"I was observing a commanding officer." She thought about that. "Well. Not observing. Living in his head. He was pretty agitated."

"About us?"

"No, even before he got the news. Did he know I was there?" she wondered, shook her head. "I have to go to Command. You'd better tell me first," she said, "what's happened here." And kept the breath slow and steady, holding on to calm.

Chapter VI

*W*RONG.

Too many people in the captain's briefing room. *Maybe that's all it is,* Hanna thought, standing in the doorway unnoticed. Metra and Cork and Cock. Bella. By holo, Jameson and Andrella Murphy.

No, not quite all. Jameson was a little larger than life, looming, the sensory effect enhanced too, color just a little richer than real. Why did he feel the need to loom when he didn't like using holo at all? And what was Murphy's apparition doing here instead of Edward Vickery's?

She looked back at Jameson. *Why,* she thought, *must he emphasize who's in command?*

Bella felt her presence and turned. *What?* said Hanna, and Bella said, *True-human politics? Something like that . . .*

Reluctantly, Hanna moved into the room and into the holo pickup field. A flash of resentment from Metra. Nothing, of course, from the holo projections. It must be the middle of the night at Admin, Hanna thought; she recognized the ghostly fragment of background as Jameson's study, not his office. Murphy too must be at home because she wore a lounging robe. She wore it like a ball gown, though.

Hanna looked up at Jameson, prepared to smile until he acknowledged her only with a sharp, slight turn of his head and said impersonally, "Hanna. What can you tell us?"

It took a moment to detach herself and say, "First, most important, at the site where the signal was received, they think their customary enemy is attacking from space."

Jameson said to Metra, "Start the greeting now," and Metra said to Cochran, "So ordered," and Cochran nodded and went out.

Hanna continued to watch Jameson. He had given the instruction immediately. He had not deferred to Murphy even with a look. Edward Vickery would have hesitated. Where was he?

Jameson's eyes came back to Hanna. "What else did you find out?" he said.

Gathering her thoughts was a slow process, and she began to understand how tired she was. Soon she would feel the full burden of it.

"I learned quite a lot, I think," she answered. "But there hasn't been time to think about it."

"Give us what you can. What held your attention for so long?"

She began slowly, "I finally found a ranking individual. The—chief military Commander—I'll speak of him that way—is named—"

The unpronounceable stopped her. "I'll call him Kwoort," she said. "He just finished directing a battle, just before he got news of what they think is an attack from space ..."

She spoke slowly, point by point. Kwoort's complete confidence in speaking with his Holy Man. No reverence there. The deliberate, planned loss in battle, tactics directed toward losing. She said finally, "He had wounded survivors. Some could have been saved. But he ordered them killed. His Soldiers did it, killed their own comrades. It's standard practice."

After a long silence Jameson said, "It's not something we'd expect humans to do. But you've told us compassion is not part of their makeup, and they do not value individual lives. What else?"

Hanna shrugged. There was more. The remembered thought of a fading image, the recollection of something from some place *where everything was green* painted on a High Commander's wall, nagged her, but speaking felt like too much effort. The hours in trance were catching up with her, along with everything she had not felt while she was in it, and her legs felt weak. She fumbled with a chair and dropped into it. She closed her eyes for just a moment—a mistake; *Yes, sleep!* said her brain, and everything receded. She heard Jameson say, "How long before we might get a reply, Captain?"

Metra said, "If they respond with no delay, four or five hours. But I wouldn't expect it that soon. I doubt they'll give up immediately on thinking we're the enemy. B—" *Bassanio,* Hanna heard, but what came out of Metra's mouth was "Lady Hanna could return to trance and keep us informed."

"She won't be able to reconnect with the Commander, unfortunately."

Hanna said without opening her eyes, "Oh, yes, I could. I could do it with this one. His personality is distinctive, we're almost on top of them, and I spent a long time with him. I could do it any time you want."

"You'll need a stimulant, then—"

No, said the D'neeran in her, the conditioned response to anything that might alter her personality, no matter how short-lived. But a more practical consideration made her open her eyes and say out loud, "If I did that I don't know if I would be able to enter trance at all, and then I wouldn't be able to conceal my presence from him. I've had stimulants before. I wasn't Adept then, but I remember how it felt."

After a moment Jameson nodded, accepting it. "Rest, then," he said. "We're closing in on direct contact and you'll need to be alert. I want a private word with you first," he added.

She felt Metra tense, that underlying unease moving toward the surface. She heard Metra think—think of her, with some bitterness—*Handle with care.* But Metra and Corcoran left without protest. Bella was gone too. Hanna did not know when she had made her escape.

Hanna found herself slumped, oozing into the chair. Soon she would be horizontal. But she straightened when Jameson said to Murphy, "You too. No monitor. No transcripts."

"I can't permit that. You'd say the same, if our positions were reversed."

He was silent a moment. Then he said, "Close out the monitors but remain as a witness. Monitor us yourself."

"Perhaps . . . unless you're contemplating holosex. Entirely too boring."

"It is boring," Jameson agreed, and Hanna said, "What?" but he went on, "It's something I'd rather Hanna heard from me. Not mission-related. Nothing you don't know."

"The Commission situation? I suppose I could anticipate just a little . . . All right. I'll start organizing a search for Edward. Congratulations, Starr."

"Premature," he told her, and a bewildered Hanna wondered if they had started speaking a language she hadn't been taught.

"I think there might be some difficulty starting the monitor systems up again," Murphy said, and her image winked out.

Hanna understood that. Murphy was giving them a chance to talk without listeners for the first time in months.

And she didn't care. She would have a few minutes of privacy, precious minutes outside Fleet discipline and mission protocol. She knew exactly how to use them.

"Mickey?" she whispered. "Can I see Mickey?"

It would take Thera a few minutes to wake Mickey. Jameson took advantage of them. "Try to pay attention," he said, because Hanna kept looking past him, where Mickey would appear. "Did you hear what Andrella said about trying to find Edward?"

She had heard but hadn't understood; she shook her head. Mickey was more important than anything about Vickery could be.

Jameson said with a trace of exasperation, "Please listen. It looks like Edward's cut his throat for good. There's been a move toward a council vote on dismissing him; some councilors who supported him agreed to change their positions tonight. He might have staved it off a bit longer, but he's disappeared. No one knows where he is, what he thinks he's doing— being out of touch with a first contact imminent! A commissioner must be able to respond to a crisis instantly. There won't be many crises if the Commission is a good one, but they happen. I'm leaving for Heartworld as quickly as I can."

She knew what was happening then, and her stomach turned over. She was abruptly wide awake. She said, "Why are you going there?"

"There will be meetings. Some of them will be very private. And I must be physically present for the confirmation vote."

"Don't take Mickey," she said. Too many people on Heartworld thought poorly of her, even contemptuously. She didn't want Mickey exposed to them.

"Hanna . . ." His face softened, finally. "It will be better for him to come. He's done quite well with your absence, but I don't want another adult in his life to turn into archived holo. You won't either, when you've had time to think. I promise you he'll be perfectly safe. And Thera will be there, of course."

"But . . ."

She hesitated another moment. And then she almost laughed.

"You are going to the most traditional, the most reactionary, of the Polity's societies, expecting to regain the highest position your council has to offer—with your D'neeran mistress's bastard son in tow?"

"They've gotten used to it," he said with assurance. "Why do you think I insisted that you meet as many important people as possible? Including a number from Heartworld I didn't particularly enjoy entertaining? Besides," he said, with a smile Hanna did not like, "I'm thinking of starting a rumor that you plan to leave me when you return to Earth, and take Mickey with you. That will allow people to feel sorry for me while being secretly relieved. What do you think?"

"I think it sounds exactly like you," she said. "I think everything I don't like about being with you is going to get worse." Echoes came back: *I must end this, I really must . . .*

But then Thera appeared with Mickey, and there was no room in her mind for anything except the sleepy, beautiful child smiling at her as if she were a happy dream.

Chapter VII

TIME FRAGMENTED.

_____

She slept in spite of the urgency of the situation. Possibly the wasted hours would have some grave import for the fate of all humanity, but probably not. *Why not enhanced sleep, save some time,* said Metra, and others, and Hanna told them she wouldn't let medics root around in her delicate telepathic brain. It was no more delicate than anybody else's, but she was wary of arousing curiosity about the anomalies she knew were there; the way she had shut out the other telepaths, the strength of that block, had already attracted too much attention. The anomalies were not likely to be noticed, in fact, in the routine production of enhanced sleep, and she knew that, too. But uncertainties were closing in from all sides. She didn't need another one distracting her.

_____

"Not a trick of the Demon. The words could be a trick but not the images they send. I have seen these creatures. I look through my past-eyes and remember."

"Maybe the Demon was there too, and makes up these images. Maybe one of his commanders does! You could think up something like this, could you not?"

"The Demon was not there on that world and none of his commanders were there. Of those who went, only I survive. The not-Soldiers ask only for a meeting, a small party in one landing craft, their ship will remain in space."

"Or Quokatk's mad brain has come up with some final trick. But if he is still this good they will not need you in Wektt!"

"I ask you with all my eyes to believe this is not his work. And though I saw no weapons in that place where the not-Soldiers lived, surely weapons exist. Should we not acquire them?"

———

Awake, cranky, sullenly accepting a cup of tea, feeling better once it was down. "I tapped into something down there in my sleep, a dream that wasn't a dream," she told Metra, but refused to say anything more until Jameson could hear it.

When she saw him he did not look—the holographic projection did not look—tired at all. He was probably using a stimulant himself. Undoubtedly, if he wasn't already doing it, he would. Hanna disapproved. She disapproved of all such substances, especially when he was the one using them. So he never did when she was entangled in his life. So why was he reverting now? Because he was reverting to being a commissioner? Talking of his imminent return to power he had been—for him—overexcited. Someone should tell him to calm down. She ought to be the one to tell him.

"I want to talk to you alone," she told him, and he said, "Sorry—" and waved a hand indicating he couldn't do anything about that now. They were in a half-real-half-virtual conference room, the *Endeavor* and Admin halves jarringly mismatched. Hanna was one of six people on the *Endeavor* side, Jameson one of only four at Admin. Murphy was there, and Zanté, and a man Hanna knew only slightly but had no reason to distrust: Adair Evanomen, head of Contact's commerce division. Nobody had mentioned commerce, so what was he doing here?

There had been no reply from Battleground while Hanna slept. Jameson said, "You want to tell us about a dream?"

No, I want to tell you about it, only you, she thought. She felt tricked. She hadn't even decided if she really wanted Jameson, but she was certainly going to lose him. To the Commission; to the Polity. Something shifted under her feet. *Bedrock slipping,* she thought, but she told them about the dream. And about its implication: that the Commander, personally, had seen New Earth.

"There was a hint of it in the first contact with him," she said. "I didn't mention it because I wasn't certain. Now I am."

"Because of a dream?" Metra said.

"A dream like this, from Hanna, carries some weight with me," Jameson said, "and that judgment is based on experience. Andrella? Do you remember?"

"Oh, yes," Murphy said. "And anyway, if it doesn't have some correlation to reality, where did she come up with that 'past-eyes' phrase?"

"She's used it before, but the meaning isn't clear," Jameson said.

Hanna growled.

"What?" said Murphy.

"I said, I'm here. You can ask me."

"All right. What does it mean?"

Hanna said perversely, "I don't know. The second pair of eyes has something to do with memory, but I don't know what—yet."

Jameson's eyes rested on her warily. Maybe he was thinking of her reputation for instability. Maybe all this holo wasn't such a good idea after all, and level, controlled voices would be better.

we were just a useful tool once, whispered the ghost. She wanted to ask Jameson, *Am I to be a tool again?*

But she couldn't say it in front of all those people. So she got up and walked out.

An hour later Communications reported a response, a senseless garble that nonetheless showed signs of striving toward a systems match, and Hanna went there quickly. She had picked Joseph and Bella to accompany her to a meeting on Battleground, and they went with her. The months of waiting had shrunk to minutes.

Metra and her officers and other people who were not usually there had come to Communications too, but Hanna's closest companion was invisible. She and the ghost watched a Communications monitor that showed just what was going out to the desert-splotched planet ahead of them: a mélange of the kinds of images Species Y did *not* transmit—families at play, physiological diagrams, works of art, landscapes and cityscapes, pictures of flora and fauna (but only cuddly fauna). The audio content was in the language Linguistics had deciphered and was

much the same as i sent before me to Zeig-Daru, said the ghost, who seemed somewhat comforted by the acceptance the true-humans in Communications extended to Hanna.

much the same as i sent before me to Uskos, Hanna said.

Cheers erupted from the main station in Communications, and Hanna listened.

"We've got a clear response! We've got them! We've got them!"

it says "you are guests," said the ghost.

it won't be that easy, said Hanna.

it never is, said the ghost.

Chapter VIII

THE MAN WHO NEVER RAISED his voice was shouting. "Mission protocol calls for at least three on the surface at all times, and together! At *least* three! Never one alone! *Never!*"

Light-years apart, they paced.

"You know I meant to take Joseph and Bella," she said. "It's not my decision to go alone. The decision belongs to these beings."

"It does *not*. That's the demand they made. The decision, in fact, Hanna, the decision whether or not to acquiesce, is *mine!*"

"And that's exactly the trouble, isn't it? I've never, ever seen you lose your temper before! I've never seen a decision do this to you! What is *wrong* with you?" Hanna yelled, realized she was yelling, and shut up.

In the silence, across the gulf, they stared at each other.

After a minute Hanna sat down. "I see," she said.

Jameson was shaking his head. At himself, possibly. He sat down too, his control back as fast as he had lost it and locked in place. He said, "What do you see?"

"Would you amend mission protocol to send Dema or Arch alone? To send anyone but me?"

"I don't know," he said. "The same reservations would hold."

"But maybe not as strongly?"

She didn't mention his guilt.

He didn't mention her ghost.

She said, "None of the New Earth colonists ever felt threatened. Certainly none of them was hurt."

"Individual lives mean nothing here, Hanna. You've had a concrete illustration of that."

The spacious room behind him, in his personal suite at Admin, was dark. The contact teams on *Endeavor* had shifted to the Holy Man's time (or maybe the Demon's) and it was not in synch with Standard. He did look tired, now; maybe he hadn't taken up the old habits after all.

He said abruptly, "I would rather send someone else. Your own people don't let parents of young children take hazardous duty. You ought to be spared this mission on that basis alone."

"My people aren't yours. Listen." She sat forward, as if it would actually bring them closer together. "I've seen you torn before, between me and what's—expedient. It cannot have escaped your attention that in matters of first contact you and I are perceived as a unit. That my credibility rests on my willingness to take risks—and yours on your willingness to put me at risk."

He said quietly, "No. It hasn't escaped my attention."

"What do you think these important people on Heartworld will say if you send one of my students to Battleground instead of me? They will say that your most vicious critics are right about you and me. That you can't be objective where I'm concerned, that your emotions override your judgment."

He was silent.

She said, "And I have a stake in appearances, too. If I don't prove myself of continuing value to the Polity, if I stay safely on *Endeavor* and let Bella go in my place, how long will it be before the restrictions on my freedom are softened? I hope for amnesty, and the Commission can give it to me, but not even Andrella would support it only as a favor to you. All of them have others to answer to. As will you. There will have to be justification, something to point at to prove I've earned it. This—" She fumbled for words. "I know you want to protect me. It's been a conflict for you since we met. But this time protection could harm me. It could harm both of us." *Transcripts,* she thought suddenly, and said, "My God, how many people are hearing this?"

"None," he said. "The appointment hasn't been confirmed, and if there were a Commission vote I couldn't cast a ballot, but in most matters I can do as I like. That includes restricting access to my communications. No one's listening, no one's recording."

He looked at her for what seemed a long while, eyes unreadable. A subtle change came finally over his face. Resignation, Hanna thought.

He took a deep breath and said, "I'll put it on record that your request to go alone is approved."

PART THREE

ROWTT

Chapter I

HANNA HAD MADE FIRST landings on other worlds with curiosity and wonder. She had done it first, on Zeig-Daru, with the conviction that she would not return alive; some years later she had done it on Uskos, with hope and (somewhat misplaced) confidence. This time wonder was elusive. She had borrowed too many Battleground eyes and seen too much that was gray. She fell through heavy cloud toward the underground complex called Rowtt and thought she saw—though of course they were not there— tendrils of fog seep into the capsule, *Endeavor*'s smallest (least threatening) shuttle.

They are all special cases . . . A whisper. Joseph's touch. *Look,* he whispered, *only look.*

She broke through the clouds and slowed. Tiny, camouflaged spyeyes had scouted the site and she saw what she expected to see. This view did not excite wonder either. Expansive fields riddled with holes—impact craters, perhaps, created not by meteors but by bombs. A few wheeled vehicles in haphazard clusters. Dirt and concrete shoved into mounds that sprouted scraggly weeds, the only visible life.

The pod touched down. The hatch fell open to form a ramp, and Hanna walked down it into desolation. The air tasted of dust.

She knew she was watched. The Y beings had specified that she would be watched.

She was dressed, by design, in a coverall as tight and flexible as her skin. If the Y beings had paid attention to the anatomical images sent them, they would know she hid no weapons. She had even relinquished the unpredictable ring to Bella's keeping—but it might have been a comfort now, the jewel a piece of sky. She missed it. The ghost did not seem to have accompanied her, either.

She kept her hands open, away from her body. The translator components had been described and detailed images shown to the beings of Battleground—microscopic circuitry at the ears, sound manipulation bank tenuous as mist shadowing her mouth, held in place by a net finer than spidersilk so that huge (by comparison) human hands could handle the network; the processing module was behind one ear, subcutaneous. Communications had explained it all to the Y beings ahead of time. Several times, very carefully. Hanna agreed with Hope Metra on one thing: if you were a stranger approaching a military base, you did not want to show up with a surprise.

Soft footsteps sounded behind her. From where in this blasted field the being could have come, Hanna couldn't imagine. But this had been specified too: one individual would greet her. Low-ranking, they had said without apology. In other words, expendable.

Check.

It stopped behind her and she did not turn, but extended her arms for the specified search. Fluid hands ran over her back and sides, seeking weapons that were not there. A scent the *Report to Archives* had not mentioned drifted around her, cutting the dust smell with a blend of cinnamon and cardamom. There was a fleeting impression of sinuous motion, and now the being faced her.

It finished its examination. Check.

Then—not planned, at least by the humans on *Endeavor*—it slipped behind her and started the whole process again. Hands-on. This time the long fingers sought something specific that was not there. *Some difference in anatomy that clothing hides?* she said to Joseph, and sensed that he made a note. The touches were different now: intimate, and sensuous. And suddenly she knew what the creature was doing. This was sexual foreplay.

H'ana?!! Joseph was shocked. Interspecies sex had not been addressed by Contact Education. Perhaps it should be.

She broke silence at last. "Why do you touch me as a mate would, host?"

It said, "We were informed that you are female, guest. I

am male. Kwoort Commander instructed me to make you welcome."

"Preparation to mate is not necessary, host. Did Kwoort Commander think it is?"

"Kwoort Commander once knew a not-Soldier female, and instructed me to welcome you as she welcomed him."

This would convince even Metra that Kwoort Commander had been on New Earth. Evidently he was the one who had gone into the woods with Mi-o.

Mi-o, thought Hanna, *you have a lot to answer for.*

"I note the intention, host. I am prepared to meet the Commander without further welcome."

She thought she detected some relief as he moved back. He said, "Guest, you will meet Prookt Commander. Kwoort Commander was called away to meet a hostile incursion."

Another one? Joseph said. *Is it heating up down there?*

Hanna didn't answer. She said to the being, "I prefer not to be welcomed as one welcomes a mate."

"Guest, I will so inform Prookt Commander."

She followed the being to an opening in the surface of the field where a mound of dirt had swiveled away to show a metal platform. They stepped onto it and it began to descend. The hatch slid shut above them.

"Host, what is your name?"

"In my rank it is not important. I am a Soldier like all others."

"Are we to call all of you Soldiers?"

"Yes, though females also are called Warriors."

Confirming the linguistic interpretation. The distinction between "Soldier" and "Warrior" was subtle, one of a whistle-pitch only. Kit Mortan's people had applied the Standard tags to avoid the clumsy "male nonhuman" and "female nonhuman."

The lift stopped and they stepped out and walked through gray concrete corridors, sealed against moisture but unpainted. The walls were bare. She was prepared for this; she had seen interior images trapped from ancient broadcasts, and identical walls through Soldiers' eyes.

("Status?"

"We observed no art in the datastream because they make none . . .")

Except for Kwoort Commander, and that trace of a painting on his wall. Hanna suspected he had put it there himself.

A room, the same concrete, already a weight on Hanna's shoulders. Tables and uncushioned benches of utilitarian design; a human would see nothing strange at first glance. A screen set into one wall showed moving images and text of the same kind *Endeavor* had recorded. It was silent.

The Soldier said, "Prookt Commander, the guest requires no further welcome."

Four Soldiers were seated at the tables. None of them got up. But one said, "I am Prookt Commander. I have four hundred and fifty-four summers."

Joseph said, *How'd you miss the greeting convention—! I wasn't listening for words! I never heard it—*

"Greetings, Prookt Commander. I am Hanna—Warrior. I have—" A moment's hesitation. She was tempted to lie. But she finished, "—thirty-six summers."

"What is your purpose here, guest?"

"It is as our communications specified, host. First, stalemate—" there was no word for peace, this was as close as it got—"between Soldiers and not-Soldiers."

The ears moved. Kit Mortan was still working on the rich repertoire of ear movements and facial expressions. The translator could not help her here, but—

What's that knot of—bafflement? He doesn't know how to respond!

Prookt Commander said finally, "Soldiers and not-Soldiers have stalemate. We wish to acquire weapons."

"I cannot assist you with that, Prookt Commander."

There was a pause she recognized as a convention, in case she had forgotten to say something. Prookt Commander had addressed the only thing that interested him. If she had nothing else to say, the interview was over.

The whole First Contact was about to be over. Good-bye, nice meeting you, see you around space-time sometime—

But so far they hadn't said no to anything. Maybe any request would do.

She said, "Not-Soldiers wish to observe Soldiers' daily lives."

She did not say there were scientists on *Endeavor* who would kill for the chance.

"Will this help you build weapons that we might acquire?"

She started an automatic reply. Stopped. Against all reason, "no" would be exactly the wrong answer.

"It is possible, Prookt Commander. Will you instruct Soldiers to cooperate with not-Soldiers in arranging these observations?"

"Certainly, guest."

"Also I would like to greet—" They were giving her commanders, she would take commanders, Holy Men could wait. "I would like to greet Kwoort Commander. I would like to speak of the not-Soldier female he once knew."

She felt that Prookt Commander was mildly puzzled. But he said, "I will so inform him, guest, if he returns."

(What is that "if"—no time, come back to it later.)

"I note your intention, host. I will leave now," she added, perceiving that her immediate departure was expected. Prookt Commander had covered everything he thought necessary.

"Very well," he said. "Survive, guest."

And she answered, knowing she did it correctly: "Survive, host."

She emerged from the pod into *Endeavor Three* to find champagne flowing. Her team closed around her—to keep a crowd of true-humans from swinging her onto their shoulders and carrying her around. If they did and Metra saw them they would be sorry.

"Conference," she said, and the team escaped.

Sinking into a familiar chair, suddenly exhausted, she admitted to herself: *Not bad for a First Contact.*

At her side the ghost said: *we've seen worse*

Chapter II

NO TIME TO WASTE, too many questions—they began lists of questions, changed lists to three-dimensional, dynamic models, posed questions that flowed into one another.

Why did an introduction require a statement of age? To establish relative status? Seniority? What were the implications of that "if he returns"? Was this conditional a special case, or did they never say "when he returns"?

All leading to the question at the center of the model: What true statement defined the worldview of beings who might live for a millennium, but appeared to have chosen a social contract that ensured early death? And how much choice did they have? *Was* it a choice, or was it hard-wired?

Hanna left the theorists to it; they had more time to think about it than she did. She was the focus in Communications for hours at a time. Negotiating the first study party fell to her—Prookt agreed to three observers as a team at a single location, satisfying mission protocol. She did not ask for more; she did not know what Prookt would regard as critical mass. He would not promise that other parties could follow. Even for this one there was a condition: she, personally, was required to return to the original contact site at the same time, and stay there for the duration of the observation period, so that any difficulties or questions that arose could be referred to a superior officer—that meant Hanna—on the ground.

All right, so there was some flavor of a hostage arrangement here. Interesting question, given the low value placed on life, did that concept play any part in their—

No time, fill in the blank later. Not the hard way, she hoped.

Consulting no one, she threw mission protocol overboard and agreed.

———

Jameson accepted the arrangement because he had to. Getting observers onto Battleground was a major advance—especially since Soldiers' obsession with war and mastery of interstellar travel (maybe lost, maybe not) meant he was under intense pressure from the Commissioners of the Polity and from Fleet. They wanted all the information they could get (they stopped just short of calling it intelligence) as quickly as possible.

But he was furious with Hanna for making herself vulnerable. Their summary sessions—at nearly hourly intervals in this period —were formal and impersonal. They were carried out blind, too, because Jameson thought that if he had to look at Hanna's face now, he would explode.

———

She would be in the gray room—a different concrete room—for about thirty-seven Standard hours, the length of a Battleground day. It had a table and a bench and a barely padded platform for sleeping. Behind a partition there were sanitary facilities that a human being could use without too great a sense of strangeness. The room was not a cell but a standard billet. The door was not locked and Hanna was not overtly guarded. It was assumed, however, that she would stay in the room. She saw no reason to leave it.

For entertainment, a screen set into the wall showed current broadcasting. Hanna might have been looking at the AV loop on *Endeavor*, except that some of it was real-time or only a few hours old. Old or current, it was all war, speeches, and public assemblies.

Still, she watched it closely for some time, and finally there was a brief reference to an alien (not-Soldier) visitation. There was even video of Dema and the two true-human scientists she escorted, but then the narrator said the guests were not interested in "our desperate situation," and that was that. Apparently if the guests were not interested in the situation (whatever it was), Rowtt was not interested in the guests. The attitude was incomprehensible to Hanna. Humans greeted first contacts with a variety of reactions, but indifference was not one of them.

She couldn't find a way to mute audio, but she could deactivate the translator. The audio became background, almost white noise. Clicks and whistles, most words spoken softly: as Maya Selig had observed, it was a pleasing language to hear. True, frequent explosions modified the effect. She listened for some hours, getting up sometimes to pace, sometimes turning her attention to human thoughts, touching the human beings on *Endeavor* lightly, telepaths and true-humans alike, careful not to distract them from what they were doing.

Most often she touched Dema and her companions. The site of their observations was a vast crèche and the study had begun well; Benj Parker, one of the true-human social scientists, was beside himself with excitement. The other, Prez Mercado, was a man who lived for data. He had never collected it on nonhumans, though, and wondered now and then if he was dreaming, but he made no mistakes. Dema's customary tranquility was almost unruffled, a solid counterweight to Parker.

Presently Hanna lay down on the platform, tired, tempted to sleep. But she thought the Holy Man might be recognizable, now that she had touched him from a dream.

She let trance draw near, let it enfold her, and went in search of him.

The Holy Man was coming to the end of her prayers. She felt an unaccustomed sense of distraction tonight.

The mechanical prayer counter at her belt ticked over patiently with each repetition.

"Be our strong arm against the Demon, chastise him, for he believes not in you.

"Be our strong arm against the Demon . . ."

Before prayer counters, there had been—

What had there been?

"Smite the Demon as he seeks to smite your faithful, we pray.

"Smite the Demon as he seeks to smite . . ."

There must have been something.

Beads?—she started back, she had seen beads in front of her eyes.

She opened the other pair of eyes and examined the full field of vision.

Nothing. It was nothing she remembered. She did not know where it came from.

The prayer counter was waiting.

"Guard the faithful against the Demon's treachery, as we guard our faith.

"Guard the faithful—"

Pebbles?

The Holy Man started trembling. She was seized with a desire to remember the crèche of her origin.

"Demonic trickery!" she roared—she began to run to the door to seek a Soldier, suddenly stopped.

She had been working hard. Praying intently. How this new occurrence, this not-Soldier visitation, might be used against the Demon, yes, that was it, that was what she had been praying about. Their Soldiers and Warriors were on this very world, this very night. Surely Abundant God would show her how to use them to advantage. Tonight's distraction was merely God's way of telling her she needed to rest.

And she wasn't as old as the others so she wasn't going—

———

—mad. Like the others. Like they always did.

Well, I found a Holy Man, all right, Hanna thought.

———

After that she tried to sleep but could not; she only lay on the platform and let alien thoughts wash over her, the pulse of something like drumbeats sounding even here. Nothing, after the Holy Man (but surely that had been a female?) was distinctive enough to hold her attention. Immersion in the heart of a city made no difference. Soldiers seemed almost universally phlegmatic; they did not think beyond immediate goals no matter where they were. Humans daydreamed, fantasized, replayed memories, started to do something and then changed course, were intensely responsive to each other, moved through emotional states at a dizzying rate of speed—and those were the normal ones. The great mass of Soldiers did not look to the past, and they did not look to the future beyond the next step of whatever task they had to perform.

What did the exceptions mean? Why was a Holy Man different, or a Kwoort?—whose presumed counterpart, Prookt, could almost have sunk into the background without a trace. Was Battleground home to two distinct sentient species? Were there classes dictated by genetic patterns, as on F'thal?

Eventually her speculations faded into a trancelike state that was not trance. It was not sleep, either, but it passed the time.

———————

"Status, please."

Jameson sounded exhausted. Others had reported to him while Hanna was on Battleground, and gauging from his voice he had been awake, personally, for every single hourly update.

"I've returned to *Endeavor*, arriving shortly after the observation team. The same team is—"

"Welcome back." Light flickered and video came to life. Jameson's eyes were cold. He had not forgiven her.

"Thank you . . ." He looked as tired as he had sounded. She spoke carefully. "The same team is returning to the surface tomorrow, Rowtt's tomorrow. I'm not required to be there this time. Do you want a personal report from Dema now on observations to date?"

"Is there a general report?"

"One will be transmitted within the hour."

"Then I'll read it when it gets here, unless there's something that requires immediate attention. Is there?"

No softening in the stony face.

"No," she said.

"And your own activities?"

"Unproductive, I'm afraid. I did finally connect with a Holy Man. Or a Demon. Who knows which is which? But the Holy Man is insane, or going insane, or expects to go insane. Because all Holy Men do."

He blinked. He seemed at a loss for words. After a pause he said, "Judged by whose standards?"

"The Holy Man's. The Holy Man is female, by the way."

"Female. You must have learned something more. She must have done something besides think about her sanity."

"She prayed. And went to sleep. And woke up again and prayed some more. That's not all she does—she's commander-in-chief, I think—but that's all she did while I was there."

"In other words, you put yourself at risk with nothing to show in return."

The deserted conference room went quiet. Then she said, "I thought we already had this argument."

"You didn't clear this little excursion with me."

"No. No, I didn't."

"Not again. Never again."

Hanna took a deep breath. He might as well have been in the room with her, she might as well have been reading his mind. He was angry with her because he was afraid for her.

She said gently, "I've been there twice and nothing has happened to me. I promise: If I feel threatened I'll tell you."

He didn't answer, but she thought she saw a softening. She went on, "There are a hundred people longing to get down there and learn everything they can, and Prookt seems to regard me as the liaison. Before I left he said I'll meet Kwoort Commander soon. 'If he returns,' Prookt said—but I'm convinced now that's a convention. That it means 'if he lives to return'—"

"Did you ask if you can bring companions?"

"No—but he thought only of me."

"Oh, hell . . ."

She waited while he thought it over. There was no rational reason for refusing, and he knew it; she saw an answer in the set of his mouth, a minute change, and knew she had won.

He rubbed his hands over his face, a rare gesture. "See Kwoort as soon as you can. But try," he said rather hopelessly, "try not to go alone."

"I'll try."

"Then go to bed now, Hanna. Rest. So I can."

Chapter III

SLEEP CAME IN FRAGMENTS, small and tormented. She was habituated to roaming through Soldiers' minds, and could not seem to stop. She did not do it consciously. She only woke—every five minutes, it seemed to her, but probably a couple of times an hour—with the weight of gray spaces on her mind, fragments of conversation, snippets of hands engaged in work; and once, like the flare of light from a faceted jewel, the being she recognized as Kwoort Commander.

I could not find the last pages I wrote, just as I could not find the pages I wrote before that when I looked for them. I have hidden them all, I think. I thought it would be systematic, that I would forget the distant past first and then the intermediate past and then the recent, but there are blanks everywhere I look and soon I will forget to look, I will forget to look for what I have forgotten. How can I serve Abundant God in the place where I must go if I cannot remember?

She was waked by a hand on her shoulder so gentle that she whispered, "Starr?"—she must tell him about the forgetting, he would be interested—before she opened her eyes to see Bella's grin.

"So you dream about the man! What'll you give me not to tell?"

D'neerans by definition were not subject to blackmail. The word had no meaning in a society where people read minds, and telepaths did not take it seriously. Except for Hanna, who knew that a discreet form of the crime was a useful part of Jameson's political strategies.

Bella got a glimpse of that, and her smile wavered.

Hanna sat up, feeling as if she had not slept at all. "What?" she said.

Bella's good humor returned, a little forced.

Message from Rowtt. The mighty Kwoort will honor you with an audience.

Hanna blinked at the flippancy. She thought there had been a time when she had a sense of humor, but she couldn't remember it. Jameson said she had never had one—

"When?" she asked.

"Evening our time. Afternoon theirs. Dema's on the surface now. I mean under it. Her team went hours ago."

Hanna did not answer. She caught at dream-fragments. Dreams could, unnervingly, be trusted. Except when they couldn't.

But there was nowhere that last fragment could have come from, except Kwoort.

She climbed out of bed, shedding the twisted sheet.

So Kwoort Commander was afraid of forgetting his past. Was he going insane too? Were they all crazy?

The Soldiers and Warriors who cared for the crèche at Rowtt's easternmost extension did not understand some of Benj Parker's questions, and his frustration began to run high. He wondered if someone who'd been through the Contact Education program could do better. Then he started to wonder—to his credit, not all his colleagues would have wondered—if it was time to take advantage of the presence of a telepath. That was why Dema Gunnar was there, after all.

Parker was one of *Endeavor*'s sociologists, a native of Co-op and at the height of his career at some one hundred twenty years of age. He differed from most true humans in being reasonably comfortable with D'neerans. He had gotten that way doing ethnographic fieldwork sixty years ago on D'neera, not long after the Polity reestablished formal relations with the telepaths. The place had been an ethnographer's dream, as he had expected it to be. Its people, largely cut off from mainstream culture for hundreds of years, had developed all manner of charming folkways. Parker had gotten a few decent papers out of the experience. He could have gotten more if only they hadn't just shaken their heads at his ignorance and reverted to telepathy so often. You *could* footnote a thought somebody aimed at your head, but he hadn't wanted to push it too far.

He switched off his translator and said to Dema, "Are these answers making sense to you? Mentally, I mean. So to speak."

"Do you mean are they coherent? Yes, they are." Dema quoted Hanna, her teacher and mentor: "You have to forget about thinking like a human."

"All right. Where am I thinking like a human here?"

Dema was no Adept, but she was good. The Warrior who was the subject of this interview was suckling an infant, and Dema could feel the female's sense of her strength pouring into the newborn.

"What is troubling you, Benj?"

"This—woman—told me that this—baby—will be on solid foods in a couple of weeks, our time. You heard that, didn't you?"

"Yes. And it's true," Dema added, feeling Parker's disbelief. "I got an image of the infant marching not long after, too."

"Marching?"

"Walking, then. But I didn't see much ... transition. A few steps—then he marches—"

"There's got to be something wrong with the timing!"

"Not necessarily. Look at her, Benj."

"All right, I'm looking." *And it's not a pretty sight.*

"How many breasts do you see?"

"Too damn many!"

"Benj ..."

"All right. Four. There might be more under that coverall, for all I know. I can't even tell the males from the females except at times like this."

"She's in crèche mode, so, yes, there are more."

"Crèche mode being—"

Dema explained carefully: "She reached a point in a biological cycle where it was time for her to come here. She's here—and so are the other adults, for the same reason—specifically to reproduce and to nurture more Soldiers. They mature quickly, and my sense of the adults is that they're devoted to the process, not the young. They know others will take over the children as soon as they're walking, and they know most will be killed in battle, many as soon as they've reproduced, so there's the absolute minimum of personal attachment. A short infancy makes sense, reduces the chance of strong bonding. They wouldn't have the kind of hormones that promote parental bonding in us, either. When my son was born, they put him in my arms right away and oh! I've never felt anything like it! I—"

"No baby stories! I'm not interested! Why can't this— female—just *tell* me this, instead of going on and on about Abundant God?" said Parker.

"Translation only goes so far," Dema said, not insulted. "I don't think it's Abundant God that's the imperative—it's the biological cycle, and that's just their way of explaining it. That's how all the religions start out, that need for an explanation. It's something I can sense that you can't. You'd work it out for yourself eventually, but I know *now.*"

The Warrior stood up and went out. She returned with a second infant; Parker knew it was a different one because its hair—if that was hair—was reddish, and it was smaller. She opened another compartment in her garment and the baby, if that was a baby, began to feed. Parker felt sick.

"All right," he said. "The translator's just not working here, not well enough. Can you just *think* to her? And to me?"

"Oh, yes," said Dema. *What else has H'ana been trying to tell you all these years?* she thought wearily, but she did not project it to him.

"But I will have to tell her what I'm doing," Dema said. "I don't want to walk around in someone's mind—not even an alien someone's—without telling her how deeply her privacy, her self, is going to be invaded."

"I thought that's what Hanna's been doing all along?"

Dema suspected Hanna paid only lip service to the scruples D'neerans were supposed to have, but it might not be good to tell Parker that. She said more or less truthfully, "That was just for background. Anyway,"—Dema was on surer ground now—"she's the only one of us good enough to do that consistently without the subject knowing, and even she slips up sometimes. So I need to tell this woman what I'm going to do."

"Then tell her!"

"You, too, Benj. I'll need to open up all the way. If your mind wanders I'll know where it's wandering. Forget about having secrets."

Parker stared at her, and felt himself shrink. Dema Gunnar, when he forgot she was a telepath, was a beautiful woman. Tall, buxom, stately—just like his spouses. When she smiled she appeared to glow. A possible wife number four—well, no. A telepath, after all. Maybe an interesting interlude, though.

"And I know exactly what you're thinking right now," Dema added. "I wouldn't have to be a telepath to know that. So forget about being embarrassed."

Parker wished he could hide behind the redness of his face. But D'neerans were pretty tolerant of lustful thoughts. He knew that from personal experience. He remembered certain other personal experiences from his days in the field—one field in particular, a riot of flowers—one telepath in particular, he had never forgotten her face—or the rest of her either—

He felt his face get even redder. Dema had started smiling at him; now she laughed out loud.

"All right, all right," Parker said. "Tell her, and let's get started."

It was better than the first landing site, that field riven by explosives. At that, it was not much: only a roughly flat space on an island in a river that snaked over and around the underground city, the only structure a low block of a building made of crumbling and neglected concrete. Trees grew spottily around it, not much taller than the building. They might have been ragged pillars, except that yellow spikes of leaves thrust into the air from their tops; when she went close to one Hanna saw that its bark had a wounded look, as if enemies had slashed at it randomly with machetes. The shallow river was flat as a gray sheet in the clouded, windless day. The air was thick and hot; an oncoming storm was less than an hour away.

"You're sure this is the place?" Hanna said to the communicator on her wrist.

"This is it," said Kaida Aneer.

No boat or aircraft was in evidence except Hanna's pod, though Communications swore they had defined Soldiers' time measures accurately. Perhaps they were wrong, or perhaps Kwoort Commander was just late—accidentally, or on purpose as a sign of authority—or maybe he had forgotten—

Or, or, or, said Bella, oddly nervous, as if she were the one on the ground. *You're supposed to know what you're doing, you know—*

A door opened in the front of the shabby building, and Kwoort came out. He flowed down the narrow steps in front and stopped. Superior officer's prerogative: Hanna would have to go to him.

She walked toward him, smelling dust, though the ground cover that caught at her sandaled feet was damp.

"I am Kwoort Commander," he said. "I have seven hundred and twelve summers. I greet you in the name of Abundant God."

Hanna, at Metra's insistence, had memorized a greeting of her own.

"Thank you," she said, knowing Kwoort heard it as *I note your intention.* "I greet you in the name of my fellow human beings *(not-Soldiers)*. Our desire is to maintain peace *(stalemate)* with Soldiers and to exchange knowledge. We are glad *(it is pleasant)* that Prookt Commander has permitted not-Soldiers to observe a crèche. We would like *(it would be pleasant)* to visit other sites. We are prepared to exchange many kinds of knowledge."

There were no beeps or buzzes from the translator. Communications had done its usual superb job.

Kwoort said, "I note your intention. I have some knowledge of not-Soldiers, because I once observed your world. It was interesting."

"That's what brought us here," Hanna said, "the knowledge that you visited a world where not-Soldiers live, though it is not the only one. There are many, and I will tell you of the others if that is what you desire. You prepared for the possibility that we would come, did you not? Is that the reason for the surveillance devices in your solar system?"

Until now only the lower pair of Kwoort's eyes had been open—not exactly without pupils, as Maya Selig had reported, though the darker segments, arranged in a regular pattern in each eye, certainly did not work the way human eyes did. Now he opened the others. It was the first time Hanna had seen the phenomenon, and suddenly she understood the nature of those eyes' field of vision, which had puzzled her when the Holy Man opened hers. They appeared different from the others only in having more of the darker dots, but they saw, literally, memories.

"I had . . . I had the satellites set in place . . ." he said uncertainly, and stopped for a moment. Then he went on firmly, "They are there to give warning if our enemy again achieves the ability to attack from space."

The upper eyes closed. He had not exactly lied. He had tried to remember the time of the satellites' building and launching and found nothing. The memory was gone; he had seized on the most likely explanation, and he would now be sure that it was true.

The hot air stirred. The storm might have speeded up. Hanna had dressed for the heat in a skimpy top and long gauzy skirt, and the skirt fluttered wildly in a sudden gust. The ring she had taken back, as if it had decided to be a weather-teller, emitted one of its unpredictable flashes of blue. Kwoort noticed. He said warily, "What is the purpose of that device?"

"It is decorative—" *Chirp*, said the translator. "It is pleasant to look at," Hanna hazarded. "That is its only function."

"What does the light mean?"

"I don't know. The stone came from a place where one great intelligence lives, and they think it is alive in some way. It flashes for reasons they do not understand and we do not understand."

"I do not know what you mean by 'one great intelligence.' And you say 'they.'"

"Both descriptors are true. It would take a long time to tell you about it. I spent the years of two summers studying this intelligence, and there is still much to learn. There are other not-Soldier beings on other worlds who are not like you and not like us." She paused, thinking he would pounce on that. It ought to have been the most interesting statement Kwoort had heard in his life.

He was not interested. He said nothing.

Hanna had never imagined having to search for a topic of conversation at a first contact. Puzzled, she said, "We can discuss that, if you wish. I requested this meeting partly to find out what you might want to tell and ask us. Do you want to ask me or tell me any particular thing?"

"The not-Soldier female I knew in that other place—does she survive?"

"No," Hanna said, thinking the question, out of all those he might have asked, an odd one. The irrepressible Mi-o, dead more than a century, kept inserting herself in the present. "Our lives are short compared with yours. Hers was long, for our kind in that place and time—" Hanna hesitated, decided Soldiers were unlikely to care about human A.S. treatments, and went on. "She had eighty summers. But she did not survive."

"Did she die in battle? I saw no fighting there."

"There was none. There has never been any fighting there. Not-Soldiers almost always prefer stalemate to active war."

He understood the words of that last statement—as words; what they meant together utterly escaped him. She almost saw them wing past the great ears and away. *No context,* she thought.

"How was it," she said, "that Soldiers went to a world of my people? It's clear from their records that war was not your intention."

The upper eyes opened again. She saw no other change in his face, but she felt his mind race. Searching for the memory.

He said slowly, "It was an experiment. There was no war then . . ."

He was silent for so long that she prompted, "Why did war cease for a time?"

The continents melted to flowing rock . . .

The quickest of visions. Hanna shook her head, shaking it off.

"You remember the molten lands," she said. "Do you remember what happened after that?"

Later she would know that was her first mistake on Battleground. Even then she wished instantly that she could take back the last words, because she saw questions form in Kwoort's mind, as startled and sudden as an alarm: *How does the not-Soldier know of the weapon we used? And how does the not-Soldier know I forget?* She said quickly, "We cannot aid you in war. Knowing that, will you allow us to stay? Prookt Commander did not seem to find us—interesting. He does not care if we stay or go, I think."

"It does not matter what Prookt thinks," Kwoort said. "The Holy Man desires that you stay for a time. She will desire it even more after this meeting."

"That is our desire as well," Hanna said; and now she wanted to end the interview as quickly as she could, because she saw Kwoort focused like a laser on her slip of the tongue. How could she have—

How could you be so stupid, Bella said—

"The Holy Man," Kwoort added, "hopes to obtain new weapons from not-Soldiers."

She tried another way of saying *No*.

"Kwoort Commander, I do not think we have any weapons that you do not have, or could not build, if you know how to manipulate the forces of the quantum reality, and to travel the stars as we do."

All Kwoort's features rippled. "Wherever there is something new, there will be a new weapon," he said. "We hoped to find something in the monstrous vessel orbiting that other world, larger than any vessel we thought could be built, but we could not proceed with our plan to remove it. We did not have enough power; we could not take it and generate enough power for our return."

He remembered that, all right. The wind blew harder; Hanna raised her voice a little. "There were no weapons on that monstrous vessel, host."

"Knowledge is a weapon," he said. "What knowledge do you have, guest, that might become a weapon? You say you studied Soldiers from space, but I think you may have a surveillance system previously unknown. Such a system could be a weapon, you must agree."

There was another gust of wind, strong as a physical push. It was time she left for *Endeavor*. Before he began to equate "surveillance system" with telepathy.

"I am recalled to my spacecraft, Kwoort Commander."

Kwoort Commander said in that language so pleasing to the human ear, "Very well. We will talk again. And I will hope to hear about new forms of surveillance."

Chapter IV

EVERYBODY WANTED TO HEAR about it—Hope Metra said—and called a conference. It was not enough that every word had been transmitted to *Endeavor*; they wanted to know what Hanna thought—Metra said. Hanna found that Metra lied. They just wanted to talk about it without end, this meeting between the telepath (her report suspect, needing to be dissected and corrected and revised) and the nonhuman Commander. Why had she said such-and-such? Why hadn't she said thus-and-so instead? They wanted to critique, that was what they wanted, Metra most of all, but Kit Mortan was not far behind.

Hanna said as little as possible, and Bella, at her side, said nothing. Neither did Kaida Aneer, who thought (but did not say) that Hanna had been splendid. Hanna doodled, a habit of Jameson's she had picked up to see her through conferences, which she disliked. His doodles were precise geometrics. Hanna drew trees and flowers. She had no artistic talent and the trees and flowers might not be recognizable to anyone else, but she liked them. Jameson was present at this conference because he could not be left out, but only partially; his head and shoulders appeared near the head of the table more or less life-size and more or less at the right altitude; he was in space, traveling to Heartworld, and there was a malfunction in his spacecraft's holo systems. Andrella Murphy appeared to be with him, but her image was fully formed and three-dimensional, and so was Adair Evanomen's. Like Bella, Evanomen did not speak. Metra and her officers were voluble, but Jameson and Murphy were not, though when they did speak it was to the point. Hanna could not say that about anyone else. Dema was not even visible, her voice patched in from the crèche where she and her companions were working. Hanna was also aware of her telepathically, and knew that Dema had begun to feel, after hours in the crèche, that the underground spaces were closing in on her.

It was Jameson—when the critics had begun repeating themselves—who said, "The salient point seems to be that Kwoort Commander should be our contact until and unless we can gain access to the Holy Man. Hanna, please pursue further contacts with Kwoort. Try to work your way through him to his superior. Secondly, Prookt consented to the original team's current visit without difficulty, but he has authorized a lower-ranking officer to be his contact with Captain Metra, and this officer balked when he was asked if other teams could come to the surface. See if Kwoort will be more receptive to our landing more personnel.

"There is one caveat." He said it without emphasis, but Hanna knew his voice better, probably, than anyone else alive, and she looked up quickly from the image she had just mutilated. "I don't like Kwoort's notion that we have a capability that could be a useful tool for war. It seems he might suspect the existence of telepathy."

Hanna had confessed uneasiness at her reference to something she should not have known. None of the others had paid much attention. It was typical of Jameson to see the hazards of that single slip.

"It would take more than one incident for him to think of it," Hanna said. "He would have to have a background of knowledge that admits the possibility of telepathy to come to that conclusion, unless it happened several times. I think technology was at the back of his mind."

"Avoid the whole subject, if you can. We weren't planning to keep telepathy a secret in the long run, but we might have to, and certainly for the present. I don't want Kwoort focused on it, or God forbid, thinking seizure of a telepath would be the equivalent of capturing a weapon. We'll amend mission protocol with a formal directive that no one is to refer to it in any way until further notice."

"That will diminish my people's usefulness—"

Hanna broke off. She had felt a ripple of anxiety from Dema.

"Will they be of any use at all?" Metra said to Hanna. Her voice implied that she doubted it.

"Just a—wait, Dema. I think we'll be safe enough if we restrict ourselves to passive observation, but we'll be much less effective—"

H'ana! Dema was almost frantic now.

"What, Dema?"

Dema gave it to Hanna in one powerful burst: her direct declaration to a Warrior that she could perceive thought.

Hanna said softly, "All right. Repeat that, please. In words. Dema, you didn't do anything wrong. Go ahead, please. Tell them."

Dema said, "We wanted to start asking direct questions, telepathically, of one of the females, so I explained what we were going to do. We practiced a little so she could get used to it—questions like, how many Soldiers have you given birth to? What is this one's name? We've only asked simple, innocuous questions so far. But she knows exactly what we can do and what it feels like when we're doing it."

Murphy said, "Just the one?"

"So far, yes."

"So this female is the only being on the entire planet who knows this."

Every head in the room swiveled in Murphy's direction. Hanna saw Jameson nod thoughtfully.

Will they discuss assassination later? When no one else can hear . . . ?

If they did he would not tell her about it. There would be other things he would not tell her about as the powers and decisions of a commissioner's role embraced him once again. He would even share control of Intelligence and Security, with its reputation for ruthlessness: I&S, which still pressed for Adjusting Hanna even though Uskos had intervened.

He can be ruthless, and I have watched that part of him gain strength this last year . . .

She was better at governing her expression than most telepaths, but when Jameson looked at her he hesitated perceptibly before he spoke. But his own expression did not change, and his gaze was impersonal.

He said, "You'll stop direct communication by telepathy, of course. Dema, if the female questions it, you don't have to give a reason. These people call themselves Soldiers, think of themselves as Soldiers, have built a military society. They appear to be good at taking orders."

Hanna was watching him recede, drifting away through a lonely future. She said with an effort, "Dissension does not exist, from what I've seen. Mostly they don't even think about the orders they carry out."

"Then if the woman questions you, Dema, simply tell her to forget it. Would she confide in anyone, do you think? A spouse, for example?"

Dema said hesitantly, "Oh, spouse. There's a male who might be her mate, or one of her mates—we haven't even gotten started on that. Whatever they have is not—I don't think it's *anything* like human relationships. I can't even give you a glimmer of what it is."

Jameson said, "Try to find out if she is on emotionally intimate terms with that male or anyone else. Do you have any sense of that?"

"My impression is that she isn't, with him or anyone; far from it. But I just don't know."

sounds familiar, said the ghost, suddenly at Hanna's shoulder.

of course . . . touching a mind so strange there are no referents . . .

he was good to us, said the ghost, changing the subject. *good for us*

for a while. only a while

"*If* you can find out, using only translators and passive observation, we need to know. Urgently," Jameson said. "If there is nothing else? No? We'll issue the directive about telepathy at once. Captain, please see to it that all personnel are notified without delay. Hanna, you'll report immediately if you or any of your team have information on whether or how far this knowledge might spread on Battleground."

He looked at Murphy, who shook her head. Jameson said, "Endit."

Chapter V

KWOORT COMMANDER WAS AWAY from Rowtt again.
"Is the Commander often called to unexpected battles?" Hanna asked Prookt Commander from a station in Communications. She had not been relegated to a lesser officer as Metra had, and Metra regarded it as a personal insult. Hanna's favored status presumably was Kwoort's doing, by order or influence.

"Often, yes. His rank is high. He is second only to the Holy Man."

"I wish to meet with him again if he returns," Hanna told Prookt.

"Very well. I will so inform Kwoort Commander."

And Hanna had to be satisfied with that, to the disgruntlement of the scientists aboard *Endeavor*, who reminded her of animals at an exotic zoo as feeding time approached. All that knowledge waiting down there! All those questions to ask, specimens to examine, discoveries (and reputations) to be made! They were viciously jealous of Dema and Parker and Mercado, who moved to a second crèche and then a third. They clamored for the team to undertake work for which they were not qualified, studies in—everything: engineering, physiology, archaeology, botany—botany? How, when they were confined to multilayered subbasements? It was Metra's job to refuse them, not Hanna's, to Hanna's profound relief.

The team was overloaded as it was, holding to Rowtt's diurnal cycle and using stimulants to override their bodies' demands (and counteragents to override the stimulants so they could sleep in the intervals on *Endeavor*). Parker and Mercado showed no ill effects, but Dema rejected the stimulant after the first trial—"I felt *strange*. Distant. Fuzzy," she said obscurely—and somehow kept operating in a haze of exhaustion. Hanna was not in much better shape, awake and available whenever the team was on Battleground. And some of the scientists managed to bypass Metra and get their demands through to her.

"Theology," she said to Jameson wearily. "I don't know whose idea that was. There aren't any theologians aboard."

"It might be helpful to have one." It seemed that he meant to say more, but she was too tired to care, and did not ask about what he might mean to say next.

"I guess that would make somebody happy, but I don't know who! Endit," she said. Prematurely, as she soon found out.

She did not bring up the fate of the Warrior who knew about telepathy, either. Presumably the Warrior was still in the original crèche, nursing successive broods. If she had spoken to anyone else about the not-Soldiers' strange way of communicating, Hanna did not hear about it from Prookt.

Days passed, and still Prookt Commander did not cooperate. Hanna repeatedly asked permission for other teams to go to the surface, and she requested meetings between Battleground experts in many fields and their human counterparts. Prookt Commander was not hostile, merely indifferent (and maybe lazy). When Hanna tried more insistently to get him to stir from immobility, he said something that translated infuriatingly to "By and by, perhaps." Accustomed as Hanna was to being in space, she was not used to staying on board a ship when there was a habitable planetary surface down there. Like Dema, she felt walls closing in.

After a week of this, the Soldiers in Rowtt's equivalent of Communications began to inform Hanna that Prookt was not available to speak with her. On the other hand, she decided, no one had said she could not simply go to Rowtt and make her way to the Commanders' headquarters by herself. Perhaps Prookt had not thought to issue orders prohibiting it.

Hanna flew to Rowtt in the same pod she had used before. Metra, wanting results, agreed to notify Rowtt that she was coming only after her departure from *Endeavor*. Hanna made no effort to notify Jameson. She didn't want *him* prohibiting it.

A figure stood on the field exactly where she had first landed and did not move as she circled before touching down. One of the Soldiers Prookt commanded? She reached out, a gossamer touch that ought to be imperceptible to its object, and knew at once who it was. She whipped the pod around the figure—an unnecessary flourish—completed the landing, and went out to Kwoort Commander. The air felt electric; the climatologist had predicted storms and Hanna had timed her arrival to get there before them.

No formal greetings this time. She said, "Prookt Commander told me you were away."

"I returned a short time ago," he said. "Prookt did not at once report your recent requests. But I was with him when he received word of your approach. He could not avoid telling me of your possible motive."

"Prookt Commander," Hanna said, "is being obstructionist."

Obstructionist was an excellent word. It translated almost one-for-one between human and Battleground tongues.

"Prookt is very young," said Kwoort.

"At three hundred and fifty-four summers?"

"He is also somewhat slow. But he has survived."

Hanna looked thoughtfully at Kwoort. The sky was overcast and a haze obscured the field, some of it dust kicked up by her flashy landing. Kwoort's face, in the featureless gray light, appeared dimmed. Hanna attempted no probe. Still, something seemed to settle in her bones: a sense of long, stretched, time.

"Kwoort Commander," she said, "what is it like to live for so long a time? The oldest of my kind survive only a fraction of the summers you yourself now have. What is it like, looking at lives so short?"

"They are flares, they are flashes," he said, and he said it dismissively. "Do you think yourself exceptional? If you are, perhaps your life will blaze like a meteorite across the night sky—but it will last no longer. Most are like sparks from a fire in the night."

"How does Prookt appear to you, then?"

"An ember," Kwoort said. "Enduring, but with little light."

"And you?"

"I? I burn."

Something leaped out of him, a desperation he held tightly to himself and could not know she saw. Her breath caught.

Kwoort Commander said, "I will instruct Prookt to make all the arrangements you desire."

"I note your intention," Hanna said. "And might you and I talk of long life? I believe you would show human beings a perspective we have never known before."

"Another time," he said. "I am not at liberty this hour."

"Survive, host," she said, turning back toward the pod, deciding that at their next meeting she would probe this being's thoughts mercilessly, relying on her skill to stay hidden.

She looked back when he said, "A request." Literally, order-with-option-to-refuse. "Disable your translation device."

"Why, Kwoort Commander?"

"I wish you to say your name and then I will say it back to you. You will know how it is heard here."

Oddly uneasy, she did as he asked. He said: *"Haknt . . ."*

The first syllable was a brutal outrush of breath, the second a dull click. She had heard her name on other alien tongues, and it had never sounded so unspeakably strange. For a moment she went quite still.

Then she reactivated the translator and said again, "Survive, host."

"Survive, guest."

She knew he watched her until the pod disappeared in the overcast, and that he thought of her for some time after.

Chapter VI

KWOORT ISSUED THE ORDERS he had promised, and *Endeavor* came to life.

Hanna was again the focal point in Communications, scheduling members of her team to accompany civilian scientists to the surface of Battleground. Like everyone except *Endeavor*'s regular Fleet officers and crew, who maintained a duty roster based on Standard chronology, she continued to function as best she could on Battleground time, wildly at odds with the circadian rhythms imposed on human biology by Earth's ancient sun. She slept badly and never reached full alertness. The two members of her team who exercised the option of using stimulants—Carl and Glory, the true-humans—were so clearly more efficient than the telepaths that she sometimes wondered if she should give in and use the organic compounds. They were supposed to be completely safe, a new formulation available only to Fleet, but Hanna kept postponing their use; they had not been tested on telepaths, and she had not forgotten Dema's discomfort. Certainly she observed no differences in the true-humans' personalities.

She had used an earlier compound of the drug before, though only under orders, and she was not even certain why the idea revolted her. To be sure, her own society was united in disapproving anything that affected thought beyond a glass or two of wine; it was tricky enough swimming in a sea of living minds when your own was clear. And, to be sure, drugs had played a less than admirable role in the histories of the men she had loved (true-humans both).

But when she found herself falling behind as Soldiers, prodded by Kwoort, worked with her to set up complicated schedules, she wondered if she was merely being self-righteous. Or self-righteous, and foolish as well.

———

Gabriel Guyup arrived and boarded *Endeavor*, to Hanna's complete bewilderment. Apparently Jameson had forgotten to tell her something. On purpose, possibly.

Warring day lengths had at this point put her in a new trough of fatigue, and she was not prepared to cope with a surprise like Gabriel. She did not look up when the stranger came into Communications, and when she realized that he had come to report to her, her first reaction was irritation at the intrusion. He told her that he had been invited to join the team by Starr Jameson personally. She said, "Well, God damn him anyway."

The man at the adjoining station perked up. She glared at him. He decided to take a break and drifted away, leaving them effectively alone.

Then she looked at Gabriel and saw that he was just as bewildered as she was. Too tired for the courtesy of words, she simply looked at his mind, and discovered:

That he expected to be awed.

That he was startled at the fierceness of her eyes and the shadows under them.

That he had hoped she would know who he was because they had corresponded.

Corresponded?

Hanna corresponded with entirely too many people, human and not. Jameson had assigned Contact staff to keep her communications sorted, organized, and answered, but she at least glanced at all but the most routine replies. She did like to see the holo, straight video, audio, or written communications from the clearly insane, which fascinated her for some reason. Once in a while there was a threat. She had ignored these until Jameson found out about them and started having them routed to him. He told her about them in detail, and since she could hardly avoid him, she always knew when someone advocated killing her. Presumably Gabriel did not belong in that category.

"I don't remember any correspondence with you," she said. "When was it, and what was it about?"

"It was about a year and a half ago," he said. He added, suddenly shy, "It was about belief systems."

She remembered then. It had been just before Mickey's birth and she had been in a state of mind she hoped she would never be in again. She could touch her baby's forming mind, growing daily in intricacy and potential, but she did not do it often; the experience of the womb was not one an adult should revisit. The wound of her grief for Michael Kristofik had barely begun to turn to scar, and she had begun to face an unwelcome reality—that Starr Jameson had been the only true stable point in her life since their first meeting; an enduring presence which had become a habit—maybe, even, a necessity. She resisted the knowledge and she resented it. But she continued to sleep in his arms every night.

It was not surprising that she had trouble remembering Gabriel.

She said, "Why did Starr contact you?"

"I don't know," Gabriel said honestly, "except that I'm a member of a religious community and have an interest in nonhuman beliefs. There don't seem to be many people like that around."

"I still don't see why you're here. Are you some kind of expert—sorry," she said automatically, but his feelings did not seem to be hurt.

"I've got, umm, I guess you'd call it a professional interest. My monastery isn't one of the cloistered ones, though, I mean, it's a teaching monastery. We're very much in the world."

No, you're not, Hanna thought—he really was awed, as if she were the goddess of alien studies or something, and people "in the world" did not usually react to her like that. She anxiously reviewed what she knew about monasteries. Practically nothing.

"So you're looking for evidence of faith in alien societies?"

"There's hardly anything in the literature. You're the one who's the expert," Gabriel said, more reproachfully than he intended, "and you haven't done anything."

"It wasn't important," she said with no attempt at tact, but his response was equable.

"Maybe not to you, but it's of great importance to many

people, and they're not all in established religions. With due respect for your own views—"

"No, no, that's not what I meant, Mister—Brother? What do I call you?"

"Just Gabriel." He smiled; she found, to her surprise, that she had marginally relaxed. There was a sense of tranquility about him, something inside him that might outlast this moment's anxiety. She could use some of that . . .

"Gabriel, regardless of any views I might have, it's not important to the *aliens*. Not to any we've met before now. Do you think so large a part of human culture was neglected in my education? I haven't done any work on it because there's so little to say. The peoples of Girritt have a variety of animistic beliefs, but they don't interest anyone but the most obsessive cultural anthropologists. The majority attitude on F'thal and Zeig-Daru is that universes simply exist, spawning one another; the beings see no reason to posit a First Cause that itself simply exists. Uskosians attribute no moral authority to the Master of Chaos and they do not regard him as a Creator. Although," she admitted reluctantly, "there are minority views in each case.

"But there hasn't been much, really, *to* study. How much did Starr tell you about this society?"

"Nothing," said Gabriel. "I didn't speak to him personally, and he didn't even admit to my abbot that there *is* a society. I inferred it. It's a closely held secret, apparently."

"So far. Well, there's a rich field for you here. I'll have— no. I was going to say I'd have one of my team brief you, but they're all too tightly scheduled." So was she. But. "Do you know where your quarters are?"

"Wherever my luggage is, I hope," Gabriel said. He was fair-skinned and blue-eyed, a wiry man undistinguished to the eye except for a mop of sandy curls; but he had a sweet smile. "I'll find my way."

"Good. Come back after that and I'll show you how to access the material we've collected so far. Go over it and then come talk to me. I'm glad you're here," she said impulsively, realizing that it was true. "This *is* new, and I don't know where to begin. Battleground is a world of theocracy and unending, perpetual war. Maybe you can make some sense of that dynamic. I can't."

Gabriel did not answer. He was looking at her intently

and she caught a glimpse of something he had barely begun to feel and had not yet recognized or named himself. She thought, *Oh, no . . .*

He seemed to wake up. He nodded to her and turned for the exit. She said suddenly, "Gabriel."

He turned back.

"Where is your monastery?"

"Alta," he said.

Hanna sighed. She was too tired to keep her face from showing what she felt.

Gabriel said, "Yes. The Abbey of St. Kristofik."

"Did you know Michael?"

"I was brought there just after he left, I think, and I was still a small child. I never head of him until, well—"

"Until he—we—became notorious," Hanna said, trying to smile.

"Until then," Gabriel said, his own smile real. "I've wondered about him, our abbey's lost son, wondered why he used that name. Do you know?"

Hanna did not know. There were many questions she had not asked because she had thought there would be plenty of time to ask them. She had been wrong. Michael was gone, and she would never know the answers.

She felt tears in her eyes and knew that Gabriel saw them. He took a step toward her, the impulsive wish to comfort her like a flash of light, as startling in its intensity as the impact of telepathy.

But he's true-human! she thought, and shook her head when he took another step.

"Go," she said. "Later," and he finally turned away.

It was indeed later when she remembered that her first remark about correspondence must have seemed, to a true-human, to have come out of nowhere, and he must have guessed she was reading his mind. And that it hadn't bothered him at all.

———

Gabriel found his quarters without trouble, tracked down his luggage (though not without trouble), unpacked mechanically.

None of the images or the writings by and about her, nothing, had prepared him for her personality, shooting off sparks, or for her mind, so quick even when she was plainly exhausted. Watching recorded lectures had not prepared him for her grace of movement, which had not deserted her even in her surprise. And absolutely nothing had prepared him for her tears.

He had frankly expected himself to succumb, at least for a while, to a schoolboy case of hero-worship for which he was much too old. Now it looked like he might be in for something worse.

C'mon, Lord. Do I have to?

Chapter VII

CAN YOU STOP IT CAN you stop it I said I order you to stop it. The Cutter only looked at me and of course I know the progression cannot be stopped. But she opened her past-eyes and said Kwler had asked her that. She said nothing about Tlorr but maybe Tlorr has asked a different Cutter. This one said though I had chosen her carefully because she is old enough she must have doubted, she must doubt but she said. We are to live in the day and Abundant God gives us forgetfulness to make it easier to obey. I wonder what she thought, explaining a fundamental directive of God to a Commander so old, but she knew what she was supposed to say.

That is what I believed when I did not have so many summers, when I did not have many summers at all, and maybe I was wrong and she is not old enough, Prookt should be old enough but evidently he is not, and maybe this Cutter believes as Prookt believes. And maybe they are right and my doubts wrong.

It is hard coming to this, I look at Kwler and remember what he was, I look at Tlorr and know she moves inexorably toward the place where Kwler has already gone and I also move toward it no matter how intensely I do not want to. I remember the summers before Kwler changed, I remember a summer when we talked about going to That Place—how long will I remember that talk, it will not be long, I think.

If we had gone

Hanna put out a hand to activate transmission to Rowtt, and stopped. After a while the man next to her—he was *always* next to her in Communications, no matter when she was there, slipping into place as soon as she came in—said her name. She turned her head slowly, and looked at him.

"Are you all right?" he said.

Hanna nodded. He was Metra's spy. She seldom spoke to him unless he spoke to her, and not always then. He didn't care, as long as he knew what she was doing.

Hanna noticed her suspended hand. It didn't seem to have enough joints. She drew it back. There were beings she would rather feel a bond with than Kwoort. If the last minutes were an indicator, however, she might not have the choice.

"Do you know where Gabriel Guyup's quarters are?" she asked Metra's man, and of course he did.

———

Gabriel woke with the reader draped over his chest. He had drifted into sleep and let it fall. It was his second day on *Endeavor*, and he had spent nearly all the time studying what *Endeavor* had learned so far. Sleep had caught up with him; the door might have been sounding the entry request for a long time.

He stumbled to it, conscious of uneasy dreams that fled as he tried to seize them. "Enter," he said, and remembered at the last second to push his hair out of his eyes.

"Oh!" he said—idiotically, he thought too late. Hanna ril-Koroth looked up at him with an odd expression on her face.

"Not ril-Koroth," she said. "Bassanio. I resigned from Koroth's House."

"Oh, that's right, I knew that—" Worse and worse. "Come in, come in!"

He didn't think at once of offering her a seat; by the time he did she was leaning against the wall, hands behind her. She was dressed with stark simplicity, but before her hands disappeared he saw the blue gleam of the ring that he knew (from his half-guilty perusal of her life) had excited so much comment.

"I want you to come with me to the surface," she said abruptly.

"Me?"

"Why not?"

Gabriel was having as much trouble waking up as usual.

He grasped for words that tried to elude him. "I'm not—trained. I haven't even been through your program, I'd like to do that if I could get permission, but it's not relevant to what I do, if I keep doing it—"

He was babbling.

"This is a better way to learn," she said calmly. "You can skip the preliminaries."

"I thought I would, I don't know, be analyzing things."

"Oh, there are plenty of people to do the analyzing! But there's not a single other soul on board who might be able to talk to these people about a god. Do you think you could pass yourself off as a human version of a Holy Man?"

There were so many things wrong with that proposition that he didn't know which one to point out first. No one knew yet exactly what function Soldiers' Holy Men served. He couldn't imagine passing himself off as a holy anything, and the implied dishonesty was repellent. Before he could decide what to object to first, she pushed off from the wall, ready to leave.

"Go to Kit Mortan and get a crash course in using a translator. I think Kwoort's at leisure; I'll see if he can spare us some time."

"Now?"

"If he'll see us. Don't worry." She smiled at him, the first real smile he had seen on her face. It blinded him; he closed his eyes and made himself concentrate on what she said next. "Engage him in a real dialogue about their beliefs, if you can. I want to—observe."

"Snoop in his mind," Gabriel translated, not knowing what he said; it might have been nonsense for all he knew.

Her eyebrows went up.

"Observe," she said firmly. "Anyway, I'm not supposed to go down there alone. Starr found out I did it again and made it clear what he thought about that. He'll be easier to get along with if you come with me."

"Starr?—oh, the director."

"Commissioner. You might as well get used to calling him commissioner. I have to," she said, obviously not happy about it, and went out.

Chapter VIII

GABRIEL'S EXPERIENCE WITH orbit-to-surface shuttles was confined to flights accomplished strictly by routine. This time he was not in a passenger compartment but next to the pilot, and she made a detour to show him all three of Battleground's moons, disregarding the pod's exasperated warnings that she was off course; shot back to the approved route at top speed (much too fast, said the pod); and finally let the craft float kilometers over the surface while she reprogrammed her translator. It resisted, scolding and issuing warnings to which she paid no attention. Navigation scolded too, from *Endeavor,* and Hanna told them calmly and mendaciously that Brother Gabriel needed to meditate before landing. Gabriel opened his mouth to protest, but before he could she shot him a glance of pure mischief, and he realized—feeling himself sinking—that he would probably forgive her anything.

He had never felt anything like this. Girls at the university he had gone to on Colony One had thought him strange as soon as he told them what he meant to do with his life. He had not had many opportunities to fall in love. Was it supposed to happen this quickly?

Probably not.

At last she seemed satisfied, and speeded up the descent.

"You took out your name?" he hazarded.

"I fixed it so when they say it, I'll hear it the way it really sounds."

He would have let it go, but there was doubt in her voice, or maybe in the air between them.

"Why is that important?" he said.

"Because . . . because . . ." The silence seemed to go on a long time. The pod continued a stately descent, swathed in cloud. Gabriel saw half-formed figures in its random swirls, vaguely threatening; he wrenched his gaze back to Hanna just as she said, "Because it's honest."

She fell silent, watching instruments. He glanced at her profile once more and away. He did not want to stare. The light in the capsule and the muffling cloud outside were not flattering to her skin, sallow against a vivid red tunic that bared her arms. He could not imagine what her last comment meant.

"Almost there," she murmured.

Gabriel had not had time to become afraid, but now he felt it like cold fog: not fear of the nonhuman waiting for him, but fear of failing. His voice sounded to him like a croak of inadequacy.

"I'm an amateur. What do you think *(for God's sake)* I can do *(that someone else can't do better)*?"

"I heard that." She paused. "I mean, I heard *all* of it. You project like a supernova." She did not stop to explain and went on without giving him a chance to ask.

"We're trying to find common ground here. You've seen my reports on Battleground. There's no real history here, no philosophy. No music, no literature, no art, nothing to start talking about. But there's religion. Of some kind."

The clouds were gone, the atmosphere sliced horizontally as cleanly as a cake. The sad little island was just below.

"Help me with this, Gabriel," she said, and executed an egregiously dramatic landing, startling him. He wondered if she was showing off for Kwoort.

He followed Hanna out of the capsule into heat under an overcast sky. Kwoort Commander stood alone in front of the decrepit building. *I don't know how he gets here,* a voice like a clear bell said in his mind, startling him. *Maybe he levitates.*

Kwoort came forward to meet them. Gabriel whispered one more prayer, and then they stood in front of Kwoort and Hanna said: "Host, the guest with me is Gabriel, a holy man who wishes to greet you."

"*Me?*" Isn't there a protocol, Gabriel wanted to say, but if there was, Hanna wasn't offering any guidance. "I'm not 'holy,'" he protested, the first thought that came to him. "I would like to be. I try to be. But I'm not."

The translators gave the gist of this to Kwoort. His ears stirred, and the bell said, *He's laughing . . .* Gabriel looked at Hanna again. Surely she had *some* plan for this meeting? *Go where he takes you,* said the bell.

"Haknt says you are holy," Kwoort was saying. "You say you are not. Who is right? Would you not know if you were holy?"

Answer, Gabriel.

At least this answer came easily. It was something he had thought about.

"Would I know? It seems to me that the holiest of our men—and women—don't see themselves as holy at all. They are too much aware of the perfection of God to think they are anything but imperfect."

"Tell me about your Holy Men," Kwoort said.

"I don't know if your Holy Men can be compared to ours. And isn't your Holy Man really a Holy Woman?"

Kwoort said, "The reproductive function falters with time, and ceases altogether when a Soldier or Warrior survives many summers. It would be more accurate to speak of 'Holy Ones,' but custom has kept the term 'Holy Men.' Perhaps at one time Warriors were not permitted to become Holy Ones."

"Only perhaps?" Gabriel said. "Many of our languages have had the same convention, but we know its origins. You do not?"

"I am not *that* old," Kwoort Commander said, and flapped his ears.

Hanna moved a little. The slight joke had caught her attention, but Gabriel did not know why. Perhaps it was only because Kwoort had made a joke at all.

She must have felt his question. She said, *He knows nothing of history except what he has lived, knows only the repetitive texts our linguists deciphered. Speak to him. Don't watch me in silence—*

It was Gabriel's first experience with telepathy, and he struggled to focus on Kwoort. He said, "Among the human beings who know my god, one becomes holy by serving him with all one's heart, all one's soul—" *Beep,* said the translator, rejecting the word. Gabriel hesitated. "All one's self," he finished. "Many of the holiest had short lives, even by human standards. But Hanna tells me that among your people it is possible to become holy only by living to great age."

"And how do you know that?" Kwoort said, not to Gabriel but to Hanna. The translator did not convey nuance. Had he said it with suspicion?

Yes, answered the bell. There was uneasiness there, but she answered promptly.

"Kwoort Commander, we obtained much information about Soldiers from space. We have seen your holy texts and heard readings of them, and other texts besides. That's how we developed our translators. I know there must be much information that we missed, too. Please—" The translator beeped. "Please" was not in its databank either. "I ask that you forgive—" *Chirp.* Hanna tried again. "I ask that you understand our ignorance. My companion only wants to know how old one must be to become a Holy Man. Are there many Holy Men?"

"Few survive long enough even to begin to change," Kwoort said readily enough. "The change begins to appear at, perhaps, three or four hundred summers. Fulfillment of the promise requires as much time again, and in that time most of the remainder cease to survive. But always Abundant God puts forth his hand to protect the one he wishes to take to himself. There is always a Holy Man, as the enemy has always its Demon. But there is only one."

Hanna was now very still. Gabriel wondered: Does she think he lies?

He evades. Talk to him, Gabriel. Go ahead!

He found his voice. "How do you recognize the advent of the change?" he asked.

Kwoort said, "How do *you* recognize it? Perhaps it is the same."

Gabriel said promptly, "We perceive that the holy one is transformed in closeness to God, in attitude, in behavior, in faith. And the holy speak to God, and God speaks to the holy. And with you?"

"The change is slow," Kwoort said. "Many traits of the mind are affected, one by one. But finally the Holy One hears the voice of Abundant God."

"What does the voice say?" Gabriel said curiously.

"To increase and obey is the first commandment," Kwoort said. "And secondly, Abundant God commands war. He commands death. What does your god command?"

"My god also speaks of obedience. But his command is to love," Gabriel said.

Chirp.

There has to be something, Gabriel thought. There were words for "love" in every language, however strange the speakers' bodily packaging appeared. But Kwoort said, "If you cannot tell me what your god commands, perhaps your god and mine do not have much to say to each other."

"They must. I'm sure of that. You and I might not understand each other, at least not yet, but your god and mine might not need a translator. They might even be the same god."

"Then tell me this. Do not-Soldiers increase in number by the will of your god? Do they go to him in death?"

Gabriel said cautiously, "They go to him in death, certainly. They rejoice *(chirp)* in his presence forever. And he cherishes *(chirp)* every life."

Kwoort responded with a twist of one wrist. Gabriel wondered if that was a shrug. Kwoort said, "If your god has anything to do with translation, it seems he does not want us to talk about this."

"Let's return to the process, then," Hanna said, "Are you becoming holy, host? You have a great many summers."

"I am indeed in the process," he said. "That will be my end, if I survive."

The ears moved now, stiffening, and the shoulders, pushing forward. Some change in mood, Gabriel thought, but he could not possibly tell what it meant.

He is angry, said the bell. *But not at us.*

"And do you wish it to be the end?" Hanna said. "Do you not fear losing your sanity?"

"How do you know that will occur?"

Gabriel looked from Kwoort to Hanna. Her eyes were wide; he thought he felt a pulse of uneasiness from her, but maybe it was his own, because she answered steadily.

She said, "In the volume of data we are collecting there is reference to the insanity that accompanies holiness. I am beginning to know you, and it seems to me that sanity is not something you would willingly relinquish."

Well, the second statement was probably true, Gabriel thought. But the first was an outright lie. There might be something in the texts, but he had read enough of Hanna's reports to know her knowledge came straight from telepathic contact.

Kwoort stared at them with all four eyes, the alarm sounding again in that intelligent, experienced mind. Kwoort said, "I recall nothing about madness in the holy texts."

"We drew certain conclusions from what is there," Hanna said speciously.

Gabriel said quickly, hoping to distract Kwoort, "Would it be possible for me to meet with the Holy One?"

"I will arrange it," Kwoort said, but he did not take his gaze from Hanna.

"I note your intention, host," Hanna said courteously, but she said to Gabriel: *We need to get out of here. Right now, I think.*

It was a mistake. Gabriel was on telepathic overload. He turned to her sharply and said, "Why?"

Quiet!

Kwoort saw. He made a soft whistle of discovery.

"We go now," Hanna said decisively. "Survive, host."

She moved quickly to the pod, Gabriel following. Kwoort did not try to stop them. But he didn't tell them to survive, either.

"He's quick," Hanna said on the return flight. No side trips this time; she let the pod follow its program, leaning back in her seat, looking exhausted. "And I'm not," she added. "I didn't learn what I wanted to learn, and what I learned I don't like. And I slipped up again. He's figuring it out. Oh, how I hate this cat-and-mouse!"

Alta had mice, stowaways in years of supply ships; Alta had therefore imported cats. The abbey had one, but as the kitchen brothers could not be prevented from spoiling it, it hunted without conviction. Gabriel understood, however, and he said slowly, making a connection, "What did you mean when you said hearing your name as they say it would be honest?"

"A reminder that Kwoort lies," Hanna said. "And so do I. Should we be here if we need to lie?"

She was silent after that.

Chapter IX

I WILL PUT THIS DOWN carefully and hide it carefully and hide reminders also so that I will not forget where I put it. But no I will put it in the sack with maps that I carry always. Though I am not likely to forget what has happened. Though Tlorr would remember. Though what if she has begun to forget things too, she must have begun to forget!—she is as old as I, and we are both older already than Kwler when he forgot battles fought hours before and began to forget all his words, at least I do not forget words and Tlorr does not either, and Rowtt does not need both of us but I do not want to go, I do not want to leave Tlorr—

It was Tlorr's idea, I must put that down, I told her I wondered about the not-Soldiers, how they knew things they could not know, how I wondered if they spoke in ways I could not hear and will they tell us how and can we use

I am too diffuse, it seems to me that my thoughts once were more clear more direct I would not accept a report from an officer that wavered so from the point

The point. I told Tlorr what I wondered. She said

See her mind is more direct it does not wander

She said Have any other not-Soldiers given evidence of this.

I said I do not know. I said no one has reported such a thing. The officers who escort the not-Soldiers only report where the not-Soldiers go and what they do. They report that the not-Soldiers do nothing that has not been approved. These are the things they were ordered to report. There is nothing else.

There would not be, she said, because those are the only things they are ordered to report.

I said the orders can be changed.

Then change them, she said, but first. First, ah, let us go to some of the places the not-Soldiers have gone.

I said I will send officers to those places.

No, she said, I mean I will go, and you. Maybe we will find out for ourselves.

Now, this is unheard of, that the Holy Man herself go into the warrens unless for namings and commendations. Kwler went, but only after he forgot words and duties and he would wander and become lost and Tlorr would send Soldiers to find him and so she became Holy Man. And sometimes I wonder if already I

I must be direct.

I said, Why do you want to do this.

She said, Maybe I am tired of praying and tired of maps and plans for the movements of others. I also want to move!

We did as she desired. We did not want to be recognized, I said to Tlorr that her image is seen many times each day by every Soldier in Rowtt, but she said no, it is the robes they see, and as for you it is not the face Soldiers see but the insignia of High Commander. So at my order Prookt Commander took uniforms from two commanders of the third rank for us to wear. He did not ask why we wanted them and he was not going to dismiss the unclothed commanders from their stations so they could return to their quarters and clothe themselves, either, but I ordered him to do that because their attention might wander if they were cold, and every Soldier in the commanders' chamber must be alert at all times. I wonder what Prookt would have done if I had demanded his uniform, no, I know what he would have done, he would have given it and remained at his post.

Tlorr said We will go where the not-Soldiers went first and stayed longest. So that is what we did. She drove us herself, she said I have not done this for a long time! It is pleasant to an extreme degree! It is not as pleasant as mating and it was easy to do the will of Abundant God when mating was the reward and not so easy when transporting myself is the most pleasant experience I have to anticipate, but this will suffice.

Nothing will suffice for the end of mating. I wonder if I asked that Cutter if she would try to find out if there is a way to draw the facilitators even in age, and would it prevent the change, would there be no more Holy Men, would there even be High Commanders, and would it not fulfill the directive of Abundant God. I said this to Tlorr, she said Ask her but she will say no.

I said How do you know did you

This is not the point.

The crèche is distant, it is the most distant from the commanders' center as Tlorr ordered at the first, indeed the female Haknt was placed at a great distance from the center also because if they had come with weapons we could have

But they did not.

We found a Warrior they spoke to, the point is what she said. They see into the mind and speak to it, she said, it is like talking but not like talking—I am certain now that Haknt does it and maybe the male who came with her could do it. And Tlorr and I are divided, Tlorr only wants Haknt to return but I am sure she will return anyway and I said besides there is this, other not-Soldiers are here, at this moment the male not-Soldier Arkt is near the commanders' center, he is with the record-keeper Kwek, it would be easy to detain him and when his time comes to mate there will be no not-Soldier mates and we will tell him he will only be released to mate if he sees for us into the Demon's mind.

But the Warrior also said the not-Soldier who spoke to her mind said Abundant God does not require these not-Soldiers to mate in his time but only when they choose but how could that be true? It cannot be true, but Tlorr says it might be true and keeping the male will serve no purpose and so we disagree but it cannot be true every creature in the world mates as Abundant God wills so how can it be true, I cannot stop thinking about it, what if it is true could they

---

If they were human, said Dema—true-human, she added—she would run from them as fast as she could.

"Why true-human?" Parker said. "You're prejudiced against true-humans."

"No." Her look was exasperated. She did not like being accused of prejudice—and wouldn't have cared if she did not, in fact, struggle with it. "They wouldn't be normal. Normal true-humans look at each other's faces, they look for affect, more than D'neerans do. What we've got here is almost universal flat affect—I mean, most of these beings show very little change in facial expression, and they don't feel much emotion, either. It's the same here in this—this school—as it was in the crèches. The oldest children here are different, but why? Why does it crop up at puberty and then disappear? It's obvious they revert before long. There's no depth. The animal species I know have more depth."

He muttered, "The more I know about them the less I like them."

Dema sighed. She said more cheerfully, "It's not so bad. Look at it this way, Benj. At least they're mammals."

"They have *litters.*"

"They don't self-clone, they don't lay eggs, they don't bear live young that strain plankton, all right?"

"Girrians are mammals. They don't have litters."

"Twins, usually, but—Girrians don't do spaceflight, either. These are *space-going* mammals, Benj. Focus on that. They are," said Dema, contradicting herself without shame, "just like us."

They were conferring in one of the (gray concrete) rooms of a sub-complex they had been assured served education. In a huge (gray concrete) chamber next door, there was a fairly rhythmic tramp-tramp as tiny Soldiers practiced marching. Prez Mercado was there too, not saying much as usual, certainly staying out of this knotty conversation.

Parker said stiffly: "They are not like us. True, we have males. They have males. True, we have females. They have females. But we do not have any goddam *facilitators!* Whatever the hell they are! I want them to produce one!"

A group of small Soldiers, already in the ubiquitous loose coveralls, had strayed from the adjoining chamber. They watched to see if the not-Soldiers would do something interesting. Parker glared at them.

Dema liked Parker, which he pretended to think annoying. She laughed.

"The mechanics of mating aren't on our agenda, Benj. That's Cinnamon Padrick's team. We're on education now."

Parker snorted. "I can just see Padrick's face when somebody tells her facilitators are Abundant God's little helpers—"

He stopped because his communicator—all their communicators—went off with a warning blast.

General order for immediate evacuation. Repeat, immedi-

ate evacuation. Prepare to return to Endeavor. *Repeat, prepare to return —*

Prez Mercado started switching systems offline. Dema called automatically, *H'ana?*

No immediate danger, but don't waste any time.

Then Hanna was gone, too busy for more. Whatever it was, she was in the middle of it.

Chapter X

ARCH HARM HAD BEEN A historian in his other life. For him, the ancient question that went "Why are we here?" was not a philosophical one.

The first time he asked that question, in a small town on a D'neeran prairie, his father had responded with an image that combined the town of their previous residence with an image of Arch's maternal grandmother, whom his father greatly disliked (though he still liked Arch's mother). This was Arch's first introduction to the reasons humans moved about as they did. He canvassed his agemates to find out why *they* were there, wondered who had first come to L'enka and started a town, and thus was launched on a path that only fascinated him more as time passed. Eventually, as a sideline, he studied the history of F'thal, was so interested that he became an expert at an early age, and took up the history of Girritt, such as it was, with equal enthusiasm. He had been an unsuccessful applicant to the Zeigan Project when Starr Jameson headed it, and Hanna, who had made that first contact, had chosen the project's handful of direct contact personnel, all of them D'neerans. Arch had not been unqualified, but there were better candidates at the time (none of whom had wanted anything more to do with Contact after Zeig-Daru).

Arch was perfect for this mission, though. He was so immersed in his subject that even though he knew Hanna well, his core perception of her was her role in history. And Hanna liked obsessive specialists. If they did not always see a larger picture, they did contribute to it immeasurably. It was Arch, therefore, who finally got to meet with a being Soldiers called a record-keeper, there being no broader word for "historian."

Kwek Warrior might have been a prepossessing female of her species, but her species was not Arch's. He only knew she was female because Hanna, informing him of the meeting, had used the pronoun "she." Kwek was not in crèche mode, and the coveralls she wore did not hint at her numerous breasts. The rooms where they met were as utilitarian as all the rest of Soldiers' spaces and dominated by a bank of equipment Arch guessed were computers and their peripherals, all looking rather scraped and dented, and so bulky that it was evident they were neither organic nor quantum-based. Faint noises hinted at the ever-present video screen pouring out war, speeches, and public assemblies, but someone, presumably Kwek, had shoved a tall gray cabinet in front of it, hiding it from view.

Arch almost missed Kwek's greeting, because his attention was fixed on one unexpected feature in the room: one of the tall, tapering tumblers these people used stood on a counter, a few forlorn-looking blossoms sticking out of its mouth. It was the first hint of decoration anyone had seen on Battleground.

He became aware that he was expected to say something, and said hastily, "Sorry, I think the translator glitched. Would you repeat?"

"Very well. Guest, I am Kwek Warrior and I have three hundred and twenty summers."

"Host, I am Arch, and I have forty summers. I am here to learn about your people's past."

Kwek said, "With which year do you wish to begin?"

Arch had decided to leave prehistory alone for now, so he said: "Your earliest written records, or maybe images of them, if you don't have the artifacts here. Those would be clay tablets, perhaps, or carved stone."

"What?" said Kwek, or so it came out of the translator.

"The earliest written records that human beings left were engraved in media like rock or baked clay," Arch explained—patiently, because Hanna had taught her students that it often took some time to get contiguous human and alien frames of reference to overlap. "Later records might survive on parchment or some other form of organic material. In some cases the content, taken in context with other data, allows dating to a particular year, or even to a particular day. Other times, we can only come up with an estimate."

He was open, as instructed, to anything he could pick up from Kwek without touching her thoughts in any way she might perceive. He was getting an odd mix now: curiosity, confusion, and oddest of all, a sense of comprehension accompanied by—fear. But it did not seem to be Arch she feared.

She said, "You must state a year."

Arch said thoughtfully, "All right. Let me see your records for the year one."

"There are none," Kwek said. With relief; she was on surer ground. The reply did not surprise Arch.

He said, "This is the year of the four thousand six hundred and twenty-sixth summer, according to transmissions we retrieved in our approach. Do I have that right?"

"That is correct."

"So you are compiling records for year four thousand six hundred and twenty-six."

He looked at her expectantly.

"Yes."

"And you have records from the year four thousand six hundred and twenty-five, counting down."

"Yes."

"How far—no, what is the lowest numbered year?"

"Four thousand three hundred and one," Kwek said immediately.

Arch couldn't take the statement literally. He said, "But that's only a little over three hundred summers ago."

"Yes. We also have records for the years four thousand three hundred two and three hundred three, four thousand three hundred twenty-one, a portion of four thousand three hundred twenty-two—"

She went on until Arch stopped her. There were huge gaps. He let it go and groped for another question.

"What are the years numbered *from*?" he said. "How do you know which year was year one? Did something happen in that year?"

"Creation," Kwek said.

"Creation?"

"Yes," Kwek said.

"Creation of what?"

"Everything. The world, Soldiers, the universe, everything. At least, we call it year one. The fact is that the counting is not certain. I think. I know my predecessor miscounted, so maybe her predecessor did, and maybe his did."

Arch was focused on that astonishing statement about the year one. He said, "You can't believe that. What about the fossil record? What about astrophysics? You must have astrophysics!" He hesitated; the translator had made a *no referent* noise for *fossil*. "Wait—" he said. Frames of reference, he reminded himself.

"Do you mean," he said—he had started to say *you can't mean*—"that everything that now exists came into existence all at once, all at the same time, in the year one?"

"Yes," Kwek said again. The answer was unequivocal. But there was an edge of doubt. A lonely doubt; an unhappy one.

I must be missing something, Arch thought.

"Do all Soldiers believe as you do?"

"Yes. It is the truth," Kwek said. Miserably. Then she added, "There are some who believe otherwise. They go to That Place."

Arch, thinking a historian's thoughts about histories of orthodoxy, thought she meant hell. To be sure, he said, "Just where is That Place?"

Then, to his astonishment, Kwek turned to the computer bank and spoke a series of instructions. A map of the hemisphere appeared, and Kwek put a finger on ocean. Arch had a wild vision of a sort of watery anti-inferno.

"It's underwater?" he said.

"No. We do not put it on maps because it does not matter."

Then Arch remembered. There *was* land where Kwek pointed. He had studied maps of Battleground intensively, anticipating that geography would play a significant role in the treasury of knowledge he expected to ransack. The land in question was not a single body and none of its units were large; humans had classified it as an archipelago.

"Does it have a number?" he asked; for Battleground designated landmasses and groupings of masses not by name but by number.

"No," said Kwek. "It is just That Place."

Then she looked quickly over her shoulder. He couldn't

read the alien face, but there was no mistaking the emotions pouring from her: longing and grief.

"I wish I could go there," she said.

The recording better come out right, Arch thought. Maybe Hanna could make some sense of this.

"Why do you want to go there?" he asked.

"Because I doubt," she said, barely above a whisper. "Thoughts come that I never had before, I ask myself questions I did not think of before. Why is history empty of so many years? Why would Abundant God attempt to deceive us by creating bones of animals that did not ever exist? Why have we never decisively defeated the Demon, why has nothing changed in all the summers of my life, why do some Commanders go away and never return though it is secretly said they survive?"

Arch thought: *I am out of my depth.*

He said, "Do you think you could get permission to visit our ship? Observe our techniques, look at our records—"

Any excuse to get her there, where others could help him sort it out.

"I do not think so. No one else has gone."

"I don't think anyone has been invited yet, Kwoort," he said, inspired. "We'll ask Kwoort if you can go. You know Kwoort?"

"Why, yes. He is ranked next to the Holy Man."

"We can get his authorization, I'm sure. I think. Will you come?"

Kwek said, "Yes. And afterward, maybe I will go to That Place, and not return here."

But Kwoort—when Hanna was roused from deep sleep to call him—denied permission. He did not even do it in person; it was Prookt who conveyed the refusal to Hanna. And shortly thereafter, an alarmed and disbelieving Arch was escorted to a room much like the one where Hanna had been a quasi-hostage—only this one had a lock on the outside.

He knew something was wrong as soon as the two Soldiers came for him, and knew before they reached the room that they meant to lock him in. He managed to go into it calmly and silently, and then he screamed in thought, *HANA!!!*

She had just left Communications, puzzled by Kwoort's action but longing to return to the dark relief of sleep—until that shout of panic made every tired muscle jerk. She lost her balance, grabbed at air, and found herself on the floor, weak with Arch's fear.

She knew a lot about fear.

Her hands were clenched. She was alone in the corridor and grateful for it; no one would distract her. She relaxed her hands deliberately, all at once and then finger by finger. She fed the sensations to Arch in a steady stream, felt the adrenaline rush begin to ebb in both of them.

That's good, Arch. That's good. Now a deep breath. Good. Another one. Let it out slowly . . .

Jameson used to guide her this way when he woke her from blood-soaked nightmares.

Again. Again . . .

Better, Arch thought.

Show me what happened.

Not much, on the face of it: two Soldiers, a locked room. *Did they take your com unit?* Images, not words.

No . . . Not a word either: relief and hope.

Use it. Report to me as if I didn't already know, as if you were true-human.

She was on her feet, running back to Communications, when he made the audible report, sounding calm enough now. She had already alerted Metra by the time she got there.

"All personnel on the surface will be evacuated at once. And I will contact Commissioner Vickery," Metra said from Command, and Hanna said, "You do that, but try for Starr Jameson first," which Metra did not take kindly. Hanna shrugged; Vickery might have surfaced, but nobody was going to pay any attention to him. Her priority was Kwoort.

But Kwoort would not talk to her. All her efforts got her were low-level Soldiers, who kept repeating, as she called again and again from Communications, that Kwoort Commander would be notified of her attempt to reach him.

"I want to go down there," she told Metra, and Metra said, "No."

"Then I'll touch him telepathically."

"No."

"He's not responding! How else am I supposed to find what he's up to?"

"Later. When evacuation is complete."

Half an hour passed, Hanna touching Arch at intervals. *Nothing's happened,* he said each time. *Endeavor*'s shuttles left and returned in flashes of light. A few specialists dragged their feet. Metra talked to those herself, the message unequivocal: *Move* now. *Or you'll be stunned and carried.* The last of them—the physiologists, the most stubborn, who had gone with Joseph—were finally retrieved. Hanna did not like Metra any better, but the captain's command in evacuating personnel was faultless. The whole exercise had taken just under forty minutes.

Then Arch said, tense but no longer afraid: *I'm free— they're letting me go—*

—thank God. Use the com unit again.

Metra was suddenly at her shoulder, angry and impatient. She had tried to reach Vickery, impotent though he might be, with no better result than Hanna had gotten from Kwoort. Vickery's staff had referred her to Jameson. Jameson had referred her back to Hanna.

"They're letting Arch go," Hanna told her.

"How do you know?"

"He told me—wait, this is him."

Voice now: "H'ana? I was wrong. I'm told there was a misunderstanding. The Soldiers escorting me were supposed to take both of us, the record-keeper and me, to a rendezvous point, so we can go back to *Endeavor* together. The captain can send a shuttle as soon as she's ready."

That is not true. Prookt said Kwoort's decision was definite.

Arch: *And the Soldiers were clear about their orders, that was no mistake—*

Metra had cleared nonessential personnel from Communications. She would have liked to clear Hanna, too, but functioning as liaison with Kwoort's proxies made her essential. Hanna had shut out telepathic communication with her team, all except Arch now back on *Endeavor*; their anxiety for Arch was too distracting. Metra had not hesitated to alert the trailing, almost-forgotten warship, but she had refused to allow Hanna to communicate with Jameson.

But finally light flashed at the module where she slumped, and the familiar voice said her name. Clearly the prohibition did not work both ways; Metra had not dared to deny Jameson. He said, "An update, please. It took some time to reach you through your captain. She's been very busy, of course."

She could not tell if he thought the delay had been deliberate. The dry tone told her nothing.

"How—" she began, and stopped. This conversation was not private. *How the hell am I supposed to function if I can't talk to you,* was what she had started to say. Before she could think of a way to put it differently another light flashed.

"Kwoort," she said. "Finally. Listen!"

Kwoort said her name, too, that strange *Haknt,* sounding like a threat as it hung between them. There was no video. "Kwoort Commander," she acknowledged, and hesitated, reaching for diplomacy, before she went on. "I'm told there has been a misunderstanding."

"There was. I corrected the situation immediately. Your Commander has informed us the remaining not-Soldier and our record-keeper will be removed momentarily. It appears all the other not-Soldiers have gone away. It was not necessary."

The translator allowed no nuance that might carry emotion, but she knew Kwoort well enough to touch his mind without effort. *The hell with getting Metra's permission,* she thought, and did it, the barest, lightest touch. She sensed him strain to feel anything like it, too, and knew then what had set him off: somehow he had discovered the real nature of the "surveillance system" he had suspected. She could not tell where the conviction came from and could not try to look for it without the shield of trance. He was so rigid with anticipation that he might even interpret a stray thought of his own as an intrusion.

But she did not have to probe further to see that he was furious. His orders had been countermanded by the Holy Man, and he was not used to it.

She said slowly, "I believe you acted properly. Disagreement between Soldiers and not-Soldiers would not be desirable."

She would let him work that out for himself. Battleground

was in no position to fight an interspecies war. As, perhaps, the Holy Man had realized, and insisted on backing off.

Kwoort said, "A Holy Man has agreed to meet with Gergtk."

He meant Gabriel. Hanna said immediately, "I will accompany him. He is under my command."

"Very well," Kwoort said. He named the location, the same as before, and a time three hours away.

"Starr?" she said when Kwoort was gone. "Did you hear? There was more that he didn't say. He found out about telepathy somehow."

"But he won't say so openly."

"Not yet. He's on guard, though."

"What was Harm doing there alone?" Jameson said, and Hanna winced. Arch should have gone as part of a team.

"I made a mistake," she said, plain truth. In the endless bombardment of detail, exhausted, she had simply missed the violation.

But the deep, calm voice that had stayed her through many bad nights only said, "Talk to the record-keeper Harm is bringing to *Endeavor*. Do it soon. Kwoort might demand her return at any time."

"Of course. But I need to find out more about what's going on inside his head first. If Metra will allow it."

"I'll make sure she does. Or Andrella will. Andrella had to intervene before I could talk to you."

Hanna made a face. "There are advantages to being commissioner," she said.

"It won't be long. Endit," he said.

———

Back to her quarters and back into trance, but not for long.

Still rumbling with anger, arguing orders. He is not without ego, and a big one, too!—flashes like this from Starr sometimes, when he talked about Vickery . . .

". . . had no suspicion of secrets when I was on their world, though perhaps they had them; we know these do! This Warrior they took to their craft—you know her cast of thought, I had already brought her to your attention, and now you allow her to go to them—we must bring her back, tell them to go away, tell them if they do not we will fight them—!"

"—oh, hell," said Hanna, scrambling to her feet, calling out for a connection to Metra.

Bella said, "What?" at her side and Metra said, *What!* from the air.

"We need to distract Kwoort and we need to do it now. He's *insane—* "

She stopped, hearing herself, thinking she had used the word too lightly. She amended it: "He's in a rage and working up to aggression—where's Gabriel? When's this meeting we're supposed to have with the Holy Man? Contact Kwoort and tell him we're ready!"

Chapter XI

" I'M NOT *READY*," SAID GABRIEL and Hanna said, "For God's sake, Gabriel, what do you have to do to get *ready?* Pray?"

"For one thing," he said stiffly.

"Don't you pray all the time, or something?"

"Ideally, just being is prayer," Gabriel said, "but I've only had glimpses of what that's like."

"I do not have any idea what you're talking about," said Hanna.

I don't suppose you would, Gabriel thought, and simultaneously wondered if she had read the thought and wished he was too kind to have thought it. She didn't seem to have noticed; she was walking purposefully ahead of him toward a starboard docking bay, her light slippers making no sound. She had put on something gauzy and pale blue which clung to her admirably, and when she glanced around, the blue of her eyes was vividly dark by comparison. She stopped abruptly, turned around and stared at him. He had hovered in her presence every chance he could get, watching the expert at work, watching with awe, and she had been too busy and too tired to pay attention to him. Sometimes she noticed him and looked puzzled. He was puzzled too — mostly because everyone around her seemed to see her as invulnerable, and he knew she was not. All that fierce attention was focused on him now like a lance of light, and he was the one who felt vulnerable.

She said, "This is not the time to be thinking of me as a woman."

There didn't seem to be any reply to that. She frowned. *Exquisitely,* Gabriel thought, and then, rather desperately, *Adolescent crush, that's all it is, just an adolescent crush!*

"Maybe it is," said Hanna, eradicating his hope that she was going to stay out of his thoughts. "Try to cure yourself of it, all right? I wish it was raw sexual desire, I can deal with that!"

"How?" said Gabriel, and immediately regretted asking.

"You wouldn't like it. Anyway, I'm not interested. I have all I want—"

She stopped short. Gabriel said, "Another lie?"

"All right. Not all I want." She glanced over her shoulder, toward the waiting pod. She clearly didn't want to take time to explain, but he saw her make up her mind to do it. "What I *want* is what I had with Mickey's father. But it's so rare that nobody where I come from expects ever to have it. I certainly didn't. And I will never have it again. It almost never happens, and it never happens twice.

"But for now, just for now, I have Starr. I respect him and I'm grateful to him and most of the time I like him and he makes love beautifully. Quite possessively, usually, but that's very exciting in a perverted sort of way," she said, and Gabriel winced at the cruel crudity of it. "Now you know what I want and what I have. What I am."

Somebody used Gabriel's mouth to say, "You didn't say anything about love."

For a moment she was absolutely still. She did not even move until she said, "I don't think I'll have Starr much longer either. I don't know if I want what he's becoming."

The somebody using Gabriel's mouth said, "What does that have to do with somebody else falling in love with you?"

"Oh. Nothing. Well, do it at your own risk," she said, and started walking again.

It's time I took some risks, Gabriel thought with new conviction. She looked back once more. It was a very thoughtful look, and he rejoiced in it as he followed her to the pod.

———

It was a rocky flight. Hanna, who Gabriel thought ought to be paying more attention to what she was doing, instead talked savagely. "If they want us to 'survive,' they should have waited for better weather over Rowtt!"

"You're the one who insisted on meeting now," Gabriel pointed out.

"I didn't know it was going to be this bad!" Billowy white clouds had turned dark as they descended and there was lightning, there was wind; the pod shuddered as it neared the surface. "Never mind, Gabriel. We'll go faster than the lightning," she said blithely, and he wanted to point out that this was impossible but thought it best to keep his mouth shut.

Still, when the hatch slid open, she stood uncertainly at the portal, looking out at the strangest storm Gabriel had ever seen. Afternoon had come but it was so dark that it might have been twilight; hot wind came in hard blasts and thunder was almost continuous, but there was no rain—not yet; there might be some in the black clouds, lit up weirdly by lightning within. The ominous light had a greenish cast.

Hanna muttered something that was lost in thunder, and Gabriel said, "What?"

She raised her voice. "High incidence of low-precipitation electrical storms. That was in one of the reports."

"I read that."

"Something to do with the magnetosphere? I don't remember." She jumped to the ground without bothering to order the ramp down, and he followed.

They were at the place where they had met with Kwoort before, the blocky, ungraceful building they had not entered, fronted by three shallow steps and a stingy terrace made of the same deteriorating concrete.

"It looks deserted," Gabriel said. Hanna walked quickly toward the door, veering at the strongest bursts of wind. Gabriel managed to resist the urge to put his arm around her, to steady her. She said softly, between stutters of thunder, "Kwoort's here, though. So is somebody else. But it's not the Holy Man, whatever Kwoort says. He lied."

He started to ask how she knew, then didn't, accepting it.

The door did not open automatically but swung inward at Hanna's tentative push. They stepped into the featureless inside of a cube. There were lights set in the ceiling, dim with grime, and dust on the floor, scuffed with tracks that resolved into footprints. Gabriel turned to close the door and Hanna stopped him with her hand on his. "No. There's been too much confinement done since we got here," she said obscurely. "Me first and then Arch. His wasn't voluntary. Don't close any doors you don't have to."

Gabriel shook his head, without a clue to what she meant. He looked down to see her brown hand against his own lighter skin, and he was distracted, lost in the sight. It might be the only time she ever touched him and his mind filled with the moment, the coolness of her skin on his.

She took her hand away and turned to the blank wall opposite the door. There was a slight sound and a section of the wall slid up. They walked through the opening into another gray chamber. Hanna glanced back, but the wall did not shut behind them; instead another panel opened, and Kwoort stood there with a personage behind him. The second figure was deep in the shadowy interior, too far away for Hanna to make out its face.

"I greet you," said Kwoort. His eyes—all of them—were on Hanna.

"Here are two Holy Men," he said, "one of my people, one of yours. You and I will leave them to converse."

"Very well," Hanna said after a moment. She seemed to have forgotten Gabriel; she had gone still and was looking at Kwoort with a directness that chilled. Gabriel suddenly remembered things he had heard about this woman that had nothing to do with her quick mind, her desirable flesh, or her tears. He wondered if she had managed to obtain a weapon and somehow conceal it.

Another panel opened, and in a moment she was gone with Kwoort without one look back, and Gabriel, feeling especially unholy, faced an alien Holy Man: his strangest dream had come true, and he was alone without any ally except (fittingly) his God.

———

Deeper and deeper into a gray warren where there were no birds to sing (*I have heard there are birds on this world*, thought Hanna, though she had seen none), and she opened her perception fully to Kwoort and saw that he thought of growing old, and of growing insane if not holy, and he knew it was happening, that he had become killer only, never breeder again, because the breeding function itself was gone, it was time to think only of killing—

—but it was not quite time, not quite, and he demanded, "How do you choose not to breed?" with the urgency of an implacable force behind it.

She had expected him to rail about telepathy and was completely unprepared for the question. She struggled to make the switch and began slowly, "It has been an easily implemented choice for a thousand summers, though exercised less in places where there is much room—"

Too slowly for Kwoort.

"That is not what I mean! We do not have room! And we do not have a choice!" he said, and she caught a momentary flash from his mind, not an image of Soldiers but of another species that lived on this world—finger-sized, dead white, hairless and blind—it lived underground, they were crowded and scrambling over one another, they turned on each other savagely and tore with sharp teeth and ate, ate—

Hanna stumbled as if someone had hit her. Kwoort moved faster, leading her on floors slanting downward, taking her deeper through gray rooms as if in fear of pursuit or—*no*—of being overheard.

H'ana!

She fastened on the call: *Joseph? Bella!*—they were monitoring her, and though Gabriel did not know it, Dema and Arch watched him.

Bella, steady, practical: *Did you know you have gone underground?*

I don't want to be underground!

I can see why!—Bella had caught her vision of tiny cannibals, too. *The captain's ordered a fix on your position. She'll come get you, if she has to.*

"Kwoort Commander," Hanna said, "stop, take me back!" She had kept track of their turns for the first three or four but at the tenth or twelfth change of direction this maze had defeated her, though now they were in a level corridor that ran straight, straight, and long, to a vanishing point in darkness, tracks of wheels showing in the dust.

The cannibalistic image had unnerved her. For the first time she was almost afraid of Kwoort. She did not know how to fight him if it came to that; she did not know his anatomy. The eyes would be vulnerable but what else, surely the genitalia, if she kicked between his legs it would hurt—

Maybe, said Joseph, who had read the physiologists' reports, *but the organs are usually retracted, the attack might be ineffective—*

Contact with Bella and Joseph had calmed her. She stopped; she would not go any farther. She said, "Kwoort Commander!" and almost said *You are angry with me*, but aloud made it a question: "Kwoort Commander, are you angry with me?"

The translator chirped. There was no match for *angry*. But Hanna had no doubt of what he felt.

He could not take her any farther without seizing her and dragging her, and she saw that he thought about doing it, but he did stop, and turned and said "Speak to me of breeding!" with fury.

Instead she said, "First tell me how the misunderstanding came about, that my historian was briefly made prisoner—"

"The lower ranks of Soldiers are sometimes inattentive. These were inattentive. They have been disciplined," said Kwoort.

The same lie.

"Answer my question!" Kwoort said. Hanna had known enough human warriors to know the tone of command even filtered through a translator. She was going to have to answer, and there was no reason not to tell the truth. But, *Something I didn't expect*, she said to Joseph and Bella, feeling their tension—or maybe they only reflected hers. *He's angry about more than telepathy. Find out what the other humans on Battleground were doing, who they were talking to, what they were studying, what else he might have found out about us.*

That had to be it, she thought. Kwoort had learned about something besides telepathy, and was outraged.

The two of them at least had stopped and were standing still in that gray corridor. Hanna did not know where it went, but she knew she did not want to go there, not without knowing what waited.

"Please, Kwoort Commander," she said. "There were students of the body here only a little while ago, and if they return they will answer your questions better than I can. Can we come to an agreement? Can you promise they will be safe from harm? That you will not try to keep them, as you tried to keep our historian? If you can promise those things they will tell you anything you want to know."

The eyes were all open and all yellowish-gray; they seemed to glow in the dim space. There was a flash of bright blue, out of place. The ring on her hand, perversely, had decided to act as if it were alive. This time Kwoort paid no attention. She could feel his effort to master emotion and with it his awareness that those emotions—for which she thought he had no words—were ever stronger and someday soon would go beyond control.

But the day had not come yet. The breathing channels at his neck pulsed more slowly. There was a fractional relaxation of all his body.

She almost whispered, "I would like to return to my companion, the human holy man. He is a gentle being un-used to communicating with nonhumans, and I do not want to leave him alone in this strange place for long—"

—just as Bella told her, tension in the thought, *Try to get back to Gabriel, there could be a problem with His Most Exalted Madness or whatever he is*—

Kwoort turned abruptly back the way they had come. Hanna followed as quickly as she could. Noting, as she went, that "gentle" had not translated.

Gabriel's first impression was that this being—this person, he reminded himself—was in constant motion. The Holy Man was robed, and Gabriel's next crazy thought was *Is there some significance to ceremonial robing among sentient bipeds, yeah, they all do it, I think we all do it.* The robe was made of some crinkly off-yellow fabric with an iridescence to it *sort of like that clingy silvery thing Hanna wore the other day oh God I shouldn't think of that—* And he thought: *Where'd the expert go when I need her?*

The Holy Man's hands were long and thin, the fingers in constant motion. Better than Hanna about reading reports, Gabriel remembered something a physiologist had observed about gross anatomy in datastream images weeks ago: *". . . observed no analogue to the human fingernail, but tegument on fingers darkens gradually which might represent a transition to more protective skin structure—"*

Maybe the subject of the report had been better at holding still than this Holy Man, whose dark fingertips danced. The being rocked from one foot to the other, and the shifting patterns of light in the fabric of the robe made it appear that the garment danced, too. The tongue tip, hardly wider than a blade of grass, protruded and flickered. Paradoxically, a line of ancient poetry came to Gabriel's mind, one that evoked stillness in eternity: *Oh sages standing in God's holy fire as in the gold mosaic of a wall*—

The Holy Man began to speak, and Gabriel forgot about poetry. There were whistles, clicks, words with a cadence that might have been speech, but the translator produced a steady stream of *not translatables*. What a time for it to malfunction!

"Holy sage," Gabriel said, reverently in spite of himself, because he faced a thinking creature of some God that might also be his, "I am here to hear about your beliefs and to tell you about mine, but I don't think the translator is working. Can you understand what I'm saying? I can't understand you—"

"Yes," said the being, "believe," and soared into punctuated babble again. The few macroscopic parts of the translator weren't substantial enough to grab and shake, Gabriel's impulse; he could only wait for a pause in what the Holy Man was saying. He waited for what seemed like eternity but was probably minutes, transfixed by the movement, the strangeness, and he began to notice things about the Holy Man that he hadn't seen at once. The creature was stick-thin, taller than Gabriel by a head; once, when he went momentarily still, he looked like a dressed-up mantis. It was when he started up again that Gabriel saw the real oddity: no facial expressions accompanied the stream of gibberish. The mouth moved with speaking and the tongue flickered constantly, but all the other muscles of the face, and the eyes, were fixed. Gabriel thought of something he had seen on Co-op as a child, after his parents were killed and he lived briefly in Gergowan with a cousin's family. The whole brood had gone to see the New Year maskers, crowding the street on a cold night while costumed men—nearly all of them were men— roared and danced to drive the dark away. One of them ran up to Gabriel, gesturing mock threats, swollen to inhuman size in animal guise. The arms waved, the legs flailed, the wild activity kept the cold away; the figure swung a torch in either hand. But the animal head was rigid and the animal face never changed. Clearly the thing was alive, but it did not have the face of a living thing, not even of any animal; it had the face of something alive in body but not in soul. Gabriel had thought of the devil then, and he thought of the devil now.

He didn't even believe in the devil any more.

The enormity of this impression was only beginning to show itself when he heard a soft whisper in Standard: *The translator's all right. He's speaking a language we haven't heard before—or else it's schizophasia . . .*

He looked at the communicator on his wrist, but it wasn't showing anything. The whisper came again: *No, no, it's Dema, don't you know me? You have to get used to telepathy. There is nothing wrong with the translator.*

"What are you—?"

Hush! Don't talk out loud! Think the words like you were going to say them.

Spooked, Gabriel couldn't think at all. The Holy Man had kept right on going, but the sounds were coming faster now, and the volume was rising. The jitters seemed to have sped up, too.

"Holy One," he said. "Holy One?"

"Kill," the translator said suddenly.

"Are you talking about killing?" Gabriel said to the Holy Man.

"Death," said the translator, picking something out of the stream of sounds. "Demon," it said, and seconds later, "Compression query—"

Kwoort burst into the gray chamber. "What are you doing to the Holy One?" he said.

All Gabriel could think was *Where's Hanna?* and the whisper said *Coming* and flooded him with reassurance.

Hanna came in then, eyes abnormally wide, anxiety a cloud around her.

"He has done nothing," she said. "Kwoort Commander, you have deceived us. This is not the Holy Man from whom you take orders. Is he even a Holy Man at all?"

Kwoort made a fast turn in her direction and seemed to catch himself on the edge of a violent movement. He said, "He is what Holy Men become."

For a few seconds Hanna was as still as Kwoort. Finally she said, "Kwoort Commander, I do not understand what you are doing. Do you understand, yourself?"

———

"That was a Holy Man, all right, or used to be," she said later, "and he's a babbling idiot."

She had barely spoken on the flight back to *Endeavor*, told the captain in an absentminded way that she would talk to her later, and taken Gabriel with her to report to Jameson. She and Gabriel, and Jameson's holographic image, this time complete, shared her small cabin instead of a common-access conference room. Probably the captain could monitor whatever happened here, but maybe she wouldn't.

Gabriel and Hanna sat side by side on Hanna's narrow bed while Hanna talked. Jameson, listening in a space hundreds of light-years distant, seemed to take up most of the rest of the room. He looked very real, and standing he was very tall, and Gabriel moved a little so that he could see both of them. Hanna was making small restless movements. Jameson made hardly any, as if there were only so many nerves between them, and she had most of them.

"Kwoort's so different from most Soldiers he stands out like a solar flare," she said.

Jameson said, "Is that an emotional reaction, or an objective observation?"

"Both, I suppose. He's being pulled in different directions, he's—I can't even conceptualize it, much less pin it down in words. It's not that there's more than one personality; there's definitely only one, a strong one. He reminds me a little of you," Hanna said. Jameson's expression changed to surprise, and Hanna said, "The intensity. 'I burn,' he told me. But your fire is controlled. His isn't."

They looked at each other in stillness for a moment. Something changed, subtly. *What's that?* Gabriel thought, then recognized, belatedly, the current of pure sensuality between the man and woman who were so far apart. Jameson had acknowledged Gabriel's presence and since then had not looked away from Hanna. Gabriel felt sick with embarrassment. And appalled, his eyes on Hanna's parted lips, at his own answering surge of lust.

Hanna took a deep breath and moved a little; the context changed. Something that had opened in Jameson's face closed again. Finally he did look at Gabriel. He said, "What were your impressions?"

"Mine?" Gabriel said, startled.

"What did you learn from this encounter?"

"I don't think I learned anything. Communications confirmed that the translator was working. But the Holy Man didn't say more than half a dozen translatable words. Was he supposed to be—" Gabriel stopped. "I wonder," he said. "Speaking in tongues? Do you know what that is?"

"More or less," Jameson said. "It's been discredited, but it's still practiced here and there."

"Yes," Gabriel said, "although I'm inclined to the view that special conditions were operating in the early church."

Jameson nodded as if he had some familiarity with the view. Hanna looked blank.

Gabriel added, "The whole meeting looks pointless. Meaningless."

"It had to have some meaning to Kwoort," Hanna said. She did not look at Gabriel; he was forgotten again, by both of them. "He wanted to know about breeding. About conception control. That was what it sounded like, but it doesn't make sense. A civilization that can develop space travel just has to have done that kind of research. Humans did; all the other Outsiders did. And he showed us what Holy Men become, that's what he called it. He wanted me to see it. Maybe he did that because of what I said about his sanity, and he wanted to show me what will happen to him, without telling me directly. That babbling idiot is his future. God! I said he reminded me of you," she told Jameson. "How would you feel if that was your future?"

"It might be," he said, and Hanna said involuntarily, "No!"—startling Gabriel, who knew something had just been said under the surface but did not know what it was.

Jameson ignored it and said, "What the hell are the dynamics of the change, then?"

Hanna said, "I think the Holy Man I touched originally, the female, is actually in an earlier stage than Kwoort, even if she's chronologically older. That one is not, fortunately, aggressive toward us. When I looked at her she was thinking only of the planetary war, thinking only of whether we could provide her with something that would give Rowtt an advantage."

"And when she reaches that final stage? Would she be replaced by Kwoort?"

"What difference would that make? He's moving toward it himself, how could he replace her? I don't know if we even need to know the dynamics!" she said with sudden passion. "What if we just file some reports and interdict the place?"

"As we interdicted Zeig-Daru, but completely this time, without the distance contact and automated trade? Leave, and make no further contact?"

"Exactly."

Jameson looked at her oddly. He said, "What happened to your curiosity? I can remember when you'd do anything to get your hands on an alien civilization."

"Then you will remember that one of them got their hands on *me*. Remember, as long as you're remembering, my apprehension when Uskos first made contact. The fact that contact with Uskos was beneficent did not negate the fear I still carried from the earliest contacts with Zeig-Daru. I'm not afraid, exactly. It's more that a series of unpleasant incidents are affecting me. How extreme must my fear for Mickey have been that it could break me out of the trance-state like it did? That's not supposed to even be possible! I hate the way they think about mating. I don't like it that there's no art, no poetry. I don't like it that a young female who wants to look pretty is going to become a Warrior who breeds on some kind of cue with whatever Soldier is getting the same cue. I don't like what happened to me when that couple was mating. I don't like—"

"What couple?" said Jameson.

"Didn't I—ah. I didn't report that, did I?"

There was an odd silence. Gabriel watched the two of them stare at each other. Finally Hanna said, "I was in contact with a couple that was mating. The pleasure they experienced was so intense that it aroused me. Tremendously. In *trance!* That's not supposed to be possible, either! I broke out of trance and damn near had sex with Joseph and Bella on the spot, right here on the floor."

"But you didn't?" said Jameson.

Hanna shook her head. They kept staring at each other.

"You don't have to deny yourself intimacy, you know."

"You are getting things mixed up," Hanna said. "If all I wanted was pleasure and release, I could have it with anybody, if I liked him well enough. Why do you think you're the only man I've had since Michael died? I would have entrusted myself to no man in the universe after that, except you. I loved Michael with all that I am, but I did not forget that I loved you first. Remember that, when you speak of intimacy."

Jameson took a step forward, as if he could really cross into the same space. Then he stopped and looked again at Gabriel, and Gabriel said, "Would you like me to leave?"

Hanna said nothing. Jameson sighed and stepped back slowly, reluctantly it seemed. He said, "No. We can discuss personal matters another time. Hanna, you seem to be suggesting that we close out this mission and never return because you find these beings ... unpleasant. That's remarkable, coming from you."

"Don't trivialize it," she said.

"I'm not doing that. But there are good reasons to continue. We might want to carry on reasonable dialogues with Kwoort after he attains ultimate authority. We can't dismiss that hope. We need to know everything about him you can get. If you can you need to become his friend."

"His *friend!* I don't see why. I don't see why we can't leave them to their godforsaken, perpetual warring and hope to make contact with some more rewarding species. Or you could give me a chance to go back to Uskos and do more work there. I like it there. I want Mickey to play with some younglings while he's little. I'll bet you could think up a reason to authorize me to do that, couldn't you?"

"Not immediately," Jameson said, "and not if you insist on prematurely writing off and abandoning a previously unknown civilization. I urge you to think of this, Hanna. You said the currently dominant Holy Man was interested only in the possibility of our providing some means of advantage in the ongoing war. But by your own account, Kwoort is now fully aware of telepathy, and sees the possible advantage in that. I wonder if, supposing we pull out now, he might, in the future, come looking for *us.* I think we should deal with him here and now instead of waiting for that."

"But he said nothing about it today. It's gotten buried under this obsession with breeding. Anyway, he'll never come looking for us."

"Why are you so sure?"

"There's no reason to think they've retained knowledge of interstellar spaceflight. Kwoort won't come looking for us because he can't."

"You don't know that; so far the evidence is indirect. I think you're trying to convince yourself—because you don't want to go through what it will take to get the answers to the questions we've been discussing—"

"God damn you," Hanna said, and got up and walked out.

Gabriel stared after her a moment and turned to see Jameson close his eyes in—exasperation? Pain? He opened them again and Gabriel said, "Is there anything I can do? Should I go and try to bring her back?"

"No. I don't know." He looked at Gabriel, expression unreadable. "These people are disturbing her. Has she said anything more about her attitudes toward them than you just heard?"

Gabriel thought about it. "No," he said. "It was new to me. I'm not sure she was aware of it herself. It might have just now spilled into her conscious mind."

"It might have," Jameson said. "She speaks on impulse, acts on impulse, quite often. This is not the first difficult conversation she's simply walked away from. Throws things, too," he added, almost to himself. He looked thoughtfully at Gabriel. He said, "You're an expert in the unconscious mind, are you not?"

"I wouldn't call myself that, no. I studied it, though, because I knew I would be working with children who had suffered severe trauma."

"Have you ever seen a biography of Hanna?" Jameson said. "There are several. They range from Contact's official version—dry facts—to one or two things so lurid I don't recognize her in them. Or myself, for that matter. Are you familiar with any of them?"

"Oh, yes," Gabriel said. "I didn't waste my time with the prurient ones, but to be frank, sir, she's almost an idol for me, so I've read everything on her that looked like it might be halfway to the truth."

"Keep—" Jameson stopped, sighed again, and said, "Keep an eye on her, will you?"

"Can you be more specific?"

"Go back to those biographies and read between the lines. Look at the trauma points and the picture that emerges. Then add in another factor: that Hanna is not true-human. In recent years she has spent every minute of her life balanced between D'neeran and true-human modes of perception, and a substantial part of it accommodating alien modes as well. Keep that in mind."

"I . . . see," Gabriel said slowly, "I will do that. I think I see what you're asking of me. But I don't think the biographies will have the truth about one more factor, and that is the bond she has with you. Will you tell me?"

"Won't she?"

"She thinks she has," Gabriel said, "and I'm taking what she said as a confidence, whether she knows her own truth or not. But now I'm asking you. What impact have you had on her life?"

"Far too much," said the other man. "Or not nearly enough. We disagree on which it is. Good-bye." He turned his head toward some receptor Gabriel could not see and said "Endit." And the image was gone.

Chapter XII

"FIND A MORE COMFORTABLE place for her," Hanna said.

Talk to the historian, Jameson had said. She would talk to Kwek. She would find a reason to abort the mission. She did not want to go back to Battleground again and she did not want to deal with Kwoort.

There is such strangeness in an alien's mind that one first has a compulsion to withdraw, as if there is a danger of being sucked into insanity. It is only a different reality, a different sanity . . .

She had written that herself, years ago. Then, she had not been concerned with the fine distinction of determining if the alien really *was* insane. But she was quite certain the question applied to the former Holy Man, and that it would soon apply to Kwoort.

She stood with Arch outside the small conference room she had used for her earlier reports to Jameson, where Arch had been explaining human history to a confused Kwek. He said, "This is as comfortable as any place on the ship. I think she likes flowers, but where would I get flowers? And I don't—"

"Flowers?"

"She had flowers in her workspace. I noticed because everybody says Soldiers don't decorate anything, and here she had these flowers."

"Wait a minute. Let me think. Kwoort—the first time I made contact with him he was remembering a painting on a wall. He painted it himself, I think, a memory he had from New Earth. It's the only trace of art anyone's seen. Now Kwek, and flowers—Arch, what is the significance of *that*?"

He didn't have an answer. He said, "We can ask Kwek,

but I don't know if she'll know what we mean. She seems sort of—stunned, I guess, like she's going through some kind of catastrophe. She's not really thinking. She's putting all her energy into holding something back, from herself, I think."

"When did that start?"

"The minute I said something that challenged their, you'd call it a creation myth, I suppose."

"They have a creation myth? They have—at least they had—the science to get to New Earth and back, and they believe in *myths*?"

"She doesn't, really. I think she's been trying to hang onto what she's supposed to believe for a long time, and having a hard time doing it. Here we come along, and she's already on the edge, and suddenly I make it impossible for her to keep trying. All her doubts, all her suspicions that what she's been told all her life isn't true, and bam—suddenly she knows. That's the catastrophe. If Kwek was a human being I'd say her mind's in bad shape right now."

"Mind as in logical thought? Or mind as in emotions?"

"They're at war. That's the problem."

It was a simple statement but took much longer to comprehend than it should have. The time lag told her how tired she was. But Arch waited, expectant. She said, "Go back to her, Arch. I'll come in a minute."

He went back into the room and she leaned against the corridor wall. She was cold. Hard rain had started while they were inside the gray building with Kwoort and the raving Holy Man, and they had gotten soaked on their fast passage to the pod—fast, because Hanna thought Kwoort might come after them. Her clothes and hair were still damp in spots, and now exhaustion welled up from her bones. She could not have gotten more than a couple of hours sleep between those mad visits to Kwoort; she could not remember when she had last really slept. It might be time to use a stimulant, regardless of how she felt about it.

Trance was an alternative, though it could not be prolonged indefinitely. The fatigue would not go away, but at least she would not feel it. *I will need it with Kwek anyway*, she thought, and let herself slide down the wall and settle cross-legged on the floor.

She had barely closed her eyes when she heard Gabriel say, "Hanna?"

She opened her eyes and looked up.

He said, "What are you doing?" and she felt something different in him, a new kind of concern. He had purposefully sought her out, and she wondered: *What did Starr say to him?*

"I'm going into trance," she said.

"Do you mind if I watch?"

"Believe me, there's nothing to see!"

"Well, then, I'll watch nothing. Why are you doing it?"

"Arch is in there with Kwek." She tilted her head toward the door. "He's going to ask her questions. I'm going to watch her thoughts and help him decide what to ask."

"Do you mind if I join you?"

"I don't know . . ." She hesitated. "If you promise not to say anything. It will be delicate, Gabriel. Arch will talk to Kwek and I'll communicate with him about what she's thinking, and maybe guide her a little, telepathically. He'll be communicating on two levels at once, out loud with Kwek and telepathically with me. It's a difficult thing to do. I don't want his concentration broken."

"I won't disturb either one of you."

"Oh, me . . . Very little can disturb me in trance."

"Some things can, obviously!"

"Yes, I'll need to be careful. Still—this is not a child's mind, so nothing's likely to trigger that fear for Mickey. You knew about that, didn't you? I felt no surprise in you when I spoke of it."

He sat down on the floor next to her. "It was in one of the reports you directed me to when I first came aboard. The other incident, the mating couple, wasn't. How did you come to hold it back? Were you ashamed of it?"

"Of course not. I just didn't want to tell Starr about it when it happened. At the time we couldn't talk without half of Contact and a dozen Commission aides hearing every word. He would have said exactly what you heard when I did tell him, and then I would have said exactly what I did say. I didn't want that to happen with true-human strangers listening."

"Thank you—if you mean, by that, that I'm not a stranger."

"No," Hanna said. "You're not. Now that I think of it, you never have been."

"That's one of the nicest things anybody's ever said about me," he said.

Impulsively, she put her hand on his. "Let me take you with me part of the way," she said. "So you can see what trance is like. I'll move away after the first stage, and you'll feel like you're waking up—oh, no. No," she said, suddenly remembering the last time she had taken someone with her. She sensed an instant's physical pain; it was Gabriel's, as her nails dug into his hand. She pulled hers away.

"I can't do it," she said. "I'm sorry."

They both looked at his hand. She hadn't drawn blood, but the crescent indentations were deep. He rubbed at them absentmindedly and said, "Tell me."

"No, I'm all right. I'm sorry."

"I know you were in trance with Michael Kristofik when he died," he said. "It's in the literature about the events on Gadrah. Is that what you were thinking of?"

"Not now, Gabriel—"

"There are some things in life that you can avoid forever," he said, "if you want to badly enough. You can decide to withhold parts of yourself, if that's really best for you. Sometimes it's a way to conserve strength you need for other things, or a way to survive in a situation that's otherwise intolerable. And sometimes it's not the best thing for you at all. But it's far better to know when you're doing it, and why."

"And I'm avoiding . . . ?"

"You're the only one who can know. Giving something of yourself to another, perhaps? Loving the man you have now?"

And tentatively he thought *The men you have now*, but if Hanna sensed the amendment, she ignored it.

"What I loved in Starr is going away," she said. "It's getting buried. Everything, *everything,* is going to be filtered through the demands of being a commissioner of the Polity. I met him when he was commissioner before. I couldn't love him until it was taken away from him. Now he's got it back again and I look at all our history and—I knew the truth but I needed so badly what he gave me, protection, stability, affection, but—"

Her voice rose and rang through the corridor. "He *controls* me—!"

She heard herself with amazement. Where had this fury come from? But she could not stop the words either. "He doesn't try to control what I think or what I feel, but just because of the position he's in, he shapes how I live my life, he's shaped it for years! I tell him there's nothing for humans here, we should leave, we'll take no good away and maybe we'll take harm—but even if he believes me, he says I've got to go on, I've got no choice . . . It's been that way since the start. I don't know what to do, and I don't know what I'm going to do when I get back! I want *out*. I don't know who I'd be without him, I need to find out—and it's never going to happen, not the way things are now—"

She ran out of words; the tiredness was too heavy a weight. She ought to be in a storm of tears, but there wasn't enough energy for tears. She was a lonely spot of consciousness, huddled on a floor in this bit of manmade metal, and infinity—emptiness—outside.

Gabriel was silent for a moment. Then he said, "I know you have to stay on Earth, but you don't have to live with him, do you?"

"No, but I'll have to keep working for him. Until the Polity lets me go, or," she said bitterly, "until he dies."

And she could feel Gabriel's puzzlement at that, but the truth about Jameson and anti-senescence was something she had forced from him long ago and against his will, and ambivalence about the way she had done it made her all the more unwilling to betray his secret.

Slowly the anger died away. She was too tired to keep it up. And Kwek was waiting.

She put her hand on Gabriel's again and said, "Relax your muscles. Clear your mind. Come with me a little way. I'll help you."

———

Kwek's perception: Odd to see this familiar room through her alien eyes. The walls a clear light blue, unnoticed by the humans so accustomed to it, not really seen for a long time. Kwek's memory: In the last crèche where she served, she had thought of painting some walls yellow, to bring in the illusion of sunlight, but there had never been time and there had never been energy, she only mated and nursed and ate, nursed and ate. Kwek's sense of the not-Soldiers: Hideous-

looking, voices harsh when they turned off the translators, the poverty of their language's range of sounds, suited perhaps to their tiny, stationary ears. And that thing, that organ, in the middle of their faces, she suspected it was for respiration, it was disturbing . . .

"I've told you what we believe about the origins of everything, in simple terms," Arch said. "I'm not saying Abundant God didn't set it all in motion, but that it was a long and vastly complicated process. Well, complicated to us. Maybe not to Abundant God."

In Kwek, assent. Encourage it.

"I have often thought—"

Afraid to say it out loud.

"Nothing you say here will be repeated to anyone on your world."

A whisper. "I think that you are right."

Fear, but—the relief! At being able to say it! She is—

"—trembling, you are trembling. Is it forbidden to say such a thing in Rowtt?"

"Rowtt or anywhere! It is never said . . ."

—I see an exception—

"Surely there is someplace where it can be said? The isles you call That Place, perhaps?"

That Place? What is that, Arch?

Wasn't a chance to tell you about—

"That Place is where you said you might want to go. What's the difference between That Place and Rowtt?"

"They say you can ask questions in That Place. That you can think of new explanations for what is."

—vague, I can't see—

"What exactly is it like to live at That Place, Kwek? Can you describe how being there is different?"

"No—I don't—"

No clear image, nothing ever seen. But she thinks there may be people there like her.

"Have you ever known anyone who went to That Place?"

"No. At least, I have known some who said they would go there, and I did not see them again. So I thought that was where they had gone."

A real landmass?

Masses, islands. We've mapped it.

Tell her that—

"Let's see."

Arch at the wall, talking to data storage. Images coming quickly and arranging themselves: geography, topology, climate, remote ecosurvey—

Hanna said: *I didn't know That Place was there.*

I did, but this is standard survey data, no detail. We only paid attention to big complexes, like Rowtt.

—and population centers.

Tiny. Figures?

Not even an estimate. But—

"People live aboveground in That Place, Kwek. We saw that from space. Did you know?"

—afraid—

"Why does that frighten you?"

—thought paralyzed, only fear—

"Is it dangerous to be aboveground?"

—no surviving—

Kwek stood suddenly. Arch had given her water and her hand jerked and knocked over the glass, splashing the tabletop.

"I am afraid to go to That Place. But I cannot return," she said.

"You can't go back to Rowtt?"

"I will cease to survive soon, there."

—the meaning is not physical—

"Your spirit will cease to survive?"

But the translator had no word for *spirit*.

Kwek could not say any more. Not would not; *could* not. She sat down again but only looked from one to another of the human beings, looking at them with all her eyes, trembling with emotion again but not able to say a word. Hanna had not anticipated this dilemma. What do you do with an alien being who does not know where it wants to go?

No longer in trance but acutely aware of Kwek's distress, she conferred with Arch in the corridor again.

"We can't keep her here long," she said. "We'll have to come up with some explanation to give Kwoort pretty soon as it is. He only let her come because his Holy Man wanted to smooth things over."

"She wasn't locked up with me. Do you think he gave her

some instructions while we were separated? About something to do here? Or learn?"

"Absolutely not," Hanna said with certainty. "If she had intentions she was trying to conceal, I would have seen it."

"Do you think Kwoort knows how close to the edge she is?"

"I have no way of knowing—unless I ask him. Unless I ask him, dammit."

"Find out if anything bad's going to happen to her if we take her back."

"Find out from Kwoort, you mean—"

There seemed to be a conspiracy to get her to talk to Kwoort some more.

"I don't like Kwoort," she said.

Arch frowned at her. "Didn't you always tell us to be careful about objectivity? Not to let human prejudices get in the way of observation?"

"Do you like these people?"

"I like Kwek, I think, sort of."

"And I don't like Kwoort. There were some individual Zeigans I liked and some I didn't, insofar as they're individuals. I don't especially like most F'thalians I've met but a few I do. I can't think of any Uskosians I dislike, but some I like more than others. And," she repeated, "I don't like Kwoort."

"You want to demand a more compatible contact, or what?"

"If I did I might get one, but the new one wouldn't be as valuable. It might even be Prookt. I'm going to have to talk to Kwoort again," she said crossly. "Did anybody find out what might have set him off? He's got to have found out about something besides telepathy, but what? How we breed, how we reproduce, or don't? He was questioning me about that. But why would that infuriate him so?"

"Bella's got the rest of the team working on it. They'd rather be on the surface, though, and so would I."

"Nobody's going to the surface until Metra's satisfied they're not at risk. And I don't want any more humans where Kwoort can get at them anyway. In case he wants to know who the telepaths are, and one of the true-humans lets something slip."

"So what makes you exempt?"

"I think you would call the reasons corrupt," she said, thinking of Heartworld's council and all the eyes on Jameson, thinking of her desire for freedom and what she would do to get it. "It won't surprise you that I think Starr will approve of them."

"It's a disappointment to stay on board, after all the training, all the work while we were getting here—"

"I didn't say it would be permanent . . . We'll see."

Bella, she thought, and quested for Bella without turning to ship's communications. It felt natural, and she wondered fleetingly if returning to a life on Earth would mean wrenching disorientation as she limited herself once more to speech—

I hate it when I'm there, said Bella—

Finding anything—?

Don't think so. But come and see . . . Cheerful. They'd been making a game of it.

That. Critically important. But so was the question of what to do with Kwek right now, for the next hours.

Hanna slipped back into the conference room. They had not turned off the translators yet, and Gabriel was talking comfortably to Kwek; she seemed less afraid.

—you have been talking about—?

This time he hardly blinked. "Nothing very interesting. My school."

"I suspect it is pretty interesting. Tell me about it someday, too . . . Kwek, are you weary? Would you like to rest?"

"Yes. Can I?"

"My sleeping platform is yours." An Uskosian concept of hospitality, extended by a human being to a Soldier.

"My cabin," she said to Gabriel. "Stay with her, if you will." *Don't let her roam, the captain wouldn't like it,* she meant, and told him that too.

"What are you going to do?"

"Talk to my team. But first," she said, resigned to the inevitable, "I'm going to get a stimulant. I've got to. I don't know when I'll get a chance to sleep again."

Chapter XIII

IT *THRUMMED*, taking effect, only for a moment. Only half a dose, but her mind speeded up, her senses cleared, her muscles were free—or felt free—of the toxins of fatigue. But she knew at once that trance would not be an option; it felt as if a film had slammed into place between conscious thought and that place of the unconscious that was the wellspring for trance. She had a moment of alarm. But what did she need trance for, right now?

She felt good, otherwise. Better than just good. She had been so tired, for so long, that she had forgotten what well-being was like. It felt wonderful.

The team had commandeered the auditorium again, and Hanna saw why as soon as she walked in. The walls were covered with images of written reports spiced with pictures, and the images shifted position, rotated, changed size, occasionally pulsated; a few drifted around the room, including one, upside down, that appeared to be Kwoort. There was an enveloping sensation, as she came in, of delight—the pulsating, especially of pictures, had been set going just for the pure visual hell of it—and she thought of one of the criticisms sometimes leveled at D'neerans as a people: *They are childlike.* Well, nobody had said that about *her* recently.

And she felt, as the telepaths turned to look at her, exactly as if she had incurred the disapproval of moralistic children; they had sensed the subtle effect of the drug immediately.

I only took half of it! she said defensively.

Simultaneously, they gave the emotional equivalent of a shrug. If D'neerans were inclined to have strong opinions about what other D'neerans did to themselves, they were also, generally, of the opinion that nobody escaped being an idiot some of the time; in Hanna's case, these D'neerans thought, that might be much of the time.

Dema said, "You might as well start with me." She had a printout in her hands. She knew that Hanna was fond of printed media, believing, on an illogical but fundamental level, that it conveyed more stable information than quantum images did. "We were in Rowtt longest, but we'd barely gotten to the—whatever it is—we called it a school, but . . ." She shrugged. "Anyway, all we'd done when the evacuation order came was talk to one of the officers in charge, and nothing that was said seemed to upset him. Then we went into another room to talk about what to do first. Nobody around us was agitated or disturbed—well, when are they ever?"

"Try spending some time with Kwoort . . ." Hanna looked around at the mad scene. She could feel her team's weariness; except for Carl and Glory, they were perpetually short of sleep. But it was oddly distant, as if strained through a filter. She felt another quiver of uneasiness about the stimulant she had inhaled.

"Tell me about the crèches you went to," she said. "That was the longest and most intensive contact any of us have had with them. Kwoort said to me, *How do you choose not to breed?* Did you say anything that might have made him ask that?"

"Well . . . I suppose so. Yes." Dema put the papers down. "It was clear these were just people doing their jobs. Part of the job is coupling to produce more Soldiers, but it's regulated by a biological cycle. It must be inconvenient sometimes, and at the first crèche we were at, I asked how they get around that. I said we don't have to reproduce unless we want to. I said there are ways to enjoy mating without conception taking place, and it was the oddest thing, Hanna. The female I was talking to became frightened. This was after the prohibition against telepathy went into effect, so I was limited in what I could pick up, but . . . She wouldn't think about it. *Wouldn't.* There was that sense of fear, and then she fastened her attention on one of those video screens we saw everywhere, and after that she wouldn't even look at me. I had to go on to somebody else. And I didn't mention it again."

"All right. That might be something important. Make sure it's in your notes, put in every detail you can remember. Who else was where and doing what," she said, focused on goals, "in the hours before Kwoort gave that order about Arch?"

Dema produced more paper, with a flourish. "Here's the list of who was on the surface."

Hanna looked at the first name and said, "Oh, is he aboard?"

"You know Pirin Zey?"

"Not personally. I looked him up once."

"Why would you do that?"

"Because Starr fell asleep trying to read something Zey wrote about projected grain yields up into the thirty-first century in the province where Starrbright is. And nothing *ever* puts Starr to sleep. He thinks everything's interesting. Except Pirin Zey."

For Pirin Zey was an agronomist's agronomist. He studied crops: their growth, husbandry, distribution, and economics. It was the foundation of any civilization, and like other kinds of foundations—the fundament of a building, for example, or an alphabet—it did not inspire sonnets.

"Zey's an expert, though," Hanna said, and Dema said, "Well, he would be, wouldn't he, if Contact wanted him. And he spent two days there."

Hanna was in no danger of falling asleep now, and tried to read one of Zey's gray reports. Then she decided to go find him instead. His brain had to be more stimulating than his prose style. A sponge would be more interesting, if it was marginally alive.

"I'm going to read your mind," Hanna told him, overrode his protests, assured him she had no interest in his personal life. "Think about what you saw on the surface. That's all I care about and that's all I'll see." She was lying, partly; she would inevitably learn some things about Zey's personality and emotions, but it was true that she didn't care about them.

Zey said timidly, "Is this going to be that trance thing I heard about?"

"No," said Hanna, "this is going to be raw telepathy," and smiled at him. It was a predatory smile.

They showed you—

What they had showed him was not on the surface, but underground.

Underground: she had touched Soldiers working the hydroponics complexes, but then she had been part of them, accepting that this was the safest way to carry out agriculture. The surface was risky; underground was certain—

—acre on acre, light diverted from the surface or entirely artificial. It might as well have been in space—

More of it.

And more of it.

And more of it.

"What?" said Zey.

"Nothing," said Hanna. Zey was using stimulants too, and had not yet taken the counteractive dose that would allow him to rest, so Hanna's thought had meshed synergistically with his, racing. But she had actually mumbled: *Now I know why Starr fell asleep.*

She hadn't thought Zey's specialty could possibly have triggered Kwoort's anger, but seeing him had saved time, anyway. She decided to see other people instead of bothering with their reports, starting with the political scientists. But they were asleep. Just as well, Hanna thought. She would try the physiologists.

Later she wondered what would have happened if she had been content with what Cinnamon Padrick, Pix Mundy, and Matthew Sweet had written about Soldiers' physiology, the facts they had put in their reports, the conservative deductions they had made about body parts and functions and put on record; if she had not found Cinnamon and her team awake and said on impulse, *What did you think? What did you feel? What did you imagine, however strange it seemed? What did you fear?*—and listened hard.

Hanna expected Padrick to be asleep, and sounded the request for entry at a volume so low she didn't think Padrick would hear anything even if she were awake. But the door said *Come in!* and opened, and Hanna moved into a darkened room that was larger than hers and spoke of comfort. The large bed and couch and a big chair were soft and piled with cushions; three walls had been turned into virtual windows giving on a nighttime forest, alive with whispering

leaves and soft nightbird sounds and the smell of herbs and
leaf mold and the rustles of small, unseen animals. There
was even a breeze, carrying a fragrance of the wild. The
room itself might have been a luxurious tent pitched in wil-
derness. A moon was rising behind the trees. Hanna had
seen nothing so elaborate anywhere else on *Endeavor;* Cinnamon Padrick had clearly used her time during the early,
uneventful stages of the voyage to ensure that she was pam-
pered. It was so dark, and so startling, that it was a moment
before Hanna saw Cinnamon, and when she did, she knew
at once that she had found the origin of the not-quite-alien
trace of thought sensed weeks ago.

Cinnamon turned large green eyes on Hanna and said in
a soft and unsurprised voice, "Oh, you're one of the telepaths. The famous one."

Hanna nodded, looking at her, trying to understand the
source of the strangeness; she saw an ordinary woman. Soft,
sleek brown hair was cut close to the rounded skull, subtly
striped; a cosmetic effect, Hanna supposed. Cinnamon was
seated at a small table, on a small (but softly padded) chair,
and she was eating, dipping morsels into a sauce and chew-
ing them daintily. Two more places were set at the table, and
there were bowls of other tidbits that Hanna identified as
meat, something she did not consume herself. No D'neeran
did. D'neerans would not eat anything that had a central
nervous system.

A second glance told her the cubes of meat appeared
fresh, or at least, just-reconstituted. And they were raw.

"Would you like something to eat?" Cinnamon said.

"Umm, no, thank you."

"Sit, then."

Hanna did, wondering why she was uneasy. Few human
beings of any sort could really disturb her any more, and
there was no threat here. Just that strangeness . . .

"I've been hoping to meet you, Lady Hanna," Cinnamon
said.

"It's just Bassanio now—"

"Oh, I don't think so. You'll always be Hanna ril-Koroth,
I think."

There was too much truth to this for Hanna to argue the
issue. She said, "Do you have a few minutes to spare? I
wanted to ask you about the work you and your team did

on Battleground. I apologize for not studying your reports first, but I—might be pressed for time. I know it's late, I'll try not to keep you long, you must need to sleep—"

"Always," Cinnamon said. "I love to sleep. It's my favorite recreation. But not so much at night." She touched a finger to the wall next to her and said, "Sweetie? Pix? Our snacks are ready. And we have a visitor."

A minute later the door said *Come in!* again. Two people came in, and the strangeness tripled.

At first glance Hanna took them for brother and sister, though Matthew Sweet was tall and muscular and Pix Mundy was short and round. It was the coloring that made her think so, the pale pinkish skin, where Cinnamon's was rosy, though they had the same big green eyes, and Pix's, meeting Hanna's, seemed to go perfectly round. Both had hair patterned symmetrically, almost identically, in black and white. "You all come from the same place?" Hanna said, looking at Cinnamon's stripes, thinking of local fashions, thinking (to herself) there was no end to people's love of decorating themselves.

"Colony One," Cinnamon said agreeably. "We have known each other since birth. Our home is in a small area on the continent Atlas; specifically, a mountainous, rather isolated region occupied by those of our ethnicity. Do you know the geography of Colony One?"

"A little. I've been there, to Atlas, in fact." *But I never saw anybody like you there.*

The others had crowded up to the little table and started to eat, Pix Mundy with a greed that explained how she had come to be round. Matthew Sweet looked at Hanna with uncomfortable intentness. She wondered fleetingly how many of *Endeavor*'s crewwomen he had seduced.

"Are you Pix's brother?" she asked.

He and Pix looked at each other with secretive amusement. "Among other things," he said.

"Yours is a, umm, pretty, umm, self-contained population?"

"Do you speak to aliens sso craftily?" said Pix. There was an undercurrent of sibilance. Hanna thought Pix's ears, inside, might be lined with the faintest layer of white down, but it was hard to tell in the dim light.

Hanna backed down. The subcultural mores of human

beings were not her field. She said, "You know *Endeavor* went on alert for a brief time because of a possible threat from the beings here, the reason you were evacuated—"

Over their protests, she remembered. It was this team that had refused to leave until Metra threatened them with force.

"Umm ... well. It came to nothing, but one of their commanders was disturbed by something, and I can't tell what it was. I'm trying to find out what our people were doing that might have made him react so unexpectedly. I know whatever it was, was innocently done. None of us on the surface have expressed hostility or displayed xenophobia or done anything that would obviously cause offense. All any of us have been doing is learning things. I came to ask what you've learned that perhaps a Commander would rather we didn't know."

"Xenophobia would not be good," said Pix. "I don't think we would like xenophobia very much."

The three Colonists looked at each other with understanding. Hanna thought about trying to see their thoughts; these humans touched her curiosity more than the Battleground beings did.

She suppressed the impulse and said, "What results have you had from your work, in this first phase?"

"They are not very interesting, anatomically," said the one called Sweetie. "F'thalians and Uskosians are much more interesting. Genetically—but then, we are very interested in genetics. It is our specialty. Are you interested in genetics?"

"Not particularly," said Hanna, whose short foray into the subject had been prompted by motherhood. She had learned, for example, that Mickey had not inherited his father's gift for music, though language—multiple languages, if he were exposed to them—would probably come easily to him.

"Surprising—since your people resulted from experiments gone wrong."

"I would hardly say they 'went wrong,'" Hanna said. "What have you learned about their genetics?"

"Oh, very little so far," Cinnamon said. "There hasn't been time so far. There's just the boring anatomy. And they don't know anything about their own genetics. We're starting from scratch."

"What do you mean, they don't know much?"

"I said, not *anything*. They haven't even done the most basic, any-child-can-do-it Mendelian experiments."

Hanna shook her head. "Of course they have. You know about the underground agriculture? Those crops have to be hybrids from nature."

"I doubt they're doing any hybridization now," Cinnamon said. "Not if their research is on a level with public health science. Because they don't have any of that. They don't know the first thing about viruses—and they've got plenty. Someday," she said, smiling at Hanna with her rosy mouth, "you're going to walk into an alien environment and find yourself the perfect host for some organism Earth never dreamed up."

"I did," Hanna said, "but the one that almost killed me was a mutation from a Terrestrial virus. It was Plague. What did you join this mission for, if you weren't willing to take some chances?"

"Curiosity, what else?" said Sweetie, as if she should have guessed.

"And the opportunity, when it's over and we've got time and our pay, to see the real Moon," Cinnamon said.

All three of them looked at the pseudo-windows, where the moon was nearly all the way up. Hanna looked at it closely.

"That's not Colony One's moon," she said. "That's Earth's."

"Yesss," said Pix. "The real Moon."

Hanna pulled herself back to the subject. "Does that seem odd to you?" she said. "I mean, does such ignorance seem compatible with the complex society they have?"

"It's not complex," said Sweetie.

"What do you mean?"

"Where do you see complexity? They are born, they mate, they fight, they die."

"They have a religion."

"They reproduce," Sweet said indifferently. "Any amoeba can reproduce. I will bet you—say, a freighter of sweet fish—"

"What?" Hanna said.

"—against, oh, whatever you would like—what would you like?"

"Freedom," Hanna said.

"You, too?" He looked at the forest again. "Is that characteristic of the products of the old experiments, I wonder? Only a hypothesis."

"The old—?" He had lost Hanna. "What are we betting on?" she said. "I don't think I could lay my hands on a freighter of fish. But if I could bet, what would I be betting on?"

"That the religion is not complex. Of course I don't know anything about it, but what I've heard suggests that it is as boring as their anatomy."

Hanna considered this. "I've assumed it has a complexity we haven't yet penetrated," she said.

"Human thinking," Sweetie said.

"Damn," Hanna said. She, of all people, should not have to be reminded of that pitfall.

"That would not be in your reports," she said. "What else have you left out? What did you imagine? What did you fear?"

"We fear the viruses," said Cinnamon indistinctly; she was licking her fingers vigorously. The dishes in front of her were empty.

"We did atmospheric sampling before I went to the surface the first time. The organic molecules we found were incompatible with anything in the human body. You *are* human, aren't you?" she added, suddenly not too certain of it.

"Our DNA is indisputably human," Sweetie said, "just as yours is. Cinnamon speaks for herself. I think it's not so much fear as horror of the emptiness the epidemics have left. Because there must have been epidemics, there must have been plagues. They are crowded together, they would not even know what caused them, and they are used to death. I think it likely the crèches we talk about are built on the bones of earlier ones, layers on layers of bones. But they deny it. They do not intend deceit, I think; they only do not remember. And there are no records. The disease we called Plague was finally contained and vaccines developed because centuries of research came before. That does not happen here. Civilization crashes and burns, they start all over, repopulate, breed and breed, *that* they remember, that they must breed—and they must breed, make no mistake. The common cycle of estrus is confined in Earthly mammals to females. Not here. We cannot see how they ever developed a civilization at all. Unless they had help. And we think that they did."

It seemed preposterous. Hanna frowned.

Cinnamon said, "Sweetie is correct. Do you wish to see the tissue samples we brought back? There is evidence of genetic tampering at a high level of sophistication, many generations ago. I do not know if you would call it help."

"Tampering by whom?"

"Who knows? I would look for traces, if I were you. I would bring archaeologists, now or later." Cinnamon smiled. "You have added a preacher to your team, why not an archaeologist?"

"Gabriel's not exactly—"

Sweetie broke in: "I would ask myself, I would ask the—preacher—I would ask an archaeologist too: What kind of intelligence finds it necessary to create thinking creatures like those of this world? Why were they created? We know why the experiments were done to create telepaths. You were meant to be spies. We are not so sure about those that made our ancestors. But here," said Sweetie, with a smile that showed sharp teeth, "we are."

Hanna might have asked another question, but Cinnamon said placidly, "I am ready to nap now." The great green eyes were half closed.

"I, too," Sweetie said. He pushed away his own empty dishes, and stood and stretched. It was a full-body stretch, languorous and fluid. He was admirably muscled. "Pix?" he said.

"There iss some food left," she said, eyeing other bowls, scarcely touched. "I will sssave it for later."

"But not much later, knowing you," Sweetie said.

Hanna, going out, had the distinct feeling that Sweet and Pix weren't going anywhere; that all three of them would curl up on the piled cushions of Cinnamon's room, call for a deeper night, and relax at once, as if their bones were liquid, after one last look at the real Moon.

———

Time to study the political scientists' impressions: Hanna went back to the auditorium and found it almost deserted, all the tired telepaths except Dema gone to bed. The report she wanted floated near the ceiling, flapping. She got the image down to eye level and steadied, with some difficulty. Jewel Guzulaitis, Nyree Olabowale, and Glenna Leatherman had written:

Political science is, at its simplest, the art of government. Our sources of information prior to direct communication with the population of Battleground were:

First, visual data extracted from the planet's datastream—

Oh, thought Hanna. They use *that* kind of language—

Second, the spoken word. Reliable transmissions for periods slightly older than the visual actually were available first, but—

Her eyes began to glaze, stimulant or no stimulant.

Finally, reports from the telepathic team led by Hanna ril-Koroth (i.e., Lady Hanna's own reports). This team was not intended to be used until physical contact was made with subject population, but Lady Hanna was utilized as an adjunct when the data described above yielded fewer results than anticipated.

The report was no more readable than Pirin Zey's, but her own name got her attention. She made a face and said, "Adjunct. Huh."

She read on. Guzulaitis, Olabowale, and Leatherman barely referred to her own reports, commenting on their subjectivity when they did. The three had accurately assigned a governing role to the Holy Man. Not surprisingly, the only governing mechanism detected had been military in structure. The commanders, it appeared, ran Rowtt.

And commanders ran Wektt, too.

I forgot about that, Hanna thought.

She went through the rest of the report quickly. There were, of course, two sides at war; but in her own mind, all the individuals she had touched had been Soldiers of Rowtt, because that was the first name Linguistics had identified with a location. Once contact was made, she and all the others had been immersed in Rowtt, buried in it. Wektt was only "the enemy," championed by "the Demon." But the people who were "the enemy" had not been clearly distinguishable by anything they had broadcast; nor could Hanna, thinking back, discern any difference between the people of Rowtt and the people of Wektt, or any other place, by what she had sensed in their thoughts or seen in their surroundings.

So what the hell was Wektt? And "That Place" had never surfaced at all before Arch talked to Kwek. Who ran That Place?

H'ana?

She turned; was this the first time Dema had called for her attention?

Distracted, sorry . . .

I think the stimulant, H'ana, it's not good for us—

I needed it.

She looked around again. Even Carl and Glory were gone now. She might as well hunt up the counteragent and get some real rest.

———

She felt it working even before she left the night-duty medic, and scarcely noticed when he pressed another vial into her hand, "in case you need it later." Her mind began to drift before she reached her quarters, and she did not even notice that Kwek must have been put elsewhere, because the room was empty. She was moving slowly toward the bed, as if she waded through deep water, when an inner voice finally broke through.

reports are not what we do best, it said, and she recognized the voice of the ghost. *others can correlate,* said the ghost. *computers do it even better*

then what should we be doing

talking to Kwoort. reports suggest questions. he has answers. always they have the answers to their own reality, the only answers that matter

So she was done with reports; she fell onto her bed without even getting undressed. *Their reality,* she thought, sinking, going under. *Theirs.*

That meant Kwoort.

Chapter XIV

*C*OME IN! said Hanna's door, though she did not remember telling it to say that. She woke slowly to see Gabriel looking down at her. "Kwoort wants us," he said.

For a minute everything was blank. His pale, strained face looked familiar but nothing came to her at the sight of it, no recognition or welcoming; the words in her ears were meaningless, neutral. She thought and felt nothing except the impossibility of moving the solid weight of herself.

He sat down on the edge of the bed, and slowly she began to wake up.

"What's Kwoort . . . what time is it?" she said, the words slurred. It was hard to move her lips.

"Standard time, I don't know . . ." He moved a hand. "Evening at Rowtt. You've only been asleep a few hours."

"I need more," she said, remembering, knowing now that this heaviness was the accumulation of weariness the stimulant had masked.

"I told him we'd come, but . . ."

Hanna sat up: such a simple thing, and so difficult. The light garment she had been wearing for too long clung unpleasantly to her skin.

"When does he want us?" she said.

"I said we'd meet him at the same place in, umm, a Standard hour, I guess."

Enough time to bathe, at least.

"What does he want? Why—?" The next question seemed more pressing. "Why did he talk to you instead of me?"

"He told Communications he would talk to either of us. And you were asleep."

"And you weren't? Gabriel, did you take any stimulant?"

"No."

"You must be exhausted."

"And you aren't?"

"Ah, hell . . ." She put her head back against the wall. The room was almost completely dark, with only a bare glow along one wall at the floor. It reflected faintly on Gabriel's face. He was not looking at her now.

"He was calm," Gabriel said. "He said he's bringing the Holy Man he answers to—Tlorr, was what the name sounded like. Do you know who that is?"

"Maybe." She got her legs over the side of the bed, two separate weights of stone. Carefully smoothed the skirt over her knees, but recognized that sitting on someone's bed in the dark and talking quietly was a familiar mode for Gabriel, with no sexual connotations, and at the moment she might have been one of the children sheltered by his abbey.

I don't know this man, she thought, *and he's worth knowing. When there's time, when we're not being driven by Kwoort—*

Held the ampoule close to her face, flicked the tab, inhaled. Gabriel held the one she had handed him and watched her silently. *Thrum. . . .*

She opened her eyes, sighed with satisfaction. "Better," she said.

He turned toward the doorway that would take them to the pod. She said, "Gabriel? Aren't you going to use it?"

"No."

"You're so tired you won't be able to walk pretty soon!"

"I'll keep it," he said. "If there's an emergency I'll reconsider. I don't need it yet."

He was moving slowly and wearily. She followed him into the bay and into the pod and took her place in the pilot's seat. She went smoothly through the sequence that allowed them to leave *Endeavor*; they descended toward the planet's night side.

"Do you have some kind of religious proscription against artificial health aids?" she said, focused by the drug, unable to let it go.

"No. Not within reason. We don't use A.S., though," he

said, meaning anti-senescence techniques, and she said slowly, "I remember that. Somebody told me that once, about your abbey. I'd forgotten. Is it hard, knowing you'll die sooner than the rest of us?"

"Hard? Yes, sometimes. Sometimes brothers leave the order just because of that. But do you know the suicide statistics among people who think they've lived too long?"

"Well, no. Is it high?"

"It starts going up at around age one hundred. At a hundred and seventy-five it's ten percent."

"And that's high?"

"Hanna, my dear—" unconscious of those two words "—that is one in ten people. Among people under age one hundred it's less than one in five hundred thousand. And there's plenty of testimony that the ninety in a hundred in the top range only go on living because they believe their family or society or God expects it of them. They wait for death as for a welcome guest."

"Starr wouldn't, if it worked right for him," Hanna said sadly. "He always wants to see how things turn out. Make them turn out the way he wants, preferably."

He caught the implication, and knew it was something he was not supposed to know, but all he said was, "And you?"

She didn't answer. D'neerans did not talk to outsiders about the dark side of their unique society, where unremitting intimacy did not depend on physical proximity. In the earliest generations so many died by their own hands that it was called the Dying Time; only now, in Hanna's lifetime, were memorials going up, and remembrance ceremonies multiplied. It still occurred, though it was rare. The deaths were grieved, but they were accepted, because not everyone born a telepath could stand it for a lifetime. Hanna understood. She had fallen deep into her own well of despair after Michael's death, and all Starr Jameson's efforts might not have been enough if it had not been for Mickey. She hoped she would never have to look into that darkness again.

The pod slipped into the upper atmosphere and Gabriel reached for her hand. "Not so fast—"

"What? Why?"

"There's no reason to hurry. You're going too fast."

"Too fast for *what*?"

"I don't know. You're going too fast."

"I just feel like—"

"It's the stimulant. The drug. What do you think you're going to accomplish by hurrying?"

"All right!" She threw up her hands—the pod was guiding itself anyway—and gave the decelerate order. They angled into clouds.

Gabriel was still not satisfied; Hanna felt it. Responding to something sensed, she dimmed the interior lights, until only the glow of changing readouts filled the capsule. He would have liked those off too, she thought, but he said nothing, and she glanced at him to see his eyes closed, his lips moving. He was praying. She thought: *What a strange pair we are.* Her own attention, in this space of stillness and darkness, was drawn to the dark city they were coming to. The second time she had gone there it had been night, and she knew lights rarely showed aboveground. Yet ten million Soldiers lived beneath the surface, packed into the space a city of half a million humans might occupy. They took meals in common in innumerable refectories—her own perception, confirmed by others' observations—but there seemed to be time and space for solitude, if they wanted it, and no sense of resentment at the unvarying focus on work, war, and the care of offspring. She had touched the minds of Soldiers assembled for the repetitive speeches, detected no rebellion against the ascendancy of the High Commander and the Holy Man—nor any particular hatred of the Demon, whoever that was, either.

Is it, she wondered, the absence of imagination that repels me? Most thoughts seem as gray as the spaces where they live and work. How could such a species envision exploring space?

The pod made steadily for its programmed landing place, unbuffeted, so far, by high winds. Hanna supposed Kwoort would be waiting. She reached out and tried to touch him, but—*thrummm . . .* Strange.

A prickle of apprehension. She tried again.

Thrummm . . .

The apprehension edged toward fear. It was like opening your eyes on a sunny day and seeing blackness. There was no improvement on a third attempt.

She had never experienced anything like it. She could not think of any possible cause except the stimulant, this time the full dose for her body mass. It was supposed to be safe, and she had brushed off Dema's warnings. Logic assured her the effect would probably be temporary.

Only probably—

And if the effect was cumulative—

The fear grew a little more. But she tried again and this time found Kwoort. Slowly, much more slowly than she was accustomed to, her perception sharpened. Finally the gestalt and the context were clear. Kwoort was with another being, and she recognized that one too. The Holy Man. *The* Holy Man, not the deposed, crazy one.

I shall go out to meet them. That was Kwoort, a pulse of images. *This place will be free from attack for a time.*

Glimpse of another city, a seacoast.

Concentrations there, a little longer. Kwoort again. *Then they are to extend operations to the north. But this city is nearly recovered from the last cycle. Attacks will resume here soon.*

But first, the centers northward . . . ?

The wind started when they neared the surface, and she slipped away from Kwoort's thoughts and thrust the fear down. She finished the landing fast, swooping into calmer air; instruments said hard weather was coming again. That appeared to be a constant with few lulls, and she wanted to get to ground. The pod would barely notice lightning strikes, except to record them, but it was too small to ignore the resulting turbulence and the brute force of wind. Gabriel looked at her when he heard the subtle hiss of increased acceleration. "Weather," she said succinctly.

"Gives a new meaning to the term 'bad climate,' doesn't it?"

She said fretfully, "Does the sun never shine here?"— thinking of the glint of light on the splashing fountain at Dwar, of old trees around Jameson's home and sunlight bright on autumn leaves, or Mickey on an ocean beach, throwing handfuls of sand with abandon in the clear, precious light.

"Sometimes," Gabriel said.

"It's always been cloudy, at least, when I've been down here, or worse than cloudy."

They came to rest at what the instruments said was the

right place, but Hanna had to cue exterior lights before they could see the blocky building a short walk away. It was closed, the steps and terrace before it empty.

"No welcome mat," said Gabriel.

Hanna turned off the light. She didn't want the two of them silhouetted against it when they left the pod.

"We'll take lights with us," she said. "We'd be blind without them."

He said, "Are you all right?" He was looking at her in the glow of the instrument panels and she saw for an instant what he saw: her face taut, eyes too bright. Then the image was gone as if a shutter had closed, gone though she had not willed it to go.

"I don't know, Gabriel. I think the stimulant is a problem. But the counteragent isn't an option. We don't have any with us . . ." Her voice trailed off.

"What?"

"I don't know. I feel, oh, walled off. Maybe I should have gone into trance instead. I couldn't now, if I needed it. Maybe I made a mistake."

"It's not too late to go back," he said.

"Is that what you think we should do?"

They looked at each other in silence, in the dim light. Presently Gabriel said, "I think that this is the valley of the shadow of death. But I believe we're not alone."

For once, the reference did not have to be explained to Hanna. It had crossed so many cultures and so many centuries that even she recognized it. But she said, "I think there's only you and me. I think I'm glad we're away from the heart of the city, where Kwoort could get reinforcements in a hurry, and that he's only brought one other with him. And that the com units have been programmed so a single word will get Metra's people down here. That's what I believe . . . Do you think you could kill someone? An alien?"

"I don't know. The question," he said wryly, "does not arise in the usual course of my life."

"You are fortunate," Hanna said.

"Yes, I am. But does it make you think less of me?"

She found that she could not lie to him.

"It could be inconvenient. In the circumstances."

"Then you must find an awful lot of people inconvenient."

"No," said Hanna. "Most of them will never have to face the choice. But most of the true-humans I know would have no hesitation if the need arose, though any D'neeran would."

Except me.

"And maybe I would have less than I think," said Gabriel. "To save a child, for example—I don't think I would hesitate. And I don't think it would be a sin. But what it might do to me later—that I don't know."

After a pause Hanna said, "I have become a violent person, I think. I hate it in the abstract—but it comes easily to my mind when there has not even been an explicit threat—when I only think there might be one."

"Does that trouble you?"

"Not much," she said, an unpalatable truth but still truth, and she got out of her seat and they went out into the night, Hanna reflecting that they were not, in any case, armed, and wondering if that was a mistake too.

The night, at ground level, was hot and still. There was thunder not far away, a low, almost subliminal rumble that did not seem to stop and that set up a vibration in the bones. They walked toward the building, pointing narrow beams of light at the ground. Outside the beams the blackness was complete and closed around them like a wall. Hanna kept looking around anyway, as if she could see something, as if some threat might come out of the dark. And she knew that she ought to be able to tell for certain if there was a threat or if there was not, but the sense she relied on always, and most of all in times of danger, was dulled.

It shouldn't be, she thought. *The drug didn't affect telepathic perception like this, not even a few hours ago, whatever it might do to trance. But this time I had twice as much...*

"It's nothing," Gabriel said softly; for a moment she thought he had read her mind, but then she said, "What do you mean, what's nothing?"

"What's making you so restless. It's just electricity. Like the air is charged."

"It is charged, isn't it," she said, not a question.

"I shouldn't have agreed to this meeting so quickly. I think that was a mistake."

They were nearly at the structure, and there had been no sign of life. Hanna stopped, shifted the light to her left hand and reached out to Gabriel with her right. He took it and they stood for a minute holding hands like timid children, looking not at each other but at the silent building. Hanna said, "The mistakes are adding up, aren't they."

"I hope not," Gabriel said.

The door opened and Kwoort came out, light behind him only for a moment before the door shut it in. Hanna felt the dark between them thicken. She reached out to touch his thought, the easy perception, easy as seeing, all wrong, sluggish. But she knew that the figure, a vaguer darkness, was Kwoort.

Kwoort did not move. Finally Hanna took her hand from Gabriel's and walked toward him.

She said, "Greetings, Kwoort Commander," the courtesy empty in her mouth.

"Guest," he said from the darkness, bare acknowledgment.

"Why have you summoned us?" she asked.

"I require answers to questions," he said.

"As do I," said Hanna, but she tensed even further.

Hanna's previous experience of beings (some human) who had required answers of her was appalling. Trance protected the practitioner from physical pain, but Hanna had concluded some time past that the optimum solution to any such threat was the immediate death of whoever or whatever threatened her. *No more goddamned unarmed First Contacts,* she thought, and felt Gabriel stir uneasily behind her.

"You have lied to me," Kwoort said.

"I have not lied, Kwoort Commander. None of us have."

"You can speak to the mind," he said. "Speak to mine!"

So he did know. But why had he not said it openly, in that earlier, aborted meeting?

After a rather long pause she said, "You suspected that we have this ability, I know . . . and it was your expressed desire to use it in your wars that caused us to decide on concealing it. We are not the enemies of anyone on this world; we will not fight with you or against you. The ability I possess cannot be taught. It is inborn, and only in a small minority. I am the only human being of this expedition to have it—" Protecting the others, if protection was needed. "It cannot be useful to you. And so it was concealed."

"You should not have concealed it," he said.

"Maybe not." Mistakes, mistakes! "But put yourself in my place, if you will. I did not know you well; I do not know you now. If you thought I possessed an ability that might aid you in war, would I not fear that you might seize me, as you seized my comrade early in this day, and try to force me to use the ability to your benefit?"

"What is to stop me, if I think it good to do that?"

Gabriel had come up beside her. He touched her hand. She knew what he meant her to do, perceive his thought, so she tried, and it should have been easy and was not. She thought the words he formed might be: *Don't talk about power, don't talk about weapons. Don't raise the level of aggression.*

"I will speak to you alone," Kwoort said. "It will not stop you from speaking to your holy man's mind, will it? But if you have finally told me the truth, he cannot speak to yours . . . we will see. And my Holy Man would speak with him about Abundant God."

"Kwoort Commander, how many summers does this Holy Man have?"

"Tlorr has seven hundred and fifty summers. Why is that of interest?"

"Because you yourself have seven hundred and twelve. Why have you not yet become Holy?"

There was a silence, and then Kwoort said, "Only Abundant God knows the time when he will take one of us to himself."

She could not sense what he felt as he said that, though she tried. But she thought of the suicide statistics among humans who felt they had outlived life.

Kwoort whispered: "Speak, I said. Speak to my mind. Speak the truth to my mind."

"I cannot 'speak' it," Hanna said. "Not in words. I can do that with humans and other beings with whom I share a spoken language. You and I do not. What I might perceive in you, and can communicate to you, can only be an amalgam of images and emotions, though our minds independently transmute them to words."

"You lie!" he roared, so loudly that his cry drowned out the translator, and Hanna saw the source of the strength of his conviction: questions asked of the Warrior who had not been, and perhaps should have been, assassinated. Her answers must have been inaccurate or incomplete.

"I do not lie! Yes, I know more, when you speak, than you say! I know that you had an informant! But did she not tell you—"

She realized then that she had trapped herself in another lie. Dema had "spoken to the mind," and Kwoort knew it; he knew that at least one other human being on *Endeavor* was capable of it; now he might think all of them were. She would have to tell him all of the truth.

Only five, she said to him, *four besides myself,* and tried to show him images of their faces. The effort was enormous and she knew that she had not succeeded. But the number had gotten through.

She watched Kwoort absorb the knowledge. Watched only with her eyes, because her mind was filled with shadow as deeply as her eyes. He could never have had this experience before, the certain knowledge that another being told the truth, and her perception of his experiencing it should have been just as absolute, but it was not. It was clouded, this sense that she most trusted was uncertain, and it seemed that even if a light shone suddenly in the night, it would illuminate only treacherous wisps of fog.

Presently he said, "The Holy Man waits for your fellow-Soldier"—a word as close to the Standard "friend" as the translator could get.

"I will not allow him to go alone," Hanna said.

"The Holy Man will not harm him."

And she couldn't tell if that was true or not; she cursed the drug that clouded her perception.

"It's all right," Gabriel murmured against her ear. "I have to do this. This is what I'm here for. The others are monitoring us, aren't they?"

"They're supposed to be," she said softly. "I can't tell!"

"Do you trust them?" he whispered.

"My team? Of course."

Kwoort said loudly, "Order him."

"We are not Soldiers, Kwoort Commander. My friend has the right to refuse."

"But I don't refuse," Gabriel said, and walked forward.

He followed a thin beam of light to the building and Hanna stood silent while the door opened and closed, shutting him from her sight.

There was a short, brilliant glow in the clouds, a louder sound of thunder from the dark. Hanna could not seem to stir, as if the weight of weariness her body did not feel had been diverted to her will. Kwoort came down the shallow steps from the doorway.

That got her to move; she backed up. She tried to tell herself it was because of Gabriel's warning—*don't raise the level of aggression*—and knew that was not true. It was because she could not detect Kwoort's intent.

She said—it was not one of the questions she had meant to ask—"Are you unusual, Kwoort Commander, in your liking for the outdoors, even in the electric night?"

"I am unusual," he agreed. He walked not straight toward her, but as if he would pass her on his way to another destination. She turned her head, watching, and at the same time sought for Gabriel. She could not feel him.

She had not shifted the light she held, pointing almost at her feet, but Kwoort, though he walked slowly, moved without hesitation. She said, "I think your eyes are superior to mine in the dark."

"Extinguish the light," he suggested.

She shrugged and turned it off. Then she thrust it into a pocket in case she needed her hands free to protect herself. The night became unrelieved black. The mutter of thunder, louder, drowned any sound Kwoort might make, but her unreliable extra sense told her he was now at her left and almost behind her. She turned toward where he ought to be. She felt unbalanced in the dark, with no visual cues. Then he really was behind her, and she turned further, uncertainly, and felt him stop.

"This speaking to the mind," he said. "Do you use it with your enemies?"

"We have no enemies."

"You lie," he said. "Everything that lives has enemies. Can you say that to my mind and not lie?"

There have been enemies, she said, felt the drugged slowness, but she could show him the shadow of a battle in space in which she had taken part. *We seek, always, peace,* she said, or made him feel, and managed to show him, though dimly, the network of trade and reciprocity that characterized the Polity. Those five worlds, at least—Earth and Willow, Colony One and Co-op and Heartworld—had never fought each other.

Her eyes were adjusting and she found that there was a little ambient light. She could just make out Kwoort, as a shadowy figure; at least she knew for sure where he was. She could see nothing of his face, but it hardly mattered. She knew little about the meanings of Soldiers' expressions, she had not even asked Kit about them; telepathy was a surer guide. Or it had been, until tonight.

He said again, almost a whisper: "Speak to my mind. This way of seeing would be useful against enemies."

"It can be useful, Kwoort Commander, but I will not— we will not—use it against your enemies. They are not ours. Is that the only answer you require?"

"No, here is another. How can you be persuaded to use it for the Holy Man?"

"I cannot think of any persuasion that would be sufficient."

"Then I would hear of your breeding," he said. "How do you breed?"

And she knew that the shift was not as abrupt as it sounded, but she could not see the transition, as she might have, with luck, if his mind had been open to her.

She said, after only a little hesitation, "Any of us could have told you that. We are mammals, just as you are. Our young are born with immature brains and bodies; they suckle until they can feed themselves; they require unceasing care for several summers, and much care for some summers more. Maturity comes much more slowly than it comes to Soldiers."

"No! I mean, what is the mechanism of conception!"

"Did our specialists in the body not offer that information? Males and females join sexual organs, and conception results. The role of the 'facilitators' among your people is unclear. We have nothing of the kind, and I do not know who they are."

"They are not a 'who.' They are a 'what.'"

There was a wave of fury and bitterness, a flash of what he felt like a jolt of static, there and gone. Hanna blinked.

"We heard of their existence, but there has not been time to pursue the subject," she said. "Nothing and no one plays such a role in our mating. Among us, a female and male mutually agree that they will mate, and develop a bond that may last for years, or even for life. They nurture, together with close kin, their own young. There are countless variations, but that is the basic model. It has proved optimally successful in the course of human evolution."

Kin did not translate, nor did *evolution*. It did not seem important.

Kwoort had circled closer. "I do not believe in your 'mutual agreement.' Bloodless," he said. There was a sound from the translator that suggested ambiguity. Hanna tried to reach into Kwoort's mind, to find out more clearly what he meant. She failed. She put her hands to her face, moved unconsciously, needing more distance between them, stumbled and nearly fell. She had never, ever communicated with an alien without full command of telepathy, a potent tool to start with, formidable since her studies with Adept masters, and she could not rely on the translator either because it could not tell her when Kwoort lied. She was blinded by more than the night, and the thunder, coming closer, filled her ears.

She tried to widen her perception, seeking the D'neerans on *Endeavor*, felt nothing; sought Gabriel, sensed him dimly. He was intent on something, perceiving no danger. But would he know danger before it had him by the throat?

"I do not know what you mean by 'bloodless,'" she said.

"Is there no urgency? It seems logical! Planned!"

"Logic often plays a part; often it does not. There may be planning, or not."

"It seems you know nothing of the body's desire to mate! That is beyond understanding!"

"I see I have given you entirely the wrong impression," Hanna said, startled. "The part desire plays can hardly be exaggerated. Often it overrides both logic and planning; ultimately it is responsible for nearly all... breeding. Often, not always, there is love as well," she said, thinking of her beautiful son and how he had come to be, and heard that *not translatable* chime. Kwoort could not know what she meant by *love* . . . which in any case came in many varieties that did not include sexual desire.

"Desire," said Kwoort, ignoring the untranslatable word. "So you do know it. And what is your reward in its fulfillment?"

He had come closer still. The sky lit up and there was a boom of thunder, deafening; Hanna moved, stumbled, retreated, and had to turn again to face him, unnerved. Other conversations with other aliens had been just as strange, but she had been able to draw on their thoughts, glimpse their goals.

She said, "At its best, there are long years of happiness."

But the last word did not translate.

"Bloodless," he said again, and again, unpredictably, the shutter flashed open and shut, and she saw that he meant immediate sensual reward.

"You are speaking of the physical pleasure of coupling, are you not?" she said.

"You experience it, then?"

"At its best," Hanna said again. She had no intention of going into the exceptions now, but she was not going to say *always* either. Unqualified statements might come back to haunt her in accusations of evasion or lies.

More thunder; a sharp crack this time, close by, and the charged air simultaneously was alight, then black again. Hanna was circling now, too. She thought: *I have never hated a place as I hate this one.*

"Explain," said Kwoort. "Explain to my mind. Make me *feel* what you feel when you breed."

"No," Hanna said, an outright refusal. Because she could (if all her senses were working properly) summon memories of men she had known who had pleased her, let fantasy summon the first tremulous excitement and the building urgency, and convey it in some form to Kwoort. But it would be an act, though mental, as generous as willing intercourse. *And I don't like Kwoort.*

"Why do you ask these questions?" she said. "What is their importance to you?"

Another crack of thunder, and she jumped, nearly lost her balance again.

"Because if it is pleasure you seek, I offer it to you. In return for your service in speaking to the mind."

"What?" said Hanna.

"You will know the facilitators," said Kwoort, but more thunder drowned out his next words, and Hanna smelled ozone. In the flash of lightning she had seen that they were farther away from the building—from Gabriel—than she wanted to be, and she started back with a sense of horror that she did not think was all hers. Something was happening to Gabriel.

"Hear me!" Kwoort shouted after her, but thunder boomed over his voice again, and the translator crackled deafeningly in her ears.

There was nothing to steady her, no clear connection to a human mind, no sure ground underfoot, no certain light. There was crack after crack of thunder, gust after gust of wind, and the lightning that blinded her left her blind in the intervals of dark. Somehow she was at the door but it did not yield to her push this time, and she began to pound on it. She could hardly hear the blows herself as thunder over-rode them, and it did not seem possible that Gabriel could hear them. Kwoort was beside her then, bending and yelling into her ear—something in her crippled mind came to life for an instant, and she knew that he yelled as much because so small an ear must surely be hard of hearing, as because of the thunder.

"Think of it," he cried, "every nerve in the body—!"

And Hanna shouted back: "That is insane! Think! My organs are not yours, the brain's receptors are not the same! This is a waste of time!" *And* you *are insane,* she thought, not caring if it got projected or not.

The door gave way suddenly, and Gabriel stumbled out and nearly fell into her arms.

She held him hard and he clutched her, rocking on his feet; she looked over his shoulder and saw the being Tlorr in the center of the bare gray chamber through the door, perfectly still. She recognized a smile.

"Gabriel," she said into his ear, her voice low, counting on pitch to make him hear it under the noise of the sky. He shook his head and his eyes were horrified, but he could balance now; she stepped back a little, still holding him, scanning him as best she could, and saw no blood or other sign of injury. She let go of everything but his arm and pulled him away from the door, down the steps and toward the pod, which was a shape from a bad dream in the flashes of light. Kwoort stalked beside her, shouting, but he did not try to touch her and she did not try to speak to him. If he attacked her they would be all the way out of luck. There was an endless interval of stumbling across the short distance while wind battered them in ever-stronger gusts. Gabriel held onto her arm but did not need it now for support; he might have felt the need for sane human contact too, but Hanna did not know, she could not hear his thoughts or sense what he felt. Only nightmares had been as bad as this deprivation; she seemed to have been robbed of all her senses at once.

The pod responded to her voice in spite of the crash of thunder and the ramp came down much more slowly than she wanted it to. Time was skewed. Gabriel hung back and she thought, *He is trying to get between Kwoort and me, he wants to protect me* — and spared a curse for human males.

"Go," she said, "go!" and he went up the ramp quickly, turning to call to her to hurry, but she was right behind him and shoved. Kwoort was actually on the ramp, still shouting, repeating the obscene offer; she thought he was elaborating on sensual delight, and she sacrificed an instant to claw at the circuitry at her ears, trying to tear the translator away and failing.

Kwoort fell back finally, the hatch closed behind them, and Hanna started the takeoff sequence before she was fully in her seat. She remembered that she had not called out to Metra for help, forgetting the communicator, and the thought froze her. *Idiot!* she thought. Another mistake; Kwoort could have attacked. It could have happened in a second.

Then they were off the ground, and it took every skill she had and every force and sensor the pod possessed to hold out against the storm until they got above it.

———

She lied to the medics, told them she was hallucinating, got them to strip the chemical compounds of the stimulant from her blood. It took an hour, and it was too late, too late, she thought, because she lay waiting for the time to pass and there was nothing but the inner sound of her own brain's electrical field where the complex mix of the medics' thoughts should be. *This is not possible*, she thought, denying it, and refused to see anyone from her team because she could not bear to tell them. They must think she exercised the block she had used before, which they thought some little-known skill of the Adept; she would let them think it as long as possible. She did not tell Gabriel the truth, either, but she let him stay beside her and could not let go of his hand.

By the time it was done she could barely move for exhaustion. She slumped at a table in a conference room on *Endeavor*—she could hardly have said which one, the thought required to place it needed too much effort—with Gabriel's arm around her. There were people in the room— Metra and some of her officers—and people who were faces on the walls, one of them Jameson, projected from *Heartworld III*. Another was Andrella Murphy, also in space in a craft of her own, and a third Zanté, on Earth; Adair Evanomen was there, too, and again Hanna wondered why. The idea of trading with Battleground for anything was ludicrous.

Real or virtual, all of them might as well have been only voices, because it was too much trouble for Hanna to keep her eyes open, and she could not feel the real presences telepathically. She kept trying to feel them, again and again, all the time holding down a tide of something that could become hysteria. She had seldom thought of what it meant to be a telepath, and now all she could think, obsessively, was that she had never sufficiently treasured what she had. The universe that was Hanna's was multidimensional in a way a true-human's could never be. *We are aliens too, we look like them, have the same ancestors, but deep down they feel it . . . no wonder they don't trust us . . . oh, God, don't make me one of them!*

She managed to speak coherently, barely. She reported Kwoort's offer, or proposition, or attempt to bribe or seduce, and saw shock and disbelief and maybe embarrassment in some faces, before she closed her eyes. Hanna felt none of those things. She was too consumed by fear to feel anything else.

"Recommendations?" said Jameson's deep voice.

Subtle sounds of movement, as people thought of answers.

"We need to find a different contact," Metra said.

Hanna put down the stifling fear once more and said with effort, "Won't work. There's nobody higher than Tlorr, and she and Kwoort are a team. He's crazy as hell and she probably is too, and they're *both* saner than the oldest one. Let's get out of here."

And let me go home please please and maybe the healers can help

Gabriel moved a little. He said nothing, but Hanna felt agreement and lost the thread of conversation immediately; she had *felt* it, sensed it, oh, God, was she going to be all right? Something had happened to her breath; she turned her face to Gabriel's shoulder and went still.

Gabriel?

And oh, yes, there it was, the sense of a complex personality, not yet strong, still dim, but unmistakably Gabriel.

"Lady Hanna?" someone was saying, but she was reaching out: *Bella? Dema?*

I'm here, what's wrong with you . . .

Me too, we could hardly feel you, it was like you were unconscious . . .

And Joseph: faint. But there. And she could tell that Arch was asleep.

They were asking Gabriel what the Holy Man had had to say to him, and Gabriel was saying it was nothing important.

It had not been unimportant. The contact with Gabriel intensified. She knew there had been something that had shocked him to the core.

Gabriel? Gabriel, dear?

She was as unconscious of uttering an endearment as he had been.

She opened her eyes and was looking into his. He shook his head. Something horrible: not clear, but it would not be at the best of times, because there were no words and no distinct images. He was not so much holding something back as holding it down, as Hanna still did with the hysteria that might, finally, slip away as she came back to being herself.

.   She looked up and caught Jameson watching her thoughtfully. Because Gabriel's arm lay across her shoulders? Jameson knew that D'neerans shared touch frequently and freely—with each other. Gabriel was not D'neeran, and Jameson also knew that Hanna did not allow true-human males to touch her casually.

She drew away, surprised at herself, and reached deep down for a last reserve of energy.

"I can't talk with Kwoort any more," she said. "I'm ineffective with him. That must be obvious now. I didn't get any new information from him, no answers to all those questions. I suppose I could . . . try one more time . . ."

But Jameson shook his head.

"I agree it's not working with Kwoort," he said. "He's dominated every meeting you've had with him. It might be as well to abandon Rowtt for the time being. There is another center of government and power on Battleground."

"Wektt," Hanna said. "I suppose Communications can identify some contacts there. Wektt would have its own Holy Man—the being Rowtt calls the Demon?—and its own equivalent of Kwoort. But maybe Wektt's Kwoort isn't quite as mad."

"I wouldn't count on it," Jameson said. "What about the area called That Place? I have a report in hand about the interview with the Warrior Kwek. Captain Metra talked to Harm about it and conveyed the information to me some time ago."

Hanna looked at Metra and picked up a clear image of an exhausted Arch answering questions. It wasn't a pleasant image, but seeing it felt normal.

"That's not the place to go if you want to communicate with important figures on Battleground," she said. "Kwoort never mentioned it. They don't put it on maps. It's an anomaly."

"Yes," Jameson said, "and as such worth investigation."

"Another perspective," Andrella Murphy said. She had spoken before, but it had been while Hanna was not paying attention.

"The hell with another perspective," Hanna said. "There's nothing for us here," and everyone but Gabriel looked at her as if she had caught Kwoort's insanity.

Murphy said mildly, "We need to be sure of that before we give up. You'll feel better when you've had some rest."

Murphy—always perfectly groomed—looked at Hanna with a critical eye, and Hanna put a hand to her hair. She had tied it back for the visit to the surface but the winds had torn it loose and it straggled everywhere. She was aware of wind-driven dust and grit caught in the shirt and trousers she had put on in preparation for the flight.

"There is no common ground with these beings," she said. "They don't have anything we could ever possibly want."

Murphy said, "Not necessarily true."

Hanna slumped against Gabriel again, staring at Murphy's face, wishing she could tell what was behind it. Because she was sure Murphy, and Jameson too, no doubt, thought there might be something here for humans that justified the whole mission. But she could not imagine what it was.

Some time later, she woke briefly. Gabriel lay next to her—was crushed against her—in her bed. They had come to her cabin together naturally, without exchanging any words about it, and neither of them had questioned the impulse. Gabriel had had to cajole Hanna into taking off her boots before she threw herself down, and she did not remember him lying down beside her. But she was glad that he was there.

She lifted herself on one arm and looked at him. The cabin was as dark as it had been when he had come to wake her; maybe it was night everywhere, and endless. She could just make out his features, which had no special beauty but had become dear to her. He was deeply asleep and was not dreaming, but even so there was a vertical line of strain between his brows. She had been too exhausted to ask again what troubled him and he had been too exhausted even to think of telling her spontaneously.

The warmth of his body felt good against hers. It would be good to get the taste of Kwoort's suggestions out of her mouth.

She thought of kissing Gabriel's mouth, softly, and gently slipping the tip of her tongue between his lips. That would be so nice. It would feel so good.

But it was customary to obtain permission first, before you did something like that.

She sighed, lay down again, and went back to sleep.

PART FOUR

THAT PLACE

Chapter I

FIVE DAYS PASSED, and nothing in particular happened.
Nothing that made it into the history texts.

Gabriel could not pray.

He knelt beside his bed. At some time in the last hours
the bowed head and clasped hands had become a head laid
in misery on helpless folded arms. He was stiff and he was
cold. He had come desperately seeking the place where ego
dissolved in the paradox containing all that existed, perceptible and imperceptible, known and unknown, that which
was at once wholly action and wholly stillness. He had not
been able to escape the prison of flesh and the chaos of
thought.

feed on us, you see, and our pleasure so intense

When he tried to pray all that came was a passionate
plea: *Take me now, take me out of this universe—*

*But You made it, so it must be good. You made them, so
there must be goodness in them. It must be I who cannot
see . . .*

The door had been sounding a request for entry for
some time before he heard it. He waited a full minute longer for the caller to give up and leave, but the annoying
chirps went on. Finally he got up and hobbled to the portal
and ordered it open without even waiting to find out who
was there. It didn't matter; he would tell them to go away.

Hanna stood there, looking up at him, and he said nothing.

She said, "I thought you might want something to eat."

He was silent. After a minute she moved forward and he
stood back automatically so that she would not have to

shove her way into the room. She was carrying a handled box. His room was larger than hers and had one of the ubiquitous all-purpose tables against one wall, where he kept an upright crucifix and some antique books of devotion, leaving no room for the box. She opened it and began taking out sealed containers, one-handed, awkwardly because the box was a clumsy thing, and something moved in his heart, as it did sometimes when he watched a child patiently work at a task that was almost beyond him. He went to her and took the box, holding it while she finished taking out the contents.

"I didn't bring any meat," she said. "I didn't know if you eat it."

"Thank you," he said, "but I'm not hungry."

"I'm never hungry when I'm upset, either. People are always trying to get me to eat. I always thought it was so I'll stay healthy enough to do what they want, but maybe it's— because it's something you can do for somebody, when you can't help them any other way."

She uncovered plates and sat down. Gabriel watched her take a bite of a creamy egg dish."This is pretty good," she said. "Please? Maybe if you taste it you'll be able to eat some more."He sat down and began to eat. It tasted like sawdust to him, but if he concentrated, he could get it down. His order did not approve of prolonged fasting, except in specific circumstances and under guidance, and especially did not approve of it as an emotional indulgence. *Take the gift when it is given and give thanks*, he had been told, and that was what he taught.Presently Hanna said, "Tell me what happened with Tlorr."

Gabriel put down his fork and closed his eyes.

She said, "It can't be that bad."

"Maybe not to you," Gabriel said, and heard the resentment in his voice. "You just observe, don't you? You're used to this. You made friends with Zeigans, for God's sake."

"Well, not immediately," she said. "And I don't 'just observe.' True-humans do that … Do you think the Polity would let me stop doing this? No," she answered herself. "They mean to get a lot more work out of me, and they've got a way to enforce my cooperation. For the foreseeable future. You don't think I'm enjoying this experience, do you? You heard me practically beg to get out of here!"

Gabriel folded his hands on the table and tried to collect his thoughts. "Eat," she said, and he said, "Be quiet," in the you-better-shut-up-*now* teacher-tone he had perfected. She looked up with laughter in her eyes, but said nothing.

He said eventually, "Tlorr told me about the facilitators."

"Tell me."

But he stayed silent and finally she said, "It might be important, Gabriel. If nothing else, it's a blank spot in our knowledge of them, because when they talk about reproduction they're vague, and when they think about it there's nothing clear, just an impression of sensation. It might be ecstasy, but memories of strong sensations are just—sketches. They don't convey substance. I went back and looked at the physiologists' reports, trying to figure out what Kwoort was offering that he thought would be fair exchange for what he was asking. I just tried to talk to Cinnamon's team again, but they were all asleep. They seem to sleep a lot," she said doubtfully; a look of puzzlement crossed her face. It cleared and she said, "So I read their reports instead. They weren't there long enough to learn much. In terms of primary anatomy, Soldiers have analogues to human reproductive organs, both internal and external. Males have penises—two to a male—and females have two vaginas for impregnation, though there's a separate birth canal. That's surprising, but—why not? Nature likes redundancy.

"Both sexes, however, have an additional external organ that seems to be specifically associated with sexual activity. Soldiers talked about it freely and didn't mind exhibiting it to the team. It presents as bodily sites that appear to be randomly distributed all over the torso, front and back and sides. The subjects said there's no special pattern in their arrangement, and individuals have varying numbers of them. When they're not in reproductive mode—and none of the subjects were—the sites appear as small, folded depressions, anywhere from one to twelve centimeters across. They probably connect with a neural network, and maybe with a separate vascular system, though that's not clear. That was Matthew Sweet's guess; the Soldiers couldn't explain it in terms satisfactory to the translator. The sites are receptors for the facilitators, apparently. But so far nobody has seen a facilitator. So what did Tlorr tell you? Is what I've just said consistent?"

"It's consistent," Gabriel said. He pushed his plate away.

"Drink some milk," Hanna said. "Come on, Gabriel. Are you embarrassed? Are you uncomfortable talking about sex? Or are you only uncomfortable talking about it with me?"

Gabriel had waked two mornings ago with the sleeping Hanna in his arms and in a state of high arousal—for a few seconds, until the memory of the benighted trip to the surface came crashing back. He had gotten out of bed—almost leaped out of it—grabbed his boots, and fled.

"I don't know what the facilitators look like either," Gabriel said. "I know they fasten onto the people—onto those receptor sites, I suppose—and there's some kind of exchange. It nourishes the facilitators. And they pump something in, or trigger something . . ."

He fell silent again. Hanna said, "Spit it out."

"I don't think the translator was working right."

"You're not just uncomfortable," Hanna said accurately. "You—you loathe it. Whatever it is."

seen that destruction with my own eyes and might live to feel God's power again

He said carefully, "They make Soldiers aggressive. Very aggressive. But only toward specific targets. Like anyone who tries to prevent reproduction."

"I don't understand," Hanna said, frowning. "You mean they react aggressively toward someone who tries to interfere with them when they're mating? You see that in a lot of species, one animal distracted by the need to fight another off. But not in all of them, and never in the sentient species we've seen until now. They do the competing beforehand, more subtly, of course, like humans—well, usually—and do the mating in private. I didn't think these beings fought each other about it at all. I thought they just did it at random, at the right times."

"It's not about competing for mates," Gabriel said. "It's a lot more complicated than that. If I understood Tlorr, it extends to destroying research directed toward population control. And massacring researchers. Tlorr said she saw it happen herself. There was some ambiguity—she might have been part of it—"

*torn limb from limb and the facilitators also inflict pain
exquisite as*

He felt a surge of nausea. Hanna said, "Gabriel?" in alarm.

"Excuse me," he said thickly, turned over his chair getting up, and ran for the lavatory.

When he came out the chair was upright, the food, to his relief, had disappeared back into the box, and Hanna was turning over the pages of a twentieth-century translation of St. John of the Cross. He sat heavily on the bed. The combination of Hanna and a bed reminded him that he had another problem at least as serious as an alien civilization he did not understand and was trying not to hate. She looked up from the book, and he wondered if she knew what he was thinking.

"Yes," she said. "You can't help projecting. Some people do it a lot. I could shut it out, but I like how your mind feels, so I don't want to."

"Do," he said. "Please."

"Why? Everyone needs to be understood. And comforted, when they're unhappy. This—*The Dark Night of the Soul*—is this your comfort?"

"You can read that?" he said, distracted.

"It's the language used on New Earth. It's changed there over the years, but I can read this. It doesn't seem like it would be as helpful as ordinary human compassion, though."

"Which is a reflection of the compassion of Christ. I can't accept what you're offering, Hanna."

"I do not," she said, "go to bed with men to demonstrate compassion. That's not what I meant."

"I'm sorry, I didn't mean—"

"That's what you were thinking about. I just meant being with you. A friend to talk to, if you want."

So tempting. So innocent. She meant it, too, and there was *Take the gift when it is given* . . .

But he couldn't take this one. The time was coming, no, it was here, to decide about the direction of his future, but he did not mean to decide on the basis of passion for a woman. Though it went beyond lust. He could not forget—he wished he could forget!—that she had reached out from her own trouble and sought to help him. That *Gabriel, dear?* had been irresistible.

He said gently, "Friendship is not all I would want, and that's the problem. Leave me alone, Hanna. For my sake."

She looked at him in silence for a moment, started to speak, changed her mind, and got up and picked up the box. At the door she did speak; she said, "Do you want me to tell you if I find out any more about That Place?"

"I guess so," he said. "But in public. In a common area."

"All right," she said simply, and left him.

The climatologist said there were, in fact, places on Battleground that had consistently good weather. He said That Place was, in fact, one of them.

Hanna was suspicious. "You mean," she said, "we go down there and the sun will be shining? Blue sky? No lightning? All that?"

"Well, it does depend on when you go," said the climatologist. "There's a storm system moving in that direction now."

"Figures," Hanna said.

No one was paying much attention to Kwek. She thought this was probably a good thing.

She wasn't afraid of these not-Soldiers ... not exactly. They were exceedingly strange, but not frightening. They only filled her with uncertainty, and that had begun before she even met the one called Arkt, when she got the casual order to tell the not-Soldier that was coming whatever it wanted to know.

The what?—she thought an animal was meant.

It is a not-Soldier but it talks, it comes from another star.

She wasn't sure she had heard that right until the minute Arkt came into her workspace, and even then she had thought she was dreaming. Strange creatures did wander around in dreams, the most unlikely things happened as if they were a matter of course, accepted without surprise—but only in dreams. The Soldier who escorted Arkt didn't seem to think anything odd was happening. But then, the Soldier probably didn't dream. Kwek had known only a handful who did; she herself had only begun to dream some thirty summers ago.

The first occurrences were far apart; she was not even sure when it had happened the first time, and she could not put the name "dreams" to what she experienced at first, thinking them memories of things she had really done. But she knew Soldiers who appeared in some of these episodes, and she soon discovered that they did not have the same memories. She still did not think of the pseudo-memories as especially strange — perhaps her recollection was faulty, or the others were wrong — until she "remembered" crouching behind a rock and taking a direct hit from a blast so huge that it devastated the whole valley around her but left her unharmed. Obviously, this could not have happened. For a time, as the frequency of the phenomena increased, she continued to mention them to others, saying *What is this, does it happen to you?* But it didn't seem to happen to anyone else, nor was anyone interested, and so, since it was relevant to nothing, she stopped bothering.

She first heard the word "dream" one day when she was in the company of two high-ranking Commanders and one of them, describing an impossible event to the other, used it. She learned then that she was, if in the minority, not unique. Dreaming was a phenomenon that appeared from time to time, she was told, and was universal among commanders. Not that she — not that any individual — had a strong likelihood of surviving long enough to become a Commander, but it did appear to be a marker of some kind, which was interesting.

She did not seriously examine the possibility that Arkt was not a dream until the two of them were on the way, with a not-Soldier described as "transport personnel," to the not-Soldiers' spaceship. But by the time her short interrogation on arrival was over she no longer questioned the reality of her situation, and she was simply relieved at being moved from place to place on the spaceship, reminiscent of the orders that moved her from place to place among Soldiers. Long stretches with nothing to do felt like normal life, and so did mild suspense at where she would end up next.

So this is real, she thought. At least, it would be advisable to proceed as if it is real, because it might be. And if it is real, maybe That Place is real too; these not-Soldiers claim to have proof that it is. I never truly thought it was.

I must have misunderstood. Forgive me, Lord. My mind and heart are troubled, give me peace. I've never even understood why Your human children act as they do. We have free will, to do good or do evil, that I know, and You don't will the evil we do. And the will to do good, to be good, until now seemed to exist among our alien brothers as it does in us, even if they don't name or worship You. I believe You did not make these thinking minds, minds that hold some image of You and the desire to bend to Your will, whose very name for you recognizes the abundance of your gifts, without giving them goodness to manifest. Help me to understand, and if my poor human mind cannot understand, at least grant me the peace to accept that I do not understand.

———

Hope Metra was—finally—beginning to feel like she was in charge of this mission. It gave her great pleasure to say: "These are your orders. You will lead a party of three—yourself, Gabriel Guyup, and the female Kwek, to the area of Battleground known as That Place. I have not decided when."

Hanna Bassanio looked bewildered. She said, "Whose orders?"

"The Coordinating Commission's," Metra said, forced to admit it. "Transmitted through Alien Relations and Contact. I'm working out a detailed plan."

"Who did you talk to at Contact?"

"Adair Evanomen. You know him."

"Deputy for trade. He's been at the conferences. Why was he giving the orders? Starr always tells me things like this himself—" *Make that past tense,* Metra thought. "Why Adair? I don't have anything to do with commerce."

"Director Jameson is on the point of taking a seat on the Commission. Obviously the Commission will appoint another director, and Evanomen's the designee. Why?" said Metra, unable to help herself. "Did you expect to get the appointment?"

"What?" said Bassanio, looking more bewildered still. But she couldn't be that thoughtless of promotion, impossible though it would be for someone in her anomalous position.

Or could she?

———

"Tell me what you think, Adair." Still on *Heartworld III*, but nearing Heartworld, the home Jameson did not think of as home. Almost summer at Admin. Winter waiting in Arrenswood; he would disembark in something not far short of a blizzard.

Adair Evanomen, the man Jameson was talking to by remote, felt like he'd been thrown into deep water and forgotten how to swim. Evanomen was confident in commerce; he had been involved in trade with F'thal and Girritt for years before the original *Endeavor* project started expanding human relations with nonhumans. He was about to take on direct oversight of the *Endeavor*s and whatever they came up with, and he was not ready—though Jameson apparently thought he was.

"I was hoping to hear what *you* think," he said.

"I'd rather hear from you."

It had to be an honest opinion; Jameson wouldn't accept less.

"I think continued contact is imperative. They might have only one fantastic intangible to offer us, but it's so big we've got to come up with something to give them in return. But conditions in Rowtt—specifically Kwoort's state of mind—aren't going to get us what we want."

"I agree. Go on."

"Why not wait until we can open channels with the other major power? I know the hierarchy in Wektt isn't as clear, but we'll identify their Holy Man eventually. I'm not as favorably disposed as you are about investigating what they call That Place. If you don't mind my asking, why are you so interested in it?"

"I'm curious. Aren't you? Better cultivate that curiosity. You'll need it, for the Contact part of the job."

Hanna briefly tried maintaining a sort of low-grade awareness of Gabriel's whereabouts so that she could avoid him, but this only caused her to be aware of Gabriel, so she dropped it. The whole thing seemed vastly unfair, when all she wanted to do was enjoy being in his presence, because she found him restful. He had not even given her a chance to point out that she still felt herself bound by a temporary quasi-promise to maintain a status quo with Jameson. And he wouldn't care about that anyway, because he (she had looked it up) was wed with a permanent and absolute promise to his God. What he would care about was that she (according to the reading she managed before she got bored) was a proximate occasion of sin, although the proximity appeared to be permissible, even if it was continuous, as long as it was involuntary.

She didn't think she had ever been called an occasion of sin before. Presumably she could not help being one, but she was not sure, and she didn't know of any experts to ask. Except Gabriel. And she had no idea how to remove herself from that unfortunate category, and he probably wouldn't either, since the assessment appeared to be subjective on the part of the potential sinner, and it was evident that Gabriel already knew where he stood on *that* question: ready and able to sin with her; just not—volunteering.

Now it does not matter now it is over now I go. Balances to be maintained. I will have no more to do with these not-Soldiers unless

Of course they might come. Would that not be the logical next step for them.

So it might happen and then I would still have to try to harness that strange power, how strange it felt, like a palpable touch. And I would have another chance to find out how they do the other thing we cannot do but even if I find out what reward could there be? What does knowing what I know, seeing what I have lived to see, living long enough for knowledge and surmise to come together, what reward has it brought?

None. Nothing. No thing.

I have lived too long, it seems I must live longer still. It does not seem too long on the days when I have forgotten much, but today it seems long. I even remember where I hid others of these pages. Not all, the most recent, only those. I will put them also in the sack and I will take them

---

"What are you doing?" said Kwek.

"It is prayer," said Gergtk, lifting his head.

"But you use no prayer counter."

"Sometimes."

He seemed to be all right, considering he was a not-

Soldier. All of them seemed to be, so far. Arkt had made sure she had Soldiers' food to eat; he said not-Soldiers who wanted to analyze it had brought it on board and he had had difficulty wresting it from them. He had come to see her several times and told her many interesting things about them, and so had this one. This time Gergtk had put his hand on hers where it lay on the table while he said quiet words that his translating device rendered mostly as signals without content. After the first short recitation he had said what might be the same syllables again, and this time he seemed to be listening to the pings, chimes, chirps, beeps and twitters for their own sake. He had just finished doing that when Kwek spoke and he answered.

"What does the prayer say?" she said.

"It doesn't matter. It doesn't translate," said the male. "Stalemate be with you, Kwek."

"What?" said Kwek.

The plan Hope Metra had come up with involved an uninhabited island, a boat, and a long walk through jungle. She put it forth in what was supposed to be a conference with Hanna and the ever present Cork and Cock, except that "conferring" implied an exchange of ideas, and Metra entertained none but her own. The plan was so shockingly dangerous and impractical that Hanna spoke to Metra's mind directly for the first time: *You and I must talk, if you don't want Commissioner Jameson personally questioning my death!*–emphasis on the "Commissioner." She threw in a judicious impression of her intimacy with him for good measure, but it was the anger, and the sense of threat, that made Metra blink.

"Dismissed," she told the officers, and she and Hanna faced each other.

Hanna said, "Are you trying to get me killed? And Kwek and Gabriel too?"

"The idea is to minimize the probability of that by allowing you to make a surreptitious approach," Metra said.

"It is not. I'm not good with boats, I have never been certified for boats of any kind, as you must know if you've seen my records. Does Gabriel know anything about boats? Does Kwek?"

"No one wants you to be killed," Metra said. And Hanna saw that that was the truth, as Metra knew it. She got up and started pacing. She stopped and looked at Metra; looked a little deeper, making it deliberately obvious and rude.

"*This* is what you want. My refusal. Why?"

"*Stop that!*"

"'That' seems to be my only defense. What is really going on here—?" Hanna said almost amiably. She dropped back into her chair and considered.

"You don't get any direct benefit from my refusing to do this. But it makes me look bad, doesn't it? And by extension, Starr? Who came up with this idea—Edward Vickery's people? I can believe Edward would like to embarrass Starr for the fun of it, but he's too cautious to set up something this dangerous just for fun. Is it some kind of last-minute effort to discredit Starr and keep him out of the appointment? You know, it just might be. So—"

Hanna smiled.

"I'll do it. I want it on record that I think it's a wonderful idea. I will take Gabriel and Kwek and the boat and stuff them all into a shuttle and go immediately. I understand storms are expected. High winds, high seas? Wonderful. Just what we need. How soon can a boat be ready—does *Endeavor* even carry a boat?—you're not recording."

"Never mind," Metra said.

"Did these plans of hers call for a boat?" Jameson said later.

"How did you know?"

"Adair told me. He didn't know about you and boats. I've told him you're not to be allowed near one. That you behave as if they're sure to fly if you only go fast enough."

"Thank you—I think. She dropped the idea anyway. It was just supposed to maneuver me into refusing to follow orders—an order to do something stupid and dangerous. I think my refusal was supposed to damage you. Would it have?"

"It's too late for that, and Edward should have known it, if indeed he was behind it. Anyway, it's all over the council that you and I are separating. That helps."

Hanna had answered his call with a light heart, pleased

at her skirmish with Metra. It took a few seconds to absorb
what he had just said, and as she did the heart slowly began
turning to stone.

She said, "You didn't."

"Didn't what?"

He looked at her with mild curiosity, but his face changed
when he saw what had come into hers. She could not speak
at all for a minute, and he said, "I told you the rumor would
be helpful. Did you think I was joking?"

Hanna still could not speak. The video projection that
took up so small a space in the wall seemed to expand. He
had reached Heartworld and was at his own provincial capital. It was night in Arrenswood and he had called her just
before going to bed. He wore a robe of rough brown fabric
that she remembered; she remembered how it felt against
her naked skin. He was at home in the city house his family
had maintained in Arrenswood's capital for six hundred
years, gilded and luxurious. Hanna had never visited it. She
had never been invited.

remember what he has poured out at our feet

The ghost.

remember kindness generosity even love

I don't hear you. I won't

himself

I won't

Finally she spoke. Her voice was thick.

"So you told them I'm leaving you, a strategic lie that put
words into my mouth. I'll make it true, then. I won't, I will
not do this any more. Being afraid I'll be used as a weapon
against you. Or used by you, for political expediency. And
Mickey, too, how could you! I will not do it any more!"

"I'm sorry—"

"Don't say it won't happen again. It doesn't matter.
And," she almost whispered, "there are other reasons."

"What reasons?" He looked bewildered now, completely
unguarded. And afraid. Not another soul in human space
could have put that look there. He knew Hanna did not
make empty threats.

There were too many answers. *I out-manipulated Metra,
and used you to do it. Used you as you have used me. A true-
human thing to do, not D'neeran. I am losing myself.*

Some part of her seemed to have been cut away, as if she

had suffered a great injury, and she felt a need to hold her breath and wait to see how much it was going to hurt. She heard a voice, knowing it was hers although it did not seem to be, say: "You are contacting me about the mission? What did you want?"

"Hanna, listen to me."

"No. We're done. Altogether done."

He looked at her for a long moment. She looked back, holding on to resolution, dizzy with it. Finally he said, "I apologize from my heart. Please don't decide now."

Too late, Hanna thought. And, *What heart?* She was shaking. She tucked her hands under her arms so he would not see the tremor. He was saying, "Later, when you've thought some more—"

"Cooled off, you mean. All right. All right, we'll talk later—" But not now. She wanted these minutes to end, they had to end, she had to go away and be as quiet as she could while the vast change rolled through her and she tried to breathe. "Say what you have to say about the mission." She tried to take a deep breath. There did not seem to be enough oxygen in it. "Metra implied that Adair was giving the orders now, that you're not directly involved any more."

"Of course I'm involved." He moved; he had been absolutely still, a sign that all his strength was needed to contain something going on inside. His voice was rough when he said, "The Commission has always been closely involved in matters of contact." A scarcely perceptible pause. He went on, evenly now: "It's too important not to be. They—we— have to know what's going on always, day to day. You can trust Adair for the most part; he only needs experience. But be cautious about what Metra tells you, Hanna. Apparently she's even more closely tied to Vickery's faction than I thought."

"Tell me—" She heard her own voice waver and tried again. "Tell me if this is true: you want three of us to go to That Place? Gabriel and Kwek and me?"

"That much is true. No boats, though. You'll simply fly there and land."

"They'll be expecting the landing, then?"

"No, I don't think they will." He said curiously, "Didn't Metra tell you anything about conditions at That Place? That's why I called. To see what you know."

Hanna eyed him warily and said, "I don't know anything. What's different about conditions there?"

"There is—" He stopped and then said with cold anger, "That woman should be relieved of command."

"Fine with me," Hanna said, "but I wouldn't have gone without information. Not even on Adair's orders."

"You might have if you thought they were mine."

"Maybe. Only maybe. What's wrong with That Place? I mean, that isn't wrong everywhere here?"

He lifted a hand and began to tick off points on his fingers. Hanna watched his face, wanting to touch it just once more. She had always loved the stark planes—

No. There was a way to leave an affair behind, or at least start to do it. *A formal Parting. That's D'neeran . . .*

"Hanna? Are you listening?"

"Repeat it. Please," she added, a little late. She heard with satisfaction that her voice was steady. She wasn't sure what her face was doing.

He started over. "The population is not as technologically advanced as Rowtt's. *Endeavor* has picked up radio transmissions, though, and there's electricity, provided by a nuclear reactor on one of the uninhabited islands—a strange combination, considering that observation indicates subsistence agriculture carried on with manual tools. There are only a dozen settlements, the largest with an estimated population of no more than four thousand. No inhabitant was seen who was not a mature adult, and there is no sign of underground structures that might serve as crèches. The extent of isolation from mainstream culture is undetermined. It does not seem to be complete; there appears to be a landing field for small aircraft, well maintained. We haven't seen any flights arrive or depart—though there was a flight today from Rowtt to Wektt and immediately back again, a surprise, reason unknown. Kwoort might be willing to tell you more, if he knows more."

"I'm not going to meet with Kwoort again! Do these people have weapons?"

"None have been seen, but we have to assume they're there."

"I can understand taking Kwek, but why Gabriel?"

"He's the only person besides yourself who's had direct contact with a Holy Man. There might be one at That Place."

"Kwek doesn't think so."

"She's guessing. It's clear she knows very little. And remote sensors recorded some kind of ritual that might be a religious rite. It occurred more than a week ago, and wasn't noticed until Captain Metra ordered observations reviewed in preparation for this mission. It doesn't fit with anything else we've seen or heard about on Battleground."

"What is it?"

"It might be burnt offerings," he said, and all Hanna could say was, *"What?"*

Joseph invited Gabriel to a Parting Observance. Benj Parker was coming too, he said, and Glory and Carl, and it would be in Cinnamon Padrick's quarters; Gabriel wouldn't be the only true-human guest. There ought to be candles and wine and some other things, he said vaguely, but none of it was available, so they would just have to make do. He thought Gabriel would find it *very interesting.* The emphasis was almost alarming, and Joseph refused to elaborate. "You'll see," he said.

Gabriel was not so egotistical as to think God spoke to him directly, but he suspected that isolating himself from his fellow humans for too long was not in the Divine plan for one of his temperament, so he accepted the invitation. He could keep his distance from Hanna in a group.

He had heard of the arrangements in Padrick's quarters but had not been there, and he felt a rush of pleasure at the shadowy forest that stretched away on three sides. All the furnishings had been taken out or shoved against the visible wall, and everyone sat on the floor in a circle.

"There is supposed to be *dirt* under us," Joseph complained, and someone said, "Really, Joseph, you are such a purist," and the D'neerans laughed, but quietly; there was the sense of a solemn occasion.

Gradually they fell silent, and finally everyone was looking at Hanna, who had said nothing. She sat cross-legged directly across from Gabriel, and she had not greeted him, only glanced at him in surprise.

She looked around the circle and took a deep breath. She said into the silence: "Love never really ends. But we part from what was, and go on to what will be. I have reached a parting from one whose life I have shared. I do not do this easily or lightly. And I do not wish to part from him with enmity, but with gratitude for what I have had. Today I sever a bond, and I honor its ending with celebration, relinquishment, release ... and hope."

Her voice was quiet and a little unsteady. An image came to Gabriel—from Hanna's mind and those of the other telepaths, perhaps all the true-humans saw it—of the candles they had not been able to obtain. The flames were golden and unwavering.

"These are the things I celebrate," Hanna said. "Sanctuary, when pain was near extinguishing my spirit. Sensual passion more intense than any other I have known. The joy of knowing a mind fascinating in its depth and complexity. A home of grace and beauty. They have nourished me. And now I relinquish them."

The flames flickered and died. They went gradually, diminishing to sparks that lingered, reluctant to go out. Gabriel felt a breath of grief—Hanna's—and felt her holding onto the sparks. She could not seem to let them go.

"These I relinquish, too: Habits of mind foreign to me: obsession with power and hidden motive. Reliance on material wealth. Suppression of the deepest part of who I am—a telepath. Fear that in being what I am, I damage the well-being of one I loved. From these, I am released."

More intangible candles went out, all at once, and these completely, as if the flames were glad to go.

"These are my hopes: A free life for my child, without the oppressive need for guards, lest his welfare be used as a threat. A home that is ours alone, reflecting our deepest selves. The self-sufficiency I sacrificed in times of trouble now past." There were tears on her cheeks.

Three new candles came to life, flames swelling slowly until they dazzled.

Hanna said: "It is finished."

And she might have thought she meant it, but Gabriel noticed that sparks still lingered in the depths of some candles that were supposed to have gone out.

Hanna said to Metra, "Is there some reason you're delaying this little excursion?"

"It takes time to gather intelligence," Metra told her.

"Intelligence you were not sharing with me in any case."

"You have it now."

"All of a sudden, yes. You could hardly keep a commissioner of the Polity from talking to me—well, I suppose he's a commissioner now, it was only hours away. But I tried to get information from Communications and at first they wouldn't give me any. And then, zap, they flooded me with it. Did Starr, or maybe Adair or Zanté, contact you directly in the meantime?"

Metra's mouth twitched, but she said nothing.

"Never mind. It's nearly morning at That Place. Is there anything else you've somehow forgotten to tell me? No? Then we're going. Now."

Chapter II

GABRIEL, a polite man in spite of (or perhaps because of) his longtime exposure to young boys, a naturally rude population, offered to stand during the flight to That Place, but Kwek declined the offer and did not even, really, appear to understand it.

"I am accustomed to standing during troop movements," she assured him, so he took the passenger seat in the pod. Sitting down beside Hanna as if nothing had happened felt odd, after the ritual he had seen a few hours ago. He thought of saying, *Are you all right?* but obviously she was, hands and eyes steady, although a shell of silence seemed to surround her. *That's an interesting folk custom you people have*—no.

He might as well have been shouting. Hanna said mildly, "You're giving me a headache."

It got her moving, anyway; she spoke to the pod and touched keypads, and the pod left *Endeavor* and moved into space. There was no homing beacon this time, and no airspace that could be counted safe, nor time to tease the puzzled Gabriel. She stayed in solid contact with *Endeavor*, letting its navigators, trained for this as well as for deep space, guide the pod by remote to a point directly "above" the largest settlement at That Place. The fall that followed was strictly controlled by antigravity, speed at the maximum the pod could take without the risk of burning up.

Down through blue-glowing high-atmosphere cloud, through separate layers of winds. Even That Place would be cloudy today, they had told her. *We're not staying for the storms, though,* she thought.

And she also thought: *I should not have been so quick to come.* She had only wanted to get it over, get it done, all of it; get back to her son, who pressed on her mind more and more insistently as the time apart from him went on. Jameson's home—that "home of grace and beauty"—would not be Mickey's any more and she did not know where they could go. She felt a wrench of guilt.

Cinnamon said girl you do not know which side of your bread the butter is on

Gabriel.

Glory said that stuff you're giving up can I have it

"Gabriel."

"What?"

"It wouldn't surprise me if we had a common ancestor not too far back—the one that got drafted into the New-Human Project."

She shut him out while he was trying to make sense of that.

"Kwek," she said.

"Yes, Commander?"

Where in hell had that "Commander" come from?

"Kwek, I want you to go out first. It's possible these people haven't even heard about us. I want you to explain to them. All right?"

"Yes," said Kwek. It was apparent to Hanna that Kwek was not used to being asked if orders were all right with her.

Through the last and lowest of the clouds, on manual control: Hanna brought the pod to a stop, hovering. She had finally gotten to see enough data to know what she would find. The landing field was grassy and unmarked by the attacks that scarred Rowtt's. This settlement, the largest population center of That Place, was near the seacoast, though tiny villages were scattered across several islands, and ocean took up the field of vision east to the horizon. The community spread out from the airfield's edge, fewer than thirty structures housing four thousand people; they were of necessity large enough to make up in volume what they lacked in numbers, though smaller outbuildings made a ragged border.

Looking at images on *Endeavor,* feeling the same distaste the first look at Rowtt had given her, she had tried to keep a negative response in check, thinking it a product of her experiences in Rowtt and with Kwoort. This was not the war-pounded land over Rowtt; there was forest Metra had

described as jungle pushing inland. There should be no
equivalent of Kwoort here; Kwek thought there was no
Holy Man. All to the good, since by this time Hanna, with
limited choices, would settle for being anyplace where a
Kwoort and a spooky Holy Man were not.

She went lower, studied the roofs of the buildings. They
told her nothing. She had seen the buildings from all sides,
in any case, as images from scanners sent to the surface in
preceding days, so minuscule no Soldier's eye had found
them. The few aboveground structures at Rowtt had been
flimsy, not expected to last long, and had punctuated the
violated landscape with grooved, tilted roofs that showed
little overhang; they would speed runoff from heavy rains
but keep wind from getting a hand under an edge and tearing the whole thing off (until some attack blew them to
bits). The structures here were built on a different model,
and presented a range of jutting ridges. A memory brushed
her mind: the House of Koroth on D'neera, a small town in
itself, which had grown by accretion over centuries, where
Hanna had lived for several years. But that House, typically
for D'neera, sang ornament even to the sky, with towers and
cupolas and graceful gables carried to the point of architec-
tural overkill. These roofs were plain.

One of the structures butted close on the landing field.
Several figures came out of the nearest door, looking up,
and Hanna reached out and felt the unmistakable signature
of the minds of beings of Battleground. Her own surprised
instant of relief told her she had harbored a little fear that
she would not be able to do this, though the paralysis of
telepathy with human beings was gone as if it had never
been there.

There was surprise on the ground, too. Not at the presence of something in the sky, but at its silence and its stillness in midair, and at the way it looked: white, not the gray
they were used to seeing; and the huge blue-black numbers
and letters embedded in its skin were in a script they had
never seen at all.

Hanna finished a slow landing. "Here goes," she said, and
Kwek went out.

Hanna folded her arms and put her head back. She was
not good at waiting. *A morning here at most*, she thought. *I
hope it is more interesting than Rowtt.*

Gabriel said, "I hope it's less revolting than Rowtt."

"Gabriel . . ." She turned her head, almost laughing. "I think you have more natural psi ability than any true-human I've ever met. Are you sure your mother didn't spend any time on D'neera? Say, nine months before you were born?"

"Nobody ever told me that before!"

"Well, you never met any telepaths before, did you? So who would notice? But you've been told—don't tell me I'm wrong!—that you have a lot of empathy? For the children you work with, maybe?"

"That, yes."

"Well, there you are . . ."

"My relatives never said a word about D'neera. Aren't there too many genes involved for that to happen anyway?"

"I was teasing," she said gently.

She watched a monitor, almost idly. Nothing unexpected; three Soldiers (if that was what they called themselves here) were talking with Kwek. Kwek wore a communicator programmed for translation. It was transmitting, and the conversation was a low murmur inside the pod. Hanna had slowly come to see Soldiers as individuals, getting beyond the strangeness to register identifiable faces, bodily variations, distinct stances, characteristic gestures. Two of the Soldiers with Kwek were male; females moved differently. *I wonder how they feel when they're pregnant*, she thought. Remembered lying on her side and trying to sleep—not that that was comfortable, but at least it was bearable, which lying on her back was not, and lying on her stomach was not even to be thought of—

("—look on the bright side."

"What bright side?"

"Your skin is lovely, and now there is so much more of it."

"I hate you—")

Hanna smiled. He had kissed her shoulders in spite of the way she looked, stroked her gently and then not so gently, discomfort faded into the improbable erotic—

She shook her head *(let it go)* and amplified the volume on the dialogue outside.

I did not believe it at first either, but that is what they are. Well, very well. What are we supposed to do with them?

*Nothing. Let them walk around. Let them ask questions.
It is all right to answer the questions.*

Are they fighters?

No.

I don't understand. Are you their appointed guide?

*No, well, I am guiding them, that's true. But I want to stay
here.*

*Don't make up your mind in a hurry. Because if you de-
cide to stay there's no going back. Do your Commanders
know your plans?*

No, they think I'm still on the not-Soldiers' spacecraft.

Their what?

Another one: *Do your Commanders know the not-
Soldiers are here?*

*Not here, not in This Place. They have been to Rowtt. Lots
of them have been to Rowtt.*

So they are fighting for Rowtt?

No! They are not fighting for anybody.

What are they doing, then?

Walking around. Asking questions.

Will they take the answers back to Rowtt?

Hanna sat up, alerted. She stopped listening to words
and listened more deeply, sorting out individuals by the texture of their thought. The one who had asked that last question had something to hide; no, they all had something to
hide, this female was only the first to think it explicitly, and
her question had alerted the others.

"There's something wrong here," she said softly.

"What?" said Gabriel.

"They have secrets they mean to keep. *Damn* it."

"What's wrong? We don't have to ask them about their
secrets. In fact, you can tell if we're getting close to them
and change the line of questioning, can't you?"

"I guess I'll have to. We don't dare get into a dangerous
situation. I tried to requisition a sidearm and the captain
denied it . . ."

She had missed a few exchanges while they spoke.

You can stay for a day or two. Or for the rest of your life.

Something else there. Something behind the thought
that was not being spoken.

If for a short time, you cannot come back again.

I know I do not want to go back to Rowtt. I am certain of that.

Remember this: we have to agree to accept you, too.

Why would you not accept me?

Do you dream?

Yes.

You will have to tell us about your dreams.

Is that what determines whether you will accept me or not?

Not altogether. It's in your favor that you dream. How does your mating time cycle? When does your time come again?

Kwek hesitated. Hanna could tell the question was significant. Kwek could, too.

Not for a long time. Not until next summer, maybe longer.

Hanna raised an eyebrow. Kwek had lied. She would need to mate very soon.

"Have they forgotten about us?" Gabriel said.

"They're a lot more interested in Kwek, obviously."

They watched, absorbed. For a time the conversation seemed to go round in a circle; Kwek and the others continued to talk, but there was nothing new. Hanna murmured, "This isn't the welcome Kwek expected."

"Me either, if they'd never heard of us. Seems if an alien landed in your backyard you'd be a little excited about it."

"You would think. But you saw the reports about the early contacts with Prookt. He wasn't very excited, either . . . Let's go out before they forget about us altogether."

And this was better, she thought, better than Rowtt at once, because the cloud cover was not solid and they stepped into slanting sunlight. Hanna sighed, feeling lighter, and looked first at the sky. It was still early in the long day and the sun was near the horizon, casting long shadows; in another patch of sky hung Battleground's largest moon, almost full, and appearing, at the moment, pink.

They walked up to the group of aliens, and Hanna froze.

I was wrong, they are different, I touched no minds quite like these from space, nor since. Do the talking, Gabriel.

"Lady, who is the First Contact expert here?" he said, and the translator broadcast it, and the aliens looked at him quizzically. *Lady* had not translated.

So few people have done this that you qualify as an expert. I want to look. With eyes and everything.

"Hello," said Gabriel pleasantly, as if greeting colleagues. "I am Gabriel Guyup, I have thirty-five summers."

Hanna gave him a surprised look. She had thought him younger. He was her age in Standard years, but as for experience—

"Let me see if I have your names right. Nookt—no, Nakeekt? Pritk. And Genkt?"

They did not use the greeting convention, no statement of age. And they did not like his using it.

"Have you lived here long?" said Gabriel sociably, and the innocence of it made something happen in Hanna's chest. Gabriel, she thought, these are not your friendly neighbors on Alta, these are not even human beings—

She studied them as closely as she and Gabriel were being studied, seeing what Maya Selig had wondered about, *what's under these creatures' boots and baggy coveralls.* She had seen the images the physiology team brought back, and was not surprised by the ropes of muscle, the extra joints in the arms and legs. This group did not wear the universal gray coveralls—only pieces of them in muddy, motley colors, exposing sinuous arms to the air in this subtropical climate, and sandals instead of boots on long-toed feet. The edges of the garments were finished, and skillfully, but not by machine, and they were patched where the original uniforms would have had insignia of rank. And the patches, in two cases, bore designs that had nothing to do with rank, one a complex geometric that resembled a mandala, the other, equally complex, the unmistakable face of a flower, built up in relief with colored threads.

Look, Gabriel. None of those in Rowtt decorate their clothes or themselves, and he put out a hand, almost touching the torso of the one called Nakeekt. "What is that?" he said. "Why do you put it on your uniform?"—*uniform,* because there was no word like *ensemble,* no words for sartorial effect.

"It has no function," said Nakeekt. "It's only there because it looks interesting."

"They don't do this in Rowtt," Gabriel said to Nakeekt. "I don't know about Wektt, does anyone do it there?"

"Only here."

"I have not done it," said Kwek wistfully. "I have never thought of doing it. I wish I had."

Gabriel, I feel rejection of her forming . . .

"But you like flowers, don't you?" Gabriel said to Kwek. "Didn't I hear you put them where you work?"

"Yes . . ."

. . . good, the right answer . . .

"Do you put flowers in rooms here?" said Kwek with the first enthusiasm Hanna had ever heard from her.

"Yes," they said, and Gabriel said, "Do you do other things just because they are interesting to look at? Show us."

Chapter III

*W*E'RE GOING TO BE HERE longer than an hour or two, Hanna thought later—several Standard hours later. That Place, which looked like something underfunded human colonists might throw together with little enthusiasm and few resources, was more different from Rowtt than she had expected it to be. And she left most of the talking to Gabriel, because she learned almost at once that some of the answers he was getting to his questions were evasions, half-truths, and outright lies, and her job was to decide which was which.

Gabriel had requested what amounted to a tour. Nakeekt, it seemed, had gotten such requests before; Hanna saw a route ready to use in her thought. *Environs first*, Nakeekt thought, in effect, and led them to a shallow freshwater stream with fishlike creatures in it.

Gabriel said, "These little swimmers are pretty—"

Translating as "interesting."

"There was a report from our geoecologists . . ."

No translation.

". . . that this world's oceans are dead in places."

"Not these streams."

"Do you just watch them swim?"

"Sometimes. Sometimes we catch and eat them, too."

"Do they taste good?"

"The taste is pleasant enough, but . . . they have one greater advantage."

"And that is?"

"They do not taste like vegetable-based protein food."

"Is that all that is eaten in Rowtt?"

"Nearly all, and the same is true of Wektt. Some of us here are from Wektt."

"When you started This Place—who started This Place?"

"The founder has gone to the True God."

She has not. She is standing in front of us.

"Is that the same as Abundant God?"

"Of course."

No, it is not.

"When you say gone to the True God—do you mean that some essence survives though the body does not?"

"Yes."

But she doesn't believe it.

"I had no opportunity to discuss continuing survival with the Holy Men I met. Of what does this life consist?"

"All who die become like Holy Men in one way. They are free of the cycle of reproduction. But unlike Holy Men, they enjoy its sensations at will."

"Is that believed elsewhere, or only here?"

"It is the belief everywhere."

"Do you reproduce in This Place?"

"It is as the True God wills it."

An evasion—there's more to it . . .

"It seems that the continuing life must be much like This Place. There are no children, for one instance."

Careful, Gabriel, that's a sensitive issue . . .

Nakeekt just said, "Perhaps it is."

———

Single file on a path. Kwek lingered behind, talking with Pritk and Genkt. Enormous, neatly tilled garden plots gave way to groves of twisted trees that would not, to an eye accustomed to human orchards, look healthy, but bore fruit year-round. Their branches—but Hanna was not really sure they were branches—vines, perhaps, big around as her waist, twisted and entwined, and the globular fruit grew directly on the skins. Or barks? The skins, or barks, were an unhealthy-looking greenish-yellow. The fruits were black.

"Very nourishing."

Caught a thought from Gabriel: *If you say so.*

"And do these taste pleasant?"

"Try one."

"Yes—"

Gabriel! That hasn't been tested! It could be toxic!

"Umm, I note your intention, but no. What does it taste like to you?"

"Not like vegetable-based protein food. Thank the True God."

"I would like to know more about the True God."

"Well, it may be called Abundant God elsewhere, but we do not think it very *(chirp)*, as it is conceived there. Why are you interested?"

That word, she means "beneficent," I think . . .

A slight hesitation, as Gabriel absorbed Hanna's thought. "I am supposed to be a man of God among my own kind. It's natural that I should want to know whom you worship."

"Is your god not Abundant God?"

The conversation seemed casual, but Hanna was on the alert.

"I have not, really, been able to get any answers about the nature of Abundant God. I have met with a Holy Man that was, who seems to have gone on into some other place of the mind, and with a Holy Man that is, who told me of horrors *(chirp)* associated with attempts to prevent repro duction. I have not – "

Careful, Gabriel!

"—learned anything about the actual attributes of what is called Abundant God. I understand that Abundant God calls for war."

"We think those who say that are wrong. At least we wonder. And here we have no war."

Gabriel, ask her again . . .

"How did This Place begin?"

"That is unknown."

Nakeekt lies.

There were things along some paths that looked like untidy heaps of vegetation, as tall as Hanna. She thought they were probably—she pulled something out of the recesses of memory, an image or a reality she had seen, some agrarian settlement, even, perhaps, Gadrah—haystacks? Fodder for domestic beasts? Though they had seen none.

She was standing beside a stack, listening to Gabriel and Nakeekt—

"How do you spend your time?"

"Growing food, collecting food. Making things that look interesting—"

And some other things she doesn't intend to talk about—

—when the stack she stood beside set up a rustling. She glanced over absentmindedly and watched it extrude a meter-wide yellow—

"Oh, my God," she said. "Is that a tongue?"

"It is called the eat-everything plant. It is harmless, except to insects," said Nakeekt, "and careless small animals." This seemed an odd combination of prey, until Hanna lifted from Nakeekt's mind an image of the things' other, hidden "tongues," which were thin and flexible and strong and moved very, very fast. She stepped away quickly, and looked around to make sure she knew where all the stacks were. Kwek, she saw, was not in sight. She quested and found Kwek; but Kwek was only getting her own tour, and was not alarmed or agitated. There was nothing to worry about. If you didn't count Nakeekt's lies and evasions.

———

More hours, and they were not even at the middle of the long Battleground day. They were given slow, exhaustive tours of one huge building after another. Gabriel conversed, commented, asked polite questions. The people of That Place—Nakeekt was accompanied by others who came and went—recognized the questions as polite (translating as "not unpleasant"). "Interesting" was a freely used word, accepted as a compliment. Hanna said little out loud, but communicated with the telepaths on *Endeavor*, making her own comments. *Nothing but "interesting" translates. Not "beautiful," or "lovely . . ." "Colorful" translates. "Skillfully worked" translates.*

This Place is all gray cubes, just like Rowtt, only extending up not down, Hanna told them; she told Gabriel that too, and felt his disagreement, but she did not know why he disagreed until—eight hours into the visit, when Nakeekt said it was time for a meal—Hanna said that she and Gabriel would return to their landing craft to refresh themselves and eat their own provisions.

The pod felt confining, and Hanna thought of suggesting that they picnic outdoors, but the day had turned gray and she had conceived a dislike of clouds in her visits to Rowtt, so they ate inside.

"It's not just that they're not underground. They build in windows," Gabriel pointed out, explaining his disagreement, munching—his appetite had returned. His spirits were lighter, he was enjoying the day, and he enjoyed looking at Hanna. "And there were representational pictures painted on some of the walls."

"Well, yes, not very good ones . . ."

"You spent a night in Rowtt, early on. Your report said there was a place for you to lie down. A standard billet, you said? What was it like?"

"Very plain. No furnishings but the bed and a bench. A few shelves, empty. There were pegs on the walls, maybe to hang uniforms on, and a video terminal I couldn't turn off. None of those here."

"So what have you seen in these billets that's different?"

Hanna smiled. "You really are a teacher, aren't you? Let me see . . . the rooms Nakeekt said were occupied had uniforms hanging up—well, not really uniforms, parts of them, like they wear here. They were in different colors. Not exciting ones, but they're not gray. And . . . tables or desks," Hanna said after a pause. "Things on them sometimes, but I didn't look closely. Flowers, some fresh, in vases. Ceramic, I think, and rather nicely made. Some dried. A few growing plants in pots, close to windows . . . I can't think of anything else."

"Stones," Gabriel said. "Small stones with striking shapes or textures. And somebody was making what looked like a necklace, drilling holes in white pebbles and stringing them on a cord. There's a major conclusion to come to here. Nakeekt showed us a sculpted—whatever it was. Want to take a guess?"

"You do it."

"These people are inventing art," he said.

Gabriel reached for another sandwich and Hanna said, "You might want to save that."

"What for?"

"I think," Hanna said slowly, "we might be here a little longer than I thought. The pod has survival supplies, but the quartermaster didn't load much in the way of fresh rations. The original plan didn't call for much."

Gabriel gave her a look of incomprehension.

"How many times did I alert you to a lie?" Hanna said. "Or something Nakeekt was ducking, or some background context that wasn't clear but that she didn't intend to talk about?"

"Why do we have to know about those things?" Gabriel said. "There's an alternate society here, it's obviously tolerated by the mainstream; why do we need to know the things they want to keep to themselves?"

Hanna said, "I have never before felt that we ought to go away and leave a society alone. *Completely* alone. Here, I do. I think it's got something to do with the things Nakeekt isn't talking about. Come outside, Gabriel." She got up, restless, scattering crumbs.

They went out and Hanna sat down on the ramp, in no apparent hurry to go anywhere. She said, "The storm's coming. Look at the sky."

It was flat with cloud; there would be no more sunlight today. The overcast was solid, and the earlier slight breeze had picked up. They sat watching what they could see of That Place, buildings mostly, each housing two to five hundred people. The peaks looked chaotic from here, as if a new decision on the optimal pitch of a roof had been taken with the construction of each one. One building of four stories was structurally unsound and was not used, Nakeekt had said (telling the truth). It was made of sand-colored stone that might have been quarried on this isle, but the doors were sealed with some flat white synthetic substance. Hanna had looked at the covering closely enough to know that it could not have been manufactured here. Evidently relations with Rowtt or Wektt included some tangible aid. The ground floors of the buildings were given over to storage and food service and workshops of many kinds. There were spaces on some of those levels that they had not seen. Those areas were more of the same, Nakeekt had said — but about that, she had lied, at least in part, and Hanna wanted to know what else they held.

She was silent for so long that Gabriel finally glanced at her and saw that she had turned her head to look at something.

"What is it?" he said.

"See that? That little thing?"

"Can you be more specific?"

"That smaller building. The one that just about qualifies as a cottage. I think it's a domicile of some kind. The others, I don't know, storage for agricultural tools? But someone's in that one, I can feel it—I think. They haven't shown us any of those."

"Maybe they just haven't gotten around to it yet."

"Let's go look."

But they had only gone half the distance when Nakeekt intercepted them. "Are you rested?" she said. "Come, then, I will show you the fields."

And the interception had not been an accident. Nakeekt had seen where they were headed and deliberately steered them away.

———

After a while Hanna found her feet aching for the first time in her life and mentally moved her next A.S. treatment—it would be the second—higher on her list of priorities. Thinking of that, unfortunately, made her think of Starr Jameson. She had not had one single, solitary instant of trouble with the anti-senescence procedures. One slightly uncomfortable but mostly boring afternoon and she had, even at twenty-eight, found herself with more energy, needing less sleep . . . no immune system crashing, no hydra-headed carcinomas springing up overnight, no brain cells disrupted, no arteries bursting, no coma that might be the final sleep, no painful struggle back to health, pushing it with dangerous haste because it would not do to be out of sight too long and risk knowledge of this weakness spreading—pitting a little more time against early death, over and over again—

Concentrate, she told herself—

At least she felt herself, for the first time on Battleground, part of a natural landscape. Surfaces that were bland masses of green from above, and hidden from view at ground level by blocks of buildings, opened into hills and valleys; mist softened the farthest hills. Green, close up, was touched with gold or deepened toward blue, and stooped Soldiers dug tubers from the ground and brought up shapes of russet or ruby red, bright purple or orange. The "fields" were rough clearings, and here, finally, there were birds, looking much like their Terrestrial counterparts, though with long flickering tongues instead of rigid beaks. They did not sing audibly, but sometimes they opened their tiny mouths and appeared to sing; Hanna could only suppose their songs went past the limits of human hearing.

Nakeekt was proud of the agricultural arrangements: *These red ovoids, you see, must be milled and then boiled because in their natural state they are poisonous. We make them into cakes. The cakes have different tastes, depending on what is baked into them. We send them sometimes to Wektt and Rowtt. The mill is behind the warren where I live . . .*

Tracks of carts and barrows showed in long grasses, winding toward the settlement. So one of those smaller buildings, Hanna thought, is only a mill. That one, at least, is no dark secret.

What is brown-red is pleasant roasted, and is often eaten with a substance that we make from fruits gathered on an island we go to when tides permit. We have not been able to grow those fruits here, so far.

They walked on a path beside a stream—another curve of the stream they had seen at first—and found a rough pavement of rocks laid for footing in a hollow that was always muddy.

Sometimes we walk these paths, alone or with others, only to look at what is around us, because it is pleasant.

Hanna had seen Kwek in one of the clearings, bending to harvest russet tubers among waist-high stalks with silver-edged leaves, learning about the work done here. Kwek had looked up with the expression that meant a smile, her ears had waved gently, and Hanna had waved a hand and turned away. She wondered if they were telling Kwek lies, too.

The sun was low when they got back to the settlement. Hanna and Gabriel had been awake for more than twenty-four hours, and the long afternoon of walking weighed on them.

"Perhaps we will return tomorrow," Gabriel said to Nakeekt.

"I think," said Hanna, "we will stay here tonight, if Nakeekt agrees. Perhaps there are rooms where no one lives, where we could sleep."

She felt Nakeekt's uneasiness at the proposition. But Nakeekt said, "Very well, if that is what you wish."

———

This time they brought food from the pod and ate with their hosts in a communal hall. It was the first time Hanna had seen so many Soldiers together in one place. They did call themselves that, Nakeekt said when Hanna asked. The word, with all its connotations, meant "people" on this world. *But they look different from those in Rowtt,* she thought, but could not think why.

After the meal she and Gabriel were shown to rooms on the sixth story of the warren where Nakeekt herself lived, rooms near hers, but they did not go to sleep right away.

———

Gabriel satisfied himself that his room—billet, Soldiers called it—was clean, that the padded platform was comfortable enough, and the lightweight spread on it sufficiently warm for a night in this climate. But he had a question for Hanna, and he found his way into a hallway and around two corners to her door.

Come in! she said when he tapped on it, and he did not hear audible words but felt that odd sensation of something inside his skull being touched, and a ripple of melancholy he thought might have brushed him along with the words, and he pushed the door open and went in.

There was a small electric light next to the bed-platform, its glow just visible in the fading light from a large window. Hanna sat on the edge of the platform, a corner of the coverlet held carelessly in one hand as if she had started to pull it back and forgotten what she was doing. Her face was serious. Gabriel had come to ask why they were staying the night—she had not offered a reason to Nakeekt—but the question vanished. Hanna had taken off her boots and trousers and loosened her hair. Her shirt was long enough for decency—barely. One leg was tucked under her, but the other extended lightly to the floor, gleaming and graceful, and abruptly she was not his First Contact expert, she was not the iconoclast whose work he had studied with admiration; she was sensuous and provocative and unbearably desirable. He couldn't find breath to speak, and then he could, and the words came out of some other man's mouth: "Would you like some company? I mean would you like, would you like me to stay with you tonight?"— aware of the ambiguity of the words, the ambivalence of his hope.

He understood much later that the long following pause came because she was bringing her mind back from some-where else—from a bed she would not sleep in again. At last she smiled. It was a gentle smile. She got up and came to him and kissed him once, quickly, on the cheek, and then she just shook her head and said, "No. Thank you."

"Ah."

He did not know if what he felt was regret or relief. He said humbly, "I'd be terrible at it anyway."

"Why do you think that?"

"No experience," he explained.

But she shook her head again. "You have a loving and generous heart, Gabriel. That's a fine starting place. Besides, I would tell you exactly what to do."

He was halfway back to his own room when the last words sank in—*I would tell you exactly what to do*—

The images they conjured made him dizzy all the rest of the way, and he forgot that he had never asked his simple question.

So once again Hanna lay on a platform in a place inhabited by Soldiers, weary again, and again it was night. Rowtt, a place of war, had never slept. There had been Soldiers awake to greet the first team of human observers; sentinels and workers had gone about their tasks, crèches demanded care regardless of the hour, and only the Holy Man, whom she now knew as Tlorr, had clearly been preparing to rest. Here the community's day wound down like an Earthly day toward night.

She had not had time to think of the difference between people here, and people in Rowtt, that she had felt upon arrival. Now she could attend to it, and her circumstances, like a refined mirror of that first night, showed her the size of the difference.

These might as well be a different species, she thought. *It does not seem right to think of them as Soldiers. They are more like Kwoort than like the others. But not like him either.*

She was not in trance, and could not, she thought, afford to go into it. It had one thing in common with the stimulants she could not use: the body would eventually claim what was owed, and the press of fatigue she felt was too strong to be safely put aside for long. She meant to do some snooping before the night was over, but not telepathically, and meanwhile it would be good and advisable to sleep. There was plenty of time; the inhabitants of This Place would sleep hours longer than she would. They might post a sentinel or two, but those could be perceived and avoided. There had been no locks on any door she had seen, and opening those she was curious about should be a silent matter.

For now she lay passive and receptive, catching fragments of thought like snatches of conversation, waiting for sleep to come when it would.

The first inner voice she heard was Gabriel's, and he thought of Hanna. She should have veered away quickly from these private thoughts, but surprise held her for a moment: he was thinking that he understood now how carnal love might be holy. *An act of worship,* he thought, *worship of creation and the Creator, a reflection of His love*

She wrenched away, inexplicable tears coming to her eyes. *What a strange man,* she thought. *First I'm an occasion of sin, now a potential—what? Partner in worship?*

Ego tempted her to see what else Gabriel thought about her; loneliness tempted her to stay near his amiable spirit; simple humanity tempted her too; she was so convinced there was nothing good on Battleground that she did not want to let herself slip through Soldiers' thoughts again. She had been in This Place long enough to know that the idyll Nakeekt wanted her to see was illusory. And secrecy implied fear.

This opportunity could not be wasted, because there might not be another, and she emptied her mind again.

Thoughts of roughing out more clearings. Difficult: there is a limit to the number of metal tools available, it will be some time until more can be procured from the mainland, and the wood of some trees is so hard that other tools are made from it, and can only be worked with metal.

One of the differences she had sensed came into focus:

problem-solving was not a habit of the average Soldier of
Rowtt. And this was not one exceptionally aged or clever
mind; several of Nakeekt's people were discussing it.

Thoughts of sounds-in-an-orderly-sequence-of-tones.

Someone thought of music. They were inventing that
too.

Someone despaired. *It's near, now's the time to withdraw
and prepare, better than my friend's fate, he waited too long
and now waits to die in numbness, in near-sleep, would he
wish mine or Nakeekt's to be the hand of death—*

Hanna sat up. She found herself shivering, she had seen
a flash of the structure Nakeekt had kept them away from,
where someone waited for death. Why? How? She wanted
to probe. Reminded herself it would not be wise. But
who—?

She lay down and composed herself again. The room was
silent. Slowly she moved toward sleep. More flashes, but
now they were perceptions of Soldiers performing routine
tasks, concrete, simple, and relaxing.

*Cleaning dishes in great openwork baskets passed from
one vat of hot water to another, mixing batters for cakes for
the morning meal, tipping food scraps from barrows in outdoor enclosures for compost.*

It was soothingly reminiscent of duties she had performed in rotation for her House.

But now there was:

*A clear image of lowering, yes, a polished coffin, into
flames, and smoke rising to the sky until the coffin and what
it contained fell to ashes.*

Not burnt offerings, then, but cremation. She would remember that, but sleep was winning. Now, finally, Nakeekt—
no, not Nakeekt, it was one sitting next to Nakeekt and he
was talking with Nakeekt in a low voice, as if afraid of being
overheard by outsiders— *That would be us,* Hanna thought,
but drowsily. They talked of a room, and hidden things in
the room. *And I think I know where that room might be, and
that is why we stay the night,* Hanna thought as she slid into
sleep, and hours passed.

She woke with tears in her eyes and didn't know why they
were there. She might have been dreaming of something

left behind: D'neera, Michael. Innocence or Mickey. Even Starr. There were so many possibilities.

Whatever it was, the novelty of this bed, this deeply dark room, brought her quickly to wakefulness, and she dried the tears with her sleeve and made herself think of what she had to do.

The chronometer in her com unit told her it was late evening on *Endeavor*, and past the middle of the night at This Place—far enough past it for the Soldiers here to be in the deepest sleep of the night, as they proved to be when she opened her mind. Many of them were dreaming, too. She had not touched many dreaming minds from space, and she had not realized then that the very rarity of it might be significant. Here, apparently, it was the norm. That must be significant too.

Dreaming is a function of the unconscious mind, as we understand the term, she thought. *What is the connection?* And now too, more alert than she had been when dinner was taken, she could pin down the visible difference between these people and the common run of Soldiers. She had seen them most often with the organs she called past-eyes open. It was the exception in Rowtt, but not here. *There is a connection there too,* she thought.

She slid off the platform and dressed in the dark. Her room was on the perimeter of the building. Gabriel's, the first one they had been shown to, opened on an inner hallway, and did not have a window. There was a steady sound of rain from outside, and she went to the window and looked out. She had given up hope of avoiding another Battleground storm, but this one was gentle. The breeze had died with nightfall and the rain fell soft and straight; it was not lashed by wind, and she heard no thunder. From here she could make out the fronts of two more buildings, and angled portions of two others. Light shone in a ground-floor room in the warren that faced her window, and there was another light farther away, on the third or fourth floor of a structure partly visible. The lights shimmered behind the quivering curtain of rain. That didn't mean no one was awake in dark rooms. She had filled some of the time on *Endeavor* with more reports, and her guess that Soldiers saw well in the dark had been right.

She stood there for a little while, deciding where to go.

She dearly wanted a look inside that cottage where someone's friend might wait for death, but the conversation
sensed just before sleep seemed more important. She had a
clear impression of the interior areas Nakeekt had avoided,
and when she turned from the window she thought she
knew exactly where she was going. She would get wet, and
it worried her. It meant she would leave a trail of footprints
when she entered the building she wanted.

She had brought a light from the pod, slipping it into a
pocket when Gabriel turned away because she suspected
that the planning of furtive acts would trouble him. She put
the translator on, though she hoped she would not meet any
Soldiers tonight, and folded the coverlet over her arm; her
white shirt would glow like a lamp to Soldiers' eyes, and she
would cover it with the darker substance. She found the way
from her room to an interior well with zigzag ramps piercing
the center of the building, and moved down them to the bottom silently, using the light at its dimmest. She heard no
doors opening and sensed no one stirring. The ground floor
was uninhabited, but she and Gabriel had gotten a thorough
look at it. This warren housed none of the hidden places. She
veered into a side hallway, well away from the major en-
trances, and went out a lesser way into the rain.

The buildings were set in no regular pattern. The one she
had left was at the outskirt of the settlement; she wrapped
the coverlet around her and made for one nearer the center,
keeping close to walls when she could, the light off now,
mud making for uncertain footing. The coverlet kept off the
rain and she was glad for it; the night was not as warm as
she had expected.

Once inside the warren she had targeted, though, she
stopped. She had used a subsidiary door here as well, and
coming in this way, she could not get her bearings. The door
opened into a hallway that showed her only other doors in
the darting beam of light, one facing this entrance and others to its left and right. One of those might open onto yet
another hall leading to an area Nakeekt had bypassed, but
she could not guess which one.

There was nothing to do but open door after door: at
first, the wrong doors. The spaces behind them were small.
Some of the things in them were homey and familiar: one
held towels and clothing and other things made of fabric,

folded neatly onto shelves, seen quickly in fast, thin stabs of light. She thought they had all been made here; there had been looms in the work areas, electric-powered. She left the coverlet there, where it did not look out of place. In another room there were neatly racked tools; in another, broken ones tumbled helter-skelter, waiting for a day of repair that might not come. Some dust, in that room. Unused furnishings were wedged into still another so tightly that the door closed, when she closed it, with difficulty. (She could almost hear someone say, human-like: *I am sure one more will fit...*) More dust, there.

It did not seem like anything she shouldn't have been allowed to see.

She had started with the first door, the one that faced her, and moved down the hallway to her right. When she was done with that direction she went back and opened the door just to the left of center.

She stepped into a much larger space.

Every door on this end of the hall opened into it. She faced a series of tables, one long line of them, running the width of the room. When she went closer she saw that there was a parallel row of benches behind them. The tables and benches were identical to those in the hall where she and Gabriel had eaten with their hosts. They were without decoration, and there was nothing on the tables. Behind those, solidly built into the wall, were cabinets or cupboards.

Hanna went through a gap in the tables. Closer now, she saw that the cabinets were really ranks of shallow drawers, and they filled up all the back of the room, floor to ceiling. The bank was made of wood that gleamed almost black. She thought it was painted, but when she touched it, changed her mind: the wood was not painted but worked to a smoothness that mimicked polished metal, and the design was utilitarian in the extreme. A single hollow was set into the face of each drawer, the depression topped with an overhanging lip to use for a handle. It had the pure beauty of simplicity.

She chose a drawer at random. It was so well made that the pressure of one finger drew it out.

Inside lay a few sheets of something that might have been paper, though it had nearly the flexibility of fabric. She took the sheets out and put them on the nearest table, and turned them over one by one. There were five in all. One had half a dozen lines of script on it; the second was almost covered with writing; the others were full, with a note at the bottom of each that might be a numeral.

She could not read any of it. She had not learned to read what Soldiers thought worth writing down.

She put the sheets back and began moving along the columns of drawers, opening them at random. Some were half-full, none more than half, and others were empty; most held sheets of the vellum-like substance.

She picked one that was covered with script top to bottom and looked at it carefully, holding the light close. The lines were not evenly spaced, and other telltales made it evident that the text had been written by hand. Using what?—she looked back at the tables and saw that drawers were built into them too, and when she opened one, there were writing implements and small ceramic containers that gurgled when she picked them up. Ink, she guessed.

The pages were important, she supposed; they must be, if Nakeekt was anxious to keep them hidden; but why hidden from alien visitors? They were unlikely to have to do with war, which apparently did not engage the people of This Place; but whatever they were about, if they were important enough to hide . . .

Hanna sighed, and called to the D'neerans on *Endeavor*. They were awake and they were bored. *Get Communications to stand by for incoming data*, she told them, and ordered the communicator to another mode. She began transmitting pictures of page after page.

After a while she heard: *They say some of it's in code!*— Joseph, gleeful at a mystery.

Then tell them to decode it!—she wondered if she was wasting her time. Possibly, but it was worth some effort to find out what was written here. Battleground's people were such a puzzle that she wanted a solution any way she could get one. She tried to remember if any alien species had ever been so opaque to her understanding before, and decided none had. Of course, she had never before pretended not to be a telepath, either, and had found other beings generous with their thoughts—

She checked the chronometer, decided she could risk an hour or two for this task and still have time to investigate that outbuilding—and a boring, repetitive task it was, too,

turning pages, sending images, more pages, more images—
time went on.

Glitch.

Nothing serious, the telepaths said. A short interruption
in reception, Metra radiating fury, someone would pay for
this. *Stand by,* they told Hanna. She shrugged, kept storing
images.

Gabriel's communicator uttered a series of plaintive beeps.
He was not, for once, sleeping like the peaceful dead, and
the sound woke him. He took the thing off and talked to it,
and it informed him that it was working just fine, thank you,
except that at the moment it was not able to communicate
with anything. Shaking it did not make it change its mind.

He sat up and looked around. The displays were indeed
working, and gave enough light in the windowless room for
him to find the switch for the electric light like the one next
to Hanna's bed. The room seemed comfortless, and he suddenly realized that if the communicator was not working,
he was cut off from *Endeavor.*

He got up and started for Hanna's room. Maybe she had
woken at a cascade of tones, too, but maybe not, and if she
did not know what had happened, probably she ought to
hear about it.

Going through the dark hallways was unnerving; he
powered up the communicator's light source just enough to
allow him to shuffle along. The halls were completely silent,
like the abbey's in the small hours of the morning, and the
swish of his footsteps sounded very loud. At Hanna's door
he called to her softly and then, when there was no response, more loudly; he knocked on it, too, and finally
opened it. She was not there. There was no sound except a
susurration of rain outside. He turned on the light and
waited a little while, wondering if she had gone to use a
communal lavatory, but time passed and she did not return,
and he began to worry. There was no cover on her bed and
no sign of it in the room, and he could not imagine what had
happened to it or to her. The communicator still did not
respond; there was no one to ask.

Could she have gone back to the pod and tried to raise *Endeavor* from there? Possible.

He told himself: *She does not need my help, whatever she is doing.* He had never faced real danger in his life, if you didn't count Kwoort and the Holy Men, and they had not attempted physical harm. Hanna—he knew now—had been born with or developed an immediate, sometimes deadly response to danger and had survived several different kinds of it.

All the same, she was alone. And protectiveness was built into Gabriel.

He left the room and went to find her. He would try the pod first.

He was pleased to discover, at the head of the downward ramps, a switch on the wall that turned on lights all the way down, and he moved down the ramps with confidence. He remembered to turn the light off when he got to the bottom, thinking belatedly that it would be good if the people here were sound sleepers.

Nakeekt was not.

She woke when she heard Gabriel knock on Hanna's door, and she heard him call out words that obviously were not meant for her because they were in the not-Soldiers' language. The creature must have disengaged or put aside his translating device, she thought. She heard him go into the female's room. Kwek said the not-Soldiers mated frequently (but without issue, somehow) and did it most often in sleep periods, so perhaps that was why the male was abroad.

Nakeekt was nearly asleep again when she heard him come out. He did not start back to his own room, but came past Nakeekt's door.

She got out of bed and peeked out.

When the male was out of sight she stepped into the hall and looked toward the female's room. The door was open and the light on, but when she went and looked into it, the female was not there.

Farther down the hall, a wall lit up with reflected light. Nakeekt knew from long experience where it came from. Why was the male going downstairs?

Her own room was directly above the main entrance. She went to the window and waited. Soon she saw the male go out and stand hesitating in the rain. Then he started walking slowly in the direction of the airfield. Were they going to fly away in the middle of the night without telling anyone?

Kwek was her chief source — her only source — of information on not-Soldier behavior. Nakeekt went to wake her up.

Joseph: *Translation's starting . . .*

Oh . . . ?

Arch: *It might be history. Can't be sure yet. Did you begin at the beginning of this archive?*

I don't know where the beginning is . . .

She pictured the wall of drawers, showed them where she had started. In the middle, approximately, and she had not attempted to reach the topmost rows. She showed them how she had proceeded, and how far she had gotten with recording images she had not been able to transmit.

Bella: *They write left to right, like us, and that's how we tend to order objects. Go to the farthest left stack of drawers and start again there.*

All right. Is it informative?

It might be.

And you've learned . . . ?

Nothing, yet. We'll need to analyze. Get as much as you can. How much time do you think you have left?

Hours yet if I stretch it . . .

It would mean more tedium, but she might have found a prize.

Kwek, unlike Nakeekt, was deeply asleep. Her usual assignments, even as record-keeper, had one obvious disadvantage — she might cease to survive quite suddenly, possibly being chosen for that fate arbitrarily (she suspected that was the case) — but they did not involve any stooping or bending or the pulling up of tough plants. Her hands were sore, her back hurt, and she had seldom been this exhausted. The whispers about That Place had not included such details as how the inhabitants obtained food.

She woke quickly enough when Nakeekt, without gentleness, shook her.

"Is it an attack?" she mumbled, not remembering immediately where she was.

"There is no attack, but the not-Soldiers have gone out into the night. They never said they were going to do that. Why did they do that?"

"I don't know," said Kwek, memory reviving.

"Do they mate outdoors? Do they go out to do it?"

"How would I know? I have not known them long enough to know their customs." She remembered one of the interesting conversations. "Arkt said they do it on the spacecraft, though. They don't have to be outside."

"I'm going to look for them. I want you to come along."

"All right," Kwek said.

She did not know it was raining until they got to the doorway to the outside. Kwek had not had to go out in the rain for some time, and she balked.

"Why do we have to find them?" she said.

"I want to know what they are doing. They might find out some things I don't want them taking back to Rowtt or Wektt."

"They might find them out anyway," Kwek said. "The male said some of them can see thoughts. He told me when I was on the spacecraft. He said it's not like reading orders, but they can find out a lot that way."

"Oh, can they," said Nakeekt.

"Where are we going to look for them?"

"The airfield, first. They might be going to communicate with the spacecraft."

"They don't have to do that either. The devices they wear on their arms do that. Anyway, the female can talk to some of the not-Soldiers on the spacecraft with her thoughts. Gergtk told me."

"Is that so," Nakeekt said, "tell me more," so Kwek did, and they caught up with Gabriel just as he got to the pod, surprising him, because he hadn't heard them behind him over the sound of the rain.

———

I'm getting sick of doing this, Hanna said.

The telepaths consulted the true-humans.

Captain says keep going. Signal's back. Everything you've got is in. Captain says get more.

I don't care. I want to sit down and rest my eyes.

Which she did. The room was peaceful. She ached; some of the muscles in her legs hurt from the long hours of walking. *I am not getting enough exercise,* she thought to herself; she had been focused on Battleground so long and so hard that she had strayed from her customary ways of staying strong. And she was tired in spite of a few hours of sleep, as she seemed to have been more of the time than not since her first tentative contact with the thoughts of a Soldier.

She tried to let her mind rest, too, shutting down directed thought, drifting. She was not likely to fall asleep, seated on this hard bench. She drifted into—

A howl—

Tearing through the dark, tearing to the sky.

I am ending I leave behind nothing nothing nothing

Then it stopped.

She leaped to her feet, shuddering, breaking out in sweat. Her hands shook. *What was—*

It had not been audible, it had been the anguished cry of a sentient mind. Not human, though: a Soldier. She reached out, still shaking, seeking,

And sensed Gabriel, broadcasting confusion and alarm, plain to any telepath in the neighborhood. But Hanna was the only one listening.

She called to the telepaths, *I thought you were monitoring Gabriel!*

Why would we? He was asleep!

Gabriel first—she grabbed the sheets that lay on the table and put them back in the drawer where they belonged, trying to stack them just as she had found them, trying to still the tremor in her hands, trying at the same time to see what Gabriel saw. Nakeekt and Kwek were with him, and it was apparent that Gabriel did not have his translator, because Nakeekt was talking and he did not understand her.

But where—?

He was wet, soaked, in fact, and in the dark. Outdoors, then, in the rain.

Gabriel! Where the hell—?

He barely perceived the question, but she got an answer anyway, a fleeting impression of the pod at his back. She shoved the drawer shut, left the room, and headed into the rain at a run.

She circled around, moving as fast as she could without light, to make it appear she had come from anywhere except the vault of documents. Mud and grass squelched underfoot, but the ground was level, and she did not fall. She heard Nakeekt's voice and turned on the light, and for an instant saw Nakeekt leaning toward Gabriel, her face almost in his, both their faces shining with rain, Nakeekt shouting as if that would force the not-Soldier to understand her. Nakeekt whirled as Hanna ran toward them and called out, "Are you going to pretend you do not comprehend either?"

"I understand. Do you not see he is not wearing the translation device?"

"Why not? Where have you been? You have been spying!"

If Gabriel could not talk to them she did not have to worry about matching his lies—or about, knowing Gabriel, any inconvenient truth he might offer.

"We lost contact with our spacecraft," Hanna said, improvising. "I came outside to see if that would help. I suppose my fellow-Soldier did the same thing."

"I don't think so," Nakeekt said. "Kwek says you can do that with your, your, head?"—she was uncertain, but she had the fundamental fact right.

Who had been so unwise as to tell Kwek about that?

"The ability is not reliable," Hanna said, thinking fast, suddenly detesting all the lies she had told, such a non-D'neeran thing to do. She had told more of them on Battleground than she could remember telling anywhere.

She swung around at something—

All for nothing nothing—

—an echo, a fainter mental howl, from the shadow that was that cottage, but she could not see it through the rain, and no one else could hear it, and Nakeekt could not be ignored.

"Is that what you have been doing? You did not say much while we walked yesterday. Is that what you did all day, look at what was in *my* head? Did you do it all night?

I should not let you go! Do you think we could not kill you here? We have weapons!" Nakeekt had reverted to active duty rapidly. "I will not let you go!"

Now she had Hanna's full attention.

We have done you no harm and wish you no harm, she said, straight to Nakeekt's mind, in words that did not register but with sense and conviction that did—finally, pure truth. And Nakeekt knew it was.

Nakeekt's breathing organs swelled and shrunk, swelled and shrunk. Hanna had seen Kwoort's do it too, the rapid breathing that accompanied strong emotion, as in humans.

"You may not wish to do harm, but others would, if they knew more! Are you going back to Rowtt? What are you going to report there?"

"We will not go back to Rowtt," Hanna said. "I think we will be ordered to Wektt, although we have not been told that certainly. But we will not report anything we have seen here that is not already known. You sustain yourselves, and you do not fight. That is known, is it not? So that is all we will say. I know nothing more except that there is much you have not told us. And I will not say that."

She was not connecting with Nakeekt's thoughts now; you could not be evasive in thought without its being perceived, and she was evading the whole truth. She expected to learn more—if not here, in This Place, then from the texts she had transmitted to *Endeavor.* Whatever they were, their nature was different from those that had made it into the datastream Communications had tapped at the start. The telepaths on *Endeavor* had told her that, not in the primary content of their thought, but in how they perceived what they saw of the first translated passages.

Slowly, Nakeekt's respiration began to ease. She was silent for a time. Gabriel had the sense to be quiet and Kwek did not say anything either. Finally Nakeekt said, "Go, then. I will let you go but I want you to go now."

This suited Hanna. She did not want to be around if anyone connected a missing coverlet with an extra one found near the vault.

"Very well," she said. "Kwek, are you coming with us?"

"I would like to go back for a while," Kwek said. "I would like to talk with Arkt again—"

"No," Nakeekt said. "You can't go. You have made your

decision by coming here with these not-Soldiers. If you go
with them and do not come back, if you go to Wektt with
them, *they* might not say 'There are things in That Place
nobody knows,' and soon they will go away, but you will not
go away and one day you might say that—no, you cannot be
allowed to do that. You will stay. And you," she told Hanna,
"will not come back. If you do I will think not-Soldiers want
to war with us, and I will make sure you do not survive."

Nothing! someone howled.

Hanna did not answer. She would not promise not to
come back. Nakeekt had not shown or told her anything
that could tell her who it was that screamed *Nothing!* in the
night or why it happened, and she wanted very badly to
know.

Chapter IV

"CAPTAIN METRA TOLD ME in confidence, before the conference, that Lady Hanna has a personal agenda."

"Hanna? An agenda?"

"That she's angry. With you, the captain said, for breaking with her."

"She's the one breaking with me, but nobody seems to believe that . . . well, I suppose it might follow that she's angry anyway, about something—but what agenda does Metra think she has?"

"Failure of the mission, was the implication. In the captain's defense, Hanna has made no secret of her dislike of Battleground."

"That is a concern, but for a different reason. Hanna has impeccable instincts. She was convinced Zeig-Daru knew of our existence and was implacably hostile long before we knew anything about Species X. I wonder what unconscious awareness she might have about Battleground that she hasn't yet been able to articulate. But she wouldn't sabotage the mission for any reason. Hidden agendas and Hanna don't go together. She would simply refuse to go on."

"She's not in a position to overtly refuse. Or am I wrong?"

"Well—admitted. She isn't. Given that, the protests we've already seen were predictable, but she will continue to comply. I would not take anything Metra tells you 'in confidence' very seriously. How did it go, otherwise?"

"It wasn't pleasant. I might have exerted more control than I did, but I wanted to get a sense of how these people are with each other. It was not like overseeing traders in F'thalian luxury goods . . ."

It had been a wrangle, the air thick with accusations, but blessedly short.

Metra to Hanna: "You had no business spying. What do you think this is? An Intelligence and Security operation? Did I authorize you to do what you did? Did anyone?"

Hanna to Metra: "You were eager enough for the results!" And then, gouging where she knew it would hurt (and drive Metra wild with fury): "I thought *Endeavor* was a first-class operation. First-class operations do not lose communications capability!"

Get out of my sight, Metra thought, and Gabriel said, "It was my fault. I should have trusted Hanna and stayed where I was."

"It was not your fault," said Hanna, and put her hand on his.

"You're right about that," Metra said. "It was your responsibility to inform him of what you were going to do and what he ought to do—but you didn't tell anybody. If you were one of my crew I'd confine you to quarters for the duration." She looked at all she could see of Evanomen, his head and shoulders, floating in the air. "I assume we're going to Wektt. I recommend assigning real humans to the contact."

She did not even bother to use the conventional term, "true-humans."

Evanomen finally said something. "It might have been a mistake to hide the nature of the telepaths."

"That was Bassanio's idea. A serious misjudgment on her part."

"I do not recall anyone disagreeing," Hanna said. She briefly considered pointing out that it had in fact been Jameson's idea, decided her own mistakes could do without examination, and went on. "Kwoort was determined to the end to enlist us in his war. Nakeekt has things she wants to conceal, and if she had known what I was when we landed she wouldn't have shown us anything. Downplaying it's still my recommendation, when we go to Wektt."

"It won't matter," Metra said, "because there won't be any telepaths in the picture. I don't want any of them involved."

"I'll take it under consideration," Evanomen said, meaning, intentionally, nothing.

"Captain Metra is speaking from prejudice," Hanna said. "Leaving my people out of it would be idiotic."

"You *are* confined to quarters," Metra told Hanna.

"I can't agree to that," Evanomen said with more authority. "I want Hanna working on the new data with Arch Harm."

"Is that what Starr wants?" Hanna said, just to goad Metra, responding to Metra's fury in spite of herself. Damned if she was going to say "Commissioner Jameson;" she felt like throwing the affair in Metra's face, over or not.

"Try not to make a disaster of it," Metra said. "The equipment you left behind was valuable. So far your accomplishments are confined to running away from Kwoort every time you saw him, and getting thrown out of That Place."

And the best Hanna could say to that was, "Well, not *every* time."

Chapter V

KIT MORTAN HAD ORDERED the telepaths out of Communications as soon as Hanna left the surface. He said he would let them access the new documents from the auditorium if that would make them go away, and that was where Hanna found them. Gabriel trailed after her, radiating guilt.

"Look at this," Bella said, depressed. Kit had supplied raw material, not the ongoing translation, and the masses of text were incomprehensible.

Hanna looked at the moping Bella, sighed, and called Kit to ask for the translation. He hesitated, but only a little; whatever Evanomen (or Jameson, or Zanté) had said to Metra about keeping Hanna informed had not lost its power, and the translations appeared quickly. She flipped through pages, muttering "next" and "next" and "next," watching them flash past.

"Metra said you should have sampled randomly," Joseph told her.

"It's a shame she didn't say that at the start. We'll have to settle for randomly sampling the samples, I guess."

She paused—at random—and read:

The one who told me about this, told me it was something that stood twelve hundred summers ago. But I don't think so. He had heard it from someone who heard it from someone who heard it from someone else and they are all dead and so is he and time is a mysterious place. He said it was a tall structure in the form of a cylinder. How tall, I said, and he said, oh, as tall as the sky. I don't think that is true either. He said there was a three-sided cap on it that was made of gold. I said where was it and he said on Continent Three, but Con-

tinent Three died three hundred summers ago. I said what was it for. He didn't know. He just remembered the shining three-sided cap standing into the sky. I said if you remember it you must have seen it. He said no. So there might have been something tall with a shiny top on it on Continent Three but what he described was only in his mind and no Soldiers have ever constructed such a thing so maybe he made it up and it did not exist at all.

"Does this qualify as history?" Hanna asked Arch.

"Damned if I know. I never did get a look at what Kwek called Rowtt's historical records, whatever they were. Aren't they supposed to refrain from keeping records? Isn't that the command of their god?"

"You talked to Kwek sometimes," Hanna said to Gabriel, politely not mentioning one of the things he had talked to Kwek about. Nakeekt would never have guessed that anyone could be telepathic if Gabriel had not told Kwek. "Did she say anything about them?"

More guilt. "I didn't ask. I just kept her company, told her a little about us, tried to make sure she was comfortable. She said she was. I prayed, once."

"Did you? What did she make of that?"

"It didn't translate," he said. "I think 'our daily bread' did, but not much else."

"'Our daily ration of vegetable-based protein food'?"

Hanna set the page-turning program on automatic. *Flip. Flip. Flip.*

"What was that about code?" she said.

"There was no code," Arch said. "It was an hypothesis that fell apart right away. It was just that this has untranslatable words and phrases that never showed up in the original datastream. Linguistics is trying to interpret them by context. It'll take a while. I'm going to get some rest," he added. "It's getting late."

"It is?" said Hanna, her sense of time skewed to uselessness. It would be near the end of the night at That Place, its inhabitants in the deep sleep before dawn, and she was so out of synch with *Endeavor*'s cycle that she forgot what chronometers said as soon as she looked away from them. She was not the only one who felt unbalanced; everyone was fading.

"I guess I'd better rest too," she said, the endless Battle-ground day still weighing on her. "We might be busy when Linguistics is done."

She expected to sleep well but did not. She dreamed of Jameson explaining that Michael Kristofik had not died after all. The explanation was obscure but sounded reasonable in the dream. A burst of joy and relief filled her, she was whole again, and blindingly happy.

She woke up and began to cry. She found herself, almost as if this was the dream, not that, stumbling through corridors until she came to Gabriel's door. When he heard her voice he came at once, rumpled but slowly waking, and held her as she clung to him and wept, trying to think of her as a mourning child, like so many he had known, trying to ignore the warmth of her in his arms.

Finally she could tell him about the dream.

"I know," he said. "I had some like that when I was a kid, after my parents died."

"But it's been so long! There are days when I don't think of Mike more than a hundred times, why is this happening now?"

"You're grieving again," he said, "because you're grieving for another man. Only this time the loss is your choice. Are you sure it's the right one?"

"It is. God help me, it is."

She was calmer now, though the deep weight of tears still choked her chest. The calmness fell apart when she turned toward the door and Gabriel said rashly, "Michael's not dead, you know. There's something after this."

"No, there isn't," Hanna said, too full of sorrow to answer with tact.

"How do you know that? There's an infinity of universes, and do you think the Creator of them all, who holds in His unimaginable thought the dance of every quark, can't shepherd a single soul from this life to another?"

Hanna turned back. She said, "And do you think every telepath who ever lived hasn't cried out for someone lost? True-humans do it too, but not like we do! We would know the scarcest, scantest trace of someone we love if a trace survived! I've felt people's minds when they died, not just

Mike's. They don't go anywhere. They just stop. What do you think I was doing," she said, the tears burning now and turning to rage, "for weeks after Michael's death? I did not speak, I had no time to speak to living humans, I was searching for *him*! I looked everywhere, I looked to the farthest stars! He wasn't there, he was gone, he's gone forever. Don't try to give me your pathetic comfort," she said savagely, "it doesn't work—"

Because you're grieving for another man, Gabriel had said, and as she went away she thought of the risk Jameson took with every venture into A.S. *I could not bear that loss,* she thought, and then she thought *But it shouldn't matter any more—!*

And now going back to sleep was out of the question, and she went back to her quarters and dressed and went wearily to Communications, trying to still the clamor of competing voices that were all hers.

Hanna did not much care for Kit Mortan, *Endeavor*'s chief of Linguistics. He reminded her somewhat of an animal native to the world of Primitive A. Her focus when she was there had been on an arguably pre-sentient species of that world, beings who had begun to fashion rough tools and use a vocabulary of perhaps two hundred utterances—whether these should be called words and phrases—language, in short—was a subject of debate, because there was scant evidence of syntax. Following these beings and scavenging their kills were creatures that the earliest observers had taken for large snakes, some as long as three meters, until someone noticed they traveled on numerous boneless appendages which carried them so smoothly and rapidly that the animals appeared to glide across the ground. It was not Kit's appearance that made her think of them, however; it was a certain sinuosity of movement, a scavenger turn of mind. She had known him on Earth; she had spoken of him to Jameson—

(*"He smiles too much."*

"Did you not, just five minutes ago, tell me that I do not smile enough?"

"He smiles when he has nothing to smile about. You don't smile even when you want to, when I can feel it in you like a light you're trying to hide—")

Kit had said something and Hanna had not heard it. She had a vague impression that he wondered whose mind she was reading and hoped it was not his.

"Sorry," she said. "What was that?"

"I said, the most striking feature of this material is that it has nothing in common with the broadcast datastream we picked up coming in. Look at this—"

It is evident that all we make must be sustainable through the efforts of our own hands. I am insistent that it be so. There are those on the mainland who wish to help us, they have promised the building of a power center. All of us see the danger of coming to rely on this center. Who is to say that the mainland might not one day be destroyed as other continents were destroyed? Then we would not be able to maintain the center and for safety would have to close it.

She said, "Is this about the reactor that supplies power for That Place?"

"I would say that's very likely. The material seems to fall into a couple of broad categories. Most of it's about the day-to-day functioning of That Place. But some of it looks like secondhand oral history, things somebody besides the writers said that the writers set down. Facts, legend, speculation—"

"'Writers,' you said. It was written by different people? You can tell by how it's said?"

He looked at her with pity for her ignorance, as if the answer should be obvious. "We can tell because a number of different handwritings appear. We'll be doing another set of groupings based on who actually wrote what. It's too bad you didn't get a sample of this Nakeekt's handwriting."

"You might have one," Hanna said. "That bit about the power center—Nakeekt might have written that. She founded That Place."

"I thought she said it wasn't known who founded it."

"She lied," Hanna said.

Kit looked at her skeptically. She ought to be used to this by now, her testimony mistrusted and discounted although her knowledge came from direct experience while true-humans' came from deduction and analysis of the written or spoken word. She *was* used to it. But she no longer wasted energy trying to convince them.

"Why don't you," she said, "load what you've got into a reader. No, two readers. One for Arch."

"You want to take them with you?"

"Yes. If that's all right," she said, thinking, *Why the hell else would I ask?* And felt an unaccustomed twinge of shame; she was irritable because she was still jumpy from a dream and its aftermath.

She said, lingering on purpose so as not to be too abrupt, "It's all in here?"

"Most of it. The categories are just a first approximation, remember. We've just started on the coded material. You'll get that next."

"Arch said there wasn't a code after all."

"First we thought there was, then we thought there wasn't. Now we're certain some of it's in code. Not much, and it won't take long, once we get to it."

She took the readers and went to wake up Arch, who was sleeping alone, for once. "Time to work," she said, and handed him a reader. They looked at the outline of categories at the start.

"I'll take the oral history," Arch said with enthusiasm. "I liked the way that first passage went—'time is a mysterious place.'"

"You know," said Hanna, "I wonder where they got 'mysterious.' It doesn't feel like a Soldier word."

He found the passage and jumped to a note. "It wasn't in the original datastream; Kit's never seen it before. There are a couple of variations, and here are the contexts, next layer down, and the rationale, next layer—they're not rushing this, Kit practically wrote a paper on this one word. Want to see?"

"When did he have time? That passage was translated by the time I got back to the ship."

"The notes are from an hour ago. He must have made a guess that worked out."

Hanna nodded. She did not have to like Kit to know that he was marvelously good at his work.

She looked at the list of categories. Many of the entries were routine. Food preparation—cross-indexed to native food sources, appearance of, cultivation of (with a note: *Refer to Zey*), cross-indexed to fiber sources, cross-indexed to fabric, production of, cross-indexed—

"Listen to this," said Arch. *"A Warrior of three hundred and one summers told me this that she saw herself. It was before I came here and she has not come here yet but maybe she will. It was in the far north region of Continent Two before the destruction and it was on a mountain. There was there, untouched, a place where Soldiers could once sit outdoors, the area having gone without attack for a long time. There were some tables and benches there and the tables had canopies over them as if to provide shade when it was warm, but it was not warm when the Warrior was there. The tables and benches and canopies were all made of metal painted red, and the tables and benches were of mesh so the rain would drain through them. When the Warrior was there it was cold and there was snow piled high on all of it and there were icicles that hung from everything. The Warrior said the sun came out while she was there and she was surprised. She said it was pleasant. She kept saying this, as if she were trying to find some word better than pleasant, and she said that it made something happen inside her when she saw it. She did not know what it was. I think now that I know what it was, I think she meant it was beautiful, the light on the clear bright ice and the white snow and the red standing out warm, and that she wanted to look at it a long time. At that time I had started to have sensations also that I did not understand and I had started to dream. So I asked her if she dreamed but she did not know what I meant, and when I explained, she said no. But I think one day she will start to dream, if she survives."*

Hanna said, "Where did Kit get 'beautiful?'"

Arch checked the notes. "Context. That was another of the untranslatable words, meaning it never showed up in the datastream. You'd expect 'interesting' there, wouldn't you?"

"I wonder," Hanna said slowly, "if they're inventing new words."

Arch consulted more notes. "Kit thinks so. What he translated as 'beautiful' started out, he thinks, as the highest degree of 'pleasant' with additions of 'interesting' and a reference to the visual. It must be a long word in the original."

Hanna looked again at the outline of contents, began to navigate through the text, skipping around. Much of it read like a series of handbooks, detailing directions for everything from maintenance of looms to forecasting weather. Here was a tide table (insanely complicated, with three moons—and Metra had proposed landing a boat?) and descriptions of ocean currents between That Place and a numbered island, the number meaning nothing to Hanna.

She began to key searches for specific topics: Reproduction. Young *(n.)*. Offspring. Infant. Child. Abundant God. God. Holy Man. Demon. As an afterthought she added: Facilitators.

Nothing.

She sat back with the reader in her lap, frustrated. How much more material was hidden at That Place? Could Kwek somehow be enlisted to obtain the rest? Could Metra be induced to let her go back to the surface and sneak it out herself? She wanted to talk to Jameson, who was now in a position to make Metra do any damn thing Hanna wanted her to do, if he approved.

She tried to put a call through to him, but it was night where he was too and he was not to be disturbed—according to the family home in Arrenswood's capital city, which had not been programmed by Jameson himself but by his relatives, and which told her she was not on the list of people authorized to reach him at any hour. Her name was on one of its lists, though. The list was called: "Banned."

It hurt. She was surprised to find that it hurt very much indeed.

Jameson was not asleep, though the house didn't know it. Mickey had tottered into his unlocked room in silence, and somehow, silently, gotten onto the bed, and started to cry abruptly, miserably, and loudly.

What the hell . . .

Mickey, with a fine sense of timing, waited until Jameson managed to sit up and order lights on before scrambling into his arms and escalating to howls.

Thera appeared in the doorway, still getting into a robe, hair wild. The adults exchanged astonished looks over Mickey's head. It was not possible to exchange words without shouting; Mickey was too loud. The Dog appeared behind Thera, assessed the situation, charged the bed and threw itself on Mickey, licking the child's face and whimpering with concern.

"Nightmare," Thera said a little later, when Mickey had gotten some words out between diminishing sobs.

"He doesn't have nightmares."

"He just had one," Thera pointed out.

Mickey had accepted a hug from Thera, but clung to Jameson. The boy's tearful face was uncertain now, but no longer afraid. Something, evidently, had been pursuing him in his dream; it had been large and threatening; that was all he had been able to tell them.

"Why now? What did he have to eat tonight?"

"Nothing unusual. He's in a new place, he's had a lot of excitement, and there's been a certain amount of tension, especially this evening—"

Jameson's sister had come to visit, and she had had a lot to say about his caring for Hanna ril-Koroth's son. He had not allowed her to say it in Mickey's presence, but even a child as young as Mickey must sense something malevolent in Portia's look, and what she had not said, at their brief meeting. Along with an unattractive satisfaction, because she too had heard the rumor Jameson bitterly regretted starting.

Later—because sleep did not come back easily—he lay awake and wondered what Hanna meant to do with Mickey when she returned. D'neeran children were raised less by a parent than by a community; the kinship group was only part of it. Surely she did not intend to swoop into the house on Earth, scoop up Mickey, bear him off without warning, and keep him to herself—she who was half a stranger to her son, her image and voice still familiar thanks to hours of holo and video recordings, but the memory of her scent and touch surely fading.

No, he decided. Hanna had changed, certainly, but she had not changed that much. She would let Mickey keep his ties to Jameson and Thera; she would not force him to break them.

Which meant, of course, that she would have to retain some tie to Jameson too, whether she wanted to or not.

We'll see just how finished it is, he thought.

Chapter VI

H ANNA HAUNTED LINGUISTICS, begrudging Kit's people their deliberate pace. She wanted to go home—back, at least, to Earth. She wanted Mickey. She wanted to make arrangements for a life.

Ejected from Linguistics, she tried to kill time: tidied her quarters, took exercise, took a meal, tried to think about Battleground, thought about Mickey instead.

Fretted.

It can't be that hard to break a Battleground code. It must be simple, a cipher made by minds and hands, no match for our computers.

"No," said Kit, "it wasn't hard. But it's strange stuff."

"Strange meaning—"

"See for yourself. I suppose you want a reader? Maybe two? What happened to the two you had? Don't lose them like you did that translator, all right?"

Hanna looked at him closely. He wasn't even trying to keep the smile pasted on his face. He was jittery. The content of the deciphered material had done that to him.

"Just send what you've got to my quarters," she said soothingly. "I'll load it from there."

I will begin by saying that I have little hope of accomplishing the goal toward which my intention is directed, because it lies beyond the farthest reach of hope. It does not even resemble a desirable dream, except in one way. Those of us who dream have in common this experience, that sometimes we do not remember we have dreamed, but later when we are awake, something moves in our minds and there is almost the memory of something we dreamed, but when we try to remember it we cannot. It is painful, to see those wisps for a moment and feel they were of unmatched importance but to see only their shadow and know they have disappeared for all time. My goal is just like that. It is impossible to reach. It is only a wisp.

I do not know if anyone has ever attempted this goal. Probably someone has. Possibly many have tried it. If they have their efforts are gone and they have left no trace. I do not think my effort will leave traces either, and I do not know why I am compelled to attempt this goal which is impossible to reach.

It is to make a history of the world. I would like to write down how we became what we are and what we have done and what has happened to us.

Nakeekt, Hanna thought, after she had read only a few words. *It can be no other.*

No such history can be complete. I do not even see how I might find a structure for it. I question and continue to question each person who comes here, asking what they know. It is not even what they know, it is what they have heard, that someone might once have known.

Those who come here are unusual. They have lived long, some so long that the end-change comes soon after they arrive. After that my questions, not hopeful to start with, find no answers at all. But I mine the memories of all of them, for all the time they have left. Everyone here has lived long enough to hear whispers, and those on whom this place has exerted its call, are those who have wondered about the whispers and so remember them.

The whispers are suspect. Some reach so far back that there are hints no God made us, but not-Soldiers that were like but unlike us. Even when the origins of the whispers might be closer it is impossible to be sure how much weight to assign to any of them. It is impossible to guess when the events or conditions the whispers are about occurred. It is impossible to assign them a chronology, although sometimes I try. Sometimes, if I let my mind travel over them enough, I can create structures. But perhaps the structures are not true.

There are the rocks, like the one Kteengt brought which I

keep in my billet, that bear impressions of the remains of animals no one has seen alive. There may be many such stones, because there are stories of others from mines, and stories about bones turned to rock that were found when emplacements were dug. Some were seen by a Soldier who is here, as I write this, in the forty-fifth summer of this place, because he was one of those making such an emplacement. I make the assumption that rocks are old, therefore these bones are old. So that is the start of a structure. Some questions do not even have traces of answers, there is nothing on which to build the start of a structure. There is nothing left to say how we know even what we know, who the Soldiers were that made the first data machines or where they were. A Warrior came from Wektt bearing an object found in the desert surrounding that place, it is a small flat object made of a substance no one else there had ever seen nor has its like been seen by anyone else here, even though all of us have many summers. I cannot break it and I cannot melt it. Who made it? When? There are not even any whispers of the makers. There are no stories.

And when there is a story, often I cannot even say that the subject is approximately old, or approximately new. I do not know how many people have passed a story from one to another or how twisted it has been in the passing, or how much of it is missing. Few survive long enough to come to the change of thought that brings them here, and for every story that someone comes and tells, thousands upon thousands must be lost forever.

There was a break in the text. Kit had added a note: *No additional references.* Hanna looked further. There were images of the original pages, in miniature; what she had just read took up three of them. She had made no effort to assign pages to groups based on which drawer they had been in, but she guessed that what she had just read was no more and no less than the pages contained in one drawer.

After a while she scrolled back and read again: *Some reach so far back that there are hints no God made us, but not-Soldiers that were like but unlike us . . .*

That was what the physiologists thought had happened.

And if they were right, just where were the makers? Did they plan on ever coming back?

I hope not . . .

She thought of calling Jameson. Remembered she could not reach him and turned back to the text.

Kit had noted, at the start of the next page, that the script was that of another person. What came next settled a chill deep in her bones.

I began to think of what could be done when I had only one hundred and fifty-seven summers. I had already begun to dream and I had begun to have strange sensations, but I did not know how unusual that was, so early in life, until another hundred summers had passed. I was learning, at that earlier time, how to fix injuries. It seemed to me then and it seems to me now that much more could be done to fix people's wounds, but there is always cohort upon cohort waiting for battle, and people do not mind dying, so it seemed acceptable to me that it should be so. It is acceptable to me even now, as long as our numbers multiply so enormously in the year of a single summer that soon everyone would die for lack of nourishment if we were not always at war. Without it we might feed on one another. It is said that has happened, although it is attributed to the influence of the Demon, and it is said the Demon's purpose is to gain so complete a victory that fighting must cease, so that all of us must turn to consuming one another.

In the year when I first began to wonder if it might be different, I was part of a troop that was ordered to Continent Three, which then was under the control of a power with which Rowtt was at war, as we were at war with Wektt, indeed we were all at war with each other. We were given the task of finding and destroying certain aboveground settlements. There were many everywhere at the time. There are fewer now, and no settlements of any kind on Continents Two and Three.

We marched across Continent Three an entire summer. My unit had heavy losses and when we were recalled, only two or three besides myself had survived the whole time. But as fighters died they were replaced by others and we continued to carry out our orders.

Near the end of this time we came upon a small town that was different. It was not on the maps provided to us and we found it by accident. There were three hundred Soldiers but there was not even one crèche, and the get lived along with the Soldiers and Warriors until they reached the time of their own breeding. It had not grown by more than fifty Soldiers within the lifetimes of those who lived there. Our scouts captured and brought back a Soldier from there who told us this unbelievable thing. I was interested in this unique settlement, and I was senior enough then in spite of my youth to have killing the Soldier delayed so that I could ask him questions.

He said that the time for mating rarely came for them and so the facilitators did not often come, and when they did, there would be only one or two issue. He said Soldiers had lived there for many summers and it was believed that only one Soldier and one Warrior had come there and started the place. It was believed that something was wrong with those two, because the facilitators seldom came from the start, many infants died at birth or were born dead, and also many born alive were carried to barren places and left to die soon after birth because they were not right, while others died within a summer or two although the reason was not apparent. This still happened, down to the present day. So the settlement had grown only slowly, though it had been there for a very long time.

That was all he said. I don't know if he could have said more. Our Commander was impatient to move on to settlements that were on the map because those were the ones we were ordered to destroy, and the Commander told us to kill the Soldier and all the rest of them. So we did that, and continued to the next target designated for attack.

In the years that followed I thought often of those Soldiers, and wished that I had found a way to examine their bodies, because it seemed obvious to me that in some way they differed from the rest of us, although there was no difference in their outward appearance. I knew that because I saw plenty of them dead, and had my part in killing them. Therefore it must follow that the difference was internal.

Although I could not examine the bodies of those Soldiers that were different, I had innumerable opportunities to examine the bodies of the normal. I do not know how many Soldiers I cut and fixed as the years went by, nor how many I killed, sometimes in battle but sometimes while I cut them, who might have recovered by themselves. In some years the orders were to fix only those whose wounds were slight and let the others die or end their lives myself. When those were the orders we were quick to dispose of the dead and there

*were few wounded to fix, so I had little chance for deep study
of the system of reproduction. What I knew at the start of my
service, what was taught to me then, was superficial. It was
sufficient to make a Soldier able again to fight or work. If I
wanted more knowledge of internal structures, I had to get it
myself, and keep the real object of my study secret, because
everyone knows what happens to those foolish enough to
wonder about reproduction if those coming to the time of
mating find out what they are doing. So I told no one what I
wondered.*

*The years that I spent, studying! Ten summers might go
by between one slight fact and the next, and always there was
the likelihood that I would not survive to find another, so that
often I wondered why I sought the knowledge anyway, and
at other times the desire seemed so hopeless that I tried to
forget it. But I could not. When I knew my breeding time was
coming on me, each time, I could not keep from trying to list
and order the sensations I felt that preceded the coming of
the facilitators. I could not write those things down. If anyone
found such a list, such an ordering, that would be enough to
draw retribution from those who were in their time, and
worse, from their facilitators, so I only kept the lists in my
mind, and sometimes I thought even that was dangerous, and
if someone looked at me in an unusual way I feared he could
see my thoughts. But even that could not keep me from wondering, though as the cycle progressed I would forget for a
time, until it was finished. I do not know why. At those times
and those times only my mind would hide its own knowledge
from itself and I do not understand why, unless somehow I
knew I could not be at war with myself, I could not both be
breeding, and at the same time think about not breeding. But
each time when it was finished, each time I emerged from a
crèche, the memory would return, and I would take up the
task again, hopeless though I thought it.*

*A time came when there was no fixing at all, there was only
killing, and I gave up my studies because there was no opportunity to pursue them. I did not think the opportunity
would come again, but it did, because some one of the powers
of the time developed a new weapon that destroyed with mag-
nificent effect. This weapon was used to wipe the power that
held Continent Three from the face of the world, and next to
do the same thing to Continent Two. Both Wektt and Rowtt,*

on *Continent One*, survived. But in those places too countless cities were destroyed with this weapon, and Soldiers were no longer so expendable as to be dispatched even if their wounds were severe, and fighting even ceased for a time.

When it resumed, for a time, there was a period when I had my chance. I became more skilled than any other Cutter in repairing injuries inside the body, teaching myself to bring life back to bodies that would have died. Inevitably the range of injuries was broad. Inevitably I had the opportunity to study the effects of the removal or disabling of this organ or that. I did this for half a hundred summers, even though the recovered were sent away to duty as soon as they were able, but I faithfully sought them out, as many as I could find of those who had suffered injuries to the organs of reproduction, because I thought the answer would lie there. But those, I found, still experienced, in the customary cycle, all the sensations that caused them to desire breeding. The facilitators would come even though a Soldier could no longer successfully join with a mate, and if it was a Warrior who could join physically but could not produce infants, that did not matter either. Still the facilitators came, and still she mated, though she bore no issue. When I determined that that was the case, I did not think I would ever find the answer I looked for.

It was a coincidence that finally gave it to me. A Soldier came again who had been sent to me at an earlier time, after more than forty summers had passed. He had been badly wounded the first time, near the end of the years when my orders were to spend more time fixing than killing, and in order to restore his lung to partial functioning I had had to remove much damaged tissue. One portion of this was an organ that is seated next to and almost behind the lung, but which has no obvious function. It is only an irregular lump of flesh, no larger than the first joint of the thumb, about the same shape, a dull yellow in color. Because of its location there is rarely an opportunity to find out what happens if this organ is removed. An injury severe enough to damage or destroy it is almost always an injury that damages the lung or a heart or all of them together, and causes death. This Soldier had not died, because of my skill. And his injury the second time was not serious. This was my good fortune, because in that year, if he had been dangerously wounded, his surviving fellow Soldiers would have killed him before they left the *scene of battle. The population had made up for those lost when the great weapon was used, and again preserving balance was the determining criterion, though I did not understand that was the reason until I came to This Place. But he did not die this time either, and when he reminded me that I had fixed him before, I remembered him with my other eyes, and I remembered everything I had done then.*

I said it was good that he had had more summers to survive, and that he had remained in health for so long. He said he was in health well enough, but he missed mating. He said that his time had never again come on him, that he had not since felt the desire to breed. But this Soldier had suffered no injuries to the organs of reproduction.

It came to me as if a great light shone out what the answer must be. It came to me as instantly and completely as if the Soldier had said it to me aloud. I cannot describe that moment. I stood there and looked at him. He did say something, talking I think of the pleasures he missed, for which he considered the immense labor of the crèche small return, but his speech seemed to come from a great distance away.

I hurried him out and walked back into my rooms in a daze. Could it be so simple after all?

I looked, then, among those who came to me, for Soldiers and Warriors with injuries that would give me the chance to remove that organ from them. I thought I would do that and then follow them all the rest of their lives or mine, follow them without ceasing regardless of my own survival, to see what happened.

But only severe injury would give me that opportunity, and as I have said, that time again was one in which those severely injured were left to die or were killed. I had myself come to an age when the cycle had slowed. But it would be many summers before it stopped altogether, and so I decided to attempt the surgery on myself.

I am old, I come to the change. But here in This Place where it is safe to say these things, I will write down exactly what I did—

"The courage . . ." Gabriel murmured

Hanna slumped wearily on his bed. Soldiers knew about anesthetics and the Cutter simply said he had used as much as he could, but he had to have remained conscious, and the pain he inflicted on himself must have been excruciating. He had not dared to ask anyone for assistance, and what must it have been to guide his own bloody hands by their reflection in a blood-speckled mirror?—while he manipulated his own organs, watched his own lung swell with breath, observed his own heartbeats?

Gabriel shuddered. She saw his eyes move faster, skimming over the cold clinical description of what the Cutter had done.

"He removed the 'organ of calling,'" said Gabriel. "A gland, I guess, from the description. Does it secrete pheromones, maybe?"

"Something like that. Something that attracts the facilitators. Whatever they are, whatever they do."

"There's nothing here to say."

Finally Gabriel looked up. She felt the question he had not asked yet.

"Yes," she said. "The ending's strange."

"Nothing, he says . . ."

"Read the last part to me. From where he says *nothing*."

Gabriel looked down again. "'It is all for nothing,'" he read. "'I am old and my end comes soon and it is all for nothing. I have seen others at the end-change but I do not think I learned this way of thinking from them. I think the end-change comes to us naturally and it is only seeing the truth. That it is all for nothing.'

"And there," he said, "it ends."

Nothing nothing nothing . . .

He went on, "This could explain why they don't reproduce at That Place, if they all undergo the surgery. But where do they do it? What with? Nakeekt didn't say anything about medical care, medical procedures."

Hanna's eyes were on Gabriel, but he had the uncomfortable feeling he wasn't what she saw. He continued talking—to himself, he suspected.

"Of course, she wouldn't show us if she thought we might give the others in Rowtt and Wektt even a hint of what they're doing."

"Armies," Hanna murmured.

"What?"

"Armies of the breeding," she said. "Descending on That

Place. Massacring everyone there ... There were a lot of areas we didn't get a look at. There's somebody in that little building. Remember? The one we could see from the landing field? Where Nakeekt didn't want us to go?"

He saw shadows under her eyes that should not be there, and it was not just the immediate lack of sleep that had put them there. He was beginning to feel exhausted, too. Everything about Battleground was oppressive. It was a weight on his thoughts, and how much more heavily must it weigh on Hanna, who had shared the beings' minds?

She said, "I wonder if Kwek could tell me who it is. What it's about."

"What are you talking about? What's that got to do with the text?"

"I don't know. Whoever's in there was crying out and he was saying *Nothing, nothing* . . . I'm going to ask Kwek."

"How? Well, she still had a com unit—"

"I shouldn't need it. I mean, I'll try telepathically first. In trance."

She got up and went out without another word. It did not occur to him until the door closed that she might intend to attempt the contact immediately. He went after her then, and caught up with her in the hall.

"Yes," she said to the unspoken question. "Now."

"Aren't you supposed to have somebody with you when you do this?"

"This isn't official. Metra's not going to know about it. Mission protocol be damned."

"Let me be with you, all right?"

"If you want."

"What am I supposed to watch out for?"

"Well," she said, "if I come out of it and beat you up there might be some cause for concern."

He looked for a smile, and didn't see one.

It was morning, and Kwek thought she would be given something to do. She had been told there were many tasks, and she would work sometimes at one, sometimes at another. She could do other things, too, interesting things. But first Nakeekt and some others would talk with her about the things she remembered, and that was what they did immediately after the morning meal, when the sun had risen only a little. *What is the first thing you remember*, they said. *Do you know where you came to life. Do you remember the crèche where you were born. What were you taught about Rowtt. What were you taught about the Holy Man and what were you taught about the Demon. Did you ever see the Holy Man of that time up close, do you remember what he looked like. Do you remember the first prayers you were taught.*

"This is an interesting experience," Kwek said. "No one has ever asked me questions like this before."

"No," said Pritk. "They don't do it anywhere else. And we will teach you to ask questions yourself, if you don't already do it."

"Oh, I do. I asked a lot of questions in my last posting. But I only asked them of myself."

"What was the posting?"

"I am Wektt's keeper of records."

Their ears curled: intense interest.

"That is wonderful," said Nakeekt. (Kwek did not know the word she used, as she had not known the word "dream" the first time she heard it.) "Did you study the records?"

"Oh, yes."

"Were you discouraged from doing that?"

"I didn't tell anybody. Nobody asked about anything except which cities were growing fastest and how many Soldiers were in them, and where the battles were and what were the numbers killed in them. That was all I was supposed to put in them. I put in other things, too, that I heard. But I didn't tell anybody I was doing that."

There was a moment of respectful silence.

"Why did you do that?" Nakeekt said.

"In case," Kwek said, "the next record-keeper—had—interest . . ."

She was fumbling; the words did not sound quite adequate.

"I think you mean, in case the next one cared," Pritk said. "What?"

"Cared. That is a new word," said Pritk, and the enlargement of Kwek's vocabulary began.

Gabriel watched Hanna. After a while, belatedly, he started to examine his motives, but he did not stop watching her.

He wanted to be with her in case something went wrong, but did some secret part of his mind whisper that here was a defensible opportunity to be alone with Hanna and just look at her?

He thought he ought to pray and he did not want to pray. He wanted to look. There was no harm in looking.

Rationalization.

His stomach began to growl. He had no idea what time it was at That Place, but it was lunchtime here.

Sublimation.

He was restless after five minutes. "Not much can disturb me in trance," she had told him, but he was reluctant to move too much. He found that his gaze had moved from her profile to the swell of her breasts. He tore his eyes away and they fell on the holo of her son. He looked at the child's exquisite, laughing face and tried to imagine Hanna with Mickey, this prickly woman's jagged edges softened, her eyes bright with love.

I will not think about that, he thought, but it was too late. He wanted her to look at him with love too; he wanted to take the still figure in his arms. When she came to him after the dream of her own beloved he had seen how broken the invulnerable woman could be, how broken she had been; he wanted to tell her she could be whole again; he wanted to be the one to make her whole. He didn't want much, he thought, and then the massive wave of what he really wanted broke and drowned him: only everything.

Not just Hanna, as lover or friend, but everything else out here too: another life. One that he might have had anyway, if a family hadn't shattered with his parents' early death.

So he had made a decision after all, and it seemed that it had already been made months ago, even years ago, and recognizing it was all that had happened now.

Hanna's breathing changed, and her eyes opened and turned to him. The blue gaze was remote.

She knows I want her and she is angry—

"No," she said. "I can't imagine being angry with you. I don't even know what you were thinking," which sounded preposterous to Gabriel; surely he had shouted it. She seemed to shake herself a little. "I couldn't find him," she said. "I think it's a him; I'm not sure."

"Him?" It seemed to Gabriel that he was talking very slowly. Certainly his thinking was slow. "Not Kwek?"

"Kwek's busy," Hanna said. "She was with Nakeekt and some other people, but they were all talking at once. There was too much going on. If I could understand what they were saying . . . I told everybody to learn as much of the language as they could, but nobody did. Including me. I will not make that mistake again."

She sighed and rose from the floor in one fluid movement. If she sensed his agitation she had chosen to ignore it.

"So I looked for whomever they've got locked away in that little building, but I couldn't find him. 'Nothing,' he kept saying, 'nothing.' I think it's someone in what they call the end-change. Not many Soldiers make it to that stage. And if this one is there but hasn't yet gone over the edge . . . this is probably the only chance I'd have to talk to someone like that. I need to go back one more time. If Starr will let me."

Hanna did not even try persuading Metra that a return to That Place could be productive. She thought of hijacking the pod and dismissed the idea. Not as immoral or even unwise; as impossible. *Endeavor* really was a first-class operation, its security impeccable. She would have to try to convince Jameson.

Contacting him, however, proved impossible. This time it was not the Arrenswood house's doing, but Metra's. While Hanna was at That Place Metra had unearthed a regulation that was ironclad, from Fleet's perspective, or at least she pretended to think it was:

You are authorized to initiate communication with the director of Alien Relations and Contact, and no one else. The director summarizes reports to his superior, the commissioner in charge. Commissioner Jameson is no longer the director. Mission protocol. No exceptions.

Jameson had approved the principle—months ago, when it ensured that Hanna could reach him without interference from Edward Vickery. He had probably not thought of the implications since. That left Evanomen, who (Metra had informed her) had been appointed director as soon as Jameson was sworn in as commissioner.

He'll never agree, Hanna thought, but when his harried

face appeared she saw something like relief come into it and revised her opinion. He said immediately, "Did you know Norsa is trying to learn Standard?"

After a moment she felt a slow smile begin. She could just see her friend Norsa of Ell, whose tentacular fingers tied themselves in knots when he was frustrated.

"He never said anything about it to me. But I haven't talked to him since I left Earth."

"I just did. But you couldn't call it a conversation."

The smile got wider. "How is he? And his grand-selfings?"

"I have no idea. Naturally I asked, but I couldn't understand the answer. I'm not sure he understood the question. He would *not* use the translation program. Can you talk to him? I do think he said something about your courtesy in learning Ellsian. Is he being courteous in turn? That would be typically Uskosian, wouldn't it?"

"Oh, very typical!"

"Do you think you could convince him he has no aptitude for languages?"

"I can't talk to anybody but you," she said, and explained the regulation. "I can't even talk to Starr unless he initiates contact."

"That has to be changed. What if I'm not available?" Evanomen evidently did not intend to put Hanna on a personal unlimited access list.

"Thank you . . . Give Norsa my regards when you speak to him again," she said. "Tell him I'll go to Uskos myself and teach him Standard, if he wants."

"Would you?" Evanomen said, and stopped short, perhaps remembering that now he could order Hanna to do just that.

"Of course. If I'm ever done here," she said. "By the way, there's a source of information I'd like to contact, but I need to go back to That Place to do it. Secretly, I mean; a quick midnight visit to someone who's sequestered from the others. I don't think Captain Metra will approve it without your authorization or Starr's."

Evanomen frowned at her. Her tone had been casual and she made sure her face was guileless.

"Starr's rather busy," he said.

Hanna discovered a developing talent for improvisation.

"This person might be able to give us some background on the documents we've got. And I suppose we're going to Wektt soon, and then we'll be focused on what's there. I'd like to be finished with That Place first."

"This would be you and Gabriel Guyup?"

"Just me. I don't think Gabriel has the—aptitude, to use your word—for secrecy."

"How long would you expect to be down there?"

"An hour maybe? Less?"

He wanted particulars, which Hanna made up on the spot, and said he would give her a decision later. She was not hopeful, but half an hour later Metra interrupted her belated lunch with a summons and started by saying, "I don't know how you did it, but—"

Hanna had a hard time keeping her mind on the rest of it because she was thinking: *I did it by misdirection, manipulation, in short, deceit. I'm turning into an excellent true-human.*

Chapter VII

THE BEST SHE COULD DO to be invisible was dress in black.

Endeavor had come openly to Battleground, gifting Soldiers with images of human society, hiding nothing. The pod did not even have a camouflage program for its white skin and *Endeavor* carried no secretive devices to make a human body blur from sight; personal proximity shields were manufactured not for spying but for casual anonymity in public spaces, and in any case were based on the parameters of human vision and might be ineffective with Soldiers. So Hanna's approach had to be as stealthy as she could make it. Her descent took her first to the sea sixty kilometers from the settlement, and she approached the clearing chosen for touchdown on manual control, hugging waves and then treetops when she reached land, ports opaque and exterior lights quenched. She kept the pod at a hover over the small field for a few minutes, probing with invisible sensors, in case an insomniac Soldier had decided to take a walk. None had, apparently. She did not even know if the Soldiers of That Place ever walked abroad in black night.

Finally she let the pod settle into the clearing, killed interior displays, opened the hatch, and moved down the ramp. The air was warm and fragrant, and she hesitated, breathing in the night. She had not been alone on a planetary surface—no Soldiers, no Gabriel—since leaving Earth.

The seductive moment passed. The path to the settlement was clear, and she began to walk. One thing at least *Endeavor* had been able to provide: membranes covered her eyes' surfaces which moderated whatever ambient light there was, so that she could see without using a light.

They gave a silver sheen to her eyes that would startle an unprepared human. But a Soldier would not know it was unusual.

The path was not straight but was easy to follow. It was banked and the earth trodden down, and the rain had ended soon after she and Gabriel left, so the ground had drained and she did not have to wade through mud. She moved along it silently. She had gotten permission to carry a side-arm in case she met with a large predator, and kept her hand near it. Big carnivores seemed to be absent from That Place, and perhaps from all of Battleground; some might have evolved, but it was not hard to imagine that centuries of war, destroying habitat, had driven them to extinction. The flora were another matter. The eat-anythings made Hanna nervous.

She had been walking for perhaps ten minutes when a flash of light startled her. It was peripheral and did not affect her modified vision, but she was horrified; it had come from her own hand, blue and beautiful and bright; from the ring that had become so much a part of her that she had forgotten it might give her away. She tried to wrench the lovely thing off but it did not want to go; she stood on the path for far too long, twisting it until it finally, reluctantly, allowed her to slide it from her finger. She stuffed it into a pocket and found herself sweating. Maybe it was the shock of knowing she might have blown her own cover with a stupid oversight. Or maybe it was fear of losing it if it was not on her hand.

Or maybe—and she realized then that she had felt exposed from the moment she stepped out of the pod—it was that since she could see everything around her, some ancient part of her brain could not acknowledge the reality that the rare moonless night hid her from other eyes. And, going full circle, it really did not. Even in this deep a darkness, a Soldier would see more clearly than a human would.

The realization paralyzed her for a moment, coming on top of the mistake with the ring and the tiredness that had underlain every thought and action for days. It seemed possible that the rest of the path would be lined with eat-everythings and their tongues would bind her like cords and wrest her to surfaces that would hold her as if glued while they began to digest her alive.

Hanna . . . It was Bella; it was a mental croon. *You're not alone. Just let me at those nasty plants!*

She relaxed a little, took a deep breath, and forced herself to move, though she clutched the sidearm hard. After a few paces it was easier, and Bella thought, *Some hero you are!* and Hanna finally smiled, herself again.

She tried to move even more quietly as she came near the cottage. Here it was necessary to leave the path and cross open ground; that part she did very quickly, in a sprint, and slipped behind the small building. She was alert for any attention directed her way, but sensed nothing.

If the cottage was meant to be a jailhouse, it was, at least from exterior evidence, a humane one. There were windows that would admit natural light, and at a height that would allow a Soldier inside to look out, though no face had showed at any of them when *Endeavor*'s spyeyes had been watching. They looked dark even to Hanna's enhanced night vision, meaning no light shone inside. The place was larger than she had thought, with four windows at the rear, from any of which she could be seen. But there was no reason to think the occupant was watching.

And now, so close, she saw that the view from the windows was partially blocked by interior bars. It really was a jailhouse, then.

She crouched, nonetheless, in a tangle of creepers, and listened for sound. There was a whisper of wind, so little she had not noticed it until now, and a faint rustle of leaves. A whir of wings overhead that made her start, a hum of insects, scarcely audible: that was all. There were not even any sounds small animals might make in the brush. If any animals were there, her approach had scattered them or made them go still.

She focused awareness then on the enclosed space in front of her, expecting the immediate sense of a sentient mind.

Nothing, came Bella's whisper. *Nobody there.*

It broke Hanna's concentration. She said crossly, *Go away.*

But she thought at first—pressing her cheek against cool stone, letting consciousness flow through it—that Bella was right.

A minute later she changed her mind. Bella was *almost* right.

Because the no one who was there had been a someone once. There was no strong marker of personality; there was less than she had felt in anyone, human or alien, infant or adult. It was certainly the mind of a Soldier. But this mind was a great, undifferentiated contentment.

It felt delicious to Hanna, stretched taut with tension for weeks.

She let herself ease into it.

Turquoise. And teal. It is water. It is above her, the transparent domed ceiling keeps it back. It is all around the circular room. And below the transparent floor. It is under her feet.

It shimmers and disorients. Shadowy halls open at angles, water-walled.

There is nothing but water and dim silence and moving light and shades of blue.

Soldiers—some of them, this one—lived under the sea once. She had not known that.

Not Soldiers, this one said. He had already been ancient when he came here. Those who made us. They say.

Who says?

There is a flicker of curiosity, so mild it is barely a trace. And no answer, but another question.

Who . . . ?

I am not a Soldier.

Then you are. One of those.

Those. Misty and ancient and vague. Does he remember, or does he only remember a story? A whisper? She cannot think of an adequate response. She can only show an image of stars, shimmering across black space.

They said.

Who?

They said.

Star-shimmer dissolves in water-shimmer.

That is what his mind is doing, too: dissolving.

So is Hanna's.

All that blue, trembling water, so peaceful. The other consciousness, so blurred, draws her in. It takes effort to rouse herself.

How many summers do you have?

She has not spoken aloud. But it is as if her voice echoes through blue spaces and turns to silver.

The only answer is blankness.

Her frustration nudges No One; he answers with irritation. And a little surprise: the surprise is at himself, finding that he is capable of feeling irritated. But nothing in this wordless exchange seems strange to him.

She repeats: How many summers?

Finally he answers: More than I can remember. Too many. They say.

WAKE UP.

That jolted No One—and Hanna, too; she stirred, feeling a cramped muscle in her thigh. She had said it to No One but Bella had said it to her first. It didn't seem that any time had passed.

You haven't moved for an hour. You're overdue.

Hanna tried to turn her attention to No One again.

Captain wants you back.

A little longer.

She said now. Conference scheduled. New orders.

Just a little.

Something's strange there—

You're telling me?

He's sick—

Not sick, I'd know—

Or drugged.

Hanna opened her eyes. Yes, maybe drugged. It had felt like a kind of unfocused trance. She felt it again, there on the other side of the wall.

Just a little.

She touched No One again, careful not to fall into that fuzzy cloud.

Are you drugged?

A slow affirmative bubbled out of the cloud.

Why?

Peace before dying.

Are you ill?

Peace before burning.

It was hard to get him to pay attention. She persisted.

H'ana, you must—

Just a little.

Pieces. She pushed and got pieces. Age, rage, disruption. Execution. Ceremonial cremation. Between the rage and the death, this time of being rendered harmless. The bits from his memory floated out of the cloud barely tinged with emotion.

H'ana!

She pulled away reluctantly from the cloud. She had to use her hands on earth and wall to get to her feet; she was stiff, and for a moment dizzy. Pieces of her own memories intruded, moments of contentment: Mickey sleeping on her lap as a tiny baby. Half-waking in the night, snuggling close to Jameson's warmth. A long-ago instant in a shadowy hall in Koroth, in her House, when she knew exactly who she was and that she belonged somewhere entirely—

Crying was inadvisable when nightsight membranes were in place.

One more question.

You are drugged. How was it you cried out in thought in the night?

She didn't expect an answer, but she got one. It was in pieces, too, and she did not put them together until she was back on the path to the pod. There was one day when the drug had not been given, the Soldier responsible for administering it distracted and forgetful, because the not-Soldiers had come.

———

"You're going to Wektt," Metra said.

They were alone. Given Metra's adamancy about keeping telepaths out of Wektt, Hanna could understand why she did not want her officers to hear this conversation.

"When?" said Hanna, not inclined to waste words.

"Around oh-one-hundred hours, Standard time. Full morning at Wektt."

Hanna tried again to get her mind around Battleground's attenuated day length. Wektt and Rowtt lay at approximately the same longitude, but in different hemispheres, with Wektt much closer to a pole than Rowtt. It would be the same time of day, or close to it, but there would be a seasonal difference. Early spring in Wektt?

"Do they know we're coming?"

"Of course. Communications made the contact a short time ago. It was much easier than it was with Rowtt. The Holy Man at Wektt already knows all about us."

"What do you mean, all? That there's a spacecraft in orbit, or what?"

"Who we are, what we look like. You were asked for by name, and the monk, too."

"What? How?"

"Their Holy Man knows you personally," Metra said, and Hanna said, "How could he?" and Metra said, "It's Kwoort."

And Metra actually smiled.

PART FIVE

WEKTT

Chapter I

*T*HERE IS RAIN ALL THE TIME. *When it is not snow. When it is not snow mixing with rain.*

Sometimes what falls is slush before it reaches the ground. And sometimes it freezes there and sometimes it does not.

I am told the weather is very good. For this time of year, before the summer, before the thaw. They say this is the thaw before the thaw, and after that it rains. When it does not snow.

I always thought, when I looked at the maps, that Wektt was at the end of the world. That was correct.

I have Quokatk's robes to put on, but I delay. I will go while there are still things to be learned from Quokatk I said, but Tlorr delayed and she delayed, I should have come last summer, no, many summers sooner than that, before Quokatk began to rave, and now he raves, like Kwler. Like Kwler, he requires Soldiers to bathe him, requires Soldiers to feed him. Except when he eats everything they bring to him in an instant, cramming it into his mouth, and screaming until more is brought. And then he has to be bathed again, and he does not always want to be bathed. It is that way with Kwler. It is not that way with Tlorr, but it will become that way. It will become that way with me.

I do not like the robes. They are the same as the ones worn by Tlorr, but they are also the same as the ones worn by Kwler. I looked at Tlorr with my past-eyes and thought that to become Tlorr would not be so bad, to become Tlorr as she is now. She is more careless now, it is true. But in most things she still listens to Abundant God. Holds to her duty, maintains the balance: Some crèches to move aboveground, to be destroyed at the proper times, and the disarming of Tvakst is projected so that it may be attacked from the ground, likewise the disarming of Prokskt. I, here, will order the attacks. The

High Commander here is named Kakrekt. She is supposed to see that the orders are carried out, as I did for Tlorr and before that Tlorr for Kwler. But Kakrekt does not want to obey all my orders. Quokatk has been insane too long, Kakrekt has been more than Commander but refused to become Holy Man, what shall I do about Kakrekt?

I am remembering well today. I remember where I hid some more pages but now it is too late, I cannot return to get them, I have only the ones I carried with me when I left. I must start all over and try to remember what I wrote, and remember to keep with me what I write because if I hide the new pages and write down the place where I hide them, I will forget where I have written down the hiding place, because I will have to hide that too.

Absolutely not, she had said, but she wasn't going to get away with it.

The conference, almost as soon as she returned, was well attended: Metra and Cochran and Corcoran, who seemed permanently attached to her, never to be unglued, and another *Endeavor* officer besides; Hanna and Gabriel sat as far away from them as possible. Arch and Bella, Kit Mortan and Cinnamon Padrick, Joseph and Dema and Benj Parker. Pirin Zey was there, and Communications staff, and two of the political science team, and even the climatologist. Adair Evanomen and Zanté were there as images from Earth. Hanna recognized the room behind Evanomen, part of the suite Jameson had used as director of Contact. Zanté was at Admin too, already in the commissioner's suite, reclaiming Jameson's old territory for him. The transition was moving fast.

And Jameson was there, of course, in all three large dimensions. Hanna had not seen his face since she told him she meant to leave him. He did not look at her at first, which left her free to look at him, which she kept deciding not to do, but she kept doing it anyway, her eyes on him again and again. He was at a desk somewhere in Arrenswood, contriving to appear both relaxed and alert. Hanna knew the look. Holo made him look real enough to touch.

It was a good thing he was not real. Touching him would be a bad idea. Thinking about him would be just as bad, so she tried hard not to think, and voices went by her in disjointed scraps.

"... a simple, peaceful contact with Wektt's Holy Man or his designee." That was Evanomen. "That was what we meant to do with Rowtt, of course. Kwoort shot that all to hell. And here's Kwoort again. How the *hell* did he get there?"

Into a brief silence, he added, "I mean that literally."

"The flight we observed, presumably," Metra said shortly.

"Well, whatever the mechanism, there's no explanation of why he's there. The other Outsiders—" it was the generic term for sentient aliens "—are peaceful, overall, but they know who an enemy is. How does Rowtt's top Commander end up being Wektt's Holy Man overnight?"

"Rowtt's Demon," said Jameson. "Wektt's Holy Man is Rowtt's Demon. Are such exchanges customary? It does not seem to be treason. It's inexplicable by our standards. We still have not taken this society's measure."

Hanna decided to ignore the deep, familiar voice. Too easy to remember how it sounded in the dark, in the night. She tuned out again.

"... capability for interstellar travel, for interstellar war," Metra said, and Jameson said, "Absolutely."

"And of course maybe the most valuable commodity we've ever run across," Evanomen said, which Hanna half-heard. She had only begun to wonder what he meant when he said, "The potential for increasing human life spans even further—and A.S. doesn't work equally well for everybody, you know. Some research here—who knows? Might be nothing there humans can use, but we've got to find out."

Hanna lifted her head at that. Jameson looked directly into her eyes.

"Find out once and for all whether their star-going poses a threat, or if they can even still do it," he said. "Hanna, that's first. And talk to Kwoort about possible trade. We might give quite a lot for research subjects. Preferably alive and willing."

She felt the ghost at her shoulder. But the ghost said nothing. Even the ghost was stunned.

She had not even imagined, how could she not have thought of it?—that whatever allowed Soldiers to live for a millennium might be studied and adapted to humans. This was why the contact with Battleground could not be terminated and dropped forever. So simple; so enormous.

Hanna did not say anything and did not move. She could not. People expected her to nod, at least. She did not nod. She was caught up in Jameson's eyes, green today, sometimes gray as a clouded sea. But she felt a wisp of greedy curiosity from Metra. The breach between Hanna and Jameson was open knowledge here as well as on Heartworld, a consequence of the Parting Observance. Silence would be read as insult. She would not do that to Jameson.

She said with an effort, "Sorry, I was thinking. We didn't take advantage of the time we had with Kwek. There were questions she could have answered that we just didn't ask."

Jameson did nod. "Can you spare a few minutes when we're done here?" he said.

"Of course," she said. Dreading a private conversation. Longing for it.

The others drifted out slowly. Hanna waited, looking absently at a reader that showed the anonymous healer's words. She had looked them up again after seeing Metra, and now carried them with her as if the being called to her across the years. The last person left and the door silently closed itself. She finally looked up.

Jameson came to the edge of the holo field and stood looking at her. He said, "You could come closer, you know."

The holographic projections had been set up for one-way transmission. Hanna would only be an image to him, a small figure in a room that seemed large with everybody gone. She got up and went closer, though.

"How is Mickey?" she said.

"He's in good health and very happy. I've been wanting to talk to you about him. About what will happen when you get back. What do you intend to do? Exactly, I mean? Where do you mean to live?"

"I don't know. Lady Koroth has some contacts on Earth besides me. If you would call her? She could get someone to help find a place near Admin for Mickey and me. And if Thera could stay with us for a while—?"

She did not like asking for the favors. But she did not have a choice.

"And I was thinking," she said, not taking her eyes from his face, "that I wouldn't go very far away from your home. So that Mickey could see you sometimes. Would you do that?"

Because favors for Mickey's sake were different.

"With pleasure. He's a delight, Hanna. I'm sorry you've had to miss these months with him."

"Me, too." She had to look away then. What she had missed was irretrievable. She forced the tears back. Some things did not bear thinking of. And a new fear seized her, full-grown in an instant.

"Sit," he said. "Try to be comfortable. Try to relax."

She hardly heard him, but she tried. She sat in one of the comfortable chairs, as close as she could get to the holo field, but she was on the edge of the seat, every muscle tense.

"I can't just come and take him," she said. "He doesn't even know me. He only knows you. It will take time. I want him to want to be with me—"

The new fear was unstoppable.

"And how can he?" she said. "He's happy where he is, you just said so. He won't want to leave you. He won't want to be with me."

She clasped her hands to her mouth as if she could force the terrible words back into it. She was certain she had lost her son. The months apart had taken him away from her and she would never get him back.

Jameson reached a hand toward her, let it fall. He could not touch her. She saw her sadness mirrored in his face.

"Please," he said, "don't think that. I've told him you'll be back and that I hope it will be soon. He has a calendar that he puts things in to tell you about. Images of the pets playing, words he's learned, stories about what he does, lists of things he loves. Yes, he tells stories, little ones; he's absorbing language fast. I hope to see him often. I'm glad you want that too."

"Yes, I do," said Hanna, and bent over with the effort not to cry.

When she looked up again, she saw the oddest expression on his face.

"What?" she said, faltering.

"You could always change your mind," he said. "I'd like that."

"About—what?"

"Leaving."

"Oh—oh. I have to," she said simply.

"Why? Can't we compromise?"

"No," Hanna said. She got up slowly. The words that came out next came of their own accord and should have been said long ago, but something inside her tore apart with each one. "You're too strong. You *have* to be strong. You won't let yourself be anything else. I've leaned on your strength with such gratitude—it's so ungrateful even to say this! I'm still leaning, depending on you for amnesty someday, trusting you to care for Mickey, depending on you to protect me from Metra's mistakes. Am I so weak?—I *feel* weak, I've let myself feel that way because you're so strong. The kind of power you have now, the kind you had already and what you've gotten back again—how could anyone not feel weak beside you? I can't let you keep being my strength. I don't even know if I have any of my own, any more. I can't keep on like that."

Then she stopped, because she had said everything important.

That strange expression was back. After a minute he said, "You're a difficult woman to love."

Her breath stopped. It was anger that stopped it, a bright flare of outrage.

"You," she said. "You're the most manipulative human being I've ever known. I've never heard you say that word—except to disclaim it! *Love!* What are you doing? Raising the stakes? I'm not playing!"

She started away, then, almost running.

"Stop it!" he said, and almost roared: "Stop running away from me!"

She did stop, but at safe distance—as if they really were in the same room, as if the light-years did not separate them. She was still for a minute. Then she said, "You've got to try A.S. again soon, don't you. You don't dare wait for results from here, even if I can get you those volunteers. You won't do it immediately, not until your position on the Commission is unassailable. But soon."

"I can't wait much longer," he said. "It's been too long."

"You always go to Heartworld for that. Take me with you."

"I can't," he said automatically. There was a hesitation first; but she only remembered that later.

She said, *"No.* Because you'll be weak. Physically weak, at the least, if you even survive. You might even be afraid, because this time might be the one that kills you. And you don't want anybody to see it. Let me be with you."

He shook his head, a fractional movement, and said nothing. But there might have been speculation in his eyes.

"Think about it," she said.

And then she did leave.

She walked out fast and nearly collided with Gabriel, who was hovering. He looked at her face and said, "What's wrong?"

Everything in her mind was a kaleidoscope and she could not focus on anything. "Were you listening?" she said, and he said, "Of course not!"

"Oh, sorry, no, I keep thinking—"

She kept perceiving him as if he were one of the D'neerans, any one of whom might have been "listening" whether they wanted to or not, unless they consciously blocked out the thoughts behind a conversation.

Gabriel put a hand on her shoulder. "You're upset," he said. "Is it about the mission?"

"No!"

She took a few steps along the corridor but stopped because she really did not know where she wanted to go. Gabriel said something she didn't hear, because she was thinking that Jameson never lied to her when they were together—but then, when they were together, she might sense it if he tried, and he knew it.

She thought: *He thinks* I'm *difficult to love?*

Gabriel moved in front of her, both hands on her shoulders now, wanting, she saw, to embrace her. Gabriel did not think she was difficult to love.

"We have to get ready to go to Wektt," she said. She only had to look up a little to meet his eyes. He did not tower over her as Jameson did.

His fingers moved on her shoulders, an unconscious caress.

"What did Commissioner Jameson do to upset you so much?"

"He implied that he loves me," she said. "Obliquely. Of course, obliquely."

"And what did you say?"

"I said—"

She stopped, then, and shook her head. "I told him to prove it," she said. "I told him to do something I don't think he can possibly do."

Gabriel wanted very much to know what that was, she saw—saw that whatever it was, Gabriel was confident *he* could do it—but he didn't ask. Instead he said, "What if he does?"

"I hope he doesn't. I think."

Chapter II

HANNA LOOKED AT THE dynamic model they had started building with such hope, given up when observers were evacuated from Battleground. Given up by others because the flow of data had been halted; given up by Hanna because she had forgotten about it.

Her fingers moved across the control pad, navigating, lingering to open précis of reports. Kit had incorporated everything Linguistics had learned or deduced from the datastream; here too were distillations of the reports Hanna had made during the approach to Battleground. But not the texts pilfered from That Place, and: *Nothing here about love*, she thought, wondering at her distress, wondering at her ambivalence.

She knew some of the truth of Battleground now; Kwoort's appearance in Wektt had given her part of the horrific mystery at its heart. Easy to kill, easy to condemn generation after generation to early death in battle when there was no honoring of sacrifice, no love felt by parent toward child or mate toward mate. One thing was certain: Battleground had nothing to do with—

Love—and neither do I, she thought.

But it would be so easy, for a woman who was weary of storms *I could play the game*, she thought, *and what was I doing, myself, except raising the stakes, playing the game after all, in what I said. He might even offer marriage according to his culture's customs, flout his society, inflame his family. I know he would, if the threat of personality adjustment became critical. And though the thought of being bound in such a way repels me, that threat would be sufficient. Who would dare to Adjust a commissioner's spouse, wife of a Jameson of Heartworld?*

No one.

The easy way, for the weary. And security for Mickey for all his life.

Arch was right to ask if that word, "corruption," meant anything to me. It's exactly what I contemplate now.

———

The model spun lazily in the air. Gabriel was enraptured.

"I haven't seen one of these in years," he said.

"Not even at your school? They're used a lot in education."

"The abbey's equipment doesn't run to frills."

Hanna's tiny cabin was dark, and the insubstantial structure glowed with light and now, enlarged, nearly filled it. The interlocking threads were color-coded, and glittered at points Hanna had decided were crucial nodes. Some points phased in and out, a brilliant blue-white: they were questions. Hanna had made alterations. She had added one that when activated would say: *Creators query?* She had downgraded the issue of whether Soldiers might be inclined toward interstellar aggression, and if their technology would support it. It had been at the center of the structure; Hanna had moved it off to the side. Another point represented the facilitators. Now she guided that one to the model's heart, intensely bright.

Gabriel glanced at her and was distracted. Rainbows shimmered on her face.

She reached out again, and the facilitator-question shone like a star at her fingertip.

"It's time to tell me the rest of what you learned from Tlorr," she said.

He said nothing.

She withdrew her hand from the model and took one of his. "Come here," she said. She pulled him to the bed and said, "Sit down."

Light shimmered on them and he thought, *Say instead, lie down. Say, lie with me—*

"I'm not trying to seduce you," she said, and paused. Perhaps *Yet* hovered on her lips. He hoped.

She sat and tugged at his hand until he sat too. The bed felt soft and springy. The warmth of her body stole around him. If she felt what that did to him she ignored it.

"I know part of what drives them, but not all of it," she said. "You have to tell me the rest of what Tlorr said. Try this. Start—"

"What part? What's the part you know?"

"The reason for their unceasing war," she said. "It's population control. Period. They avoid starvation and survive as a species only by killing each other in enormous numbers. The average Soldier doesn't have any idea that's the reason he's dying; he thinks he's doing it for his god, he thinks the enemy's goal is to force starvation and cannibalism on the defeated, he's been told that from the crèche onward no matter which side he's actually on. In fact the sides are interchangeable. The Holy Men cooperate for maximum mortality; they even move back and forth and fill each other's places. The capacity for imagination is there in all Soldiers, but it's suppressed through the prime breeding years, so the capacity for inquiry and dissent is suppressed too. Those who survive long enough—begin to wonder. To question. And if they live to a very great age, like the Holy Men, they understand the truth. But they do nothing to change it. They do nothing, or can do nothing, to exert control where it could be used without turning to war—reproduction. Controlling birth instead of killing each other. Why? Tell me what Tlorr told you."

He hesitated still, trying to absorb what she had said. Said so bluntly, as if there were nothing terrible about it.

"Tlorr didn't say why," he said. "It seemed to be a given."

"Tell me what she said anyway. Start slowly." Her voice was impersonal. "You prayed, I remember, as we went there. We came out and walked forward and saw Kwoort. He wanted me to order you to go in to Tlorr, and I wouldn't. You chose to go. That was brave."

"I didn't feel brave," he said.

"No, but you went. You went through the door. Was Tlorr there already? Waiting for you?"

"Yes, she was there."

"Just standing, walking around, what?"

"Just standing. Why?"

"I'm trying to see the context," she said, and he understood suddenly that she meant to turn him toward objectivity.

"Yes," she said. "They're just pictures. Just words." She

went on, "I only got a glimpse of her. What does she look like? Does she look like the first one, the completely crazy one?"

"They all still look alike to me," Gabriel confessed. "Don't they to you?"

"Not at all. No more than you and I look alike. Did she act like the first one?"

"No," Gabriel said with certainty. "The first one was restless. He never stopped moving. Tlorr stood still. Just gestured now and then. She opened the upper pair of eyes when I came in. She did something with her mouth."

"Smiled?"

"I don't know what it was."

"It looks like this."

He nodded at the image in his mind. "Yes. She smiled."

"Who spoke first?"

She reached up suddenly and smoothed the curls at his temple. He looked at her and began to smile, turning his head to her touch. The dark memory became lighter.

"She spoke first. She greeted me and told me her name."

He looked at the skeins of light cradling them and thought back to that gray chamber.

You are not really there now, Hanna said, *you are only watching. Only listening.*

"I had to keep trying different ways of saying things," Gabriel said slowly. "Listening for the 'untranslatable' cues, finding other words. She said—"

What did you think we are here to talk about?

Umm—Kwoort Commander said you wish to talk about your god.

What did he say he wishes to talk about with your fellow-Soldier?

Speaking to the mind, I think.

Is that what you want to talk about?

No, I want to talk about your god.

Kwoort has already told me about your god. You can't explain it. Your translating devices are good, but they fail when you talk of your god.

We can find common words, surely.

I'm not so confident. Have you seen your god manifested? Have you seen its power?

I see him manifested in the kindness with which—ah. That did not translate.

You see.

Tell me then how yours is manifested.

In his power.

Mine has power too. But that power is too great for me to comprehend. So is his love—oh. His—the ways in which people express his—the best ways in which people act toward each other and the best sensations they have with each other—those are images of my god's actions and sensations with his people. That is how I see him manifested. Good. That translated.

Yes. It did. But I still do not understand what you mean. My god is the fire of life and it is our duty to make his fire blaze brighter in our increasing numbers. To experience his fire in the creation of Soldiers and experience it ever more strongly in death.

Well, we are less concerned with numbers than with teaching the young how to live rightly—oh. Teaching them to live as God would have them live. But we cherish—um, we encourage life. We nurture it, as a parent—oh. As, as a crèche does a child.

Kwoort has been told that your people circumvent the creation of life. Your god does not seem powerful enough to stop that.

I don't understand you.

Kwoort has been told that you are surprised at the abundance of our breeding. The not-Soldiers who went to crèches expressed surprise.

It surprises us, yes.

Why? Why does your god permit your interference in this? Ours does not permit it in us.

I still don't understand.

Abundant God has made us so that we must join at the times of his choosing and sends his facilitators to ensure this. He has given us the means of making crèches so that our young survive until they are old enough to fight and kill and die.

Yes, I understand about the crèches. We also have the means to build homes—ah—places for our young. And the means to feed them and ensure their health. But I don't understand why you have no choice in the joining. You speak of mating?

Yes, the union of Soldiers and Warriors and facilitators.

I don't understand about the facilitators. What is a facilitator? I don't think any of us have seen one.

Have you seen mating?

No.

Then you have not seen facilitators.

"And I don't want to see them," Gabriel said. "I can't give you rest of the conversation as accurately. I started feeling—"

Sick. Sick with horror.

Hanna had stretched out on her stomach, frowning as she listened. Gabriel found that reporting the first part of the conversation had muted the impact of the rest. It was at a distance, far away from this small darkened space with the rainbow-lights shining like a child's grand toy. He found himself telling her about the dual role of the facilitators: the ecstasy with which they rewarded the mating act and the nourishment they somehow got from it, and the part they played in destroying anyone who might threaten generation. Tlorr had not explained how they forced ordinary Warriors and Soldiers into merciless mobs.

But Hanna said, "There was something about that in what the Cutter said, the surgeon. If word gets out ... and spreads to the people who are actively mating ... and there's some sort of symbiotic relationship with the facilitators, some kind of feedback loop that activates the behavior ..."

Her voice trailed off. She did not say anything for some time. It was Gabriel who broke the silence.

"Do you think what they get out of mating is the most intense thing most of them, maybe any of them, ever feel?"

She was resting on her folded arms; when she moved it was to clasp her hands and put them lightly on his knee. It was too much; he could not help touching her hair, and he felt the sensation in every cell. She sat up quickly, breaking the contact.

"Pay attention," she said. "We've only got a few hours," and Gabriel thought: *She could teach me a lot in a few hours.*

"Not now," she said, but there was a glint of laughter in her eyes, the first he had seen in a long time. And *not now* wasn't *no*. "Stop it," she said. "Concentrate, all right? You might be right about the intensity, especially if Matthew Sweet is right about that neural network. I'll tell you something, though. When I was with the mating couple? You heard me tell Starr about that. Well, I was aware of the male and the female, but I did *not* perceive a third sentient being with them. I don't think the facilitators are sentient. I wish I knew what they are."

"You can identify non-sentient life too, though, can't you? Can't you observe the minds of animals?"

"Oh, yes. But there was nothing—well, nothing I was in any condition to notice."

"What do—oh." He remembered. *I was aroused*, she had said. *Intensely.* And suddenly he was, too.

It hung in the air between them until he reached for her. But she stopped his hands, taking them in her own.

"You said you'd made an absolute break with Starr. You're free now," he said.

"But you're not."

"I am," he said. "I don't know who I'll be when we come out of this, but it won't be who I was before. It's not because of you. It was time. I think, I think I understood that I wasn't being fair to the children. Some of the older men who'd been in the world before even tried to tell me. That hard as I tried I still only had this narrow perspective. Maybe someday I'll go back. But it won't be for a long time, and I won't be who I was."

"All the same . . ." They looked at each other, not moving, holding hands lightly in the air as if they were preparing to dance. Words were there too, words she did not say because—he saw before she did—she did not know what she wanted to say.

"I think," he said, "you're afraid of hurting me."

"Yes," she said. "I love you—as a friend. But only that. That would be enough for me, if we became lovers for a time. I don't know if it would be enough for you."

They were almost whispering, hands still clasped, the barest touch.

Time to take some risks . . .

"I'm willing to find out."

He leaned forward finally. "One kiss," he said, "just one," and touched his lips to hers. She let go of his hands and cradled his face, her fingers like feathers or tender new leaves, and his hands on her back were light as shadows, a communion of cells. Light flowed over them and through them, caressing. They kissed softly for a long time, and he found his inexperience no burden; he had, it seemed, a natural talent for kisses.

The door closed and Hanna turned back into the glimmering room, feeling very young. She had forgotten the sweetness of being regarded as a precious treasure; she had almost forgotten what it was to feel this heat. Now she knew she could desire Gabriel as he desired her. She had said, *We should take this no farther* and he had said, *But only not now* and she had said, *It would only be a little, for a while,* and he had said, *I don't mind.* And maybe, she thought, he would not.

Reluctantly, aware of time pressing, she turned her attention to the mission and thought of what she might do with the hours that were left before the descent to Wektt. Seek information, she thought. That was the only thing she could do, and there was only one way to get it. She would have to do it in secret, though; in trance.

She moved through the glowing model and spoke the command to shut it down, and darkness fell.

Now there was nothing but the slight glow from the base of a wall, too dim to cast shadows. She sank to the floor and in the dark bowed her head and reached for the inevitable: Kwoort, of course.

Chapter III

H E IS PACING. Is this—
Is this the same restlessness that afflicts Kwler?

A strange gait, the extra joints, of course, but I've known kinetics as strange. He is studying maps, I see, some animated, some material and stacked, but all flickering—in reality? No, in his sight.

Rowtt has nothing like this encircling web of ways. Rowtt is smaller in extent and it does not go so deep either, near all of Rowtt is occupied and much here is deserted. A Soldier could lose himself in the old outer ways and Kakrekt Commander could lose me too in the depths, if she took me that way. I must learn all of them! And look even harder at these surface maps too, not Wektt but Rowtt, all Rowtt's territory. Troop dispositions and details, points vulnerable and points building, significant sites and command personnel. Kakrekt knows them thoroughly, but I will not leave it all to her. Tlorr did not leave all of it to me, the study of Wektt. And I cannot trust Kakrekt—

How odd, the images blinking—

I cannot shut my eyes, the eyes of now or the past-eyes. I do not know what I see and all of it tangles together. That globe half-buried in ruins long past on Continent Three, the color deep and rich, Soldiers do not make such things, what could have been its purpose and what made it and why do I think of it at all   it was the color of that not-Soldier's eyes, I think—not-Soldiers have no past-eyes, they have less to remember—

I do not like it that he thinks of my eyes. Does he feel me watching?

Saw the shining thing when I was young, saw it in a desert where there was nothing left to destroy because whatever had been there, was long dead. Would not-Soldiers make such a purposeless thing? Would they make it on that world where they lived?

New Earth.

Those who are here now could tell me—no, that is the kind of thinking Kakrekt does. I only have to find out how they perform the speaking to the mind, can we do it. It cannot be taught, the female not-Soldier said, was that true. If it cannot be taught, how, then—

How explain the New-Human Project, and how it might parallel his origin? What good would that do?

Tlorr said I must find out the means they use, she wanted me to use their seeing of the mind. A trick, a way of spying, I must initiate surprise, Tlorr said. We are too obvious she said, if we do not make more surprises even young Soldiers will see the truth, and they will not want to die if no Demon threatens them with hunger, if no fire of the god waits for them. And then soon they will eat each other.

How small is this cadre that knows death is the object? How long has this gone on? Push a little, just a little . . .

How long has this gone on? Records risk too much, truth cannot be written down for any Soldier to find. Was more of this world once green, like the one where not-Soldiers live? There are others, she said, are they green? Past times there must have been others like me. Writing frantically, hiding what they wrote. Commanders turning Holy Men as the truth and the end come near. But so many disappear before they come to the time I have come to now.

Disappear—?

Disappear, we say. Destroyed in battle, lost on reconnaissance, gone prematurely to Wektt, we say. But Kakrekt says none of those I knew came here. Kakrekt says commanders vanish from Wektt too. But I know that none came to Rowtt. If that is not what they do, then I know what it was, I have thought of it myself more than once. Slipped away from a billet, slipped into a company by night, there to die in battle and come to an end. Or—I think of Xtaapt, I think of Wtent-kagt. Assassinated we said, but weapons near their hands and no assassin to be found. Because there was none. Real assassins proceed with circumspection, sow the end-change in food, death in drink. I know what they did to themselves, those two, and others as well, I have almost done it to myself.

He thinks of a recent past, his own past, but what of—

All the countless summers. Generation on generation, dying before they grow old. Before they begin to think. Bleeding, dismembered, burned, disemboweled, crushed, vaporized, eager to live in god's fire forever. This is what we tell them in the crèches, this is what we tell them as they are trained, as they yield to the facilitators, as they feed the young and train them in their turn. This is what we believe summer after summer, surviving. Until we have survived so long that the past-eyes open and the mind begins to move and will not stop. And one by one we drop away. Killed by enemy action, if we are fortunate, before the first questioning swells too far. Killed by the facilitators' will if questions go that dangerous way, killed by order of the Holy Man if we look like turning assassin. Oh, knowing another's mind would be useful there!

Think of—

Are you here, not-Soldier?

And before Hanna could stop herself, she thought, *Yes.* She had gotten an overload of information and become—

Careless! she thought, and *Yes, you are,* said Kwoort; and if she did not understand the words he formed, as he could not have understood the Standard *careless,* the meaning was clear.

I can, thought Hanna, *communicate full meaning in this way. I have done it before—*

She slid into a contemplation too diffuse for him to follow. Stay inside the protective shell of trance?—she had lost its concealment when her concentration slipped; maybe she wasn't as good as she thought she was. Run to Communications, switch to the translation program, open a voice dialogue, with the distance from emotion speech enforced? Or—

She let go of trance. It was like taking off all her clothes.

You want to know about speaking to the mind? she thought without words. *Here it is.*

They regarded each other bleakly.

Are there assassins around me?

How would I know? I would have to examine each individual that comes into your presence. And why do you care? Don't you want to end it in any case?

Not today. Duty compels me today. It compels me to consider the possibilities I see in you.

Not words. Hanna stirred, aware of the people of *Endeavor* around her going about their lives, in a space that for once seemed warm and comforting, while she stood outside them, outside humanity, and this alien considered her.

Your Commander agreed to send you here. Come now. Why wait?

Whenever I come, I think I will come armed.

There is no need for arms, he thought, not in words, and Hanna sighed. He meant it—now—but he was volatile, changing. She would like to go armed. But she did not think Metra would allow it.

Chapter IV

CLOUD. Always. This time, all the way to the ground.
There was a beacon, a pulsing whine to the ear. It did not get louder as they neared it, but the pod spoke mechanically during the descent, counting off Ks. At point-one Hanna expected to break through the cloud at any moment, but seconds passed with no perceptible change. And when the naked-eye monitor showed something besides fog, they were so close to the ground that it seemed possible to open the hatch and simply jump out, onto a surface that made the cratered landing field at Rowtt look sophisticated, and the little island in the river, lush.

The pod set down, and Hanna and Gabriel looked in bewilderment at what was on the monitor. They were some distance from Wektt's chief city, but they had expected some sign of habitation, even though advance observation had found none. But there was nothing here: only dust and desert and outcrops of rock, gray-brown in the fog, and livid patches of moss.

More bewildering still was the figure that stood next to Kwoort, as tall as he, gray uniform blending with the surroundings just like his. Hanna thought she was seeing double for an instant, until she extended a tendril of awareness and met a hostility that made her open her lips to cry *Abort!*—then the certainty came that the hostility was not directed toward her; that there was indeed another Soldier with Kwoort; and that the hostility was that of the two for each other.

Her wariness had seeped out to Gabriel. He said softly, "Who's that?"

"I've no idea . . ."

God only knew how the aliens had gotten to this desolate spot; there was no sign of conveyance. Something that looked like a large satchel was slung over Kwoort's shoulder, and another hung carelessly from the other's hand. Next to them was a cone-shaped artifact, wider at the base and tapering toward the top, a bit over half a meter high. Hanna eyed it distrustfully until she realized it was the beacon.

She muttered, "If we'd come in blind we might have landed right on top of them."

"Accidentally squashing a couple of aliens wouldn't look great on your CV."

"Is that supposed to be a joke?"

"Displaced anxiety. Kwoort's never brought anybody with him before except a Holy Man, and he *is* Holy Man here. So who's this?"

Kwoort did not, evidently, intend to wait for them. He began walking toward the pod, and without hesitating, the other did too. *Female,* Hanna thought, watching the figure move. She shook herself and got up and went to the hatch. Then they were outside, and the sense of seeing double vanished as the pair came close and their faces were clear.

"I greet you, host," she began, but Kwoort interrupted.

"I am your guest. *We* are guests. I could not avoid telling this fellow-Soldier of your arrival and your origin. She insists she must show you something and show it to me too. We will go in your aircraft."

We will? Hanna thought, but she was not going to refuse. She could tell without effort that Kwoort was in a rage; and there was a keening impatience in the other.

Gabriel was oblivious. He said easily, "I greet you, fellow-Soldier of Kwoort! My name is Gergtk, and yours?"

"I am Kakrekt Commander," she said. "We will go now. Unless this *Holy Man*—" the translator could not convey a sneer, and Hanna could not read it on the Commander's face, but she felt it—"has deceived me about your willingness to do his bidding."

It was not until much later that Hanna remembered Kakrekt had not stated her age, but by then she had seen that many other things were different about Kakrekt.

"There," Kakrekt said. "Do you see where a landing place has been cleared in the vegetation? I send workers to maintain it. There."

"A waste of Soldiers who could fight," Kwoort said.

"It is not waste. These not-Soldiers will see that even if you do not."

For some time they had moved slowly over a solid mass of green, at treetop level, assuming those were trees down there. They had flown for an hour to get there, after nearly three hours of consultation with *Endeavor*, and finally broken free from cloud near the end. Kakrekt had brought detailed coordinates in her satchel, but *Endeavor*'s navigators had had their hands full adapting the script to human terms and programming the pod to follow them. They had stayed in contact through the hour of flight, too, hovering in spirit, making Hanna hope she would never be as over-anxious a mother as these navigators were for their charges—and giving her no chance to draw back in silence and delve into the bitterness she felt between Kwoort and Kakrekt. She had ventured only one question—"Kakrekt, what is your position in Wektt?"—and Kwoort had answered for Kakrekt: "She is my High Commander. My High Commander!" with a fury that made Hanna blink.

She thought it would be a relief to escape from the pod, but they got out of it into vicious heat. Hanna's face poured with sweat before she had taken three steps. So did Gabriel's, and so, Hanna saw, did the aliens'.

But Kwoort just said, "Pleasant," and smiled.

"Aren't you hot?"

"I have been cold since coming to Wektt. This is pleasant," he said, and Kakrekt made an untranslatable sound that might have been the equivalent of a snort.

They walked a cleared path that was a suffocating tunnel walled and roofed with trees and vines. The air was swollen with humidity. Kakrekt walked swiftly, leading them; Kwoort followed more deliberately, and Hanna and Gabriel slowed to his pace. Tough creepers caught at their boots and in places rose to Hanna's knees. Kakrekt's workers had not been here for some time, or the undergrowth reclaimed territory quickly no matter how brutally it was cut back.

The narrow trail wound between lofty, rounded green mounds which Hanna began to suspect were overgrown ruins. Kakrekt was soon out of sight, but they could not mistake the path. Kwoort walked in silence; his legs appeared to ripple, with a strange boneless quality, when he wanted to avoid especially dense tangles. Hanna and Gabriel swerved with less grace. Then the track took an abrupt right-angle turn, and they faced an opening that might once have held a door. Vines had been clawed away on either side but were trying to take the portal back, thrusting out new shoots that waved, questing, as Kwoort followed Kakrekt through them into darkness. He went in silence, in no mood for speech. Hanna felt him think angrily of the humans, anticipating how they would react to what they approached. Kwoort had not even seen it yet, but he had already made up his mind—

Hanna hesitated an instant, glanced at Gabriel. They followed Kwoort into the dark, just in time to see a flare of light.

Kakrekt stood before a panel of newly polished copper inset with bright gold, holding the light. Hanna was too startled to speak. But Gabriel whispered: "Is this a temple?" (*Chirp*, said the translator on the last word.) He hesitated and went on, "How old is this place?"

"No one knows," Kakrekt said. "A scout found this, I think it must have been a city, by accident. I came myself, I found this structure myself, I found the way in myself."

She stroked the surface of the panel, fingertips lingering here and there, as if she could absorb information from it. Hanna moved closer and saw that the panel bore the image of a face, half life-size. It was not stylized; the individual would be recognizable if he walked into the chamber now. A series of written characters framed it.

But it was not the face of a Soldier ... assuming those slits were eyes, that protuberance a nose, the rounded appendages at the top ears, that fleshy blob at the bottom a mouth.

"Can you tell me what the writing says?" Kakrekt was saying. "This Holy Man says you have experience, can you tell me what that not-Soldier is—"

Hanna could not speak. She had even stopped thinking.

Presently Gabriel said very quietly, "There's nobody." *Nobody that looks like that.*

"No." By now Hanna had gone through the same sequence of images that Gabriel had—as if she had not known immediately, as if flipping through the mental catalog, like a child's picture book, would make it not so. No

F'thalian looked like that, no Zeigan, no Uskosian. No Girrian, and Girritt had not developed spaceflight anyway.

She looked finally at Gabriel, and then at Kakrekt. She said, "I don't know what this is. Have you found other artifacts like this?"

"There are other such images in the deeps below Wcktt. I want to know what they are."

Hanna turned away with an effort. She said, "I didn't know you speculated about such things. I didn't know anyone did. Isn't it forbidden? Why have you been permitted to do this?"

"There was no one to tell me not to," Kakrekt said. She swung around and looked at the silent Kwoort. "There is still no one," she said.

Kwoort erupted, at that. "Do you think I cannot fight this war without you?" he shouted. "You are mistaken!"

Kakrekt took her hand away from the wall. She said nothing, but Hanna felt the oddest conviction in her: that Kwoort would not stand in her way for very long. She could not tell why Kakrekt thought that, but eyed her thoughtfully.

She said, "What does this place—its maintenance, its investigation—have to do with your war?"

"It has nothing to do with war," said Kakrekt, and Kwoort snarled, "This Warrior only found it because she was left to her own devices too long, and that was the fault of Tlorr."

"Tlorr! How does Tlorr come into it?"

"Prookt was next senior after me in Rowtt. Now that I am gone, Tlorr is left with Prookt as High Commander. She resisted that necessity, she postponed it again and again. My departure for Wektt was delayed much too long, summer after summer after summer. And for all those summers while Quokatk descended into madness, this Warrior has refused to become Holy Man and has done as she pleased, ignoring the directives of the god, with no one to prevent her, because Tlorr did not want to let me go."

"I don't see—oh. Prookt."

"Yes. Would you like to rely on Prookt as your High Commander?"

"He is—a little lacking in imagination." Translating as *foresight*. "So—"

"This Warrior—"

Kakrekt interrupted. "This *High Commander* chose to investigate the report of the site. I shall continue to investigate. Look at it! What do you think? Do not-Soldiers have sites like this?"

Hanna began, "There are many—" but Kwoort had swelled with fury again at the interruption.

"It's of no importance what they think! I will have the place destroyed! And if this Commander has made records of it they will be destroyed too!"

Kakrekt said very calmly, "I am sure there are other places like this. They will be reported to me."

"It does not matter. In time you will forget. In time it will all be forgotten," Kwoort said with dreadful satisfaction.

But Hanna said softly to Kakrekt, "One of our people said to me that he thinks all your crèches are built on bones. Layers and layers of bones, he said."

"Yes," Kakrekt said. "But I do not think they need to be."

"It has always been that way!" Kwoort's voice was loud and got louder, he trembled and seemed almost to vibrate in the dark. He shouted, "It will always be that way!"

Hanna held her breath; she thought he would strike Kakrekt, but he did not. The passageway was stifling and except for the radiant wall everything seemed black. Kakrekt turned suddenly and moved deeper into the passage, and Kwoort hurried after her as if afraid to let her out of his sight. There were more of the ceremonial panels, but Kakrekt's Soldiers had not cleaned the rest. Copper was crusted with green oxidation, gold with layers of grime. The passage dead-ended in rubble after only a few meters and all of them stopped. Kwoort did not turn around. Hanna suddenly backed up a pace and bumped into Gabriel. He put his arms around her but he did not seem to be aware that he was doing it. Hanna touched Kwoort's mind and found that he was staring at the rubble with hatred, and that Kakrekt was staring at it too—but she was absorbed in contemplation of what might lie beyond the rubble, the knowledge there.

Hanna said very quietly, "We could help you learn more."

Kakrekt whispered (Hanna felt the leap of hope), "How could you do that?"

"Not-Soldiers know a great deal about their past. The civilizations that led to the present have been traced in detail, cities like this excavated, the lives of rulers and ordinary people examined. We have done this through the cooperation of many sciences. We could teach you the sciences; we could help you reclaim the past."

Kwoort said, "It is of interest to no one. Except to the few who live too long."

The dark weighed heavily, stone and earth and riotous jungle overhead, and Hanna wanted to break for the outside. She resisted the urge to run and said, "Why is it of no interest? What is the authority that says Abundant God forbids the study of history?"

"The Holy Men say so, they have said so forever. Always, it is remembered and written down again, everywhere in every time, in the holy books found in Rowtt and here too. Only, I wonder if those Holy Men said it because they knew they would forget, that all forget."

"The end-change, the forgetting—"

"Don't speak. I do not wish to talk any more. Go away. You too," he added to Kakrekt, but Kakrekt did not move.

Hanna was glad to obey. She turned and urged Gabriel before her back through the passage, dimly visible in reflected light; they turned a corner and saw the opening to the outdoors, and went to it and stepped with relief into the tropical day.

The heat seemed to have gotten even more stifling in the minutes they had spent inside the mound. The air felt thick, like liquid, and it was hard to breathe. There were sounds, bird sounds, Hanna supposed, though the birds she had seen had been silent to human ears, but she did not hear the calls she might have expected somewhere else. She heard small moans like intermittent cries of pain. Gabriel started to say something but she put a hand on his arm and said, "Hush."

"Hush," Gabriel repeated, and quoted, "'Don't speak.' 'Go away.'" He sounded exasperated.

Hanna shook his arm a little. "I want to see what Kwoort is thinking. So hush."

She expected fragments of a quarrel, but the aliens were silent now, Kakrekt watching Kwoort and taking hope from his concentration. For Hanna that concentration produced abstractions, few concrete referents, hard to decipher:

. . . and others have come to this point and must have

known what I know that I will leave nothing behind nothing that I write until the end all that came before lost because I have forgotten it and forgot where I hid it and in time I will even hide this sack and forget where I hid that too. As they forgot. Nothing but the end and what would happen if I shouted to them before then shouted you are wrong! All of you are wrong, you have always been mistaken, the god you believe is false! They will say I am not in my right mind I have come to that change and they will feed me and bathe me and seek another Holy Man and all will go on as before

"It's all right," she said. "You can talk. Kwoort's thinking about forgetting. I would bet the chemistry of memory is tied right into that second pair of eyes. That there are tiers of memory—it would take forever to untangle the relationship, even if we could get some of them to volunteer to be studied. I wonder . . . I thought they're not interested in us enough to volunteer. But Kakrekt's different."

"Volunteers is what we want, isn't it?"

"And Kakrekt might be willing to order them to do it, if we can help her learn some history. I wonder," said Hanna, "if we should concentrate on her instead of Kwoort."

"Or on . . . whoever they were? Whenever they were here?"

"No! Not now. It's been a long time since 'they' were here . . . One problem at a time."

They sat on the ground and waited. Sweat crawled on their skins. There were insects, too, some of them with wing-spans like Earthly eagles, but the insects were not interested in human fluids. Hanna and Gabriel scrambled up when they heard the aliens' voices drawing near. Quarreling about where to go next, but Kakrekt had just conceded.

Kwoort said to the humans, "It will not be so hot at the next place. Maybe you are pleased to hear that."

"I don't know," Hanna said. "Is it another place of ruin?"

"Ruin. Yes."

More interminable consultation with Navigation: at least it was cool inside the pod. Eventually they flew toward the southwest, until— "You're *landing* on that?" said the navigators.

"It's just a desert, isn't it?" Hanna replied.

"Not exactly," they said, but she didn't know what they meant until she got out of the pod and they began to walk across a glassy surface barely masked with windblown dust.

The damn stuff was slippery and lumpy. It had solidified erratically, so that the uneven ground in places had edges that would have cut bare feet to shreds—for a change Hanna had sensibly worn tough boots, and even those started to show damage—and in others betrayed balance as badly as ripples of melting ice. The sun was well up but there were black shadows that made rounded humps look edged and hid the depth of ankle-turning pits beyond edges. And where winds had swept the dust away the rock was shiny, and reflected light in disorienting flashes like a forest of tiny mirrors. It lay all around them in hills and hollows, red-brown and brown-black, and though the sun beat on it, fog lingered from night air meeting heat retained from the day before, and mist lay in strata here and there, damaging depth perception even more. Not that it was cool. They had not changed latitudes by much, and the climate was only cooler by comparison.

Kakrekt hung back stubbornly by the pod, but Kwoort wanted to walk on the tormented surface. He did it easily, with inhuman balance.

"Why," said Hanna, "and how far?"

"I wanted to see this with my own eyes. A weapon was used here at its most powerful—a test, perhaps, of its ultimate formulation. Most areas of the dead continents are like this, I think, but I have not been to them since the weapon was used. There are blasted areas in Rowtt and elsewhere in Wektt, but not like this."

"Do you intend to cross all of it on foot?" She raised her voice; Kwoort had already gained ground on the humans.

"Perhaps," said Kwoort, who must know they were fifty kilometers from anything resembling ordinary landscape, but he did not mean it. Since the translator could not convey the complaint in Hanna's tone, he must have deduced it, because she saw that he certainly recognized her reluctance, and responded as if she were a whining Soldier. And however far he meant to go, he obviously expected Hanna and Gabriel to accompany him, because he stopped and waited for them to catch up. They did not hurry. They did not dare; the footing was too treacherous. Hanna hoped

Kwoort would not linger long. The ambient radioactivity here was slightly elevated over the norm of other places she had been to on Battleground; short-term exposure should not be dangerous, but she would not want to live there.

He waited at the top of a shallow rise, but when they got there they saw that the other side descended much more steeply. At the base of some tortured hillocks lay a pair of pools. Hanna could not tell how far away they were; in the absence of anything for comparison, distance was hard to gauge, and the hillocks might really be respectable hills, the pools small lakes. There was heavier mist over them, and the water, at a distance, looked milky.

Perhaps it was not water. Hanna thought she probably would not want to breathe the mist.

Kwoort started downhill, toward the pools. Hanna called after him, "We are not going there!"

He was moving fast, and his voice barely floated back to them. "I order you," he said.

"No," said Hanna, not raising her voice this time, but directing a negative to his mind so that he could not ignore it. He swung around, surprised. No one ever disobeyed orders. Except, maybe, Kakrekt—if he dared to give her a direct order and find out.

Look at us. Do we look like Soldiers?

The answer was grudging, but at least it was *No*.

It made no difference to Kwoort, whatever he intended to do. He turned and continued walking down the long slope, toward the murky pools. After a minute Hanna set her communicator for visual imaging and recorded the scene. Gabriel watched her curiously.

"Why didn't you do that back at the other place?"

"Because I didn't think of it, all right?" said Hanna, and cursed herself for it.

Kwoort got to the pools and stood motionless for a long time. He had almost forgotten about the humans; he was thinking of the power it had taken to turn once-fertile land to rock, thinking of the spaceflight that weapons technology had accidentally made possible, thinking the population had grown again and would soon explode, wondering if the world would survive.

"They are self-destructing," Hanna whispered, "and he knows it."

For the first time she felt pity—for Kwoort, for Kwek, for Kakrekt and Nakeekt—and she resisted. It was a good deal less painful to hold onto dislike. And when Gabriel asked her to repeat what she had said, because he had not quite caught the words, she only shook her head.

After that they went far south, toward Wektt proper, and followed the curve of the world still farther south to someplace where it was the end of winter, as in the city, but with temperatures colder still, and they had followed it too to the middle of the night. The sky was black and without stars (because there were, of course, clouds), and Kakrekt stalked ahead of them into a cave of ice, and they went through two scts of doors and walked into warmth and light.

"What," said Hanna after a moment's silence, "do you call this?"

"Waste," Kwoort growled, "wastage of labor and energy."

But Kakrekt said with simple pride, "It is only an adjunct to my billet. It is not physically proximate, of course."

Gabriel said, "It's Kakrekt's garden." His cold hand took hold of Hanna's.

It used hydroponic principles, but no protein-based vegetable food was grown here. Flowering vines climbed the walls and containers studded them, dripping with leaves and more flowers. There was rock underfoot, in erratic paths that led between banks and beds of more flowering plants. They had been planted without, apparently, regard to any plan.

Kakrekt said calmly, "Perhaps they make things like this at That Place."

No grasp of design, Hanna was thinking, the implication of Kakrekt's words escaping her at first.

"Then why did you not go there?" Kwoort said to Kakrekt. "It would be an excellent move for you to go there now."

And then Hanna was all attention.

Kwoort turned to her and said, "Is that where my former record-keeper went? Record-keepers have a high incidence of going to That Place. I myself was Rowtt's record-keeper for some time."

Hanna looked up at Kwoort and saw the thrusting smile. His ears unfurled and flapped. Laughter at what he knew must be her surprise.

"How much do you know about That Place?" she said.

"Why should I answer your questions? You offer nothing in return."

Hanna looked at him in silence. *Spyeyes. Fuel modules. Weapons that kill organisms but leave structures intact. Shall we give them the fruits of our mastery of death?*

"I think," said Kakrekt, "they will offer me the knowledge I want."

And Hanna was still silent, but now her thoughtful gaze was on Kakrekt.

Deserts and lakes and mountains and rivers and deserts. And more deserts. Sites of battles, Kwoort plotting courses on maps he took from his satchel and unrolled. Human voices, *Endeavor*'s patient navigators. An incongruous stop to relieve themselves, Hanna and Gabriel behind separate bushes: Hanna made sure there was nothing in sight that looked like an eat-anything. After that, the changing border with Rowtt, flying low though Kwoort assured Hanna they would not be detected and fired on this far from Rowtt's chief city. It was hard to stay alert hour after hour, and the tension between Kwoort and Kakrekt became both grating and monotonous. Talking of military matters they were amicable enough, but it was evident to Hanna that their final goals were very different. She could not tell exactly how they differed. The discordance was too great, their thoughts jangled like orchestras at war, and her own mind went numb in response.

"Hanna," said Gabriel. He was not standing behind her now but sitting on the floor, back to the back of her seat and leaning against it. He was tiring, too.

"What?"

"I thought I heard a Communications signal."

Hanna opened her eyes and saw a blinking light. It was green: not an emergency. But she activated the link, and to her surprise, instead of hearing a voice, she saw words scroll across her field of vision. Kwoort and Kakrekt could not read them, and obviously they were not meant to hear them.

Say nothing that might threaten ongoing talks. Maintain friendly relations at all costs until further notice. By order of Commissioner Jameson.

"What does that say?" said Kwoort.

"A routine status report," Hanna lied. Gabriel got up and looked at the message as it repeated. He said nothing, but Hanna heard the question he did not ask. What the words said was clear, but why someone had found it necessary to send them was obscure. She wondered what had happened.

Jameson, returning to Earth on *Heartworld III*, reflected that he really had missed the yacht.

He meant to make some changes—Edward's taste was not his—but the vessel would do for now. He could reach anyone from it, just as he could from Admin, and access any information he needed; he could conference, debate, field questions and demands, as easily as he could on Earth. His staff was just as accessible, his working days just as frequently interrupted even in deep space. All the old authority was back, complete with accoutrements and image.

Maybe not the image.

"Answer," he said automatically at the communications signal, and did not think of the picture he presented until he saw the astonishment on Karin Weisz's face.

"Oh," he said, and looked down and around. Mickey was sprawled across his lap, asleep. The Dog took up all the space on the seat to his right. The Cat was wound tightly against his left hip, a gray ball of fur with one protruding white paw. None of them looked like waking up.

"If you can spare the time," Weisz said.

"Go ahead . . ."

He rolled up the reader he had been holding (rather uncomfortably) just above Mickey's head and put it aside. On the Cat's side. The Dog liked to play grab-and-keep-away. If he was very lucky, the animal would outgrow the game—

Irrelevant. The Dog wouldn't be living with him much longer. Or the Cat, or Mickey.

Weisz said, "I just saw the last *Endeavor* conference. Why didn't you alert the rest of us?"

"What's the urgency? You've seen it now . . ."

"We could be the Commission that doubles human life spans, or triples them, or more! How long have you known?"

"Known what? Hanna found out how long-lived these people are the first time she made contact with one of them. That does not automatically translate into longer human lives. We're looking at years of research that might come to nothing."

"I want all the information you have."

"You already have it."

"I have précis. I want everything."

"I'll see that you get it," he said equably—he would inundate her with it, millions of words, billions of numbers, every scrap of information on the Battleground mission.

"Immediately."

"I'll call Zanté as soon as we're done. What do you mean to do with it, by the way?"

She said after a perceptible pause, "I just want to be fully informed."

"You understand the secrecy here?"

"The existence of the mission is not secret. People are wondering publicly if there's been a contact, and if so what we've found."

"I hope you don't intend to answer those questions."

"Of course not," she said.

"Good-bye, then. Let your staff know the data's coming. Endit . . ."

She was gone, her eyes in the last seconds speculative. He was speculating too, but he was sure he did not show it.

She had lied about maintaining secrecy, he thought. Colony One had a high turnover in commissioners; for several weeks Karin had been looking at the prospect of becoming another commissioner *emeritus*. Crying *Live for a thousand years!* might gain her quite a lot of time. And if she did that, Jameson could not afford to be seen standing in the way. Kwoort's cooperation—or the cooperation of *somebody* in authority on Battleground—had just become critical.

"Enough," Kwoort said finally. "Enough for today. Return us to the plateau where the beacon is placed. Come back tomorrow."

"That is acceptable," Hanna said.

"I did not ask you if it is acceptable. You will do it unless you want to end all contact with Wektt. You could return to Rowtt, of course, and deal with Prookt."

"Or Tlorr," Hanna said.

"Tlorr will not cooperate. I told her you will not consider aiding any of us, and she has no further interest in you. At best she will delegate Prookt to deal with you, and then where will you be? Where you started."

"If you believe we will not help you, why do you want us to come back?"

"I myself lied to Tlorr," Kwoort said. "I still intend to obtain your assistance, but I already knew that I would come here, and then Tlorr would be my enemy. So I lied. You are assisting me now. That is what you have been doing all day. You have nothing to show for it. Come back tomorrow, and maybe you will get something of what you want. Come and stay. Yes. Come and stay some days. Stay until we agree."

Gabriel said, "Will we be able talk with Kakrekt Commander as well?"

"Yes," Kakrekt said, but Kwoort said, "Why do you want to talk to her? Is talking to me not enough? Kakrekt is very busy. I was very busy as High Commander—busier than I am likely to be as Holy Man. It is my duty to pray, however. That will require much time."

"You had time for us as High Commander of Rowtt," Gabriel said. "Surely Kakrekt can make time, if she thinks she can get something useful from us."

Hanna looked at him in surprise, but Kwoort's ears moved on the edge of laughter.

"You are more demanding than I thought you would be. Very well. Kakrekt may find some time for you, if you stay long enough. And if I do not order her to be too busy."

Chapter V

FOR ONCE HANNA AND METRA agreed on something. Continued contact with Kakrekt was worth pursuing, if Hanna could find a way to bypass Kwoort.

Bypass, or "Neutralize—" Metra said.

"Neutralize?" Hanna said. She had been around true-humans—around Jameson—long enough to develop some synonyms for that. *Discredit. Disgrace.* She said unwillingly, "Kakrekt is already pursuing something like that, I think."

"Evidently. In any case, negotiations need to be ongoing."

"Is that what you call what we were doing? Negotiating? It's ongoing, then. If that's what you call it."

"What are you doing to prepare for tomorrow?"

"It's already tomorrow," Hanna said. It was after midnight on *Endeavor*, early evening in Wektt. She had not previously worked on a world where day-length was so drastically skewed from Standard. She was tired. But then, she had been tired since the first telepathic contact with Soldiers.

"Your plans?"

"I'm going to rest."

"Me too," Gabriel said.

But he did not.

Abundant God cast forth fire for he was fire. He commanded the sky to make it cool and of it he made the great stone of the world, and cast forth again and gathered fire together and set that fire in the sky. He took the sparks that spun away and set them also in the sky. He made the fiery portion move and made it begin to wheel around the world and the sparks he

*also set in motion. Thus day and night in regular succession
we see the gathered portion that is the sun, and then the many
sparks.*

*Abundant God then seized the world. He struck off many
shards of stone until he made a sphere, but inside the sphere,
he placed fire.*

*He took the largest of the stricken shards and made the
moons and set them whirling too around the world. Others
he took and clenched in his fiery hand until water poured
from them, and in this way formed the seas and rivers and
lakes. And with the other hand of fire he touched the sea and
made cloud, and rain began.*

No hierarchy here, Gabriel thought, *no demigods. This is
hands-on.*

Plunged into the tangle of Hanna's reports and those of
the first on-site observers from the moment he boarded *Endeavor*, he had not read the texts Communications had intercepted, the wellhead for translation programs. He did
not think Hanna had read them, either. She would have
seen no need for it when she could live inside other beings'
minds. A blind spot, he thought. Everyone had them.

*Abundant God looked at the fires in the sky and at the
cooled world, and saw that though they were made of his
own substance they were separate and did not know their
own existence. They did not know him.*

*Abundant God thought well and took some of the stone
from the world. He held it in his hands and breathed fire
upon it and the stone lived and multiplied into different
forms. These forms he threw upon the world and living
plants began to cover it, but they lived without knowing that
they lived. He took more stone and infused it with a greater
breath, and it lived and multiplied into other forms, and he
threw them upon the world and they were animate. But despite the fire of his breath, they did not know Abundant God.*

Gabriel rubbed his eyes.

Abundant God, it seemed, had had a hard time of it. The
animals he created went about their business without paying any attention to him. The flame in them glowed fitfully
when they mated, but then when they were finished, it subsided. Abundant God tried out a smarter version, and tin-
kered with it until the new animals had tools and weapons.

All right, Gabriel thought. Abundant God must have

given them proper hands and pulled them upright, too, though the writer or writers of the text, ancient or not, blithely dispensed with evolution and anthropology.

The god's experiment, though, was a dead end. (Not the words of the text; Gabriel's assessment.) The creatures hunted lesser animals with the weapons and the fire in them was hot when they killed, a hopeful sign. But once fed, the upright creatures preferred to sit around and exercise their linguistic skills (also new, Gabriel inferred) to no particular end, or to mate in a desultory way. In short, they were lazy. Disappointing, really.

Abundant God kept on tinkering.

Abundant God looked upon his creation and saw that his creatures passed through life with the indifference of the sparks in the sky. Abundant God desired that they know him and determined to make them aware of his power.

Abundant God once more cast forth a fiercer fire, and of it he made the facilitators, and placed them among his creatures. And he said, "You shall know me by these. They shall be inseparable from you and without them you will perish." And those of his Soldiers who wished to have congress with one another learned that they could do so only in the presence and power of the facilitators, and the facilitators would not be denied. And when Soldiers had learned this, Abundant God also said, "Now you know me and know my power, that my authority is absolute; and so that you will remember this, you will increase according to my dictates, and I will not be denied."

Gabriel read until it was time to leave for Wektt. When he got up to go his leaden legs told him how tired he was. He joined Hanna near the pod, and he thought she saw his weariness and would say something about it, but her communicator sounded—Metra wanted her, here at this last minute—and there was no time.

Metra's private conference room, looking dreary; the walls were light, a silvery-gray, but gray nonetheless. Metra loomed in it, her dark green uniform looking almost black. *Something is missing,* Hanna thought, but she did not know what it was.

Metra was impatient, though Hanna had come at once, detouring from the route to the pod.

"New orders," Metra said. Her voice was tight, and so was her face. She did not make an effort to hide her dislike of Hanna, but, of course, she never had.

She expected some reply, and Hanna could not think of anything to say except, "All right."

"First—this is per communications from Wektt—you will meet Commander Kwoort in Wektt proper this time. We're loading supplies for two weeks, but you'll stay as long as it takes to produce results."

Hanna nodded.

"Secondly, Admin has communicated this to me. You are to find a way to make some concession. It's imperative that we get volunteers to go to Earth."

"What kind of concession?" Hanna said.

"Find something Kwoort wants. Anything. You ought to have some idea what that is by now!"

"He wants weapons. Contact's charter strictly prohibits supplying weapons."

"You can hold out the possibility—"

Cork and Cock were missing. Witnesses.

"You *will* find *something.*"

Or else—what? Hanna thought. She did not say it; she did not want to know what the "or else" might be. Someone might even have thought of things she could lose that she was not already afraid of losing.

"I would like to speak with Commissioner Jameson," she said without heat, because heat would be counterproductive.

"Not possible. You know the regulation."

"Director Evanomen said that would be changed."

"He must have forgotten."

"I will speak to him, then."

"I have told you exactly what he told me to communicate to you. There is no need for you to speak to him."

"Yes. No doubt," Hanna said, and went out to Gabriel and the pod.

Chapter VI

WEKTT'S CAPITAL WAS IN BETTER shape than Rowtt's, probably, Hanna thought during the last of the descent, because it was so much farther away from the amorphous, ever-changing border between the two. Wektt's primary city had aboveground structures still intact, tucked into mountain gorges, hidden in the lee of cliffs, huddled low to the ground along stony rivers. There were even a few trees, though they were stiff and sparse, and distorted by prevailing winds.

If Rowtt had been pounded by electrical storms, Wektt had its own scourge—wind. It was cold and steady and Hanna shuddered as she stepped from the pod to greet Kwoort. She was lightly dressed; she expected to be underground most of the time and wore a loose tunic and trousers of thin fabric. The tunic hid a weapon at her waist. *For demonstration if needed,* she had told Metra, and on that basis, Metra had agreed.

Gabriel watched thoughtfully while Hanna handed their supply of meal tabs over to a waiting Soldier. "Do you really think we'll be here two weeks?" he asked.

Hanna shrugged. They stood on the landing field and looked toward a looming mountain. They had come before dawn, and the mountain was only a deeper darkness against the sky. There was no way to tell how much of it had been hollowed out and no way to guess how many Soldiers were inside. *Endeavor* probably knew, but Metra had not given them any figures, and there had seemed no reason to ask. She said, "I have no idea how long we'll be here." She looked at Kwoort and said, "Does it matter to you how long it takes, Holy One?"

"No," he said.

"Nor to my commanders, I suspect."

"You understand I must take your weapon. Yes, I thought you would have one. I want also any other devices that you have."

Kwoort held out his hand. Hanna looked up at him, her face expressionless. Then she took the weapon from under her tunic and put it in his hand. He put it into his satchel and held out the hand again. After a moment Hanna took the com unit from her wrist and gave that to him too. She said, "You did not tell my Commander that you would not let me speak with her."

"Why do you need it, when you can speak to her mind?"

"She will not listen," Hanna said, and added, *She finds even the thought of speaking to the mind unpleasant to the highest degree,* and Kwoort felt the truth of it. Perhaps he had forgotten that other telepaths remained on *Endeavor,* or thought, since they were not officers, they did not matter. Hanna had not expected that and was not going to tell him otherwise. She was prepared to cherish any advantage she could get.

"I will give the device back to you if it becomes necessary. Give me yours also," Kwoort said to Gabriel.

He did it, slowly. *All right for Hanna, she's a telepath,* he thought. *But if something happens to her . . .*

My people will watch over you still, came Hanna's answering thought.

Kwoort turned and started uphill, Hanna and Gabriel behind him. It was even colder now. The ground was wet, and a few snowflakes drifted down. *At least,* Gabriel thought, *we're not trapped, the pod is here,* only to hear the familiar almost-voice inside his head say: *Look back.*

He glanced behind them and thought he could make out something like a fence that seemed to have sprung up around the pod.

Guards. Lots of them. No going back.

It was a rough, cold walk and Kwoort used no light. The wind strengthened and diminished at intervals, but never stopped. It drove straight through Hanna's clothing. She started to shiver and could not stop, and then became light-headed. She and Gabriel stumbled often in the dark, but Kwoort walked ahead of them steadily. Hanna wondered how quickly these long-legged, multi-jointed creatures could move if they were in a hurry. She could not outrun them, she was certain. She was out of breath quickly, and the dizziness worsened. Then she heard Gabriel panting, caught a flash of worry from him, *headache, where'd that come from,* and something came back to her, a memory of other mountains she had visited in better times. Altitude sickness; they were very high up.

She kept her eyes on the path, afraid they must trudge all the way to the top. She did not want to see how far they had to go.

When her feet hit paved level ground, she did look up, and ahead was a vast cavern cut into the side of the mountain. It was open to the cold and filled with dimly lit machines and figures that moved over and among them. Close up, only one or two of the workers even glanced their way. Deliberately, she focused on a Soldier who had not looked up, drawing his attention. He responded, though sluggishly; she had to touch him a second time before he turned his attention from the engine he was repairing and the mental schematic of its parts. He looked briefly at the not-Soldiers in their strangeness, and there was a clear instant of discrimination that translated to *not-a-threat.* Then he thought of his work again, incurious, dismissing the two figures with his Holy Man.

Into the cavern, where a Soldier waited to act as guide; Kwoort had not been here long enough to move unerringly through the huge warren by himself. The guide led them straight through the cavern. More machines here, more workers, engine noise. Kwoort and the Soldier did not slow down and Hanna and Gabriel were well behind, gasping, when they came to the back of the space and into a corridor that led deeper into the mountain. On and on they went in dim light that barely glimmered from the ceiling, past many corridors and doors and arches that branched off, all the hallways and openings spacious and wide. After a while the guide began to take turnings, and there were ramps that led to other levels, sometimes up and sometimes down. Soon Hanna was more lost than she had been in the maze under the riverside outpost in Rowtt, and though the walls were posted with signs that might offer information, she could not read them. She did not know in which direction she should go if Kwoort abandoned them. The dizziness increased and her chest hurt when she breathed.

Then Kwoort did abandon them, turning them over to the guide at a junction marked with more unreadable signs.

"A billet is designated for you," he said. "This Soldier will take you to it."

"And then what?" Hanna said.

"I will have you brought to me so that we can talk. When I can spare the time," he said, and there was that smile again.

The billet and lavatory cubicle were standard, sizable enough, the sleeping platform comfortable enough, though sleeping on it at the same time would force them close together. They didn't care; they fell on it like exhausted children. Hanna had just gotten her breath back when the door swung open and another Soldier came in, dropped the package of meal tabs on the floor, and left without speaking. The package looked pitifully small. The knowledge that each tab was dense with nourishment did not help. Hanna sat up and looked at a familiar screen set into a wall, where a Soldier urged action against the Demon. She said, "Oh, hell. I hoped they didn't have those here."

"Twenty-four hours a day." Gabriel was still breathless. "Thirty-six point-eight? Whatever it is."

Hanna pulled the fine skein of the translator carrier from her hair and the audio became white noise. "It's not so bad this way," she said.

"The, uh, what he's talking about. The Demon."

"What?"

"I wish I'd read more of the creation myth. I never got to the Demon."

She looked at him closely. His fair skin was still blotched from the cold wind, and she did not know what he had been doing before they came, but it had not been sleeping.

"Tell me later," she said gently. "Why don't you rest?"

"Maybe—all right. That might be a good idea."

He took off his translator too and dropped it on the floor. His eyes closed, and she felt him think again: *Lie with me* ... But the thought trailed off sweetly, and he was quickly asleep.

Chapter VII

SOUNDS SPILLED FROM the video unit into her dreams. She woke slowly, swimming up through deep water, when they became louder. Gabriel touched her shoulder and she opened her eyes to see a Soldier standing over her, talking. The gossamer net of her translator lay abandoned on a shelf. She stumbled to it and got it on in the middle of a statement: "—will see you now. You must come with me. He orders it."

She muttered, "Wait, wait," and the Soldier stood patiently enough while she used the lavatory, ran cold water (the only kind) and splashed her face, hoping it would thin the fog in her head, but it did not. She came out to find the Soldier standing in the same place, Gabriel facing him, translator on. He looked around and said, "He only wants you."

The thought of leaving Gabriel behind in this maze made her uneasy. "I'm not going without you," she said.

"The Holy Man does not want Gergtk," the Soldier said.

"Tell the Holy Man he must see both of us."

"I cannot tell the Holy Man he must do anything. He tells me what I must do. He tells you what you must do."

Hanna sat down on the sleeping platform and simply looked at the Soldier. After a minute he took something from a pocket and put it in his ear and asked for instructions. She knew what they were before he said anything. *Wait for reinforcements; bring the female by force.*

The diffuse sense of threat she always felt on Battleground sharpened. She gave up and went.

In the hallway, unnervingly, there was a vehicle, a flat cart with rigid seats. She sat in it beside the Soldier while a second stood on a platform at the front and steered by means of levers. There was plenty of clearance for another in the hall, and it moved silently at a good fifteen kilometers an hour. She appreciated the reason for ramps now—and soon, the reason for the bar in front of her; the Soldier driving did not slow down much for corners. The machine had no other features, not even a display to show how fast it went. The Soldier must have a map of this warren in his head. Hanna did not. She was conscious of the increasing distance between her and Gabriel, but she could not have gotten back alone to where she had started.

She had been right about the dreadful distances they would face if they had to get out of this vastness on their own; the convoluted route to Kwoort took half an hour to travel. There were a couple of upward ramps, but more going down, and more activity in the lower levels, more of the silent open carts, many more Soldiers who registered the strange sight of her without fear or hostility, though there were flickers of awareness; she would have bet money on correlation between a Soldier's age and the degree of interest. Sometimes the cart skirted huge open areas. In one, hundreds of Soldiers were engaged in mock hand-to-hand combat; another enormous space held at least a thousand beings who were scarcely moving but swayed rhythmically— marching in place—while someone on a platform harangued them. She finally began to understand a little about the underground extent of Wektt's habitation. At that, if Kwoort's maps were accurate, it had once been much greater.

She would never find the way out on her own.

Presently they came to an open space that seemed to be a hub for other ways, doors instead of archways opening off it. "We stop here," said her escort, and she got off the cart and followed him through a door that led—exasperatingly— to narrower corridors, more doors. He took her to one of these and stood aside, and behind the door was Kwoort.

He was robed now in yellowish iridescence, exactly like Tlorr. He sat on a bench and was doing, apparently, nothing. Another bench faced it and Hanna sat down on it.

She said, "If I did not know you so well I would not be able to tell you apart from the Holy One of Rowtt. And yet to Rowtt you are the Demon."

"I would play both parts at once, if necessary, and be

Holy in Rowtt as well as Wektt. I would not be surprised if it has been done."

She said curiously, "Do many Soldiers know that Rowtt and Wektt communicate about the status of their Holy Men?"

"Not at this time. At other times there have been more who knew."

Hanna was silent, the thought dizzying; or maybe the dizziness was only, again, altitude.

"Kakrekt returns soon," Kwoort remarked.

Hanna did not know that Kakrekt had been away. Possibly she had gone to "repel hostile incursions," as Kwoort had done for Tlorr.

"What does that have to do with me, Kwoort Commander? Holy One?"

"She will want to talk to you. She may summon you herself. I want to be certain you know one thing: she is under my command. The things she talks about are only dreams, and as long as I am Holy Man her desires do not matter. Not to me and not to you. Do you know what I mean by dreams?"

"The things that happen in the mind while you sleep?" she said uncertainly. *Dreams* could mean other things to human beings.

"And sometimes to Soldiers who are awake. They happened to some of us many summers ago. That is when our builders found out how to go through space, and some of us went there, where not-Soldiers lived. But it was a dream. It was not real," he said, and Hanna caught a flash of something she had not been certain of before. The knowledge of *how to go through space* was firmly in the past, and safely— in humans' judgment—lost.

She absorbed the nugget with relief. One question answered. She said, though, "But you really did go to the place where some of us lived."

"It was an aberration, it was nothing. Kakrekt will see that her dreams are nothing, if she survives. Do not encourage her. Tell me now about the weapons you know. Tell me what they do. Tell me how to make them."

"I don't know how to make them. If I tell you what they do perhaps you can make them yourself. But you will have to give us something in return."

"And what do you think I have to trade?"

"Order Soldiers to accompany us to our worlds. We might gain useful knowledge from studying them."

"Then I must have the weapons first. I must have them in my hands."

"No."

"Then we have nothing more to talk about."

"Allow us to return to our spacecraft, then."

"No. Think about what I have said, and I will think about what you said."

Hanna thought of Kakrekt and her "dreams." Kakrekt might settle for knowledge.

"Very well," she said.

Chapter VIII

TIME WAS PUNCTUATED BY the meetings Kwoort required. It could not be measured by the intervals between them, which were sometimes long and sometimes seemed very short. Hanna made no discernible progress demanding research volunteers from Kwoort and he made no discernible progress demanding weapons from Hanna. At least they had defined goals, even if they weren't moving toward them. Kakrekt sometimes saw Hanna too, along with Gabriel, interrogating them fiercely about the kinds of knowledge not-Soldiers could help her get, but she could not do anything but talk about it because she was under Kwoort's command. She had something in mind about changing that, though, and Hanna began to guess what it was. But she did not tell Gabriel.

Time dragged. The supply of meal tabs dwindled. Hanna's reports to the telepaths carried no useful content.

Kwoort called us to him again today. He demanded that I "see into the mind," as he calls it, of Tlorr. I told him I couldn't, because I don't know Tlorr well enough to find her again.

That might be true, said Bella.

Or:

Kwoort demanded that I tell him how my sidearm was put together. He had a Soldier take it apart and the Soldier got sick and died. Radiation poisoning, I suppose. I told him I don't know how to make them, I only know how to use them.

That's true, said Bella. *You're technologically challenged.*

Or:

Kakrekt had us brought to her. She wanted a history lesson. Human history, I mean.

From you? That must have been a short conversation.

Gabriel's a teacher.

Not so short, then.

Pretty long, actually.

Did you learn anything?

I dozed off, actually.

The door was not locked. On the second day Hanna had opened it and walked down the wide corridor outside, between rows of flat gray panels and other doors. In one direction they stretched so far that dim lighting and diminishing perspective made the walls appear to converge in the dark. At the other, closer, there was a T-junction, but when Hanna got to it there was more of the same on either side. A Soldier came out of one of the doors and looked at her. The Soldier did not say anything, and Hanna went back to the room she shared with Gabriel while she still could; she was afraid that if she went around more than one corner she would not find the way back. The Soldier had not said anything to her but might have reported what he had seen, because the next time Hanna opened the door there was a guard outside who said they could not go anywhere.

She closed the door and looked at Gabriel. He shrugged. "You weren't going anyplace anyway."

In fact Hanna had begun to think it was possible. She had nothing to take notes with, but why could she not mentally recite lefts, rights, ups, and downs while another telepath accompanied her in thought and made a three-dimensional map?

Too late now. She would have to find other ways to pass the time.

One way was easy and, in retrospect, inevitable. Hanna's scruples about Gabriel's heart dissolved; in the early days of their enforced intimacy she acceded to mutual seduction, and found that heart tougher than she had supposed. Gabriel might be sexually inexperienced, but he was an adult more mature in many ways (Hanna admitted) than she was,

and she was pleased to offer him the adventure she suspected was now his real desire. He was moving beyond in-
fatuation, she thought. He was looking ahead—here, in this
place where he could see nothing—to a larger universe than
he had known before, and to the man he might become.

"If I could give back to you," he said once, "what you're
giving me—"

"How can you think you're not . . . ?"

He smiled down at her; she was moving a forefinger in
little circles on his chest, memorizing the texture of his skin.

"I mean loving you is going to affect the rest of my life.
I'll certainly never think of women the same way again."

She moved the hand to his disarrayed curls, memorizing
those too.

"You're keeping me human," she said. "Helping me shut
out these thousands on thousands of Soldiers' minds.
They're as heavy as all the concrete and rock—"

She shivered, reminded of that unbearable weight. Gabriel kept it from crushing her.

If you could get Metra's attention, Hanna said.

I got Metra's attention. Bella's thought signaled bad news
coming.

And? said Hanna.

Adair can't get the Commission's attention.

Hanna issued a burst of annoyance. Tinged with fear.

Why not?

*Something's going on with Colony One. Something about
virtual lives, alternate existence—*

Those things are nothing new!

Something about armed conflict.

Oh.

At another time Hanna might have been slightly interested in the matter.

Are you telling me nobody, nobody, *is paying attention to
this mission? Not even Starr?*

*Nothing's happening where you are. I guess that's satisfac-
tory for now. I bet he'd pay attention if we tried armed conflict, though.*

*That is not funny. What did Metra say about food? Did
you tell her it's nearly gone?*

She said the local food's non-toxic, so eat it.

Hanna had already admitted to Kwoort that though their meal tabs were down to a day's supply, Wektt's food-stuffs wouldn't poison humans. He had, in effect, also said: *So eat it.*

She could not make love to Gabriel all the time, and time had its own weight.

I could do, she thought, *what they give me all that credit for.*

Contact paid her well. Until now she had diverted almost all the credit to Jameson's household accounts. He then, over her objections, diverted it to a depository in Mickey's name but with himself in control. Hanna could not retrieve it after that, and she could not make him take it back. Arguing about it had proved a reliable source of entertainment.

Ultimately she was paid for being a telepath. She was sick and tired of Soldiers' thoughts, but finally resigned herself to doing what no one else could do, and prowled invisible through other beings' minds.

Kwoort prayed. He did not do it very well.

Smite the Demon but I am the Demon. Tlorr prays Abundant God to smite me! And I pray in return: Smite the Demon with your strong arm, and I mean, smite Tlorr. Does she pray with as much sincerity as she did when Quokatk was Holy here? I wonder did Quokatk merely go further into Holiness and we call it madness. Kwler was mad we said, Tlorr and I—

I am distracted. I neglect the prayers.

Guard the faithful against treachery am I supposed to say other prayers here I wonder. These are all I know. But they were prayers against Quokatk, so now they are prayers against me. How can I say them, I once thought there might be no Abundant God but he did not smite me for thinking that, instead he has made me holy and supreme in this place, so what does that mean. Except that I am the Demon.

It was better to be High Commander in Rowtt, I moved outside the citadels, I saw things—

Bones, said the not-Soldier female. All the crèches are built on bones.

If prayer had ever had a place in Kakrekt's mind, she had evicted it. Kakrekt was on the coast, planning a maneuver conceived before Kwoort appeared from Rowtt.

We have the advantage already, the Holy Man confirms it! Move troops from here and here and here, feint and use missiles to destroy opposing troops at this point, at that point, march, march to Rowtt—

Win! she thought. But Kwoort would not order it so the plan could not be carried out until he was gone.

*Someone is going to win this wa*r, Kakrekt thought. *I will win it. The Holy One will not be here to stop me. And then I will change the world.*

Quokatk no longer had any interest in war. Kakrekt was determined that what had happened to him was not going to happen to her. Holy Men came to think nothing could ever change, and that inevitability crushed them in the end. As long as she believed in the possibility of change, she was convinced, she would be sane.

Sometimes she wondered if thinking she could escape the end-change might itself be the beginning of insanity. But she refused to believe that. She had refused to believe that she would die in battle in her early years, and she had not. If the tactic had worked for that, why not this?

Sometimes Kwoort's prayers were fierce, accompanied by images of battle and carnage. And sometimes they were bitter as he prayed to an Abundant God in whom he did not, that hour, believe. Sometimes he thought of the long sweep of history that was irretrievable because the records of it had not been permitted to survive, and these thoughts left him prostrate on the floor. He had no word for what he felt, but Hanna had done her share of shuddering on floors, and knew that it was grief. At other times he tried to remember his life, and saw the raggedness of memory, and groaned with—not his word, but Hanna's—anguish. It was impossible for Hanna to determine which was the "real" Kwoort. They were all real.

———

Kakrekt fell into conversations with companions, officers subordinate to her. Sometimes these conversations were not about war. *Have you ever heard of. I have heard it said, have you. Who in this company is oldest?—summon her. I wish to protect my Holy Man, I have heard whispers about assassination, I have heard a rumor of poison.*

———

When Hanna came out of trance she thought: *So that is what Kakrekt means to do. I thought it possible and now I know. If I tell Kwoort I wonder what he will do—*

But then she had a second thought. It was a non-D'neeran thought, it was as far from transparency as it was possible to get.

Kakrekt would be easier to deal with than Kwoort. I will mention this to no one. Not yet . . .

Chapter IX

HANNA WALKED INTO the familiar chamber (cramped, gray) and looked at Kakrekt with surprise. She had expected Kwoort.

"Where is Kwoort Commander—I mean, the Holy One?" she asked.

"He sleeps," Kakrekt said. "His great age requires it. I do not want him to know of this meeting. There is something new I wish to discuss with you."

Hanna sat down on the hard bench. Her bottom was getting very tired of that bench. She said, "Do you want to discuss your intentions for the Holy One?"

That was risky, though it was exactly what Kakrekt "wished to discuss;" no one was supposed to know she had intentions for Kwoort. Hanna felt subliminal movement in the Commander's hand—a reach toward her sidearm, stopped before it started. She looked at Hanna carefully.

"Yes," said Hanna. "I have seen it in your mind. Kwoort has told you of this ability, has he not? I have not informed the Holy Man of what I saw in you."

Kakrekt stared at Hanna for a long time. It was the unnerving flat gaze of a lion; only the color was different.

Truly alien. Not one of us. Only a thing.

It was impossible for Hanna to have such a thought. That was Kakrekt, thinking of Hanna.

At least Hanna thought so.

Kakrekt's long hands moved, those deceptively slender hands. The silence ended when Kakrekt said, "We can't often meet together, we two, without the Holy Man's knowledge, and he will demand to know what we speak of.

Quokatk had ways to listen from a distance, and perhaps this Holy Man does too. But," she added as Hanna stirred impatiently, "we will be able to talk as much as we want in his absence."

"It would have to be a long absence!"

"It will be," Kakrekt said calmly.

Kakrekt did not add *It will be forever,* but she did not have to.

And then I could go home, Hanna thought, *true-humans could take over—*

But at such a price. Such a price to what Hanna suddenly thought of—perhaps she had been around Gabriel too long—as her soul.

"Be careful what you say," Kakrekt warned her, and embarked on a long, circuitous description of what happened to truly ancient Soldiers, the fading memory and episodes of rage—the same thing that happened (Kakrekt hinted) to those given a poison that mimicked the change. How, Hanna wanted to ask, will you get it into his food and drink? Whom will you employ? How employ them, or order them, with surety of their silence? But after Kakrekt's caution about "ways of listening from a distance" she could not ask openly. She did not even know if she could cooperate in this—well, this homicide.

Of course not.

But then again. And on the other hand . . .

She was taken back to where Gabriel waited without seeing anything. A horror of gray spaces was sinking into her bones. She looked at her hands and those looked gray, too. The blue stone in the ring was the only color in her life and she looked at it often, falling into blue for minutes at a time. It had become more active lately, as if it knew she needed to see the sky in it.

Gabriel sat on the floor, meditating. It was what he did instead of snoop in alien thoughts. His eyes opened when she came in and he started to smile, saw her face, and stopped.

She threw herself on the bed facedown; she did not want him to look at her.

All she had to do was nothing. She could even leave

Wektt now, insist on it to Kwoort, insist that Metra back it up with force if needed. Say to Jameson *Wait a year until Kwoort falls,* because she had seen, while Kakrekt described its effects, that the poison was long-acting. She would not have to tell anyone else the truth; she could say he already showed the signs, naturally. As, in fact, he did. Kakrekt proposed only to speed up the process.

Well, and murder him.

Gabriel said her name—he might have said it several times—and simultaneously she heard it like a tickle in her mind: *H'ana.*

She kept her face down and ignored Gabriel. The nudge to her thoughts could not be ignored. Not Bella this time, but Arch.

Captain says it's time for a report. Why've you been out of touch?

Reflexively, she curled her consciousness into a tight ball, as small as she could make it. Her muscles tightened, too, and she felt Arch react.

Concern! Alarm!—he might as well have been beating on the outside of her head like a drum.

Stop it!

She felt the answer as *BANG! BANG! BANG!*

And flipped over in a flurry of temper. Gabriel, hypersensitive, advanced on her; she shot a warning finger at him and he froze at her expression.

What are you hiding?

Only corruption, Arch, she thought wearily, put him off while she sat up and pointed that finger at Gabriel again, making him back off. His eyes were wide.

She lay back down and closed hers. She could not close out Arch's clamoring—she wished Dema had been the nearest telepath when the captain decided to demand a report, or Bella or Joseph—anyone but Arch!

Ten minutes, she pleaded. *Then Dema or Bella. Not you.*

Arch was gone, with a lighthearted pretense of being offended. She opened her eyes and there was Gabriel. "What is it?" he said. "What did Kwoort say?"

"Nothing. It was Kakrekt, not Kwoort. It's not important."

She rolled off the platform and went to the door, which,

of course, did her no good. Rock pressed on her like a presence, and the wall screen yammered propaganda. She would do anything to get out of here, anything. *I could get Kakrekt to give me a weapon and kill Kwoort myself. Metra would approve. The Commission would approve. It would be our secret. And Kakrekt would give us all we want and I could get OUT of here.*

Gabriel had turned to watch her and she met his clear eyes. He would not approve. Nor would her D'neerans.

Back to the bed. She could not hold still, she wanted her face to stay invisible: she threw an arm over her eyes. It did not stop her perception of Gabriel's worry. She removed the arm and turned her head to look at him.

"I wish you knew how to stop projecting," she said.

He said nothing. He knew the signs of secrecy and guilt when he saw them.

"Just what do you think I'm not telling you?" she said.

"I don't know," he said. "You've done something you knew you shouldn't. Or left undone something you knew you should have done."

She continued to look at him. The sounds from the wallscreen, the whistles and murmurs and clicks, seemed very loud. He said, suddenly certain, "Or have you not yet done the thing, or left it undone? Have you not yet decided? Is that what weighs on you?"

She said slowly, "I don't think it will make a difference, in the long run, to what happens. No difference to anyone but me."

She would not say any more about it. She had to concentrate on blocking this thing from her telepaths. She put the arm back over her eyes and lay without moving.

———

She could not make love any more, with this secret between them, and she could not tell Gabriel why. She slept, when she could, as much as she could. She was not used to such appalling amounts of sleep and woke with headaches. Time meant nothing. It means nothing when there is no sun to rise and set, when there is not, at least, a clock to measure seconds and hours. The wallscreen's endless flicker included, at one corner, a marker for time as it was counted on Battleground, but since Hanna had not bothered learning to read native script, she did not understand it.

In Standard chronology, however, it became the month of July.

Chapter X

JULY 1: Mickey Kristofik Bassanio was developing a concept of time. Day followed night followed day followed night. An "hour" was a long time. So was "a minute," when he wanted something. Months were beyond him, so far. "Summer" apparently described absolute joy: rolling down hills on cushions of emerald grass until he was dizzy, brilliant flower colors, sunlight so loud it boomed, intoxicating smells of leaves. He begged to stay up late and got to do it as soon as Starr (which came out "Tarr") and Thera ("Tera") understood that he wanted to watch the sky change until at dusk it was the same color as Mama's eyes. ("Mama" came out always, clearly and from the very start, "Mama.")

7th Siege of Twetsk: It is remarkable how much better I remember, now that I am here! It has become warmer and often I walk in a near valley where the clouds fall close, and today in the valley I remembered what the not-Soldier female said, of wishing Soldiers to go back to her world. I went back and summoned her and the male and said I will send them if you will show me how your weapons work. She said you have destroyed the one you took from me but if you allow me to talk to my Commander I will ask for another. I must talk to her soon, our supplies are gone, if you mean to keep us here we must get more. I said but you eat. She said I do not think your food nourishes us well. I think we are becoming ill. I must talk to my Commander.

Then I said, only if you think she will give us many of the weapons and send not-Soldiers to teach us how to use them.

I do not know what she might have said but the male immediately said no, he said it very loudly! And then he said

*their Commander would not endanger other not-Soldiers by
sending them here where they might be made captive.*

*I said you are not captives, you will not be here long, only
until we have discussed all we need to discuss, such as the
weapons. The female said, I also am ordered to continue discussions, and then she said she would like to walk in the
clouds in the mountains with me and I said no. And I remember all of this by the will of Abundant God.*

July 4: *What do you mean, make the captain contact Kwoort?
I can't make her do anything!*

Hanna conceded the point. She did not share Joseph's
alarm at the idea of demanding something from Hope Metra, but it was not likely to gain anything.

Besides, said Joseph, *you can talk to us. Why should Metra talk to Kwoort?*

I would like him, thought Hanna, *to be reminded we're not
alone and forgotten. And we need food. What's in this stuff
they eat? We're eating it, it comes out looking just like it looked
going in! I don't think we're absorbing any nutrients at all!*

I'll find out . . .

*But I really want Metra to insist on talking to us. To insist
on that assurance we're still alive.*

But she knows, because we *know,* he said, meaning the
telepaths.

*Kwoort doesn't know she knows. I told him Metra won't
let me communicate with her this way and he seems to think
that taking our com units has cut us off completely. It might
be good to keep him thinking that.*

I'll ask Metra to contact him, then. But what if she won't?

Then I'll *soon think we're forgotten . . .*

July 6: Jameson had gotten reaccustomed to the trappings
of office, and sometimes he wondered why he had ever
missed them. He could do without the implant, for example.
He could do without anything that required his presence in
the official Commission chamber, too. Every time he walked
into it he thought: *The builders were insane.*

It was really very high, immensely high, so that the upper
reaches melted into shadows and even, at the very top, into

darkness out of reach of all light. It dwarfed, incongruously, the small group of immensely powerful people who were at the bottom of that well, in the brightest of light, on a dais along one small arc of the circular hall. The materials acknowledged no debt to the past. The meeting place constructed for the earliest Commissions had been more human in scale and ornate, embellished with reminders of human history, reminders indeed of prehistory; when not in use the chamber had served as a museum. It still stood, its only function now to reflect the past. But the designers of the current structure, working four centuries ago, had not thought the past a proper subject for contemplation. The white wall—one could not say "walls" when a chamber was circular—was not even the natural marble of earlier times, but a synthetic whose reflectivity increased incrementally from the top of the dome to the floor below, so that at the lowest level it dazzled. It was meant to dazzle, literally—meant to induce a daze in lesser beings who approached the commissioners when they sat in formal session.

Lilifair, Co-op, wanted the disbandment, possibly by force, of a nearby settlement where God-sanctioned practices horrified even the locals, whose standards were fairly loose.

Approved. Fleet task force to be dispatched.

Almost over, Jameson thought. *I had forgotten what a gift a really short session is.*

The newish colony of Hostem, barely hanging on, wanted assistance. They wanted some of—a lot of—the servos that saturated Earth. They could not pay for them, but this just made their demands louder.

Denied.

There would be plenty of time, today at least, to play with Mickey.

Such a loss to me if—no, when—his mother returns.

Willow's own Coordinating League, unable to reach consensus, wanted the Commission to take responsibility for deciding on the semi-sentience, or lack thereof, of a native species, thus deciding if it should be protected or left to the mercy of an expanding human population. Andrella had finally gotten the belated controversy forced to Commission level; she was all for protection.

Protection is recommended.

And time later to see Catalyna. Why not? Since Hanna

*says never again. Honey hair, honey eyes, honey all over, I
suspect, and her mouth as delectable—worth pursuing, this
one. Worth pretending to believe a few lies . . .*

And once more the issue that preoccupied all of them:
Colony One. An old controversy coming to a head: How
strictly should escape into alternate, virtual realities be
regulated? The attrition of citizens addicted to the practice
was the dark byproduct of a huge industry. Figures on loss
of productive lives fell inside acceptable limits elsewhere,
but Colony One's rate was alarming. Worse, a major city
was on the edge of revolt at a proposed tightening of restrictions, and others were voicing support. Riot was imminent, Karin Weisz's position at risk.

Further discussion required.

Large matters and small, on and between the five Polity
worlds and many others besides.

Endeavor was not on the agenda.

July 10: Gabriel poked at the slab of something on his plate
and thought about steak. There was also a pile of shredded
something and a heap of mashed something. It was all the
same color. It all tasted alike to the human tongue. It was all
at room temperature. Perhaps it was supposed to be eaten hot,
and cooled as it was carried to the out-of-the-way billet where
he and Hanna were lodged. Or perhaps not. It was hard to tell.

Hanna was not there, but her platter would wait for her.
Kakrekt had summoned her.

He wondered if they were plotting something. No, he
was pretty sure they were.

He returned his attention to the food. He remembered
Hanna remarking on ideological differences between the
Soldiers who stayed in Rowtt and Wektt and those who fled
to That Place, assigning them to stages of intellectual development. But maybe it had nothing to do with that. Nakeekt
had talked of spices and varied foods, so maybe the exiles'
motives were simpler: the food was better in the isles of
That Place.

July 13: The telepaths had taught themselves to talk out
loud when true-humans were around. This was changing.

Deep down they had never completely trusted Carl and Glory, because deep down they had never trusted any true-humans (though they kept forgetting that when it came to Gabriel).

Now they didn't even trust Hanna.

The silent four-way conversations swelled in number and filled up with homesickness.

Does she know . . .
. . . what she is doing . . .
. . . this hiding . . . ?
Is it even important?
It must be, it's that wall, that impenetrable thing . . .
Maybe (lighter) *it's just that she's sleeping with Gabriel . . .*
Oh, she doesn't hide that!
Something, though . . .
. . . and there's all these . . .
. . . true-humans so-called . . .
. . . so that we hide, too . . .
. . . we don't want . . .
. . . true-humans . . .
. . . to know . . .

July 14: Hanna walked through a meadow sweet with the symphony of a long, cool spring. Every blade of grass was unmarred green. It wasn't a large meadow, and all around it thick, old trees spread new leaves. On the edge, smaller trees floated in clouds of white and pink and red. She knew that beyond the trees ran a clear stream fringed with bluebells. She did not have to leave the place. She would never leave.

Gabriel woke her. She was summoned.

Once more the interminable cart-ride through the caverns of spice-scent, though this time it was night and quieter, fewer cars and Soldiers on foot, no clamor of training. At the end of it, the prospect of another interminable conversation with Kakrekt.

Kakrekt had almost given over *What can your scientists* (translating as *investigators*) *do?* Now she asked *How will your investigators do these things?* Hanna could answer only with generalities, she was no archaeologist, no seer into the past. All the while she would think *Just give me your scrawny body, any Soldier's body, for research.* And all the while she would think *We'll send no scientists to work here for weeks, for months, where any moment they might be blown up!*

But Kakrekt surprised her this time.

When Hanna came in Kakrekt threw something soft at her and said, "Put this on."

It was a coat, heavier than any Hanna was used to and much too big for her. But she put it on eagerly, because Kakrekt meant to take her outside.

The dream of spring had lingered; it went away with a deep wrench of loss when they stepped into Wektt's early spring, which felt just like winter. She took a grateful breath anyway, glanced up, and was transfixed. For once the sky was clear and the Milky Way blazed across it. A glow over the peaks to her left suggested a near moonrise, but it did not diminish the glory of stars.

Kakrekt had personally driven her through many hallways and brought her to a door that was probably little used, since it opened on nothing but a barely discernible path that straggled off across the hillside. Kakrekt started off at a fast pace that Hanna could not keep up. She had long since adapted to the altitude, but she and Gabriel both were perceptibly losing strength, and she soon called to Kakrekt to slow down.

"This is far enough, I hope," Kakrekt said; she stood and looked back the way they had come. They had gone around an outcropping of rock and nothing of the complex was visible, only brown grasses flattened by frost.

"Far enough for what?" said Hanna.

"Far enough that no one will hear."

Still Kakrekt looked back, head up as if sniffing the air, though the respiratory tubes showed no unusual movement. Hanna caught herself thinking that and shook her head; there was no evidence that the organs housed Soldiers' sense of smell.

There was a puff of cold wind. Hanna pulled her hands into the too-long sleeves of the coat. Her hair blew into her face. It felt stiff. It was past waist-length now, dried and dull from the harsh liquid Soldiers used for personal cleansing, and the only comb she had was her fingers. If she had access to a mirror and looked at her face she would probably see a gray cast to her brown skin.

I am becoming gray, she thought in a moment's panic, *I will fade into this place and never get away,* and stilled the thought.

"I can't get the poison," Kakrekt said almost dreamily, looking at the sky. "No one here has heard of it."

"Then how do you know there is such a thing?" Hanna asked practically.

"I heard of it from Quokatk; it was how he became Holy Man, he used it on the one who came before him. But he is too mad now to ask, mad without poison, only with age. And all the others are too young. Except the new Holy Man himself; maybe he knew of it in Rowtt."

Hanna could think of nothing to say to that, and there was silence. Her feet, in the light shoes she preferred and had worn to the surface, were noticeably cold.

Kakrekt said, "This thing called speaking to the mind . . . It is more complex than that."

She looked at Hanna, and Hanna saw that Kakrekt's past-eyes had opened. This was important, then. Hanna did not answer, waiting.

"It is also," Kakrekt continued, "listening to the mind, as you listened to mine. The Holy Man believes it will be useful for spying."

Hanna said nothing, but she was indeed listening, and knew what Kakrekt would say next.

"Listen to the Holy Man's mind," Kakrekt said. "Find out about the poison, and tell me."

After a long hesitation Hanna lied, "I will try. As you said, the matter is complex. Once when I tried to listen to the Holy Man's thought, he perceived that I was doing so, and he also knew what information I sought. You would not want that to happen."

Four eyes regarded her, pale glints in the night. Hanna was afraid Kakrekt would demand telepathic assurance that what Hanna said was true. Some of it was, but Kwoort had sensed her touch only because she had been impatient and careless. She could do as Kakrekt requested. She only did not want to.

"When will you try?"

"I don't know. It will have to be a time—" lying, solemnly—"when he is particularly receptive."

Kakrekt seemed satisfied.

"Try as soon as you can. I will speak with you soon. Come now," she said.

They went back the way they had come, Hanna dragging behind, trying to prolong her escape into the open air if only by seconds.

———

July 17: The roses had been tampered with and bred back a century, and a century more and a century more and more centuries before that. They were small, and as inconspicuous as simple pink, red, and yellow can be against deep green leaves. The stems bristled with thorns. But their scent was as intoxicating as any drug, and potent on this bright summer evening.

Jameson had almost forgotten about them. He seldom came to this obscure corner of the gardens, having ordered the roses set in place twenty years ago only because they were rare.

Adair Evanomen waited for him here, a good walk away from the people who sipped drinks and swallowed luxurious tidbits on the terrace or strolled the grounds nearer the house. Their voices were inaudible from here.

I must bring—Catalyna here, Jameson thought, knowing his first impulse had been to share this sensuous luxury with Hanna. Who surely already knew about it; who knew far more about what grew on his lovely property than he did.

He nodded to Evanomen and raised an eyebrow but said nothing. It was the other man who had requested a private word.

"I'm sorry to take you away from your guests . . ."

"Never mind. What is it?"

"A conversation I had with Captain Metra today. Daily report, status quo for the most part. There was one troublesome aspect . . . How well do you know the telepaths on board? Besides Hanna, the others?"

"I've met them all. Carl and Glory, too."

"I didn't mean them. It's the telepaths—"

Evanomen looked around uncomfortably. He sat down on a bench almost hidden by roses, looking for words.

"Metra said the telepaths have stopped mixing with true-humans altogether, if they can possibly avoid it. When there's more than one of them and a true-human's present, they'll communicate with each other telepathically—an obvious parallel conversation to whatever they're saying to the true-humans. They didn't do that before, at least as far as anyone knew. Metra wonders what they're talking about."

Interesting . . . "What do you think it might be?"

"It could be anything, obviously. Metra suspects they're hearing things from Hanna that they're not passing along."

"What about Glory and Carl? Are they part of this supposed conspiracy?"

"The others have shut them out too. I'd like your advice on what to do. If anything."

Jameson did not answer at once. The sky had finally begun to darken, perfectly clear, as it had been all day. A couple of late butterflies drifted by. Mickey called them flying flowers.

Presently he said, "Get complete transcripts—word for word—of the telepaths' reports to Metra. Route them to me, too."

Evanomen's face was a question.

Jameson said, "Metra summarizes what they've said for you, and you summarize what she's said for me. 'Status quo,' you say. Things go missing in summaries of summaries. Get the originals."

"Hanna's the source, and we can only get what she says through the others. The issue is what *they* might be leaving out."

"We'll start with what we can get. Then we'll see."

July 18: Gabriel meditated on the simplicity of the tiny chamber. There were so few objects in it that space alone defined them; or did the objects define space? The question was elegant and beautiful, prompting gratitude for the purity of the place, gratitude for the moment, for the privilege of being at play in the fields of the universe—the experience of simply being alive.

He was honest enough to admit that creeping physical weakness might have something to do with this focus on lofty thoughts. Healthy, he might be preoccupied with lust. Or maybe he could accommodate both.

A Soldier came in without warning—there was never

warning, never a knock—and said that Kwoort wanted to see Gabriel alone.

This was a new demand, and Gabriel wondered if he ought to be afraid. He looked at Hanna.

She had lain down again as soon as the Soldier made it clear she was not wanted. He said her name and she looked at him, her eyes the only color in the room. She sat up, still holding his gaze, and he relaxed a little as her thought touched him.

You're worried? I'll be with you, if you like. Like this . . .

The cart, the caverns, all echoed with noise. He had not been out of the billet for some time, and after such isolation the warren felt like a mad cacophony. But, *I'm here,* Hanna said, and he leaned into the feather-touch, a shield against chaos. Being told things telepathically resembled, he thought, a mild electrical shock inside his head. Hanna was not telling him anything, she was only letting him feel her existence, in touches soft as the petals of flowers. It was her personality that he felt, and he drank it in. He was not aware of passing time until the Soldier ordered him out of the cart and he went slowly through a doorway to Kwoort. This was an anteroom, and he and Hanna had never gotten past it. Gabriel had seen Kwoort here a dozen times, sitting, standing, pacing. Today his posture on the bench where he sat was one Gabriel had not seen before, the long, flexible back curved, the head drooping.

After a minute Gabriel said, tentative, "Holy One?"

He had to repeat it twice, and go closer, before Kwoort looked up, and it was another long minute before the alien said, "Ah. The not-Soldier male."

Time, already slowed by endless inaction, slowed further. Kwoort appeared content to remain still forever. Finally Gabriel prompted, "You wanted to see me?"

Another minute.

"I did. I must have. Or you would not be here."

He looked down at something in his hands, sheets of paper or some other material. Gabriel took another step.

"What do you have there?"

"I wrote this, I think. I wrote it, I do not remember writing it! I found it in my satchel and perhaps another Soldier put it there but it is my hand. I must have written it."

He dropped his eyes—two eyes that looked dulled, the other pair closed—and began to read aloud.

"I cannot remember the prayers. I hear them in the walls and I know that I know them, I have always known them, but when I do not hear them I cannot remember them."

He went on, but his voice fell to a mumble. Gabriel thought of boosting the translator's volume, but then it was too late. Kwoort had fallen silent, staring at the papers in his hands. The satchel that accompanied him everywhere lay at his feet, more papers spilling from its mouth.

Presently Gabriel pulled another bench around and sat down on it, facing Kwoort, so close his knees almost touched Kwoort's robe.

Hanna's touch again, faintly questioning. Gabriel had no answer but patience.

A long time passed. Gabriel was not even aware that he had slipped into a meditation, contemplating the miracle of self-reflective consciousness, God's greatest gift, the attribute in which intelligent creatures most resembled Him. Simply to *be*, to know that one *was*, here in this gray cubicle, was miraculous.

"Teach me," Kwoort mumbled.

Gabriel said gently, "What would you have me teach you?"

"Teach me to pray!"

"I would if I could," Gabriel said, with a sadness lost in the translator.

Kwoort stared at him (*hungrily,* whispered Hanna's thought). *Why can't you teach him—oh!*

"Compassion," said Gabriel, knowing that Kwoort heard *cooperation,* the closest match the translator, after all this time, had been able to find. "Humility." *Possessing low rank.* "Kindness." *Cooperation,* again. "Pity." *Acknowledgment of another's inferior performance.*

He could have gone on and on, because he had done more than meditate and make love to Hanna. While she slept or stared at the ceiling and wrestled with whatever she withheld, he had listened to what the wallscreen was saying, explored what the translator could tell him about it, analyzed the results, and seen the implications.

"What you hear," Gabriel said to Kwoort, "is not what I'm really saying."

"That makes no sense!"

"I think," said Gabriel, "you're wired differently. I think we exist in—" He hesitated, looking for something that would translate accurately. "I think we exist in—in brain-states, we might call them—you're not capable of having. I think it has to do with the relationships we have with our young, where you have none. Because of that much of our language will not translate as we mean it, and those brain-states are active in our prayers."

Hanna sighed in his mind, *Give him something, Gabriel. Think of something!*

So Gabriel did. It did not seem like much, but it was all he had to offer.

"Listen to the wall," he said simply. "When you hear prayers, write them down. Then you will not have to remember them."

"Go," said Kwoort in a whisper, and called for a Soldier to take Gabriel away.

———

July 20: Bella was a darker brown than Hanna. Her round, blunt-featured face was not beautiful, but she looked open, honest, and trustworthy—as if all of Bella shone out of her face.

This was a trait shared by successful confidence tricksters, as Jameson had reminded himself when they met. He reminded himself again. The image from *Endeavor* showed only Bella's head and shoulders; there would be little body language to rely on. But he saw that her eyes—deep true green eyes, those indeed beautiful—were wary.

She did not have a nervous disposition, but after he had stared at her a little while in complete silence, she licked her lips.

He said in a voice like velvet, "I can't communicate with Hanna directly. You can. Establish communication with her, please."

He expected her to balk, and she did, throwing her head back and saying *"What?"* as if he had proposed something obscene.

"I need to talk to her and I can't," he said patiently. "Not with technology, not with telepathy. I'm asking you to be, so to speak, my interpreter. Contact her now, please."

"It's not that easy—"

"Of course it is. You do it frequently. The conditions might be a little different; you won't be doing any after-the-fact editing."

"We wouldn't do that," Bella said, looking innocent.

"You're doing something, and hiding it so poorly even Metra has noticed. Talk to Hanna for me. And don't leave anything out."

Unexpectedly, Bella grinned.

"We're pretty bad at it, aren't we?"

She still looked at him, but her eyes refocused on something inward that he could not see. Jameson knew the look.

Bella said, "She's asleep."

"Wake her."

This time her resistance was in earnest.

"She's dreaming. I don't like going into dreams. A lot of it comes from a preverbal level, and it's crazy in there."

"Show her a door and knock on it. Keep knocking. Make her hear the sound."

A look of respect. She had not known how much he knew about telepathy. He ought to; Hanna answered questions readily. It was only being its object he did not like.

It seemed to take a long time for Hanna to wake. The silence was the first still interval in Jameson's long day, and in it he became aware that he was tired to the bone. There had been two nights of violent storms, and Mickey had been afraid and come to Jameson, not Thera, for consolation. He was short on sleep and more storms were promised for tonight. He had already told Catalyna he could not see her. The affair was likely to die before it even started—

"She says you wouldn't want her now. She's all gray and thin, just bones . . ."

He couldn't read Bella's face; there were too many emotions, passing too quickly.

"Is she awake?"

"Yes."

"Is she sick?"

"Maybe . . ."

Surprise now, and grim disapproval.

"They ran out of supplies, they're eating native food. It's not poison, but they wonder if it was nourishing them. We knew that. Hanna says now she's sure. She says they can't live on it. She doesn't mean it's not sustaining them well enough, she means there's no nourishment at all."

"Why the hell wasn't that in your reports?"

Bella focused on Jameson fully. "We reported what we knew to the captain. I don't know what happened. And Hanna wasn't positive before, and now she is."

"I'll take care of it." *Somehow.* "What else is going on?"

A pause. Then Bella said, "Nothing. Nothing's changed. They've come to some hypothesis about the translation program—Gabriel's come to it—"

"Go over it in the next report. What's she not saying, Bella? Or are the rest of you hiding something, all of you?"

Bella's mouth opened and closed again. She said finally, "It's not us. Hanna's keeping something back."

"Ask her what it is."

"If she won't tell us, she won't tell you!"

"Ask her."

The unfocused look again. Then perplexity.

Disbelieving. "She could tell you, but not us?"

"Then I'll find a way to talk to her," he said, though he could not see how.

Bella said, "How is Mickey?" with a longing that must be Hanna's.

"He's good . . ." Jameson hesitated, but Hanna deserved more than that. "He's afraid of thunderstorms. He wants to be in my lap when they come, he's fine then. But Hanna would be better. She could do more with thoughts than I can do with words. Soon—I want her—he wants her home soon. But he's safe, and loved. He's very much loved."

"Don't cry," Bella whispered, and he actually put a hand to his eyes before he realized she meant the words for Hanna.

July 21: Back to Kakrckt, a commute so familiar by now that Hanna dozed on the way. She surfaced fitfully from time to time, to snippets of thought, memories of talk.

"You'd think starving people would notice sooner . . ." Her own voice.

"No hunger pangs. We eat as much as we can stand. You were already too thin, and so lethargic—the word doesn't start to describe it. But I couldn't understand why my clothes

were getting loose, or why I feel so strange . . . All I want to do is sleep."

"You are here," said the escort, and Hanna straightened, resisting a hysterical laugh. *You are here,* universal guide to complex maps: here at the edge of the explored universe, trapped and weak and alone.

No, she thought; only conditionally trapped; Starr might decide to move that warship up, and Battleground wouldn't stand a chance with Fleet. Nor alone: there were D'neerans on *Endeavor.*

But weak, that, yes. It took more effort every time to crawl out of the carts.

She did not have to crawl out. She was hauled out by Kakrekt pulling on her arm.

"Come, come—"

This was a febrile excitement she had not felt in a Soldier before. Kwoort was prone to something like it—

"But the language has no words for these emotional states because most users of the language don't experience them after a sort of, think of it as priming the pump, at the start of puberty. After that it's gone for years, for centuries." Gabriel. *"Most don't live long enough for, oh, for the circuits to activate fully—"*

She was dragged through Kakrekt's quarters, through doors, through narrower corridors she had not seen before.

"Slower!" she gasped. Something had finally taken hold of her spotty concentration. It was the heaviness in her legs.

"You are always slow, now you are almost standing still," Kakrekt said impatiently, but she slowed as if for a pet that would not be hurried.

The narrow corridors gave way to wider ones with Soldiers coming and going, the hush to a rumble that stirred Hanna's memory. They came abruptly to the space Hanna had seen on her arrival here, the hangarlike cavern with Soldiers crawling over machines in many stages of construction or repair, using noisy tools, shouting at each other. She stumbled through the chaos, dizzy, following Kakrekt's sinuous figure. A gray glow of natural light grew ahead of them, and they came out onto a familiar plateau. Snow fell here, big feathery flakes. The wet ground showed that earlier flakes had melted, but the air must have cooled and now there was a thin layer of white over everything.

Kakrekt did not hesitate. She grabbed Hanna's arm again and dragged her into the snowfall. Hanna's feet slipped on treacherous rock; on a wave of fury she tried to pull away, and failed, off-balance and weak. This slithery walk went on forever, downhill, minute after minute, until Kakrekt suddenly stopped and Hanna looked up again, freezing, snow splattering into her eyes, and there, like a precious mirage, was the pod.

She couldn't stop herself, the code words burst out of her mouth, the translator was programmed not to twist them and the hatch whipped open. She wanted to rush for it, and Kakrekt's hand held her just long enough to think that would not be wise; and anyway it would be a stagger, not a rush.

"I know where you can go," Kakrekt said.

Yes, to Endeavor, *only there*

"If anyone has what I require," Kakrekt continued, "it will be Nakeekt, or others on her islands, the oldest ones. That is where you will go."

Her grip had relaxed, and Hanna twisted free. She said, "That Place must be the worst-kept secret on this world. I've been there, and Nakeekt told me not to come back. What makes you think she will give me any help?"

"She would not, but she will help me. She must, if she wants That Place to survive. You will show her this." Kakrekt's long fingers dipped into her coverall and came out with something flat and gray. "The directive is in here. It is detailed. She is to give what I demand to you, not to your escort, not to anyone else."

"What escort?"

"Wox." Kakrekt raised her voice. "Wox!"

A shadow in the falling snow turned into another Soldier, shorter than Kakrekt, a little stockier than the norm.

"Wox has a hand weapon," Kakrekt told her. "He will not kill you. But if you do not go directly to That Place, and come directly back again, he will hurt you, only not so much that you cannot fly this craft. And if you attempt to call your Commander, he will disable you enough so that he can reach into your mouth and cut out your tongue. He has a knife for that purpose."

She gave Hanna a shove toward the pod's entry ramp. Wox was already making his way up it, rather slowly and suspiciously.

Hanna ducked another shove, more startled than alarmed by the direct threats, the first from anyone on Battleground.

"Wait, wait! Kakrekt Commander, as soon as I start to power this craft, a signal will go to those who sent me. They will immediately try to communicate. If I don't answer I don't know what they will do. Think it taken by someone unauthorized and destroy it from space, maybe. I will have to answer them, and what could I say? I do not want—"

"Wox! *Wox!*" Kakrekt's shout soared to a warbling whistle; Wox scrambled back down the ramp, and Hanna thought of making a dash for it—

move fast, get the ramp up, take off and—

—but Kakrekt's hand clamped on her arm again hard enough to bruise, and when she tried to jerk free Kakrekt said something and Wox's bigger hand came up and hit her so hard that her head rocked.

When it cleared she was in the pilot's seat in the pod, tasting blood, and Wox stood behind her with Kakrekt.

"I would go with you but I can't," Kakrekt said. "Your Commander has demanded to talk to the Holy One and I am determined to be there when she does. I will say, you will say when you are asked, that you have gone to perform a task for me. To learn about our history, you will say. Wox knows what you are allowed to say. Go now. Go *now.*" And Kakrekt was gone.

Wox poked Hanna's shoulder. "Ramp up," she said automatically, thinking *Is my cheekbone broken, I don't think so, just hurts like hell*, "power up," *shaky, long time since I was hit*, and the readouts came alive. The first one her eye fell on showed the date, and her breath caught. The days had blurred together, she had never asked the D'neerans what day it was in Standard time, preferring to believe her imprisonment was not as long as it felt. But that was wrong. She had been in Wektt for six Standard weeks.

Chapter XI

A SOLDIER CAME FOR HANNA, but she was not there. The Soldier looked for her—it was almost funny, Gabriel thought, because where could she hide? The room was a gray box. The bathroom—literally, "water-cube"—was just a setback behind a partition that gave the humans welcome privacy, but was only there to keep water from spattering into the rest of the box, keeping down the mold that had to be scrubbed away. Soldiers presumably were supposed to do this for themselves, and no cleaning crew had showed up in this billet (Soldiers did not use servos), so Gabriel had appointed himself mold-scrubber-in-chief. As his energy waned, however, the mold had begun to win.

The Soldier went away, scratching his head in an eerily human way. Gabriel lay down and sank back into torpor. After a while, a minute, an hour, the door slammed open again, jarring him out of it. Three more Soldiers charged in, and then, amazingly, Kwoort himself.

"Where has she gone?"

Gabriel didn't bother to sit up. The weakness that had been growing on him—and on Hanna—seemed to have taken a quantum leap. Every move demanded thought, a determination of how much energy it required.

"I don't know. Nobody tells me anything. Somebody came and got her. If you don't have her, maybe Kakrekt does."

"What would Kakrekt want with her?"

"What she always wants, I guess. Whatever it is. What do you want?"

"I am to speak with your Commander. And your Holy Man. I—"

"What Holy Man?" Gabriel said, but Kwoort went on without hearing him, "They want to see her. To see if she is well."

Gabriel said nothing. Kwoort ordered his entourage into the corridor and gave more orders Gabriel did not hear, though he heard Kakrekt's name. Then Kwoort came back and stood inside the door, at first very still, and waited. Presently he began to fidget. *He's getting just like the first one, just like Kwler,* Gabriel thought vaguely, but then he dozed again.

———

Jameson had used, in some desperation, a stimulant. Kwoort had been adamant about the only interval he could spare from his devotions, and then he would only do it to confer with a not-Soldier of equal rank. Jameson, in further desperation, had allowed himself to be temporarily and falsely designated Holy. The interval happened to fall at three o'clock in Jameson's morning. At least Mickey had finally gone to sleep around midnight, though thunder still rolled through the sky. *I am too damn old for this,* he thought, inhaling the vapor his contact guaranteed was black market Fleet issue.

He summoned official transport, less conspicuous in the night sky than his personal aircar (which shouted of privilege). Before he reached Admin he learned that Kwoort had arbitrarily canceled the conference, but he did not turn back. The telepaths had told Metra almost simultaneously that Hanna had been forced to leave Wektt—and wouldn't tell them why. At least she was in control of the pod; but Gabriel was still deep underground.

———

The telepaths all knew about the aborted conference, and they were all awake, and they all knew where Hanna was, and called for her attention.

But she could not hold two conversations at once, and the one she had to have aloud, with Communications, was delicate.

"A task as a favor for Kakrekt Commander," she explained, ears pricked for Wox with his knife.

"What kind of task? Where are you going?"

The voice was familiar, but the man's face and name escaped her. She did not answer at once; she concentrated on climbing up, straight *up*, past the snow, through the clouds, up and up until she could see the sun just beyond the terminator, and the pod filled with golden light that made her gasp and made her eyes water. Sunlight at last! She drank it in, every cell in her body rejoicing.

The voice began, "Team leader Bassanio—"

"Yes. Sorry. Uh, the task is a matter of historical research. An observer is with me. I'll report when I can."

"Very well." The scantest hesitation; Wox would not find it significant. "Your team will await word from you." Telepathically, was the implication.

"As soon as possible. Over."

Definitely not alone, and not so trapped, either, but—she began to feel the weariness born of hunger again—she would still keep to herself Kakrekt's reason for sending her to That Place. A plan of murder would not suit her D'neerans. She didn't want to deal with their combined righteousness, not yet, not when she thought murder might not be a bad idea at all.

———

Soldiers had a nice line in invective, Gabriel was interested to find. There were a lot of references to what the translator prissily called "excrement," and many accusations of laziness ("lapse in industry") and dereliction of duty. He listened for references to sex, that staple of human mudslinging, but the closest Kwoort and Kakrekt got was mutual accusation of failure to breed. After a while he deactivated the translator and listened to a cacophony of top-volume clicks and whistles, punctuated by spoken (shouted) words. Hanna should be here, he thought. The scene would add something to her theory that emotional life developed with Soldiers' aging. These two were certainly old enough to emote!

———

The telepaths wanted a conversation, but Hanna didn't. She told them about Wox, the watchdog, but nothing else. You didn't have to be Adept to slide an all-purpose veil over your thoughts, though it helped, and that was what Hanna did, hiding behind shutters. She could not escape the awareness that everyone knew—the true-humans, too—that she hadn't told them everything. She would have to do *something* about that soon—eventually—

But she was busy. The pod was capable of getting back to someplace it had already been without help from her or from Navigation, so she told it where to go and began a search of every storage compartment in its interior. Maybe she had overlooked a meal tab or two.

The search was short and unproductive. At the end she found herself face to face with an intruder, a frightening face on the wall, bruised and strained. Who . . . ?

She blinked at her reflection in the medical cabinet door, which did not blend with the matte tan of everything else but was shiny and purposely made to stand out. It was unlikely to hold anything edible, but she opened it anyway. No food. She started to close it and her eyes fell on a neat row of tiny vials. Stimulants could substitute for food. For a while.

Wox was not watching. He was looking out with mild curiosity, and some trepidation, at something he had never seen before: the brilliant white masses of cloud below.

Hanna pried the vials from their nest and slipped them into a pocket.

I can't use them, I can't risk it, but maybe Gabriel . . .

They talked about foodstuffs for Gabriel that could be delivered by unmanned transport, and about starting continuous transmission to Wektt requesting permission to come get him or, failing that, a demand that the supplies get to him.

"Last resort, we'll go dig him out," Metra said.

"Do you know where he is in that maze?" Jameson asked.

"Only approximately."

"You're risking casualties, then."

"I hope not. I'm thinking we'd move the *Admiral Wu* into the system and borrow some combat servos. Use minimum personnel."

Evanomen looked strained and said nothing. He probably wished he had stayed Deputy Director for Trade.

Bella, part of this meeting over Metra's protest, said, "What about H'ana?"

"We can't intervene while she's in transit with an armed Soldier," Jameson said. "And she's not likely to overpower him. Not if she's been starved for a month."

Metra looked up from a readout. "She's definitely headed for That Place. Just confirmed by contact with the pod's navigation systems. Why does Kakrekt want her doing historical research?"

"She doesn't," Bella said. "It's a cover for something else. I don't know what."

"Can't you tell? Why not?"

"She's shielding. H'ana can shield better than anybody I know. You people throw around the word 'Adept' and you don't know what you're talking about. There's only a few hundred on all D'neera, and there's only about ten of her caliber. She might be better than any of them. Listen, the food. I could just take the other pod, with supplies, and go to That Place myself."

Metra sorted that out. "I don't think we want them to know we're tracking Bassanio," she said.

"Are you going to let her starve? I could expect it of you," she told Metra, "but *you?*" This was for Jameson. "That guy with her, he hurt her. Hit her. I picked that up trying to read her, she saw her reflection and her face is swelling up."

He was silent under Bella's green gaze. The passion in her face reminded him of the unguarded moments that had once come easily to Hanna, though not so easily now. She had become miserly with emotion, Mickey excepted; she had done her best to leave behind the young woman he had first known and loved. He had tried to find out why and she had refused to tell him, leaving him to guess. Best guess: the devastation of Michael Kristofik's death had been so terrible that she was afraid emotion, if allowed its freedom, would destroy her.

She had put out her hand to him years ago, with her heart in it. Unforgivably, he had undervalued the gift. Now he thought he might go on paying for that for the rest of his life.

He abandoned talk of strategy and said so gently that all of them stared at him, "We won't let her die."

You'd think she could think to me . . .

Gabriel thought of turning over, just for variety, but the effort required too much commitment. He remained on his back.

If Kwoort and Kakrekt had not chosen to have their explosion in this room, all spice and fury, he would have had no idea that Hanna was not still in the complex.

He was cold. Somebody must have turned down the heat. If Hanna were here he could huddle against her, though lately even slight pressure seemed to start up inexplicable bruises.

He thought of Cory, the starved little boy who had been found abandoned in a demolished domicile in some place of war. Cory was not starved by the time Oversight brought him to Alta, but there were images in his records. Gabriel wondered if he would look like that at the end, skin barely, obscenely, veiling naked bone.

No! somebody said.

"Bella?" he said out loud.

Hold on a little longer. We'll get supplies to you. Or get you out.

In the thought he saw servos marching as implacably as Soldiers, fire and dust in the teeming caverns. Soldiers dying.

"Not because of me!"

Not your decision.

"Just supplies, only that. Please. But Hanna. Kakrekt sent her away."

I know. Don't worry. Starr Jameson said she won't die.

"You believe him?"

I've seen them together. He'll get her back.

The Parting Observance popped into his head. "Even after . . . ?"

Even. Be patient. Food is coming.

He didn't feel hungry, but he said, "Send chocolate."

He drifted off into prayer, into Psalms. *I will satisfy you with the finest of wheat. I will feed you with honey from the rock . . .*

Chapter XII

THE SUNLIGHT DIDN'T LAST LONG; Hanna dropped the pod to a lower altitude, back to night though still above the clouds, and the pod flew toward a morning it would not reach. All three moons were visible, neatly lined up, the nearest round and full, the others crescents of partial eclipse. Hanna wondered how often this conjunction occurred; she thought of tides and Metra's stupid boat proposal. *We wouldn't have lasted long near land. And how would she have explained* that *to the Commission?*

Then remembered Metra had never meant the expedition to happen. It had only been meant to force Hanna to mutiny.

Hunger was affecting her memory, her thought processes. *I must remember that I am forgetting . . .*

She thought to herself that she sounded like Kwoort.

H'ana . . . whispered Bella in her mind.

She acknowledged the contact wordlessly.

Please tell us. Please tell me what's going on.

She did not have to hide everything. Not homesickness, though she no longer knew if she longed for D'neera or for Earth. Not the exhaustion of hunger, not the pain where Wox had hit her, or the loosened teeth, or the swelling headache.

This blow, it's the first time they've hurt you, is that significant?

I don't think so. I think it was just encouragement, Soldier-style.

Hanna drifted. She felt Bella thinking to herself, a quiet background murmur. Oh, this was like home, where being alone was a choice, and nothing stayed secret forever; she could not cut herself off from this. If she acquiesced in Kakrekt's plan, abetted it, still someday, if she wanted to stay D'neeran, she would have to acknowledge what she had done and face the consequence. There would be no judgment by a court and she would not be punished. The consequence would only be that D'neerans knew the thing she had done. Would that be enough to stop her doing it?

———

Joseph wanted to lay things out logically. "What is H'ana's exact status? Medical condition, mental condition, how is she going to be received, where's the reports on when she was there before, we should look at those—"

Arch said, "There's Gabriel, too—"

"Oh, him."

"You never liked him."

"And he's very likable, for a true-human." Dema added.

"I don't *not* like him."

"You don't like him," Arch said firmly. "You're jealous, you don't see why H'ana wants a true-human friend when she's got us. That's so parochial."

"Will you all shut up," Bella said.

"I am not parochial. I've been to Earth, I spent months—"

"On *Endeavor,* before we got here. We know. And you're still parochial."

"You're projecting—"

"Shut up! Playtime's over!"

They subsided and Bella said, "We know Gabriel's status. He's safe for the moment, if we can just get him food. But H'ana could be headed for—" A thought like a glimpse of darkness. "Nakeekt was hostile when the last contact ended. She might kill H'ana before she can deliver Kakrekt's message."

"I think she threatened to do that if H'ana came back. If memory serves," Dema said.

"Arch here, though—" Bella shot him a glance, as if she could not believe what she was saying. "Arch has an idea."

Arch beamed. "H'ana's got one friend there," he said. "Kwek. We should talk to Kwek. And she knows me, too. She'll listen to me."

———

Kwek was not asleep. Sleep had been scant for two nights and she knew why, but even if it wasn't *that* how could she sleep when the rain made that noise outside and the wind moaned like a dying Soldier? She should have stayed in Rowtt, in dry tunnels with whispers of ventilation and the reassuring clink of machinery.

—*all those not-Soldiers' fault, they brought me here*—

There, someone said, practically, *is where you wanted to go.*

Not to stay! thought Kwek, not immediately aware that she was not alone.

The communicator she had worn when the not-Soldiers brought her here appeared in front of her eyes. How had it gotten here from wherever she had put it, did it move about by itself? She made a grab for it.

No, it's a picture in your mind. Think, Kwek! I'm speaking to your mind!

It was Arkt!

I do not want to be here!

The communicator, Kwek.

She remembered where she had last seen it, and scrambled for it.

"It is about time you contacted me! I have been thinking about you day and night! Where is Gergtk? I want to talk to Gergtk!"

"Gergtk has gone to Wektt. Haknt is coming to see Nakeekt, though. You will see her soon."

Silence. Then Kwek said more quietly, "I, I want to talk to Gergtk."

"You can talk to me, Kwek. We've talked before. What do you want to say? Has something unpleasant happened to you?"

"I have to work," Kwek said. The translator could not convey sullenness, but Arch, the thread still stretched between their minds, felt it. "I have to work in the fields and forest, I have to make clean the building where I live, I have to care for the grass on the landing field and elsewhere, I have to prepare food, I have to make—" *Chirp.* Some product, untranslatable. "I have to do this, I have to do that, I thought there would be more time to talk and remember and write things down and learn!"

"It's not what you expected," Arch prompted.

"No, it is not! I had to do many things in Rowtt, but not all at once! I had only one assignment at one time!"

"That's because you're in a small community—" *Chirp.*

"A small complex. Everybody must do everything, in such a small place. Everyone does a little of everything in the places where we live, too."

"It is like this where not-Soldiers live?" Kwek said dubiously.

"It's like that in many places on the world where we live, those of us who speak to the mind."

"But it leaves little time to do what I want!"

"But you didn't want to go back to Rowtt," Arch said. "And there isn't any other place except Wektt."

"In Rowtt they say Wektt is worse because the Demon is there. What is Gergtk doing there? The Demon will not let him survive!"

Arch said incautiously, "I don't think it's worse, but you could ask the Soldier who is coming with Haknt. He lives in Wektt."

Kwek gasped, "A Demon Soldier is coming here?"

"No, no, he is not—"

"What is Haknt doing with the Demon? Has she gone over to his side?"

"Not exactly... Kwek—" she was making ambiguous noises, and he raised his voice—"You were having some doubts about what's believed about Abundant God, weren't you? Doesn't that mean you have some doubts about the Holy Man and the Demon, too? Aren't some of the people at That Place from Wektt?"

"Yes, but they do not belong there, that's why they came here—Haknt is with a Demon Soldier? There is one on the spacecraft?"

Even the translator managed to invest the words with Kwek's horror.

Bella muttered, "You shouldn't have mentioned Wox. Kwek, Haknt is not on our spacecraft. She is in the small craft you traveled in with her and Gergtk, and she is close to you. They are coming to That Place—"

"She is coming with the Demon?"

Arch thought contacting Kwek might not have been the best idea he had ever had, but he had another one. The Commission would crow over a voluntary specimen, wouldn't it?

He said, "Forget about the Demon. If you don't want to go back to Rowtt, and you don't want to stay at That Place, and you don't want to go to Wektt, we could let you spend some time on our spacecraft. Do you want to do that?"

"Will the Demon be there?" Kwek said suspiciously.

"The Demon will not be here."

"Nakeekt will not allow me to go."

"Haknt can talk to Nakeekt about it. If she agrees, will you come?"

"Oh, yes," Kwek said. "And maybe I will just go away with you when you go. Maybe I will never come back to this world again."

Yes! Arch thought, but not to Kwek.

"You won't have to, if that's what you want. But for now, Kwek, now—"

Now took a few minutes to establish, because Kwek dithered. But she agreed at last to go for Nakeekt and tell her Kakrekt had sent Hanna to her. It ought to make Nakeekt think, at least, before she pulled out a weapon.

Kwek did not like being outdoors. Record-keepers did not have to go outdoors often, and she had been record-keeper for twenty summers, when she was not breeding, and when she was in a crèche she had not had to go out either. It got hot in the groves where she harvested the things that grew on trees, even more hot in the clearings where she dug and pulled other things up (with more effort than she was used to) from the ground. She wasn't sure she ought to be going to Nakeekt on some Demon-consorting not-Soldier's instructions and besides, Nakeekt was suspicious of the not-Soldiers to start with and had sent them away and besides, Haknt had a Demon Soldier with her and maybe Nakeekt would not like that either and besides, it was raining. Getting wet with rain was even worse than getting wet with her own sweat, which had never poured from her so copiously as it had since the not-Soldiers brought her here. And her billet in Rowtt had stayed cool, but her billet here sometimes remained hot all day and all night.

Kwek went, though; she knew what building to go to, and ran to it through the rain. Inside she started up a ramp. She got to the second level and realized she did not know which billet was Nakeekt's, so she pounded on the first door she came to, pounded and pounded, and eventually started shouting.

Another door opened and a cross face peered out.

"What do you think you are doing? Why are you making noise at the door of a billet where no one sleeps?" said a Soldier she knew as Mwintsk.

Kwek thought Mwintsk was an unpleasant Soldier. Yesterday he had told her she was not digging fast enough, and then when they were eating he had told her not to jump around so much, and when had she said her time for breeding would come? But she said, "I have something to report to Nakeekt."

"Whatever it is, it can wait!"

"I don't know. Are you an officer?"

"I *was* an officer."

"And it can wait?"

"Anything can wait! What can't wait?"

"The Demon is here," Kwek said.

"You have been dreaming. Go back to your billet and go back to sleep."

A clear order from an officer overrode everything else.

"Very well," Kwek said, and retreated down the ramp. That was an order, to be sure, but on the other hand this was not Rowtt, and she did not know where to find Nakeekt, and a Demon-Soldier was coming and Nakeekt had told Haknt never to come back and Nakeekt would not like Kwek bothering her about Haknt and—

Wox poked Hanna's shoulder. She came slowly out of—not sleep. An energy-conserving half-consciousness in which she spent more and more time, brain idling, systems at minimum.

One poke, but the intrusive fingertip would leave a bruise.

"What?" she said.

"The craft spoke."

The pod was no longer over cloud but under it and in fact was on the ground. It had brought her back to exactly where she had specified: the landing field at That Place. Outside there was nothing but blackness, but a readout said the land was covered with steady rain again (or still, for all she knew). She touched a control point for outside audio, and heard the downpour's monotonous drumbeat. No light showed in any direction and there was no sound of an alarm.

She felt Bella's familiar touch in her mind.

Kwek was supposed to wake Nakeekt, but she . . .

Images. Kwek had run away, overwhelmed, into the rain. She was not even on a path, but she could see well enough in the dark to keep from running into things.

Have you tried . . .

Arch has tried, but she just keeps saying nonono . . . She has a com unit, but she doesn't respond . . .

"I wish you hadn't done that," she said aloud.

"What?" said Wox.

"Nothing."

Why? Bella said.

Hanna could not think of a reason. Something in her had sounded a warning, saying it was a mistake to add Kwek to the mix of uncertainties. But maybe it was only a short circuit in her own brain.

"I will go to Nakeekt now," she told Wox. He got up immediately. He would stick to her until Kakrekt's orders were carried out, unrelenting as her shadow.

The hatch seemed to take a long time to open, the ramp to descend. She knew it was not long, that her perception of time was skewed. She thought of the ghost for the first time in a long time.

where are you, ghost? you were good with a knife. could we get Wox's knife do you think

And heard:

i think not. we're too weak

She fingered the vials of stimulant in her pocket.

No! said Bella. *Don't even think about it! Telepathy's the only advantage you have! And what if the blackout's permanent next time?*

Hanna and Wox went down the ramp and out into the rain.

You would think. You would think an artifact as sophisticated as the pod would give its passengers a way to keep dry outside. It carried plenty of supplies (minus, now, edibles) but it did not carry a single portable, one-person rain deflector. Hanna, from a plainer culture than the Polity's, would have settled for a simple umbrella.

The landing field had been scythed almost to the dirt—
Kwek had done a good job in spite of her objections, or
others had worked with her—and the dirt had turned to
mud. Hanna's feet sank into it until she got to the edge,
where the ground cover was thicker. Her clothes were plas-
tered to her body, but there was one advantage: people who
were dripping wet did not look so much like threats.

She supposed she would find Nakeekt in the same warren as before, the building in which she and Gabriel had
slept, and paused to get her bearings. It did not matter how
long she stood in the rain. She was already sodden. In the
stillness she opened her mind and heard dreams. Oh, there
was plenty of dreaming here!—and Soldiers' dreams were as
absurd as humans'.

Wox poked her again. She was two meters away before
she knew she had moved. He took a step toward her and
she hissed, "Don't *do* that! Don't touch me again!"

Something had ignited inside her, but he could not tell
that from her face or her voice. He said, "You were not
moving. You are to go to Nakeekt."

She thought of the knife again. Wondered, if she cracked
a vial of the stimulant next to one of those breathing tubes,
would the gas affect him, knock him out, something—

H'ana.

Bella. Calming.

"Leave me," she started to say aloud, but Wox would
think she spoke to him and he would argue, or just hit her.

Leave me. Don't distract me.

Bella knew evasion when she felt it. *You're not talking
about distraction—you mean you're doing something you
want to conceal! What, H'ana? It can't be good!*

It's something I have to do. Leave me, I said!

Wox's long finger reached out again. She stumbled backward, almost losing her balance on the slippery ground. She
wanted to kill him.

ghost, you never worried about weakness before!

that was before we went to

gadrah. i know

Hanna turned and started walking. Attacking Wox
would be futile, and she had a low opinion of blind courage.
She was convinced Michael Kristofik would be alive if he
had not been without fear. If he had had the sense to be

afraid they would never have gone to Gadrah in the first place.

H'ana, you are not thinking straight—
Get out of me! Get out!

She felt Bella leave, with the lingering impression of a hand—gentle, soothing—laid softly on her head. There might have been tears in her eyes. She could not be sure because they were full of rain. The adults who reared her had done that when she was a child, she would do it for Mickey if only she were there, let him go through a storm of anger and tears and wait patiently until he was calm and could accept love again. Especially if he had done something wrong.

She did not seem to be walking any more. She seemed to stand on a strip of grass and it carried her through the rain to the warren where Nakeekt lived, and then she seemed to stand on ramps that carried her up. Somewhere along the way she remembered to seek a light control. She knew where Nakeekt's chamber was. It was near the one where she had briefly slept, and the Soldier who escorted her past it had not so much thought of it explicitly as been aware of Nakeekt's door. The walls of the warren closed in, like the walls of underground Wektt, like *Endeavor*'s, like Jameson's dominance, Earth's restrictions. All choice seemed to have been suspended.

Kill Kwoort. The solution.
not hard. i don't even like him
are you sure
i don't
you don't like Metra either. would you kill her
well why not

The ghost seemed to be considering this. Hanna left her to it.

She was at Nakeekt's door. The sense of being conveyed had been illusory; her legs felt ready to give way. She put a hand on the wall to steady herself. She had caught a peripheral image from Bella of Kwek knocking, knocking at a door behind which no one waited. Nakeekt was behind this one.

Her own knock was tentative. Wox gave her a look, lifted his fist—Hanna flinched at that—and banged. Nakeekt opened the door almost at once. When she saw Hanna all her features changed, the great ears stood out for a moment and then wrapped tightly to the head, fast, and the breathing tubes swelled with a great intake of air.

"What," said Nakeekt, "what are you doing here? Who is this?" and Hanna felt the Warrior's impulse to shout for reinforcements.

"Kakrekt sent me," Hanna said; she leaned against the doorframe in exhaustion, holding out the sealed message. "Kwoort is Holy Man in Wektt now, and he is standing in Kakrekt's way. She wants to kill him."

Absolute silence. There must have been a murmur of rain from the room beyond Nakeekt but Nakeekt's astonishment, and Wox's, outweighed it. So Wox had not known Kakrekt's purpose—

Only seconds passed, perhaps, seeming longer. The rain became audible.

Presently Nakeekt said, "Come to my workplace." She wheeled and went to a coverall hung from a peg on the wall. She threw off a robe and stepped into the coverall. She was back at the door in seconds, sealing the front of the garment, pushed past Hanna and headed toward the ramps and down, moving fast. Hanna tried to hurry, and felt Wox shove her and shove her again. Then he gave up and almost carried her the rest of the way, talking to Nakeekt, explaining his role as guardian or captor, and they came to a room where Nakeekt stopped and when Wox let go, Hanna slid to the floor. The two Soldiers were talking and she could not understand what they said, but the translator was not at fault. She was losing comprehension along with strength.

Her hand fumbled at a pocket, nightmare-slow. She nearly dropped the vial of stimulant, and hardly had the strength to break it open. Something seemed to say this was a bad idea, but what else could she do? She got the thing cracked, and started to inhale.

The only advantage you have . . .

Chapter XIII

THE ROOM CAME INTO FOCUS. Desks, benches, writing materials: a human would call it an office. The twisted halves of the vial lay where Hanna had thrown them, as far away as her weak arm could manage. Nakeekt and Wox stared at her.

"What was that?" Nakeekt said.

"Something for my well-being."

She hoped she had not absorbed more than a few molecules of the vapor before coming to her senses and hurling the vial away. She waited for the *thrum* . . .

Nothing.

There were more vials. If she got desperate enough she would have to use them. But not yet. Adrenaline, from the surge of fear at what she had almost done, made her alert, however briefly.

"Can you get the substance Kakrekt requires quickly?" she asked. "Will the wait be long?"

Silence. All Nakeekt's eyes were open. So, surprisingly, were Wox's.

"What is it?" Hanna said as the silence went on. "Is there a reason why you delay?"

Nakeekt said, "Kwoort has cooperated with This Place to the highest degree."

Wox said, "Kakrekt Commander would assassinate the Holy Man?"

Hanna looked from one to the other and thought, *Oops.*

Nakeekt didn't want Hanna, but she wanted Wox. She assumed, perhaps correctly, that if left to herself Hanna would make a run for the pod and disappear. Not that Hanna could have moved fast enough to escape if she did run; but Nakeekt did not know that. So Hanna was thrust into what evidently was a closet, which was without a lock and would have been crammed with heavy objects if Nakeekt and Wox had not taken them out and piled them against the door to keep her in.

Hanna had been shut up in worse places. Only, after she sank to the floor, feeling dust under her hands, feeling a patch of damp that argued for a crack in a wall somewhere, waiting for her eyes to adjust—the space was not sealed, there was light at the edge of the door—she missed something. She put her hands to her ears, touched her mouth. She had not even felt the slight tug when Nakeekt, knowing what it was, jerked the translator away just as the door closed on Hanna. She ran her hands over the tangles of her hair, last chance, maybe the transparent web that held the parts together had gotten caught in it.

No.

She sagged against the wall, shivering with relief that she had not breathed in the stimulant. The hypothetical question posed months ago had been prescient: *Suppose they take your translator away and you need to know what they're going to do to you . . .*

She could listen to alien minds, any minds, with a better chance of concealment in trance, and she had entered trance in worse places, too. So she thought of it, but rejected it. It would drain her body's resources just as if she had used the stimulant; drain them too far, and it would only mean a quicker death.

Concealment without it might not be possible, but she had to know what was happening around her. She risked discovery, and sought Nakeekt.

Nakeekt did not trust Wox any more than she trusted the not-Soldier female, what was her name, Haknt? Wox might let her out, or rummage through the workplace and make it untidy. Nakeekt did not like disorder. So she took Wox with her.

She collected Pritk. No, do not speak now, we will all talk—

On to Genkt's billet. The unusually persistent rains were a nuisance (and a worry—how much crop will we lose?) but

Wox at least bore it like a Soldier, not like the ever-complaining Kwek—

This was the second time that not-Soldier, that Haknt, had arrived bringing an uninvited, uninvestigated Soldier. Is she doing it to annoy me—

This is Wox, he came from Wektt, come with us, no, wait, go and get—

She sent Genkt for the others and jogged back to her own warren with Wox and Pritk. Best not to leave Haknt on her own too long, who knew what not-Soldiers could do, perhaps she could burst out by herself—

Kwek, Kwek has had dealings with these not-Soldiers, here is Xext, you, Xext, go and get Kwek.

It was a good thing they had not executed Kwek yet—

Nakeekt's head hurt. This happened frequently; she thought something might be growing inside her head.

(Hanna thought the headache might be hers; it kept getting worse, slowly filling up her skull. Starvation, or Wox's blow? She tried to see why Nakeekt thought of killing Kwek, but it just made Nakeekt's head ache more. Hanna desisted.)

How can I explain this, should I wait for Xext? No. Listen.

Strong personalities. Stronger than she remembered, except for Nakeekt, but on the first visit to That Place she had been focused on Nakeekt and had not paid much attention to the others. Wox might as well not be present. A little uneasiness in him; he had heard of assassination, but it had never made much of an impression. Certainly he had never expected to personally confront a question of loyalty. And loyalty was not the issue for Nakeekt and her band. It was— how very humanlike—the survival of That Place.

Does Kakrekt mean to become the Holy One, and who will become High Commander, who would she put in her place?

Nakeekt asked Wox, but Wox knew nothing.

There was the sound of heavy objects being thrown about. The door opened, Hanna was dragged from the closet, the translator was shoved into her hands and she dropped it. Nakeekt made a sound of impatience and picked it up and closed Hanna's hands around it, shouting unintelligible words, though Hanna knew she cried, *Utilize it! Make it work!* She fumbled with it, clumsy. Her fingers did not want to work. The beings crowded around her, jostling. Then the filmy net did not want to fit over the tangled mess that had once been her shining hair and she mashed it down and adjusted the parts and suddenly it functioned. She heard Nakeekt say, "Why does Kakrekt want to do this thing?"

Hanna hesitated. She thought she saw Wox start to raise a fist, and winced reflexively, but no one had told him to hit her, and he had hardly moved.

"Kakrekt wants change," Hanna said finally. "She wants an end to war. She wants to learn about—to learn everything about Soldiers and where they came from. She thinks, she thinks someone else made them, other not-Soldiers. Kwoort does not think Soldiers ought to learn these things, and Kakrekt does not want to wait for his natural death."

"Kakrekt's brain is malfunctioning, then," Nakeekt said.

"You want to learn about what came before, too. You try to do it here."

"Here. In this small space. Because we are hidden, because we are known only to a few. We can do it because we do other things which are forbidden. They cannot be done everywhere. They cannot even be known."

"Why not!" The translator did not convey Hanna's tone and Soldiers could not read her expression, but she made up for it in volume. "I don't understand! Why can't all of them just stop, if you can do it here?"

Stop breeding, was what she meant, but some subconscious instinct for self-preservation stopped her. If she said it aloud she would never leave the room alive, and if Wox heard it he would not either.

The room swayed. Something crushing approached—nothing material, and it approached only Hanna. She recognized despair when she saw it; she had known it before, but this time it was different. The woman who talked to aliens, who understood them, who at least had never failed in that before, looked at failure.

———

There was a jumbled hour that Hanna could not, later, remember with clarity. Kwek missing from her billet. Of course. *Find her!* Nakeekt ordered, and more Soldiers were roused to search. A memory that insinuated itself and brought a half-life to Hanna's reluctant muscles; dogged by Wox, she made her way to the billet where Gabriel had slept. He had carried something to it because— *We might be here a little longer than I thought,* she had commented, and when they brought supplies from the pod for the first meal in Nakeekt's warren, Gabriel, the good planner, had brought . . .

Meal tabs for another day. You could dissolve them in water or swallow them whole. She could still think clearly enough to be cautious, and begged a tumbler of water from one of Nakeekt's lieutenants. No one tried to stop her from dropping in a tab; she sipped carefully at the brew. For a long time every cell in her body was focused on it. *Sip.* Low voices that seemed to come from a great distance, talking of poison. *Sip.* Kwek could not be found. *Sip.* So tired, she wanted only to sleep, but presently something was different, it was not so much that she was stronger but that she had stopped losing strength. *Sip. Sip.*

Nakeekt began to wonder aloud if it was worth searching for Kwek any more tonight. The not-Soldier seemed to have said everything she was going to say and sat quietly in the corner, drinking something she said was nourishing, apparently not interested in anything else. *Maybe Kwek has stumbled into the tides and drowned, one less task—*

Hanna drifted into half-sleep, but not so far that she lost her hold on the precious nutrients. She thought idly of Kwek, who would die tomorrow in any case—

Sopping wet, exhausted, dragging herself miserably here and there, with no idea where the settlement lay. Cold, too. And unaware that tomorrow she would—

Die?

Kwek stopped. For a moment she was too startled to be cold. She was not going to *die*, it was not *that* cold, and if she could not find her way back she was sure Nakeekt would send Soldiers to find her in the morning. Nakeekt wanted to see her in the morning, she had said so.

That is because they are going to kill you in the morning. Why are they going to do that, Kwek?

She looked suspiciously at the communicator pulled tight on her slender wrist. The words had not come from it. But it wasn't Arkt, either.

It is Haknt. I have listened to Nakeekt's mind. You will be killed tomorrow.

The speaking-to-the-mind left no space for doubt. Kwek began to run again. The night was not impenetrable to her Soldier's eyes and she did not bump into anything. She still felt Haknt in her mind, but now there was a dim sense of another presence she did not know and then another that she knew.

"Kwek," said the communicator, and kept repeating her name. Finally she slowed and stopped and leaned against an eat-anything plant. It would be sluggish in the rain, and Pritk had told her that in any case an animal the size of a grown Soldier could escape it easily enough.

"Who is talking to me?" she said.

"This is Arkt. Haknt said she told you what is going to happen tomorrow."

"She said, she said—" Kwek couldn't repeat it. "Why would they want to do that? I know they are not satisfied with me but there are others who don't work even as hard as I do, and nothing happens to them!"

"What is different about you? Never mind now," Arkt added quickly. "We would like to remove you from That Place. Will you come?"

"Yes, yes, if they are going to—to do that to me!"

"You know where Haknt's aircraft is? On the landing field?"

"Yes, but I'm lost, I don't—"

"Listen to me, listen, listen."

Now he spoke to her mind, just as he had on the spacecraft. He was calm and certain. He knew where the aircraft was. He knew where Kwek was, too, because of the com unit. He could guide her to the aircraft. The hatch was open and she could go into it and hide there, and then when Haknt returned, go with her.

The rain came down harder. Kwek slapped away a questing tongue, pushed off from the eat-anything plant, and set off, following Arkt's directions.

This is a complication, Hanna said to Bella. Nakeekt and her Soldiers had eventually come to some decision and two of them had gone to get something that Hanna thought was the poison Kakrekt desired. They would not return immediately. They would have to make it, or mix it, or something. Kwek's predicament had made Hanna more alert, but she had been too distracted by it to pay attention to the discussion going on around her.

It is a complication, but you don't want to leave Kwek to die, either, or you wouldn't have broken silence. What's the silence about, anyway? Bella asked, trying to be crafty, and Hanna shot a barrier into place. Her reflexes were slow and Bella got a glimpse beyond it first, but it was not enough to tell her any more than the telepaths already knew.

Wox will not want to take Kwek along, Hanna said, closing the door firmly on her reason for being at That Place.

Kwek will not want to go with Wox! Bella said, and showed her Kwek's reaction to the prospect of the "Demon's Soldier's" arrival.

Hanna finished the last drops of her drink.

Tell me about Gabriel.

Asleep. Not really unconscious. Somewhere in between.

I found meal tabs.

So that's why you're better.

Better. Not good.

She felt for the reassuring lumps of the meal tabs in a pocket. Someday, when there was time, she might sit down and weep with gratitude for Gabriel's forethought. There were five tabs left. Three had to be saved for Gabriel; at least three. Wait, or swallow another one now?

She thought of the likely scene when not only she, but Wox as well, got into the pod with Kwek.

She asked for more water.

Chapter XIV

*O*N OLD EARTH, *it was dawn at Admin. Commission staff signed in from locations across human space; those living nearby began to arrive on-site. Jameson spent a few minutes, as he did each morning, walking the corridors of his own floor of the vast complex, speaking to individuals regardless of status. He had found that the practice fostered loyalty. It was a normal morning,* Endeavor *the first thing on no one's mind. Except his.*

He had not consulted his colleagues about the action he had ordered Captain Metra to take. Resupplying Contact personnel hardly required a Commission vote, and Metra had offered no dissension; allowing those personnel to starve to death, knowingly, was not something she wanted on her service record. But Jameson didn't want to embark on discussions after the fact, either, because inevitably they would lead to speculations about the future.

Commissioners were pragmatists—even Jameson's most likely allies, even Andrella Murphy. If Hanna and Gabriel failed to produce an experimental subject, they would consider the option of starting over again with new envoys. Someone would observe that if Gabriel Guyup died on Battleground his abbey might be satisfied with calling his death martyrdom. Someone might even think a kind of secular martyrdom would be an acceptable way of getting rid of the troublesome Hanna ril-Koroth. No one would say that. At least not in so many words; at least not in his presence. But someone would say something. He meant to keep them too busy to propose discussion.

The crisis on Colony One, he had decided, would swallow hours, giving no one time to be sidetracked to Endeavor. *Civil war threatened; a Fleet presence had become necessary to remind would-be rebels what they risked if they did not stand down. If their response was intemperate, Polity detainment of certain citizens would be required. Personally and privately, Jameson wanted the dissidents got out of the way for good, because the half-life they advocated was ghastly. Perhaps he would suggest summary executions, cloaked as accidental deaths. That would provoke lively, and long, discussion.*

It would keep Karin Weisz too busy to revert to hypothetical improvements in A.S., too. If the situation on her homeworld could not be resolved, she could be gone from the Commission in a matter of days; Colony One's council was pragmatic, too.

In Wektt, Gabriel focused on examining his conscience, suspecting that he had come to his last chance for contrition. Of course, it was possible he was not dying; that was up to God. Examination of conscience was never amiss, however. It was not a painful process. Gabriel knew God well understood the imperfection of His human creatures and in the infinity of His love, readily forgave their fallibility.

Oh, and here was the Angel of Death! The Angel was a woman. Why not?

Angel? Nobody's called me that before!

"Dema?" He wasn't sure he had actually made a sound.

Hang on. H'ana's found some meal tabs. Can you hold on a few more hours?

"If God wills it."

The most extraordinary feelings flooded his mind, all of them Dema's. Exasperation, affection, anxiety. Resolution. Dema was going to keep him awake, keep him alive, until help arrived. Or until she had to let him slip away.

Chapter XV

HANNA EXPECTED SOMETHING EXOTIC. A small, carved container, perhaps, filled with a deadly powder, maybe engraved with Soldiers' equivalent of skull and crossbones.

Instead Nakeekt loaded her down with a woven sack big as her torso. "Here," she said economically, peering down at Hanna over the sack, and Hanna got slowly to her feet, pushing against the wall for support. Her joints hurt, her muscles ached, her clothes were still damp from the rain, and she was cold. The sack looked large and the pod seemed a long way off. Hanna took the burden in both arms and stumbled under the weight. Even if she had been in peak condition the mass would have been respectable. Now she would stagger if she tried to carry it.

She stood unsteadily, swaying and trying to hold onto it. The muscles in her arms trembled.

We can use this, said a whisper in her mind.

How? Bella! Where's Bella! she thought in panic, because the whisperer was Arch. He and Joseph had developed a plan; she had been given to understand that. And to understand that her part was to do as she was told. *Because you're addled,* Joseph had said. It was true, and she was at the mercy of a pair of D'neerans who were having a wonderful time with their plot.

You've never had to fight for your life! she protested. She wanted Bella, who was at least not absurdly gleeful.

Neither has Bella! And she's been commandeered to keep an open line to your director with the funny name—

What?

Evanomen. By order of your very own commissioner. Not that she's told him what we're doing about Kwek.

Hanna could not hold the sack any longer, and it fell to the floor, lumpy and slack. Before Nakeekt could think she was refusing she said, "I can't, it's too heavy." Arch prompted her and she added, "Wox is strong, he will have to carry it."

"It is to be given only to you," Wox said.

"Then you'll have to carry me along with it."

He hesitated, and the clicks he made were probably a growl, but he picked up the sack. Hanna felt Arch and Joseph cheer.

Nakeekt said, "Tell Kakrekt she must distill what she wants from the leaves in this sack. Tell her water will suffice for solvent, she is to steep the leaves for at least ten days, beginning with a like ratio of water to leaves and adding only enough to keep them moist—"

Hanna looked at the bag again. She could see wet patches on it. Nakeekt's Soldiers had not mixed or made anything; they had gone out into the night and stripped leaves from stems or branches. Many leaves: the distillate must have to be administered over a long period. Nakeekt went on for some time, but Hanna could not make anything after the water stay in her head. That did not matter because at the end Nakeekt thrust a rolled paper at her and said, "I have written everything down, Kakrekt must read it. Go now. This is the second time you have disturbed my sleep. For the second time I tell you: don't come back!"

They went, Hanna trailing behind Wox, feeling as addled as Joseph had said she was, her mind a jumble of the external (the rain had diminished), and the internal (she was a little stronger, not much—and her stomach, waking up, howled with hunger). Behind her she felt Nakeekt put the episode into the past, attention already turning to tomorrow's work with drowned crops. Arch watched through her eyes, and she felt a tendril of his consciousness extended to Kwek, strong and sure.

Have you ever thought about Adept training, she thought muzzily, *you're very good.*

Too much work, he answered, *now pay attention. You're almost there. Get ahead of Wox. Make him slow down.*

How can I—

Give him a reason. Order him. He's conditioned to obey. Lie to him; you're good at that. Tell him—

They were nearly at the foot of the ramp to the pod.

"Wox!" she said sharply. "Wait. I instructed this craft to repel intruders when we left it. I must go first and tell it to
allow your entry."

He hesitated; she edged around him and he followed
slowly. At the top of the ramp she turned and said, "Give
the cargo to me."

The translator made it an order. She held her breath; she
felt Arch hold his. But Wox stopped.

You can do this, Arch said, and she managed to take the
sack without falling and started to turn into the pod.

And Kwek was there like lightning, seizing the bag, hurling it behind her, shoving Hanna in and with a mightier
shove throwing Wox off the ramp. Kwek sprang back inside.

Lift! Arch said urgently, *override the failsafes, the hatch
doesn't matter!* and Hanna gave the order, but Wox was on
his feet in a second, grabbing for the end of the ramp and
somehow getting hold of it. He hung there as they rose into
light rain, pulling himself hand over hand with grim determination, and fingers appeared at the lower edge of the
hatch. The pod was still lifting and Hanna seized manual
control and shot it down and forward, skimming treetops.
She heard them thump against the dangling ramp, but
Wox's fingers still clutched the edge of the hatch, and she
took the pod up again, fast, zigzagging, desperate to dis-
lodge him.

Kwek stomped the implacable fingers. She did it again
and again with all her strength, smashing stubborn joints
until the fingers jutted at pitiful angles, until it seemed Wox
could bear any hurt, could haul himself into the pod with
one fingertip—but he could not. The hands disappeared.

Hanna had shut out Kwek's viciousness, Wox's excruciating pain, while the endless seconds went by. Now she looked
at the altitude readout. Wox could not have survived the
fall. And through the whole brutal attack and the plunge to
his death he had not made a sound.

The horrified silence in her head was Arch. Kwek was
crowing, saying, "I can still fight!"—burbling, excited,
bouncing around the cabin. But all Hanna listened to was
the emptiness that stretched between her and Arch. Finally
he said, *He's dead?*

What did you think would happen?

We thought, I didn't think he would try to—

Hanna managed to give orders, voice breaking; the ramp retracted, the hatch slowly closed, and the pod steadied into the course back to Wektt. Adrenaline had drained away, and she let her head sink onto her folded arms. They ached from the brief weight of the sack, but it was nothing compared to the way her head hurt. There would be a remedy in the medical cabinet, if only she could make herself get up and get it. She should have thought of that hours ago.

We just thought, if he and Kwek were together it would be chaos, we just wanted to keep him from boarding—

I hoped, she said, *I hoped we could get out of this without killing anybody. I wanted, when we got here, for a minute, to kill Wox. But now I wish it hadn't happened.*

She tried to shift her focus to Nakeekt. Nakeekt had withheld some knowledge about the poisonous leaves; did she even know how to be straightforward? There was something unreal about the last hour, a tinge of deceit in what Nakeekt had said of the leaves, but Hanna did not know what it was. Touching her now did not help. Nakeekt was only saying: *". . . have to cut new channels, start now, start with this field, it must be drained, always there is either not enough rain or too much . . ."*

Thoughts of crops. Nothing else.

Now Kwek sat down beside Hanna, still bouncing, making the seats vibrate. "Now we will go to your spacecraft!" she said—and there was something unreal about Kwek, too. Something different, at least. Or were all Hanna's senses playing tricks on her?

She turned her head slowly

"No," she said. "First we have to go to Gergtk."

Chapter XVI

K AKREKT WAS FUMING (though she had no such word for it). She should have heard long since from Wox, who carried a radio transmitter, or from Nakeekt. The not-Soldiers had been surprised to learn that Wektt and That Place communicated—as did That Place and Rowtt, and Wektt and Rowtt, for that matter. Communication was sporadic, true; perhaps that was the reason the not-Soldiers had missed it. So much for their technology! So much for listening to the mind!

"You have been asleep," she accused the sentry in the station that looked in the direction of That Place. Like the others, it commanded a view of the physical terrain in case electronic surveillance failed and Rowtt succeeded in invading overland.

"I have not slept," the Soldier said. "There has been no communication except from the not-Soldiers above, which does not cease and does not change and only repeats demands. There is nothing in the air, there are no missiles, there is nothing."

Kakrekt resisted a need to kick him. It seemed that her life consisted of one internal imperative after another, many of which she prudently resisted. She remembered distinctly that once she had had few needs. Young Soldiers did not need much: to eat and drink, to sleep, to mate and feed the young, to carry out orders; to fight, to die. She had been the same, until one day the formula Soldiers repeated to each other upon parting—*survive*—had ceased to be a matter of rote and became a personal priority. Soon afterward, in an engagement where continuing to fight was hopeless, she had run away, taking care that none of her fellow-Soldiers saw her do it—not that it would have mattered, because they had all died. She had suddenly *needed* to survive, as she understood later when she examined her actions. Examining what she had done was new then, too—

The sentinel was wrong. Something was coming. Kakrekt's sudden conviction of this was absolute.

It was not to be fired upon.

Also absolute.

A rather shaky image of the not-Soldier aircraft formed in the air before her eyes.

Not eyes.

Now she understood that it was an illusion, the image was in her own brain, and in the next instant she understood that this was the not-Soldier female "speaking to the mind," the phenomenon that so interested Kwoort, but which Kakrekt had not yet experienced herself.

It did not, at the moment, seem to have any advantage over Wox's radio, and why did he not use it?

"Now there is something," the sentinel said. She saw him begin to move a hand and said sharply, "Do not fire," and waited until she was sure he understood the order before she left the sentry station, immediately breaking into a run, because it wouldn't do for Kwoort to find out the aircraft was returning and get to it first with questions.

The sentry, however, had additional orders. He had not told Kakrekt about them because she had not asked. He moved his hand after all; he signaled Kwoort.

———

Hanna had tried to spend the flight locked away from the telepaths—and they didn't understand why and wouldn't let her alone. What could be so terrible that she had to conceal it? *Maybe it's not so awful,* they tried to tell her. *Maybe it's something you've blown bigger than its size, looking worse the longer you hide it.*

Never mind that, she said, *help me think up something to tell Kakrekt. She'll want to know where Wox is.*

Tell her he stayed. Why not? Nakeekt doesn't talk to Kakrekt.

She talks to somebody. Kwoort's been "cooperative in the highest degree," she said. *I've got to get past Kakrekt. I have to get to Gabriel, I can't reach him, is he even alive?*

Alive, Dema said as if from a great distance. *Stable.*

And Endeavor's *sending supplies, loading now. Don't worry.*

But Hanna worried; she couldn't quit seeking Gabriel, it didn't seem fair that Dema could touch him and she couldn't. There were reasons, in the tricky logic of telepathy, and she knew, she *knew* what they were. She just couldn't think of them right now.

Calm down, they kept saying. *Calm. Calm. Have another meal tab.*

I can't, I'm saving them for Gabriel—

Try to rest—

I can't—

to relax—

I can't!

Over and over, round and round, with Kwek slowly subsiding from exuberance into suspicious watchfulness, as it sunk in that they were going to the Demon's chief city. But it was a good thing Kwek was there, because twenty minutes out from Wektt she said suddenly, "The Demon will fire on us!"

Oh! everyone said; and then Hanna had to focus on Kakrekt and warn her to hold fire, and so she lived to land the pod in Wektt.

She got out of it and swayed where she stood. Two meal tabs had barely replaced the energy she had spent on this little trip; at least she had raided the medical cabinet again and the headache was better. It was still dark and the air was impossibly cold after the comfortable twenty-one degrees of the pod. Wind slapped her face, bearing crystals of ice. She heard Kakrekt, shrill and whistling and coming closer, a light bobbing in her hand. She was aware of the telepaths far, far above, not thinking to her, not even breathing, a great stillness; nobody knew what would happen next. Kwek had drawn as far back into the pod as she could get. Hanna just stood there. She couldn't think of anything else to do.

Now Kakrekt was inside the translator's range, and now she was in front of Hanna.

"Quickly, quickly, where is it? What do you have for me?"

"It's vegetation," Hanna said.

Kakrekt looked at her as if the translator was not working.

"In there," Hanna said. She gestured wearily over her shoulder. "Nakeekt sent somebody with it," she added. "Wox stayed. She wanted to show him things to report about to you. She said you must send for him later."

Kakrekt's ears lifted and tightened and her face shifted. It was the human equivalent of a shake of the head, dismissing the unimportant.

"What use is vegetation?" she said.

"Here are the instructions on how to use it."

Hanna lifted the little scroll from her pocket, careful not to allow it to catch on a single meal tab, afraid of losing one, or the stimulants that might have to serve if something didn't change soon, and Kakrekt seized it.

She never remembered very well how she got back underground. She remembered trying to walk up the mountainside and falling; the earlier snowfall had stopped, but she had staggered off the roughly cleared path and snow came up over her ankles. She might have gotten up and tried again. She must have been terribly cold, but she did not remember that. She must have tried to connect with her D'neerans, but she could not concentrate because Kwek distracted her with unceasing grumbles about the weather (*I would not have come if I had known!*—forgetting that Nakeekt had meant to kill her) along with Kwek's indignation at having to carry the sack. It would be dropped for later retrieval if Kwoort should appear, but he did not; meanwhile Kakrekt had read Nakeekt's instructions with disbelief, puffs like steam coming out her breathing tubes in the cold air, followed by indignation nearly as great as Kwek's.

Then maybe she had fallen again; she only remembered that there had been a bustle of more Soldiers, Kakrekt hooting orders, a rough ride uphill on an open platform. After that, nothing, until she opened her eyes once more and found that she was crowded with Kwek into a cart that moved silently through the gray maze. Kwek no longer had the sack. No one else was with them except the driver and a guard.

She pulled upright from her slump and managed to say to Kwek, "What are they doing with us?"

"Kakrekt Commander has sent us to your billet. Both of us! We will have to stay in the same billet!" Kwek's complaints had not diminished. "I did not have to inhabit a billet with anyone in Rowtt at any time unless I was in the field! It was not necessary at That Place either—"

The driver's ears pricked. Hanna was starting to think again, though slowly. She wondered fleetingly how old the Soldier was. Old enough to have heard a rumor of That Place; old enough to be interested in it, too.

Her toes hurt, and her fingers. Her hands appeared unharmed when she looked at them. Finally she realized they must have gone numb with cold, and now circulation was coming back.

———

The billet had not come with niceties like tumblers to drink from, but Kakrekt had seen to it that Hanna and Gabriel got one so they did not have to drink from their cupped hands. Hanna filled it, swallowed a meal tab for herself—acknowledging the telepaths' gentle insistence that her own collapse would do Gabriel no good—dissolved another, and got Gabriel to take the liquid. The change in him frightened her. She had only been gone a few hours, but the hollows in his cheeks were even more pronounced and his eye sockets looked cavernous, and though he roused enough to be conscious of her presence, she had to help him sit up, and his hand fell away when he tried to take the tumbler for himself. Kwek hovered, not in anxiety but demanding his attention—for a few minutes; then Arch intervened, explaining why she must back off. Kwek sat on the hard bench after that, looking at the ever-yammering video unit and jeering at what she saw. This was not the shy and uncertain Kwek Hanna had known on *Endeavor*. Something, clearly, had changed. Hanna remembered the evasiveness with which Kwek had answered Nakeekt's question when they first went to That Place—*How does your mating time cycle?*—and suspected what the change meant. How she was to share quarters with Kwek and stay sane was a question for later.

She spoke to Gabriel from time to time as he slowly

drank, small meaningless words meant to reassure—*"It's all right"*—something she could not do with her thought, because she hoped rather than believed what she said—*"everything will be all right . . ."*

But it might be, came Dema's whisper. *Metra's been transmitting nonstop for hours that she wants you to return to the ship, and if Kwoort won't consent to that she'll land supplies.*

What's he said—?

Nothing. No response at all. But another pod is coming anyway. Starr's orders.

Images: A servo would put packages and bins on the ground and return to the pod. The pod would take off and Soldiers would gather up the cargo. That was how it was supposed to go.

Gabriel had slipped into a light doze, still leaning against Hanna. It was sleep, though, not unconsciousness. She woke him gently and fed him another life-giving drink. By the time he finished it he was more alert.

He touched her cheek and said, "You were gone a long time." His voice was hoarse but there was some strength in it that had not been there before.

"Yes, I'm sorry, I didn't know I would be gone so long. Kakrekt sent me away."

"I know about that," he said, not altogether accurately, because he did not know the reason. "Do you need to rest?"

"Yes . . ." Badly.

He lay down again, making room for her on the pallet. She let herself stretch out next to him and felt sleep close in almost at once. Gabriel murmured, "Do you think we could just walk out of here?"

"You know," she said drowsily, "we could try, if we get desperate enough."

"I'm just about that desperate. Are you?"

"Yes—" She was starting to be afraid she would never see Mickey again. "There's still a Soldier outside the door. I don't know what he'd do to stop us. If we got past him maybe we could just go out to the pod and—but I don't know the way."

"Couldn't *Endeavor* help us with that?"

"Maybe." She woke further. "Kwek has the com unit we

gave her when we got to That Place. I think they could track that, even underground."

"Suppose we try it? Soon?" *When I'm stronger,* he thought. He said, "A few more meal tabs. Then we'll try."

But there was only one tab left.

Chapter XVII

*THEY LIED THERE IS NO thaw only snow, there is ice,
they did not tell me about the ice! I wonder if Kakrekt
has made the seasons go in reverse, why would she not try
to order the seasons, she orders everything else! The not-
Soldier female went to That Place at Kakrekt's order and
what did she do there? Nakeekt cannot see the past, no one
can! We do not will ourselves to forget so it must be the
will of Abundant God and so we cannot choose — we must
all forget, we are all to forget. Kakrekt will forget and perhaps she does now, she has five hundred summers she says
but I wonder if she lies and she has more, many more,
maybe even more than I, because she is mad! Mul to want
to remember and if she is mad then she must forget!*

*The not-Soldier communication repeats and repeats. It is
not audible here in my chambers. But I hear it! I have called
Soldiers to listen and they do not hear it but I do, I think the
not-Soldiers have done something to me and that is why I
hear what no other Soldier hears or maybe Kakrekt has done
it to me or all of them together. But the not-Soldiers must
stay, they must be made to make weapons for us and it is a
lie that they are hungry, there is food in abundance, they eat,
they eat so much they must be growing fat. I do not know
what they are supposed to look like and it would not surprise
me if they were fat. I will order their rations cut. So it cannot
be supplies that will be landed, I do not know what they have
sent. Spies to watch our movements? Fighters to come here
and disarm us? I will not allow it! I will not!*

Spyeyes circled the pods, and Metra watched what they saw.
The second pod was at rest beside the first, identical, the

two a pair of solid workhorses for tasks needing little equipment and one or two crew. Wektt had made no visible response to the landing. It was now one Standard hour after Wektt's dawn, the supply drop undertaken in full daylight for a reason, to show Kwoort the humans hid nothing. Metra thought it surprising Kwoort's Soldiers hadn't tried to take the first one apart. Or maybe not so surprising, since just the attempt to dissect Bassanio's sidearm had killed a Soldier. The pod looked dingy after a month and a half on the surface without upkeep. *Overhaul as soon as it returns,* Metra thought. That would be very soon, if Kwoort refused the supplies. Because the next plan was all-out rescue, and retrieving the pod from this moronic society would be part of it.

She had watched for an hour, standing, arms folded. She did not move; she was a monumental statue. The crew was not so much afraid of her as in awe of her, and here was another reason. Her brain was not idle, though; she registered every detail of every square meter of the terrain. And she noticed that Bella Qu'e'n, who would not even have been in the command center if Metra had had her way, stood nearby—and didn't move either. A bright bead on Qu'e'n's collar was a direct conduit to Adair Evanomen, but there was nothing for her to say.

After exactly an hour Metra gave the order to trigger the hatch and have the servo show itself. It appeared at the hatch and started down the ramp.

Servo and pod went up in a blinding fireball. Metra barely blinked at that, but finally moved, shock overriding control, when the first pod, the one that had faithfully served Hanna, went up in flames too, and snowmelt flooded melting rock and the spyeyes recorded gouts of steam before shock waves hit them and they went blind and were hurled far away.

Hanna dragged herself up from sleep, not at first certain what had waked her. She lay for a while with eyes closed. She hoped always now for dreams of summer: flowers, leaves, sky, sun, colors so saturated they appeared elemental, the colors of childhood remembered.

She had dreamed of something gray instead. She did not try to remember it.

She did not sense the telepaths seeking her, and she did not seek them, though their silence seemed odd. Perhaps they had no more to say just now than she did.

Slowly she realized the background noise of the video screen was not the only Soldier voice in the room. But she did not know until she opened her eyes that Kakrekt had come in, and was conversing—calmly, it seemed—with Kwek.

The translator lay on the floor where she had dropped it. She sat up, moving with leaden slowness, and picked it up and put it on.

"So you are awake at last," Kakrekt said. "It seems you do nothing but sleep! No Soldier would be allowed to be so lazy!"

There was something different about her expression. Hanna felt an edge of anxiety in her that might have accounted for it. Next to Hanna Gabriel stirred, and she glanced at him. There was more color in his face, and she thought with relief that he would be all right until supplies arrived.

"It is time for the Warrior Kwek to mate," Kakrekt said. "I did not notice when she arrived. I will conduct her to a breeding ground for that purpose momentarily. Perhaps you wish to observe."

Hanna bit back what she wanted to say with some difficulty. *We could have observed at any time, instead you have kept us—*

Hidden. And Hanna suddenly understood that Kakrekt wanted to hide them further, far away, and the "breeding ground" was very far away indeed.

She thought uneasily that Kakrekt had come in the first place to see to moving the humans; that recognizing Kwek was in breeding mode had only prompted the choice of destination, perhaps different from the one originally intended. She did not know whether to be alarmed at that or not. At least it would solve the problem of getting past the Soldier at the door.

Gabriel was as awake now as he was going to get. He sat up and she put an arm around his shoulders.

"Can you do this?" she asked.

"Of course," he said, but his movements were slow and painful, his weakness apparent.

One meal tab left. But more coming.

Not again. Never again. How does she get herself into these things?—conveniently overlooking his part in getting her into them.

At least she was not presumed or feared dead this time. She was only—

"Trapped there to starve to death?" Andrella Murphy suggested.

"Absolutely not. We'll blast a way in and get her out."

"Not the best idea you've ever had! We're committed to nonaggression toward any sovereign species, and that's what they are—"

"Who's decided that? They're not a sovereign species till we say they are."

"We're going to say that. How could we not? We can't use violence except under clearly defined circumstances."

Jameson knew quite well what the circumstances were. Imminent war, threat of invasion, clear and immediate danger toward humanity as a whole . . . that last was the "wiggle room" clause, but even that didn't apply here. He looked around at the others' faces, aware that he had been running his hands through his hair and it must be standing on end. That if any other commissioner had held onto a smidgen of belief in Jameson's ability to think calmly about Hanna, it was gone now. But none of them had believed it anyhow.

Adair Evanomen was part of this conference; he had interrupted today's conclave as soon as he got Bella Qu'e'n's spluttered report. The move to get relief to Hanna and Gabriel had gone disastrously wrong, provoking Kwoort to violence for the first time, and Jameson could not keep the situation to himself. They were not in formal session. No two commissioners were even in the same physical location, some not even in the Commission complex; they were banks of faces to each other, which Jameson thought was bad enough, considering what his must show. He asked Evanomen, "What has Hanna said about their destruction of the pods?"

"She doesn't know about it," Evanomen said.

"How could she not? Bella saw it happen. If she knows all the telepaths must know."

"All but Hanna. They held off telling her, and now she's otherwise occupied . . ."

The D'neerans' first impulse had been to tell Hanna at once. *Wake her up. Make her do something. Make her tell us what to do!*

Bella had put a halt to that just before a communal shout would have roused Hanna.

She needs the rest, needs the strength. What can she do?
You just don't want to be the one who tells her!
That, too.

And when Hanna said they were on the move and said *Can you track the com unit Kwek's got on*, Bella just said *Acknowledged* in a flash of pure surface thought so fast that Hanna picked up nothing more. Bella might have been proud of herself if she hadn't felt a little ashamed.

Back through the interminable maze, with long ramps and endless tunnels tending more to one direction, as best as Hanna could tell, than any other—though there were intervals of turns and more turns, on Kakrekt's orders, that Hanna suspected were meant to disorient the humans, as if they were not already confused enough. After a while she tried to estimate the vehicle's speed to determine how far they had gone. This machine was faster than the others that had carried her, and it was larger, too, more bus than cart, perhaps meant for work crews. The two humans, Kwek, and Kakrekt, a driver and the Soldier who had guarded the door, did not come close to filling it up. But it slowed when it passed groups of Soldiers and put on bursts of speed when the corridors were empty, and finally she gave up the effort. At least she knew they weren't going deeper underground. In fact the trend was certainly upward; but they must be moving farther and farther out from the center, to the most distant reaches of Wektt.

Endeavor tracked the com unit. It was evident that the group was moving slowly toward the surface. At the same time, if inexplicable detours were discounted, it was headed in an almost straight line through honeycombed mountains toward a series of surface plateaus and passes. No one could guess how many centuries had gone into excavating these warrens and making them usable. Probably no one in Wektt could either.

"Find out exactly what's around them," Metra said to Bella. "Get Bassanio to give you descriptions. Living quarters? Armories?"

Bella hesitated. She was not going to be able to shield all her anxiety from Hanna in extended communication. After a minute she said so.

Metra, surprisingly, seemed to understand. She said, "She'll have to know about the supplies soon."

"I'd rather have a solution to offer when I tell her. Can't I wait a little longer?"

"No, and I don't want the aliens' attention drawn to that com unit. Bassanio has to get it back from Kwek. Until she does it's up to you. Can't you hide what's happened to the pods? Can't all of you shield yourselves to some extent?"

"Yes," Bella said reluctantly. "She'll know I'm hiding something, though, and she could dig it out if she wants to, because I can't shield like she can. But that wouldn't be polite. She probably wouldn't do it right away."

Bassanio? Polite? Metra thought so clearly she might as well have shouted, and Bella scowled, even as she reached for Hanna. She was sick of true-humans. Trying to soothe their fears, respond to their reality, without letting them know you saw the truth of them when they tried to hide it—how could H'ana stand it for years at a time?

And how did she stand—

What? came Hanna's blurred answer.

This. Now . . . It was Bella's only response for a moment. Hovering on the edge of Hanna's perception felt so strange it took a minute to adjust. She saw dimly lit passages and shadowy figures, heard a clicking sound the vehicle made, and indecipherable utterances from beings outside the translator's range. She absorbed Hanna's knowledge that she was going into something no human had ever seen—

Yes, breeding chambers. Maybe the heart of the mystery . . .

But the thought, which ought to have been eager, was sluggish. For the first time Bella perceived the real depth of Hanna's weariness; probably Hanna was not even aware of

it herself. Imprisonment and malnutrition and gray days following one another without demarcation—would she ever
get over it?

Bella. I've gotten over worse.

But Hanna said it without optimism. She was grim.

Bella drew a deep breath. It was shaky.

What's around you? The captain wants to know.

Walls. Walls and more walls.

What's behind them, she means.

Why?

Because we might have to come get you.

*If you have to, but—people could get hurt. Ours and Sol-
diers. Could we get out on our own? Where's the pod relative
to where we are now—?*

And that was that. Bella couldn't stop her spontaneous
reaction, and Hanna saw just what Bella did not want her
to see: the escape she hoped for gone up in flames, along
with the precious supplies.

A long minute went by. Then Hanna said softly, "Translator
off." *Yours too, Gabriel.*

He didn't stir; the vehicle's motion had sent him back to
sleep.

She patted his cheek gently and felt the dry slack skin;
spoke the code again to deactivate the translator he wore.
"Gabriel. Gabriel, listen . . ." His eyes opened and drowsily
he turned his head, brushing her fingers with chapped lips.

Kakrekt had not been paying attention to them, but now
she looked around. Hanna said quickly, "We have to get to
the surface if we can. The pod's been destroyed, and the
supplies. We have to get into position to be picked up."

Kakrekt said something, meaningless clicks, and Hanna
said, "Listen, listen, stay with me, whatever happens, don't
lose sight of me."

He nodded, slowly comprehending, and she fished in her
pocket and brought out the last meal tab. "Can you swallow
this without water? Take it. Please try."

He looked at it and she saw the fate of the supplies sinking in. She felt no surprise in him, as if he had gone beyond
surprise. Kakrekt was speaking again, louder now. Gabriel
said hoarsely, "It's the last one. You take it."

"I'm holding up better than you are. Don't try to be gallant. Quickly!"

In a minute Kakrekt would get up and demand to know what they were saying. Hanna said swiftly, "I don't know what's going to happen. Bella said something about—it could be armed rescue, I think, but we'd be at risk if they do. Best to avoid it. But be ready for anything."

Now Kakrekt was beside them and Hanna reactivated the translator and heard Kakrekt say, "What are you talking about? You must have no secrets!"

Hanna watched Gabriel anxiously. The big tablet did not want to go down.

"Answer me!"

A twinge of pain crossed his face, but he turned his head and nodded. Hanna nodded back, relieved, and finally looked at Kakrekt. "Very well," she said calmly.

She did not say any more while the endless ride went on. She only took Gabriel's hand and held on.

"Another sixty meters up and we could guide them where they need to go," Metra said. "I'll show you."

Two more faces had joined the conference, Metra necessarily, Bella at Jameson's insistence. Both of them were looking down at a three-dimensional map of Wektt's subsurface. Presently it appeared, vertically oriented, over Jameson's huge desk. At first it was blurred and wobbled a bit. When it sharpened he was surprised. He must have expected something that looked organic: curved passages like blood vessels, chambers like organs—though he could not imagine where that fancy had come from, unless something in him suggested Battleground was trying to swallow Hanna whole. Instead most of the map was straight lines and right angles, a series of rigid grids. He heard Peter Struzik complain that he could not see it and said absently, "Come here, then," and ignored the rest of the protests. Commissioners would turn up or not, as they chose. He did not hear Andrella Murphy's voice. She was probably already on the way to his rooms.

"The red dot is the com unit," Metra said. "We can pick up its signal, but we don't quite have the capability to map what's around it at that depth while the coordinates keep changing. The open area that appears to surround it is actually two to three levels above its real location. We think the levels above that area look like this—" The configuration changed and then changed again, and again, and once more. "Accuracy improves with each level we go higher. And finally—"

One more change. "This is the level closest to the surface. If they can get to the upper levels we can direct them to passages leading in any direction. Actually getting to them physically—"

Metra looked up.

"We've no heavy machinery, no explosives. We have nineteen remaining servos that could dig down to them in one to four hours, depending on what level we have to reach and the geology of the site. The *Admiral Wu* has heavy-duty laser generators that can be calibrated to pinpoint accuracy. Those could do it in minutes."

"The *Wu* was ordered to proceed as soon as the pods were destroyed," Jameson said. "Its ETA is twenty hours. Much too long."

"They're a moving target. Starting to dig now would only alert the population and cause tremendous damage. We'd have to fight our way to them, and they might be killed before we get there. We should wait till they're stationary, wherever they end up, if that's at all possible."

She turned at Bella's murmur and said, "What?"

"I said, they've just moved up another level."

"Good. The closer to the surface the better."

"Maybe," said Bella hopefully, "that's where they're taking her."

"There is another possibility," Metra said. "There are shafts to the surface. Some of them are sheer verticals, others rise at an angle. They're probably for ventilation, but they should be accessible. There might even be ladders in place in the verticals."

Jameson said, "If you were obsessed with potential invaders, would you leave ladders handy? I wouldn't count on it. And I'd question whether either of them has the strength left to climb."

"Alternatively, if we can guide them to a shaft we should be able to pull them out," Metra said. "Depending on the resistance we meet."

"Pull them out alive, I hope."

"They're getting out alive. I won't settle for less," Metra said, and for the first time Jameson almost liked her.

———

Hanna saw Kakrekt's attention sharpen, apparently at nothing. She heard Kakrekt whisper, apparently to nobody, and focused her own awareness. She had forgotten the small devices Soldiers used as communicators; Kakrekt had one tucked into her ear, invisible under an inner fold, and had just gotten bad news. Hanna waited to hear about it, but Kakrekt did not even look at her. She asked outright, finally: "Kakrekt Commander, is something wrong?"

Kakrekt looked at her, debating an answer. Finally she said, "The Holy Man is displeased that you are not in your quarters."

Hanna said, because it seemed important though she was not sure why, "Does he know where we are?"

"No," Kakrekt said. "No one knows where we are going." *Good,* Hanna thought, but then Kakrekt said, "Not yet. But there are Soldiers who will tell him which way we have passed, and he may deduce our destination."

Bad, Hanna thought, because she understood now that Kakrekt did not only want to hide them from other humans; she thought they would be safer hidden away from Kwoort.

———

Another ramp, up again. Bella said Hanna had to seek out the thoughts of more Soldiers. Hanna didn't want to. She had begun to fade in and out, and think in scraps. Perhaps if she had not given the last meal tab to Gabriel . . . but he had needed it so badly . . .

Bella prodded her: *What about the communicator?*

No chance of getting it while Kakrekt's watching.

What about what's around you? Captain wants to know.

Why? Hanna had absorbed the knowledge that the upper levels were being mapped as rapidly as possible.

In case you don't go any higher. Even if you do, a map doesn't show what's inside. Soldiers? Are they armed?

Hanna made a half-hearted effort. *Soldiers and Warriors mating*—a great blast of it, she knew what that felt like, the cauldron she had almost fallen into once before. *No!* she thought and shut it out, looked for something else. There were Soldiers working in—

Crèches, she said. *There are crèches here.*

All the Soldiers nearby, in fact, seemed to be performing crèche-related tasks.

Makes sense, said Bella, *if you're getting close to breeding grounds. But are they armed?*

Ask Dema. She didn't say anything about weapons in the crèches she saw.

Good, said Bella, but then came a doubt. *If there's fighting. Children, babies.*

Hanna thought of the Soldier-children she had touched. There had been nothing, nothing, to remind her of human children or the young of other sentient species she knew, their eager curiosity and quick emotions. But they were children. Their parents would not care: the horrible difference between Soldiers and humans and, for that matter, other sentient species too. Soldiers would not spare Mickey in a like situation. But still. They were children.

Hanna did not remember sliding into a doze, but woke to find that she and Gabriel were slumped together like rag dolls. He was awake, though; Bella had been communicating with him. Hanna didn't know where they were. Wherever it was, there was even less light.

Bella said, *Gabriel says you've gone up another level. And you've moved even farther south. There's a plateau over you now. A couple more levels and you'll be right under it. We've got a good, sharp map of the level you're on now and the ones above.*

Kakrekt leaned forward and said something to the Soldier-driver. The translator did not pick up her soft words, but the thought was so clear Hanna did not have to probe for it.

We're almost there, she said to Bella, *but I don't know what it's like.*

There's a huge grid of rooms just ahead. Small ones, with thick walls. Exterior corridors that turn back to the city. There's one that doesn't—it's way ahead, let's see, my God, that grid goes on forever! Nothing else for almost two

*kilometers—just those spaces. Definitely not a crèche layout.
Are those the breeding grounds?*

Must be—

The vehicle stopped. "Out," Kakrekt said, and Hanna
saw that the corridor had narrowed and they could not ride
any further. She climbed out, feeling her legs protest and
almost give way. *Not good,* she thought, *two kilometers to
any way out—* Too far to go, with nourishment and energy
so desperately depleted. She turned to help Gabriel, for
what her help was worth, and his hand on her shoulder felt
crushingly heavy. Kwek was suddenly there beside her,
looking ahead, breathing fast and sweating. Kwek looked
quickly at Kakrekt, who said, "You may proceed. Follow
her," she said to the humans.

So they followed, not knowing what else to do; and a
little later Gabriel thought for the first time, but not the last,
of the circles of Hell.

Chapter XVIII

KWEK PLUNGED THROUGH the opening ahead of them, seeking a mate. There was a high, dim chamber with a guarded gateway at the opposite end, otherwise empty except for two male Soldiers who paced nervously but turned when Kwek came in; both started for her but hesitated, less because of the not-Soldiers behind her than because of Kakrekt's insignia. Commanders, it appeared, were not seen here much more often than alien life-forms. It did not stop them for long. "Now," Kwek was muttering, *"Yes!"* and she headed for the nearest of the males. The pair walked quickly toward the far doorway, already touching each other, sinuous fingers plucking at uniforms, reminding Hanna unpleasantly of her first landing at Rowtt.

The guards had moved forward but retreated now; if the other male had been there first, they would have intervened to be sure Kwek went with him. Kwek had only appeared to have a choice.

Bella had seen through Hanna's eyes. She said, *Don't lose Kwek. Get the com unit!*

But Hanna hesitated. Immediately past this chamber there was a maelstrom of noise and compulsion in which she could detect not one single conscious thought. It would be a hothouse, too, because this outer hall already was perceptibly warmer, much warmer, than the corridors they had come from.

She was afraid. What if her perception of that fury of desire took her out of herself again? What if she threw herself on Gabriel and begged him to couple with her, not caring who he was?

Block it, Bella said. *You weren't blocking then, just the opposite. Block it!*

But I'll lose contact with you—

Then get the com unit. You have to anyway. It's all we'll have to track you with.

Still Hanna hung back. She did not want to watch Soldiers mate; the prospect revolted her. Sex was supposed to be a kind of present people gave each other, and honoring the value of the individual Other (or Others, if that was your bent) was part of it. So she had been taught, and so she believed. Nobody in those rooms ahead was giving presents. She understood now, seeing Kwek with the stranger-mate, that it was not even Soldiers who gave pleasure to one another. The neural network was responsive to the facilitators alone.

For just a second she thought of the inquisitive Mi-o once more. Kwoort must have gone into breeding mode while he was on New Earth. But Mi-o could not have given him any satisfaction, nor anyone else, in the absence of facilitators. He must have been desperate—

"Did you not wish to observe?" Kakrekt said, and finally Hanna moved forward, Gabriel behind her, following Kwek—

—while Kwek and her partner sought eagerly through a hot maze of rooms for a cubicle with space for them. The floor was earth here, and the walls, and the air so saturated with heat and spice smell that Hanna thought she might faint. Overwhelming too was the perception of sensation, the blind ecstasy so intense it had once torn her from trance; she obeyed Bella, threw up the telepathic block, and Bella vanished from her mind and she was horribly alone. She moved forward through darkness, one dim light high up in each room barely enough to show the figures on the floor. She did not dare let the block attenuate enough even to think to Gabriel, the only human contact she had left. The rooms were connected by wide arches, and in the dark she could only see moving shapes, most prone, thrusting against each other. They stumbled over bodies in the act of copulation, two by two, bodies strangely changed, torsos almost covered with pale lumps as if mating spawned gross tumors. The cacophony was indescribable; indecipherable, too, because wordless, so the translators filled their ears with a chorus of whistles and screams. Soldiers did not need words to mate. But then, humans did not either.

Then—eyes slowly adjusting to the near-dark—she saw the sick growths on the feverish bodies for what they were. For a moment she was back in a tunnel with Kwoort, in Rowtt: *another species lived on this world, finger-sized, dead white, hairless and blind—it lived underground, they were crowded and scrambling over one another, they turned on each other savagely and tore with sharp teeth and ate, ate—*

They were the facilitators. And they were eating now, but not with teeth. They crawled out of the earthen walls and floor and onto the twisting bodies, and extended glistening filaments that sank into receptor sites that gaped open to take them in. For a frozen instant Hanna focused on one of the things and saw the filaments pulse and knew she saw an exchange of fluids.

An exchange. *They pump something in,* Gabriel had said, and it had not seemed important at the time. But now a tiny, distant part of her mind said it was wildly important, but revulsion silenced it, and Kakrekt said loudly, close to her ear, "They come when it's time. They know. We don't know how they know."

Kakrekt glanced down absently. One of the things had wriggled onto her boot. It paused and wriggled off. Kakrekt was not in season. There was nothing for it here.

Hanna whispered a question, but Kakrekt could not hear her over the din and bent her head, one ear extended. Hanna raised her voice—with effort, because she was not sure she wanted to hear the answer—"Where do they come from?"

"They are everywhere in the earth, even at That Place. It does not matter where a couple is when the time comes on them. These always ascend from the ground. It is not like that with other animals, only with Soldiers."

Then Soldiers, if they were native to this world at all, had been altered to breed like this. *There must have been containment and control,* Hanna thought, but what had happened then? Did the creators leave, did they die? Did they free facilitators into the earth, did the creatures escape? If it was purposeful, to what end?

She could not think about it now. All her fading energy was spent in fighting the chaos that filled these dark rooms.

Kwek was out of sight. She had hurtled through another

opening, still searching for space. And Hanna could not see Gabriel either. He was gone too.

She had gotten just a glimpse of Kwek before she disappeared. Hanna ran after her, fear soaring to panic, surely Gabriel had gone the same way—if he had not she would never find him—

But he was not in the next space, or the next, or the one after that, there were arches everywhere going in all directions, but she hoped, how she hoped he had gone in a straight line, because maybe Kwek had done that in her haste. Hanna ran blindly, fear taking over, trying to avoid the shapes on the ground, reason dissolving in horror. She crashed into a wall and reeled away, tripped and fell over a mating pair that did not even notice her. Something squirmed disgustingly under one breast and she scrabbled to her feet. One of the slugs clung to her hand and she flailed until it spun away, her scream lost in the tumult of sound around her. She staggered to the moist wall and fell against it and mud flaked onto her face. Movement caught the corner of her eye and she turned her head and stared straight at one of the things. The leading orifice was open and she saw its teeth and behind them the filaments, writhing, beginning to extrude; it reared like a snake, half out of the wall, and she saw other features. Appendages with chitinous ridges for digging. Suckers for climbing walls or bodies. What if it scented Kwek's pheromones on her? What if it thought—

Another scream rose in her throat, only she could not get the breath for it, she could not breathe at all.

The thing popped out of the wall and tumbled to the floor. It had not mistaken her for a Warrior in heat.

She finally gulped in air thick as water, and it came back out in sobs.

Something touched her and she gasped and jerked away, ready to run, but her legs would not move, and then she recognized Gabriel and sobbed again in relief. She clutched at him and his mouth moved but she could not hear what he said over the tumult. She struggled to focus her thoughts, stood swaying on tiptoe to shout in his ear.

"Where did Kwek go?"

"This way!" he shouted back, and grasped her hand and stumbled away through the dark, trying to pull her after him, but there was little strength in his grip and he was unsteady on his feet. He was at his limit, too.

We are both going to collapse, she thought, *we are going to fall here in this hell and not be able to get up.*

It came to her in flashes that she ought to question her revulsion. She had seen animals mate, she had done plenty of mating herself; she had been raped, if it came to that. *But we were conscious of each other,* she thought—dodging a male who rose to his feet, tripping over his companion's foot, somehow staggering into another room. *All the sentient creatures we know*—Gabriel turned to make sure she was behind him—*feel emotion for each other in mating.* She shied away from an earsplitting scream of ecstasy at her feet. *Even in rape there is emotion, even if it is hate on either side. Even an animal wants one mate more than another, when there is choice.*

She focused on Gabriel like a beacon; he had found Kwek and was just as focused on her, and they were close behind. There seemed no end to the maze. Hanna had not asked Bella how many of the rooms there were, there might be hundreds of them, thousands, and how many must they pass through to reach the way out? Fear was the only thing that overcame her weakness, and perhaps it drove Gabriel too.

Ahead of them Kwek and the male had become impatient. They paused now and then, touching each other, opening clothing to touch the sensitive ports that in this stage of arousal looked like open sores. Over and over they did this, the pauses becoming longer and more frequent, until their uniforms were bunched at their waists. They did not kiss. Hanna had seen no one kiss. It must be unknown here.

The pair came completely to a stop. Another couple occupied the room but there was space enough, and Kwek and the Soldier tore off their uniforms altogether and fell to the floor. It was littered with the heaving white things, and they surged toward Kwek and the male at once. In a last convulsive move to divest herself of everything that might bar their way, Kwek wrenched the communicator from her wrist. It fell among the facilitators.

Hanna and Gabriel leaned together, breathing hard, and stared at the spot where it had disappeared. Facilitators crawled across it. It was visible in flashes as the things moved over and around it. In a minute they might not see it at all.

Hanna stopped herself from thinking. If she thought about what she had to do it would be impossible. She couldn't bring herself to kneel on that floor. She grabbed Gabriel's hand and said in his ear, "Don't let me fall!" — and stooped and reached, dizzy with heat and noise.

She had never been squeamish and rather liked snakes with their dry, cool skins, but the things her hand met were moist, and hot — not warm, but hot. She groped in the mass of them and gagged at the touch but she did not dare pull away or she would lose her nerve forever. *No, oh, no,* she thought, *no,* she was thinking as she groped for the com unit, and *No!* but she did not pull back until she had it in her hand.

And then she had to throw up, but there was nothing in her stomach, and Gabriel snatched the translator away from her mouth and held her up while she retched.

"Bella? *Bella,* where are you, come in!"

"She's in Command with the captain. This is Aneer." The voice was calm. "Is Guyup with you?"

"Yes—"

"Are you alone?"

Hanna had not been able to force herself to move; Gabriel had dragged her through another room, with difficulty, because there were no less than three busy couples in it. The one they had come to now had only one pair.

"Alone!" Hanna said, "No, we're not alone!" Gabriel had had to force the com unit onto her left wrist because she couldn't stop rubbing her right hand against her clothing long enough to use it. As if that would get it clean! She heard her own voice changing pitch when she spoke, out of control. *Where do all these couples come from?* — the emptiness of the pairing hall was deceptive; but if a Warrior only had to wait for the first ready Soldier to arrive, the couple could be processed in seconds. That *was* the process, all the process there was. It crossed her mind that Heartworld's founding families might negotiate for years before they signed a contract that authorized a couple to produce children. She began to laugh and was crying.

"Don't." Gabriel shook her, so surprising a move that she stopped crying immediately, from shock. "Are you thirsty? I am. I haven't seen any water sources here. We're sweating. Don't waste moisture."

He spoke loudly, but it was not a shout. The overall decibel level seemed a little lower here.

She began to think again. Rational thought felt like a strange relief; she clung to it. "There must be lavatories somewhere."

"How would we find one? Ask somebody? Tap some guy on the shoulder and say, excuse me, could you stop what you're doing and tell us where to get a drink?"

She felt a giggle rising and forced it down. She couldn't afford more hysteria.

"Bassanio?" said Kaida Aneer.

"All right. I hear you. There are Soldiers around, but they're busy. They haven't noticed us. I don't know where Kakrekt is."

Now it was Metra's voice: "Get moving while you can. We can track you, let's hope she can't."

"Which way?" Hanna said.

"Just start moving! Go!"

Chapter XIX

"GO RIGHT. Keep forward."

"Check, turning right ... Can't go forward here. Two doors to the right, one to the left."

"Left, then."

"All right, we're through. Doors left, right, ahead."

"Go right."

"All ri—dead end."

"Turn around and go back. Straight ahead."

"We're through. Doors ahead and right."

"Try right again."

"Dead end."

"Turn around and go back. Then right."

Talley Hong gave directions, easy, so few choices at each move: left, right, ahead, aiming for the farthest reach of the complex, where the outbound corridor might open from the breeding ground; if there was no opening, *Endeavor*'s servos would start to dig. But sometimes Bassanio and Guyup had to go back. Too often, the last hour, back. They were barely moving, pushing the limits of exhaustion, and they could not afford the extra steps. There were signs that directed Soldiers to exits, and they had experimented with transmitting and translating the script, but the exits led back into the city. No good.

And Bassanio was afraid, screwing the tension tighter— not afraid of being found by Commander Kakrekt, who seemed to have misplaced them, but of the creatures she called facilitators. Hong couldn't imagine why. Images Bassanio transmitted from the breeding ground had moved the crew to incredulous laughter. Hong's own first reaction had been to suppress a chuckle and shake his head; surely this wasn't the first time Fleet had needed to retrieve crew from brothels, though presumably the brothels had not been alien. The situation was too ridiculous to seem dangerous, or even lewd. He controlled himself, though, because he was in Command with the captain, and the captain didn't allow laughter on duty. And Bassanio, no novice to dangerous situations, was unquestionably scared. He could hear that in her voice.

He kept giving directions. *Left. Right. Ahead. Back. Back again . . .*

After a while she said, "These things are getting interested in us."

"Interested how?" Metra said.

"Starting toward us when we cross a room. There aren't as many people here. The farther we get from the entrance the fewer there are. Some of the rooms are empty. Except for the, um, these *things*. There aren't as many but there's always some crawling around and every time we go into a room they crawl toward us. They can move pretty fast when the floor's clear. It's getting obvious—doors left and right. Wait, I can tell you now, the way left is a dead end. So is— oh, damn it, so is the way right! We've got to backtrack again. Can't you get us out of here?"

She sounded on the edge of tears. Hong heard Guyup's voice under hers, a soothing murmur.

"We've almost got a program done to calculate relative density of the walls. That should tell us which walls have openings. Give us a *real* map. It'll be ready to run in a few minutes. Why don't you take a rest?"

"No, no rests, if we stop I don't think we can get up again and these things are coming at us—"

"You don't have the receptor sites the aliens do. What can they do to you?"

"They have *teeth!*"

The commissioners awarded themselves a break from wrangling. Jameson's strategy to keep them focused on Colony One had succeeded, though events had overtaken his motives; they had spent hours arguing what to do about the incipient rebellion and what to do with, or to, its ringleaders—pitching data at each other, consulting experts, proposing options and shooting them down. He had seen too many of these sessions to find them entertaining, and if the others' attention was fixed on something besides Battleground—leaving that to Metra and Evanomen until something happened—his own mind wandered. The map of the breeding warren still hung in the air where he could see it and he had positioned it so he could follow the red pinpoint without being observed, except by Andrella Murphy, who had joined him and watched it too. A transcript of the transmissions between Hanna and *Endeavor* scrolled through the air beside it in real time.

He got up, after voting a hearty assent to the recess, and Murphy said, "Where are you going?"

"To see Mickey." He ordered map and transcript directed to a portable reader.

She said thoughtfully, "You do that every day, don't you?"

"When he's on the grounds, yes."

Mickey was enrolled in the play group nearest Jameson's private suite, housed in an interior space full of color and things that moved and things that grew; it flowed into a large courtyard park, roofed in winter but open in this season. Thera sometimes stayed with Mickey, sometimes not. Today she was not there. She was engaged on other business with Zanté and, by remote, Lady Koroth, to whom Jameson had loaned both of them. To his regret. He had not imagined the pursuit of housing for Hanna would occupy so much time. All three women were enjoying themselves far too much.

They went down a long spiral stair into the park. The sky was gray and the air hot and humid, but the roof was open. Most of the children had elected to stay indoors where it was cool; only three, one of them Mickey, were outside, clambering noisily through a tangle of tubes and tunnels, with one sharp-eyed caretaker moving around to keep them all in sight. He was fully qualified as a child companion and he was also fully qualified in security. He nodded to Jameson and Murphy as if he thought they might be abductors in disguise and he the children's last defense.

Jameson stole a look at the reader while they waited for Mickey to emerge from the maze. The red dot was not as motionless as it looked. And a jagged green line had begun to extend from it: the modified mapping program was online.

Murphy said, "What do you suppose Kakrekt's up to?"

"She left them there on purpose, obviously. Left guards where they came in, probably, thinking they'll be hopelessly lost and she can retrieve them when she's ready. She has all the personnel she wants at her disposal. A thousand Soldiers would track them down quickly, even in that labyrinth."

"We should pull out of there altogether, you know."

Jameson nodded. The telepaths had reported casually that Hanna was now certain, confirmed in a conversation with Kakrekt, that no power on Battleground could travel between stars in this era, and perhaps none would ever achieve starflight again. The civilization fell outside Contact's mandate. But the mandate wasn't going to hold up.

"Information is starting to leak. Karin's doing, and she's going to push the longevity issue as long as she's still around," he said. "We're not going to get out of this without results. Research volunteers would be enough. Or—"

Or unwilling captives. He wasn't going to say it out loud even to Murphy.

She glanced sideways at his face. Andrella Murphy, still in love with her husband after seventy years, was convinced against all evidence that Hanna ril-Koroth was exactly the right companion for Jameson. "Suppose we need a long-term contact on site?" she said. "Hanna would be the obvious candidate. What then?"

Mickey popped out of an opening a few meters away, saw Jameson, and ran to him laughing, face flushed, eyes shining. Jameson picked him up and kissed his check. He said, "She hates Battleground. She would hate me."

Murphy waited until he had put the child down and they had turned back before she said, "That wasn't an answer."

"I don't have one," he said.

They moved faster, now that Talley Hong could weed out dead ends before they ran into them. They could almost have run, Hanna thought, if each separate step didn't require a separate act of will. If she didn't keep getting the directions mixed up in her fuzzy brain, turning right when Hong said left and vice versa. If it wasn't so unutterably confusing when a wall had two openings and it wasn't clear which was the right one so that she had to actually form words and convey them to Hong.

I'm slowing Gabriel down, she thought illogically. *He could be out of here by now—*

She looked around to tell him so and he wasn't there.

The communicator made noises she didn't listen to. She wanted to run back the way she had come screaming Gabriel's name and knew that she physically, absolutely, could not. Even breathing was an effort, her body telling her she had finally used it up. She managed to say to Hong, "I've lost Gabriel." *Think,* she told herself, but she couldn't.

Her hand thought for her, fumbling in a pocket. It brought out a stimulant vial. If she were to find Gabriel, if they were to get out of this place, she was down to her last recourse.

She knew that after she used it telepathy would be lost to her, and she was afraid. But fear for Gabriel was sharper.

She stood with the capsule in her hand and looked around, trying to find a reason not to use it. There were no mating Soldiers in this room. But there were half a dozen facilitators on the floor and as many again clinging to the walls, and they began to crawl slowly to the floor, head-down, and those on the floor began to ooze toward her. There was no question the humans were becoming targets.

She did not know why. It didn't matter. But if Gabriel had fallen they might already be on him.

She snapped the vial and inhaled the gas. *Thrum,* said her nervous system. But faintly. It really did not want to keep going.

For a few seconds nothing happened and then energy began to flow into her muscles and her mind. The drug would not affect telepathy immediately and she dropped the block she had been holding—cautiously, but now that she was not in the middle of a mob of Soldiers and Warriors, she found she could shut out the roar. And when she reached for Gabriel, she sensed him, but he did not respond to her.

She took a step, testing herself, and had to stop, for a moment wildly dizzy. But her voice was stronger when she said, "Guide me back, the exact way we came."

Metra's voice said, "How long's it been since he was with you?"

"I don't know. It doesn't matter."

There was a silence that stretched too far. Hanna moved to the door she had come in by and looked through it; that room was empty of Soldiers, too. She could not remember which of the three entries into it she had used—but she saw facilitators, only four or five left here, all slowly moving toward one opening.

She said, "Gabriel is not expendable," just as Metra said, "Five minutes."

Hanna had no intention of giving up after five minutes, and she could move more easily now, the artificial strength in her legs growing. She would take another dose if she had to and the devil with telepathy.

"I need directions! Hurry!" she said—she was sure she could follow the facilitators but also sure they moved toward Gabriel, and there was no time to wait and watch them, and why were so few visible here? Did they have underground routes that were more direct?—of course they did. There might be many more on the move.

Hong began to recite directions. Hanna dodged right, left, left again, trying not to step on facilitators. She had been too tired to think of that before, had managed to keep the disgusting mess on the bottoms of her shoes away from consciousness. She thought of it now and thought she would be sick again. *Is that the reason? We are trampling them, killing them, and they will not stand for that—*

There was a terrifying instant when she thought of hundreds of them turning on her with those teeth—

And maybe worse.

Anyone who interferes with reproduction . . .

It would be word of mouth, spreading to the breeding grounds so that the Soldiers and Warriors and facilitators surged out of them and sought out the unbelievers, the researchers and they were—

Torn limb from limb—

How long before the mating Soldiers behind them connected the strange intruders with the trail of trampled facilitators? The fluids coursing through them, essential for reproduction: what else did they trigger?

No time to think, no time—

Less than a minute more but it seemed forever: she found Gabriel facedown, one hand beneath him. He could not have been there long and the way he had fallen gave him some protection. The fear that she would find him bleeding from a hundred wounds or already eaten alive was wide of the mark—though perhaps it would have been different if she had been longer getting to him. She dropped to the ground and tore two of the sickening things from an ear, one from his scalp, three from the exposed hand, two more from a wounded cheek. Flesh came away with them, in their teeth.

I'm sorry, I'm so sorry— If only she had seen him go down; how could she not have noticed? Her blood mixed with his when one of the things turned in her hand and nipped her as she flung it away. He didn't answer her call and she turned him over easily, with a strength that would have been impossible a few minutes ago, and broke a vial under his nostrils and shook him. "Breathe! Gabriel! Gabriel, inhale!"

There were a score of the slug-things here and they were all crawling toward the humans.

"Breathe . . . !"

Unless he had died in the last seconds, unless he wasn't breathing at all—but then the blood wouldn't flow so freely and of course she would know he was gone, she had sensed the deaths of people she loved less—unless she could no longer sense anything—

His eyes opened. He put a torn hand to the torn cheek and groaned.

"Quick," she said, "quick! Talley, I've got him, let's go!"

Kakrekt plowed through the city, scattering Soldiers. She had gone straight back to the Holy Man's quarters and found him gone. Now she was after him as fast as her vehicle could go, by herself, with no subordinate's weight to slow her down.

She thought—jerking the acceleration lever, clipping a corner, clipping a Soldier who did not dodge quickly enough—that she ought to have anticipated how fast *he* might move. Kwoort had gotten reports on where he was headed with his "guests" and had rushed out, apparently, just as she arrived at Mating Complex Four with the not-Soldiers. She wondered if she would chase him, and he chase her, around and around in circles.

Except he was chasing the not-Soldiers instead of Kakrekt.

She had been outside when he ordered the two aircraft destroyed; she had seen them explode (along with some nearby Soldiers) and gone to him at once.

"Why did you do that—?"

"They will kill the facilitators!" He had ranted some more, but Kakrekt had not stayed to listen. He might be closer to the end-change than she had thought, he saw enemies everywhere, and she was afraid for the lives of the guests. Kwoort's wild accusation was already in her thoughts when she saw that Kwek was ready to mate, so she thought at once: where better to hide the not-Soldiers than a breeding ground?

She had to keep them safe. If the not-Soldiers on the spacecraft had not been hostile before, they would certainly be hostile if those two were killed, and even if they did not retaliate they would go away, they would never assist her in mastering Rowtt, never share their knowledge—and now she had to intercept Kwoort and keep matters from getting worse.

––––

They could run. The strength might be artificial, but Hanna exulted in it. Pain did not slow Gabriel, and they flew though the maze as fast as Talley Hong could direct them. The population of facilitators dwindled; when Hanna said so Metra interrupted with *Bring specimens,* and Hanna and Gabriel glanced at each other without slowing. *Pockets. Teeth.* "Did you hear that?" he panted, and she said, "Hear what?" At the end of it all a final arch led into the corridor *Endeavor* had mapped. It led up almost immediately to the highest level of the underground maze, and from there cut away from the city, part of a complex web. Some routes connected Wektt's major city with other population centers, Talley Hong said. Some were blocked with substantial barriers and assumed abandoned, but this one—with many intersections and complex branches; he cautioned them to follow his directions precisely—appeared to be open all the way to a dead end under the plateau. That was how Kwoort and Kakrekt had gotten to the desert meeting place, Hanna thought, through a tunnel like this one. The floor was the same concrete used throughout Wektt, old and thick with dust, cracked but intact, inviting speed. The air was close and felt unmoving, but it had to come from somewhere. And there were indeed shafts ahead, said Talley Hong; some appeared to be blocked, but others, farther off, were open to the surface.

We're finally getting some breaks, Hanna thought.

Yes! said Bella, and Hanna laughed out loud, breathing easily as she ran. The way was unlit but the communicator's light-source function was enough. And she could feel Bella's personality as vividly as if they stood side by side; this time the stimulant had proved safe.

We're out of here! she thought.

Arch said, *I know how we can celebrate* . . . Teasing.

After this place? —I'll never want to have sex again!

She was giddy with freedom, and free of Kakrekt's plot to kill Kwoort, too. If Hanna hadn't been there Kakrekt would have sent someone to That Place anyway; she had only sent Hanna because the pod was the fastest transport on Battleground. Hanna wasn't responsible for what happened next: no gnawing conscience, no conflict, no guilt.

Finally confident, finally free, she reached for Kakrekt. Checking. And stumbled.

Kakrekt was coming after them and thought Kwoort was too; she touched Kwoort also, and had just time to register fury and despair before everything went black.

She was absurdly flying, arms flailing; something came up and hit her so hard it shook her bones.

For a second or two she did not know where she was. Then she looked up from the ground in bewilderment, slowly understanding what had happened. She had come to a dead stop and Gabriel had crashed into her so that they had both gone sprawling. The tunnel was no darker than before; the black void was in her mind. She could no longer feel Bella's presence or anyone else's. She could see Gabriel with her eyes, see the look of surprise on his face through a veil of dust disturbed and settling, but she could not feel it. The curtain had descended not gradually this time but all at once.

Hanna picked herself up slowly. She made futile motions at brushing dust away. She was trembling.

"What — ?" said Gabriel, getting up too, not finishing the

question, as if he expected her to know what he meant to say. But she could only guess from context, like a true-human.

"Lost my footing—"

He didn't know. She hadn't told anyone except the telepaths exactly what the stimulant had done to her before, as if it were a shameful weakness.

"Hanna? We have to get moving. Come on."

She said, "Kwoort and Kakrekt are after us. They're not together."

She heard Metra say, "Where are they? Do they know where you are?"

Even Metra, perhaps without knowing it, had come to value telepathy.

Hanna said—no choice now—"I don't know. Listen, listen, this is important." Her voice was unsteady again. "We had some stimulant from the pod, we used it. It knocks out telepathy. Ask Bella, she knows. That's all I found out. I can't see any more, I can't tell anything else about them. I can't know anything that's not in front of my face."

The shakes were still there, and violent. She couldn't run yet. She wasn't sure she could walk.

Faintly she heard Metra ask questions, Bella answering. Metra understood quickly.

"You're perceptible on sensors now you're out of a crowd," Metra said. "Anybody after you will be too. Keep going. We'll keep watch."

Hanna could not stop shaking. They started to move again, but she could not run. Neither could Gabriel, as if the shock of falling had thrown a switch. The stimulant had too little to work with and energy was already flagging; their muscles, lately so little used, were worn out too, weak and aching. *Endeavor*'s medics joined the conversation, worried about hallucinations: Hanna had had them when she used the stimulant before, hadn't she, and was there any evidence of them now? Explaining that she had lied would take more energy than she could summon, and she just said, "Not yet." She even thought of taking more, but Metra relayed urgent warnings from the medics to both of them: *No more. In your condition it could kill you.*

The fear she had thrust away when Gabriel's safety was at stake flooded her now. *If it doesn't come back. If it never comes back.* She kept moving, but her brain felt paralyzed. *Crippled, crippled forever. Blind and deaf on D'neera. Blind and deaf everywhere forever.* There were voices from the communicator but they did not penetrate, as if they came from a long way off, echoing on the edge of hearing in the shadows of the endless tunnel. She didn't answer. After a while Gabriel stopped her and took the com unit from her wrist, clumsily, because he could only use one hand. She didn't object, but it roused her enough to help him.

The voices kept sounding while they moved ahead, which felt like crawling through liquid mud.

She heard Bella say, "All right, I can think to Gabriel and I can read what he thinks. That'll have to do. H'ana's a blur, not even as clear as true-humans. She doesn't hear me when I think to her, I don't know why, even true-humans do."

Forever.

Hong: "—off to the side, fifty meters ahead. Looks like there was a shaft there but it's filled in. Don't go that way, keep straight."

"Be easier digging there, wouldn't it?" Gabriel said.

Metra answered. "We don't want to attract attention. The optimum's getting you out without being noticed. Get as far out as you can."

"We can't go much farther."

"Do the best you can. If anyone's after you there's no sign of it yet. If you can make it another three Ks, there's a shaft we know is open."

Hanna had lost the thread of conversation.

I don't want to live like this, I can't. . . .

Her feet went on without her noticing.

Soldiers told Kakrekt Kwoort's route. They had no reason not to. He had given no order for silence and Kakrekt was High Commander. Word that she was looking for the Holy Man sped ahead of her, Soldier to Soldier, and replies sped back to her ear. *He rides a one-Soldier conveyance*—two wheels, that meant, fast and maneuverable.

What of his robes?—Kakrekt hoped for robes catching in wheels, the machine spinning out of control, the Holy Man flying headfirst into something ungiving.

He wears the uniform—so she had to give up the gratifying vision.

As she neared the breeding ground, at the edge of a power complex, she pulled up to question an informant who had news. Kwoort had seized a Warrior to accompany him.

What for?

He said he wants Woke to make records—

Records?

The up-ramps slowed her and made her furious.

She had often seen Kwoort writing, writing, when he was not looking at maps; she never knew what he wrote. At least a rider would slow him down, and she thought of Woke Warrior clinging to the Holy Man with one hand, frantically scribbling with the other, and her ears unfurled and flapped. But he had stopped again, a Soldier's voice said in her ear; he had taken another Soldier's weapon, complaining that Woke was unarmed.

At the thought of what he might do with it she tried to get more speed out of her own machine, but it had no more to give.

———

A long time had passed.

"Down to one K," Metra said.

"We can make it," Gabriel said. He glanced at Hanna and was not so sure. She looked in the dimness like a walking skeleton; like a ghost.

———

The not-Soldiers are not in the breeding ground, I searched it, I went myself. Have you seen not-Soldiers, I shouted, I roared. Who sees anything while they mate? To my amazement some had seen. A Warrior sat up and said she knew the not-Soldiers, they took back from her a communications device they had given her I do not know when, I would have her executed but she will soon be quick with young so I will not. Then I found a couple rising to retire to a crèche who said they had seen two strangely shaped Soldiers pass through who talked to such a device, so the not-Soldiers are talking to their Commander despite all my precautions

*against it. I write this so that if I cease to survive all will know
what they have done. Sent machines to destroy us. Sent machines against the facilitators, my High Commander herself
sent the not-Soldiers into the warren against them! They have
crushed facilitators under their feet, I have seen the remains!
I will not allow it! When I get them back they must be torn
apart!*

*I think I know where they have gone. If they have not
been seen in the city then the only way out goes through the
deserted places*

Gabriel was on Hanna's right, his undamaged hand clamped
firmly on her wrist. He took every turn specified by Talley
Hong, but other corridors and downward ramps meandered
off everywhere, and he began to wonder what they led to.

Hanna did not seem to notice. She appeared to have
shrunk.

After what seemed a very long while he said suddenly,
"Wait a minute."

Hanna stopped obediently, but Metra's voice said, "I
wouldn't advise it. Someone behind you now and closing. A
single vehicle, maybe one individual aboard, maybe two.
Interception in ten minutes at current rate of speed."

Gabriel had felt a puff of cold air against his cheek. He
let go of Hanna and licked a finger and lifted it into the
dark.

"How far away did you say that shaft is?"

"Less than a K. You're not going to make it before the
pursuit gets to you. Keep going, though. We'll send servos
in ahead of you."

Gabriel started walking, but he had—maybe, if they
were lucky—a closer goal in mind. Hanna lagged behind,
and after a minute he stopped and waited for her. When she
got to him she stopped too, but she didn't look at him. She
was an automaton, her mind shut down or somewhere else.

He touched her face and said her name. She finally
looked up. Her eyes were dull. She whispered something,
but it was unintelligible.

"I don't know what it's like for you," he said. "I can't
know. But you have to come out of it."

He sounded different even to himself, as if something

drained from Hanna had passed to him. The blurred out-
lines of the cavern seemed to sharpen. He recognized that
though Hanna might be helpless, he was not. He leaned
forward and pushed both translator mouthpieces aside and
softly kissed her mouth. When he pulled away and looked
at her again there was a little more life in her eyes.

"Stop it," he said. His voice was loving. "When we get
out of here you can spend all the time you want feeling
sorry for yourself. If you even need to. The blackout didn't
last before; why should it this time? But now you have to
stop. That's for later. I need you now."

A spark for sure.

He kissed her again, long and hard. This time there was
a response. Just a little at first, but then it was stronger, and
then it stopped his breath. Ludicrous they must look, two
bags of bones, skulls kissing, but there was life and heat
here. And no one to say *ludicrous*.

"Get moving," Metra said from orbit.

They started walking again as fast as they could. Hanna
had not said a word, but her footfalls were quicker, and
firm.

Kakrekt had not wasted time finding out if the not-Soldiers
were still in the breeding warren. It had already been
searched on the Holy Man's order. Her ears flickered with
amusement when she heard that he himself had charged
into the warren, raged through it, strode over the couples
oblivious to him as they obeyed the god's imperative and
got on with breeding.

And *he* had lost time, because he had had to return to
the common entrance to resume his vehicle and the assistance of Warrior Woke.

There was only one point where the not-Soldiers could
have left the warren without being turned back toward the
city. Kwoort probably knew it, thanks to his endless perusal
of maps.

She had wasted no more than the space of a breath wondering how the not-Soldiers had found that point. She had
not imagined it was possible when she left them there. But
if they had been in communication with their spacecraft,
perhaps by "speaking to the mind," other not-Soldiers

might have guided them somehow. Not-Soldiers could do seemingly impossible things. And certainly the guests had gotten out.

She had set off again as fast as before, certain now that she could catch up. She knew the same maps the Holy Man did, but they showed only the uppermost level of the city's extent in forgotten times. He might know lower levels existed under the plateau, but he could not know how to move about in them.

Kakrekt, though, had explored them over many summers. No life stirred in those strange depths, though facilitators must lie dormant in the floors and walls of abandoned breeding warrens. Kakrekt had seen ancient crèches there, refectories and vast hollow kitchens, living quarters, dried-up crops and processing facilities, transport centers filled with machines drained of fuel, echoing administration halls, silent machine shops, emptied storage facilities, armories bare of weapons, hollow assembly halls. Deepest of all were empty chambers where faded pigments showed faces of Kakrekt knew not what, like the one in the overgrown structure far from the center of Wektt. Other things, too, that she did not recognize and could not explain. The not-Soldiers could help her find out what they were. And always the corridors and roads, silently waiting for Soldiers, connected by ramps in an unending web.

Kakrekt knew shortcuts.

———

"Do. Not. Go. There," said Talley Hong.

But the side passage Gabriel had found led upward, and a breeze flowed from it, fresh and cold.

"I don't think you'll have to dig," Gabriel said, and turned into it. Hanna trotted after him. He couldn't remember the last time he had felt fresh outdoor air, and he took great breaths of the cold draft.

"That tunnel's not on the schematic. It doesn't exist."

"We're inside it, so it must. The walls are different. Have you accounted for solid rock?"

"The geology says there can't be—"

There was a silence. The incline was shallow, but it was long, and they trudged up it with heads down, breathing hard. There might be light up ahead—surely dawn had come to Wektt by now—but the communicator's light obscured it.

"All right," Hong said finally. "Rock. A sinkhole or something not far ahead. Might be an exit. There's a shuttle on the way—" *Yes!* thought Gabriel—"we'll redirect. Look, there's a lot of levels below you, and somebody's moving on the next one down. Coming your way. Captain says get a move on. It's closing fast, and so is whoever's right behind you on the level where you're at."

Hanna said, finally sounding like herself, "Too late. They'll think we kept straight, like we've done all along."

Gabriel, however, turned for a moment to shine the light behind them. The dust on the floor was thicker here, and damp, too; there might be mud ahead. Maybe Hanna hadn't noticed the clear trail they had left. He thought a droning noise touched the edge of his hearing. The tunnels echoed and it was hard to decide where sound came from, but this could only be coming from behind them. *Closing fast.*

Slowly, he turned the light back ahead of them. Hanna had seen the footprints now, and heard the drone, but she did not say anything about them, and Gabriel did not either. There was no need.

———

Through the last few meters the mud turned to ice. The incline rose more sharply and they skidded with every step, the light skewing wildly from Gabriel's wrist, dimming as they drew near daylight. At the very end there were rocks and boulders, a haphazard camouflage still effective against eyes outside, but time had loosened and tumbled them and there were gaps. The following drone had become a roar. Hanna and Gabriel squeezed through separate cracks into a deep hollow. There was frozen mud underfoot, the color of drying blood in dim morning light.

Hanna thought she could not take another step, but Gabriel grabbed her and pulled, squinting in natural light that blinded them, though the lowering sky was gray. The wall of the hollow rose more steeply yet and they half-climbed, half-crawled up it, grasping at handholds with fingernails, and they made it to the lip of the hollow and over it, a meter farther, two meters, four, before Hanna collapsed on stony flat ground, too numb to feel the cold of snow scattered over more ice. She heard Gabriel say, "Where's the goddam shuttle?" and could not answer, but he had said it to the communicator.

"ETA five minutes," said Metra's voice, and Gabriel said, "*Why?* Why isn't it here?"

Hanna would have cursed too, if she had had enough breath. She had counted on that shuttle, like Gabriel; she had thought it would be there if they made it this far. Below them, at the end of the tunnel, machine-roar swelled and died with a cough. Gabriel spun to face it, and where in God's name had he gotten the strength to move so fast, Hanna thought, and saw that his eyes were wild. She had never seen him angry until now; threat piled on threat had stripped him to instinct, to pure self-preservation. He looked like someone she had never seen before. He looked murderous.

In the silence there was a scrabbling in the barricade, out of sight from their vantage. Gabriel bent and picked up a rock with his wounded right hand. It must hurt, but he curled his fingers around it in a practiced, complicated grip. She wanted desperately to think *No!* to him and tried but there was nothing, and when she tried to shout it she did not have the breath; and why would she want him to hold back anyway if this was Kwoort? That last glimpse of Kwoort's mind had shown that he meant to kill them. Gabriel drew back his arm, and she did not know what to hope for: that his wasted muscles could not throw a rock with fatal force, or that a final burst of energy would cave in Kwoort's skull.

But Kwoort's head appeared and Gabriel did not move. Kwoort's shoulders now, and now his hands: one held a spindly weapon. Kwoort came all the way out of the hollow and raised the weapon, and Gabriel hurled the rock.

To Hanna's complete astonishment it connected cleanly with Kwoort's wrist. He yelled and dropped the weapon at his feet.

Hanna tried to get up and could not. Her mind would not obey her and now her muscles would not either. She made it to all fours and saw Gabriel launch himself at Kwoort, for a second he seemed horizontal, feet off the ground, and Hanna thought *He is flying* and Gabriel's head rammed hard into Kwoort's chest.

They disappeared, tumbling back into the hollow.

Kwoort's boot had jerked against the weapon and it vanished with them.

Hanna crawled toward the edge of the dip in the land. Time stopped. It would take forever to get there but she had forever. There was time to feel each separate ice crystal in the mud under her hands, each frozen shred of some dried-up creeper that would not part from its roots. The wind had stopped and she heard a faint sound from the hollow, a desperate sucking noise, and more sounds from the rough barricade, and finally a voice. It was not Gabriel's. She crept to the top of the incline and looked over.

Kakrekt was there, crouched by Kwoort. The sucking noise came from his breathing tubes, and he heaved on the ground in his struggle for air; Gabriel's hard head had knocked all the breath out of his chest. But what had it done to Gabriel's skull and neck, his spine?—he lay near Kwoort, unmoving. A Warrior Hanna had not seen before hung back among the barricading rocks. Kakrekt said something to Kwoort and turned to Gabriel, took hold of one shoulder and shook him, but Gabriel did not respond. There was another voice, too, coming from the communicator, but Hanna could not tell what it was saying, and Kakrekt suddenly pulled it from Gabriel's wrist and stood. Kakrekt looked at the communicator closely.

Hanna had once seen a mortally wounded animal, savaged by a predator, struggle to move toward some illusory refuge. She moved as mindlessly as that animal, toward Gabriel, rolling over the lip of the steep decline, clutching for handholds by reflex but mostly sliding to the bottom. Somehow she was on her feet, stumbling to him and sinking to the ground again, a hand floating to his chest. She felt the slight expansion of a breath. Her hands moved of their own accord, stroking his chest and his forehead, tangling in his hair, trying to think his name to him and finally calling aloud, "Gabriel, come back, come back!"

His head turned a little and his lips moved. The breath that came out might have been her name. Then he moved a hand.

She helped him sit up, a slow process. Her mind began to work again—within limits; she tried to remember what she knew about concussion and failed, tried to think of what she might do to get them out of this and failed at that too.

The weapon that had gone over the edge with Kwoort lay between him and Kakrekt on the mud, but she could not get to it without being noticed.

The hollow was full of eerie silence. Wind had started up above their heads, a distant whisper. Not even the communicator made a sound. Then Gabriel muttered, "Better."

"Are you hurt?"

"Head hurts . . ."

Slowly Hanna became aware of movement around them. Kwoort had gotten his breath back and he struggled to his feet, calling for Warrior Woke. The Warrior came up to him; she held the satchel Kwoort had carried everywhere. Kakrekt had backed away a little from the four of them. There was a weapon in her hand, but she was not aiming it.

"Shuttle," Gabriel said. It was still hard for him to speak.

Hanna looked up into the low clouds, but no shape darkened them. "It's not here," she said.

"Tell them. Get back."

"Holy One," she said. "Kakrekt Commander. You should move away from this area. An aircraft will be here momentarily to remove us."

Kwoort snarled, "If I had known that I would have brought an army. I would have brought missiles."

Hanna opened her mouth to start the *We mean you no harm* speech. Closed it. She was tired of saying it and it wouldn't do any good.

Kwoort started toward them, stumbling. Kakrekt moved forward swiftly and tripped him, and he fell again. There was a constriction in Hanna's throat and she recognized it as pity. It was the last thing she had ever expected to feel for Kwoort.

Kakrekt was plainly in charge. Hanna said softly, "What are you going to do now?"

Kakrekt's mouth moved. It might have been the beginning of a smile, but it was gone at once. She turned, lifting the weapon, and it hissed. *What?* Hanna thought, because nothing happened for a second, and then Woke went down all at once and without a sound. There was no blood, no charring, nothing.

Colloidal disruptor, Hanna thought, but the thought was automatic. No more complex thought occurred. She was not capable of complex thought.

Gabriel said to Kakrekt, his voice faint but calm, "Why did you do that? What did this Warrior do to you?"

"She did nothing. She was only present. Now there will be no living witness to carry the facts back to Wektt."

"Witness to what? Do you mean to kill us too?"

"Not you," Kakrekt said. Her eyes—all four open wide—turned to Kwoort. "I could not do this openly. But if there is no witness, I do not have to wait any longer. When I am asked why the Holy Man did not come back, I can say anything."

Kwoort got up. His eyes were all open too, as if he meant to remember this episode well—as if he thought he would live to remember it. The smile Kakrekt had not produced pushed out from his face, and his ears lifted and waved. Laughter.

"You see incongruity, old Soldier?" said Kakrekt.

"Old Warrior, how much do you forget?"

"I forget nothing," said Kakrekt.

"Never? You do not say 'Why did you attack that point?' and hear 'It was your order'? You do not make notes to yourself of this and that because you find, more and more often, that if you do not write things down, you might forget?"

"Nothing of the kind has happened," said Kakrekt.

"I do not believe you," Kwoort said. "I think you lie. I am sure that you do. But perhaps you have not yet come to the next passage—you have not begun to forget that you forget. Do you think you are different? Do you think you will not one day desire the final madness—one day when you know you have forgotten nearly everything and worse, the day when you want only to forget what you still know—do you think you will not want to cease to survive? Wanting to know the past will only hasten that day because you will see—"

He took a step toward Kakrekt and she shifted the weapon. He began to talk again, his voice getting louder and louder. "You will see that it is no use, nothing is any use! Soldiers will breed and breed and if we do not encourage death they will find the Great Weapon again in the end and all will die! It nearly happened in my lifetime, I saw the summer when it happened, I saw the end of it—I am sure you did too, I am sure you lived then! Do you not know it will be your duty, it has been my duty, to send Soldiers to their deaths in multitudes to prevent it happening again!" He screamed now: "We all come to this point! All the Holy Men! We forget, we see we must force others to forget, we must tell them God demands that they forget, because breeding allows no change, it is how we are made, and it is too bitter to live with this knowledge—that we leave nothing lasting after us, only the same death over and over! I have not forgotten quickly enough! Kill me! I order you, my last order! Kill me!"

And Kakrekt, her hand now shaking, lifted the weapon and it hissed once more.

———

If only he had died at once, Hanna thought later, over and over.

He seemed to stretch, arms flung high, reaching interminably toward cloud, and he swayed, bending now forward and now back as if his bones had dissolved to liquid, head lolling, feet rooted in the mud, but all his eyes were open and looked everywhere. She felt Gabriel's hand behind her head, urging her face to his chest, an instinctive gesture of one used to protecting children, but she resisted, even though she had seen enough horrors, as if she owed it to Kwoort to bear witness to the end of a millennium of life. So she saw Kwoort take two last staggering steps, convulsing, arms still flailing; then she did turn to Gabriel and close her eyes, but she heard the monumental crash, surely louder than a single Soldier's fall should sound. She heard someone moaning. She did not understand until later that she had heard herself.

Crushed in Gabriel's embrace she did not hear, either, the faint sound that made him tense and shift, looking upward; but she finally opened her eyes and looked up too, following Gabriel's attention, and saw the shadow that broke through the clouds: *Endeavor*'s shuttle at last.

She heard Gabriel say to Kakrekt, "I would put that away if I were you"—he nodded toward the weapon, and Kakrekt made it vanish.

And now they will not have to go away, Kakrekt thought.

Hanna whispered, "Oh, my God"—she had heard the thought.

The shuttle eased onto the plateau and wordlessly they began to climb upward again, holding tight to each other. They did not say anything to Kakrekt. She had not moved and did not speak either. They had made little progress when two figures appeared above them. "Keep going. Board the shuttle," one said; they were machines, many-armed servos, and they started down the steep incline, sure-footed, and passed them without stopping or speaking again.

"What—?" said Gabriel, starting to turn around and almost falling; Hanna saw blankly that he had picked up Kwoort's satchel without her noticing, and the weight, however slight, affected what was left of his balance.

"I don't care. Come on," Hanna said. Another difficult step, and another: she had never been so glad for the Polity's rescue. "Come *on!*" she said. But Gabriel stayed where he was and she felt—*felt*, yes!—his uncertainty on the steep slope, and finally she turned around too and saw the servos' purpose. They went to the bodies of Kwoort and Woke Warrior and picked them up and started back after Hanna and Gabriel.

Kakrekt still had not moved. Telepathy had shut down again and Hanna could feel nothing of her thought. If Kakrekt was anxious or apprehensive there was no sign of it.

Something touched her arm and said, "Do you need to be carried?"

It was another servo. Gabriel said, "No, but let us hold on to you. Go slowly."

From just below them Kakrekt finally called out: "Come back in a summer or two and see what I have done." And she was not finished; there was another shout. "Nakeekt lied!"

Hanna stopped at this, and the servo obediently stopped too. She turned, but still she did not speak.

"Yes," Kakrekt said, more quietly, but every word carried through the cold air and pierced Hanna's heart. "I get more information than you know. More than Nakeekt knows. Those leaves, prepared as she said—the distillate is a pleasant beverage. Nothing more. Was it difficult for you, deciding what to do? There was no need. It would have made no difference. It was your fellow-Soldier who made the difference, here and now, when he put the Holy One alone and unarmed into my hands. The Holy One never gave you what you want, but I will."

Kakrekt lifted a hand, the one that had not held the weapon, and Hanna saw the communicator.

"You will return. I will be waiting," Kakrekt said.

Chapter XX

THE SHUTTLE WAS CONSIDERABLY larger than the pod, but it seemed crowded with servos sent to dig or fight. Hanna—falling into a seat, steadying Gabriel (or being steadied by him) as he fell into another—saw one human being, Corcoran, in the pilot's seat, and shrank from the horror on his face as he looked at them. Possibly the servos looked more human than they did. It did not stop him from accelerating upward so fast that the layers of cloud blurred. *Now* he's hurrying, she thought. She must have projected it uncontrollably and unknowingly because he said, "Got what I came for, no reason to wait around. They blew up two transports, didn't they?"

And just as uncontrollably Hanna saw that she and Gabriel had been secondary objects. Soldiers—specimens—had been the first. Metra had held the rescue back deliberately, allowing them to remain in danger, looking for one last advantage without putting the shuttle at risk, probably with spyeyes transmitting the last flurry of violence—

And in that second's flash from Corcoran—oh, telepathy was back, all right, back with a vengeance—she knew that Metra had not done it all on her own responsibility. She had done it with Commission approval. Starr's approval.

Metra's voice came into the capsule, urgent.

"Maximum speed, at once. Incoming data indicate Commander Kwoort is still alive."

Hanna froze. Next to her Gabriel whispered, "Thank God."

But Hanna thought: *If only he had died at once.*

PART SIX

OLD EARTH

Chapter I

SHE WAS SLAPPED INTO *Endeavor*'s sickbay so fast her head spun. She was injected with nutrients, someone cut off much of her hopeless hair, and she was admired as the only case of starvation the medics had seen outside textbooks; Gabriel, she was assured, was equally admired. All this she gathered in dozy fragments, finally surrendering to exhaustion and a sedative she did not want or (in her opinion) need. In another fragment she was walked carefully through *Endeavor* and transferred—somewhere—with measured haste, where the same things happened again, though she would not let these new medics shear off any more hair, the importance of retaining it swelling out of all proportion.

When she was allowed to emerge naturally from the haze she found that she and Gabriel were on the *Admiral Wu*. They were prescribed gentle exercise and slow progress with real food, combined with short periods of debriefing and long ones of rest.

There was time to assess the damage.

———

Hanna, as soon as she could leave sickbay, spent as much time as she could in a lounge reserved for important passengers. It was large (that was in its favor) and one wall looked out into space, giving the specious impression that there was an escape route at hand. She had not suspected how important that would be. She had not understood until now that during the long captivity in Wektt she had vigorously suppressed memories of other occasions, more brutal but much shorter, when she had been a captive. The *Admiral Wu* was moving fast; even given that a course, once painstakingly charted, could be retraced at enormous speed, it seemed to be proceeding too fast for comfort, and the staccato Jumps that made for rapidly shifting starscapes were disconcerting. All the same, Hanna would have slept in the lounge, if it had been allowed, just so that she would be reassured, when she opened her eyes, that she was no longer confined to the tiny room deep under Wektt.

She suspected she had become claustrophobic. Time would take care of it, she thought. It didn't seem important. She had, as she had said to Bella, gotten over worse.

Gabriel's default for damage control was prayer.

Should I not, Lord, feel penitent? It was my hand that disarmed Kwoort and left him helpless before his enemy, even though I pitied him, even though he was Your child as much as I. But all I find in my heart is sorrow, I find regret, but I do not find guilt. I live. A woman lives and goes home to her child. That must be enough.

Still there is need for penance. Show me what You would have me do. Lord, I listen . . .

Hanna touched him in one of these private intervals, but only once. He seemed to her remote in a way that eerily resembled trance. It was not detachment she sensed, though, but passionate engagement with . . . something.

How brave he was, she thought, after what he had seen, to still believe.

The two of them had a secret. *Don't bring it up,* she said in an urgent pulse of thought just before debriefing began, and the question in his mind meant, *What if they ask,* and she said, *They won't.*

Later he came to see her in the lounge, which she had already begun to think of as her personal property. Uncharacteristically, he was frowning. He sat down next to her, leaned close, and whispered, "Is anybody listening?"

"Eavesdropping, you mean? Here? No," she said in surprise. "Why?"

"Nobody asked me about *that.* What you told me not to tell them about."

"That's because I never reported anything about it. It

never seemed to be the time for it, when everybody was talking about negotiations. So-called."

"But we've got to tell somebody."

"Well, of course we do. Oh. No, no," she said. "Did you think I'd keep *that* to myself? No! But," she said, "it's too important for just anybody to hear about. I'm going to tell Starr. And I'm glad, I'll be so glad, when it's the Commission's secret, not mine."

———

Eight days after they left Battleground—*Wu* pushing protocols and moving from Jump to Jump at battle-ready speeds—they were on Earth. Hanna refused to do anything until she had seen Mickey, though much of their reunion was given over to an explanation that sometimes people cried not because they were unhappy, but because they were so filled with happiness that it could not be contained.

After that she had to go and do something else. The path led, inevitably, to Starr Jameson. It always did.

Chapter II

"WE'LL HAVE TO SEND someone back," he said. "Not you personally, I hope"—he wasn't promising, Hanna noticed—"someone else. But there's no hurry. We have enough to go on with for now."

They were in the quarters Jameson had reclaimed, the commissioner's suite that was a kind of warren of its own, though this room, his most private office, opened out to water and sky and land. Hanna turned in her seat to look out at the river, merged flawlessly with interior space, just as she remembered. The water was blue today, like the gloriously clear sky above it. The last time she had been in this room with Jameson, not long before first contact with Zeig-Daru, they had hardly known each other, but on that occasion she had recognized the attraction between them for the first time. Now that she was physically in the same room as Jameson once more, she recognized something else. She might go away, but the attraction was not going to. In spite of her declaration of freedom, exasperatingly, she could not help wanting him. The bond between them might be attenuated, but it was not broken.

She knew that for his part he was not shocked by how she looked, which was better but still bad. Nor was he repelled by her emaciation, as he had not been by her pregnancy. She felt his desire to take her in his arms, take her to his home just as he had when she returned, battered, from other missions. He wanted to give her all she needed to get well and more; he wanted to give her everything he thought she should want.

This time she would not allow it, bond or no bond. And the first thing she said was a reminder of all the reasons why she would not.

"That's what the delay with the shuttle was about? To make sure you got what you wanted?"

"We needed a Soldier out in the open, alone and isolated from a population center. Kakrekt gave us two. She'll gloss over their disappearance for her own purposes. Whether Kwoort will ever be conscious again is questionable, but he doesn't have to be. The other can be dissected down to the cellular level and beyond. If we can't get what we need from those two specimens there's always Kakrekt. Willing to trade."

"I don't think so," Hanna said.

He waved a hand with uncharacteristic vagueness. He seemed, Hanna thought, to be divided. He thought Battleground was sorted out, and now that he had Hanna in front of him again in the flesh (what was left of it), he would like to return to his peculiar brand of courtship. She was almost sorry that she had to tell him sorting out Battleground was about to become the least of his concerns.

She said, "We could help Kakrekt to the knowledge she wants, but when she's gone, who else will want it? And she won't remember much longer that she wants us to help her change the world. She'd never do that anyway. No one will."

"A world is a hard thing to change, but it can be done. What makes you so certain this one can't be?"

"It will be in my final report," Hanna said. "About what I saw in the breeding ground. The facilitators weren't just taking nourishment. They were pumping in fluids at the same time. This is a guess, but I'll bet you. When you dissect poor Woke I bet you'll find something missing from her ova, or whatever she has, and the same from Kwoort's sperm: great big chunks of Soldier DNA. That's what the facilitators carry and that's how they've evolved their power—they're a delivery system for the rest of the DNA. Making more Soldiers is their only function. The Holy Men don't know the mechanism, but they understand it can't be fought. And the facilitators are mindless. *They* control Battleground. Kakrekt never will."

He might have questioned her further, but then she said—she had to take a deep breath first—"There's something else."

He knew every shade of her voice. He did not ask what she meant. He only waited.

"Somebody else made Soldiers," she said. "To fight, maybe. Well, of course to fight. What else can they do? Somebody took a native mammal—if Soldiers are even native—and bred a sentient species just for that purpose. The physiologists told me there are traces in the genetic makeup. That was the first hint I got. And there's other evidence. Memories of artifacts that don't have any referents in this civilization. Whispers handed from Soldier to Soldier down through centuries. A portrait in an ancient, overgrown—something. Maybe a temple, or an administrative structure. I said 'ancient,' but it's not all *that* old if Kakrekt's people could just stumble on it. The face in the portrait wasn't a Soldier. It wasn't like anything else we've ever seen."

He saw the implications immediately. "Are you sure?" he said, but it was not necessary. He knew her; he knew she would not have said so if she was not sure.

She nodded, and watched his eyes lose all warmth. A few minutes ago she had been talking to a man. Now he was all commissioner.

He did not move while she described the physiologists' findings, the overgrown structure Kakrekt had shown her, the stories Nakeekt had compiled. His attention did not flag. He would retain every word.

She finished, "What kind of creatures would do that? Why would they need enormous numbers of completely expendable fighters who aren't afraid to die, who only live to die? The creators didn't care what might happen when Soldiers got old, about the increase in intelligence and self-will, or maybe they didn't even know. They might have expected Soldiers all to die before they reached that stage. Possibly, if they didn't die, they were slaughtered. I don't think," she said, "we want to meet beings who would do that."

But humankind was moving inexorably outward, and Hanna knew as well as he did that an eventual meeting might be unavoidable.

Jameson's gaze turned inward. Hanna did not have to read his mind to know what he would think, because she had already thought it. That meeting should be avoided as long as possible.

And the creators, even if they had been gone for centuries, might return to Battleground. There must be not even the slightest trace of humankind there for them to find.

After a while Jameson said, "We'll have to get back everything you left behind. Kakrekt has the communicator you gave Kwek. What else?"

"Gabriel left a translator at That Place. That's all. We went into Wektt the last time with nothing but the clothes on our backs. And not nearly enough rations," she said with some resentment.

"Are you sure that was all? Kwoort took a weapon from you when you arrived. We know what happened to that. But you had com units, didn't you? And he took those too?"

"Yes. I forgot . . ." Hanna rubbed her face. She still tired easily. It seemed she could not trust her memory yet, either. "Maybe Kakrekt can put her hands on them. She might not want to return them, but I suppose . . . I suppose you can get them one way or another."

"Mmm," he said, already thinking of something else.

Hanna said it for him. "Equipment is tangible. There is also memory."

He met her eyes across—again across, still across—an official desk, their positions unchanged.

"How many do you think you will have to assassinate?" she said.

He heard accusation in her voice. Instead of answering directly, he said, "You were prepared to collaborate with Kakrekt in eliminating Kwoort, were you not? How is that different, except as a matter of scale?"

"I never really had to decide," she said quietly. "Events made it unnecessary in the end—and Nakeekt cheated anyway. What she sent Kakrekt wouldn't have killed Kwoort."

"But you considered it."

"I considered it."

Something hurt in her chest. She heard Arch say: *Does the word 'corruption' mean anything to you?*

"You wouldn't have to kill anybody," she said. "Kakrekt . . . Nakeekt . . . Tlorr . . . they're all aging. They'll forget soon."

"Maybe in Wektt and Rowtt. But at That Place?" he said. He watched her closely. He would know there had been time, in the journey to Earth, to think the situation through. "Nakeekt will be writing everything down, filing it away in her archives. And what of her lieutenants? What of the rest of the Soldiers there? Soldiers don't go to That Place unless they've reached a certain level of development. You can be sure that even if Nakeekt is gone, others will remember. And they'll write things down too."

Silence stretched between them. Jameson would not break it.

Hanna said finally. "I thought what you're thinking. But then I thought, there's another way. Could you bring them here, the people from That Place? If not to Earth, to a colony. New Earth, perhaps?"

"Nova. They've decided to call it Nova, at last report. Unless they've changed their minds again."

Hanna ignored the digression. "You want to study Soldiers. If it's that or killing all of them . . ."

A longer silence this time, while he considered the possibilities.

Finally he said, "There would be problems, but advantages too." Hanna only nodded, but she felt herself relax a little. It was enough that he was willing to consider it, and she did not doubt that if he approved, he would be able to convince the rest of the commissioners. And she thought that on reflection he would approve. Thousands of living subjects who could be studied in comfortable surroundings would be a tempting prospect.

It was not ideal. All the Soldiers who lived at That Place would be torn from their home, their way of life dissolved; they would be sundered from the younger peers who might have joined them one day. There was a chilling parallel to the history of Hanna's own ancestors, exiled from Earth.

But it would forestall mass murder. Hanna had not been able to think of any other course that would.

She had one more thing to say. She had to, though she said it without hope.

"Starr . . . I want to go home."

"Go, then." He smiled. "Zanté and Thera insisted on showing it to me. It's beautiful, and you've hardly seen it."

"No, I mean *home*, to D'neera. I know I can't stay, because of Mickey, but—just to be free to go there, to leave Earth when I choose—Do you think the Commission would pardon me now? Haven't I earned it?"

He took in a long breath and let it out. He said almost helplessly, "Oh, my dear . . . you've earned it, certainly. But after what you've just told me, especially . . ."

It was not going to be good news; she knew that before he got up and came to her. He held out his hands, wanting her to stand up so he could hold her, but she did not move, and finally he let his empty hands drop.

"Battleground will be interdicted," he said. "We would have done that in any case, because Soldiers' inability to travel in space is sufficient reason for withdrawal. We meant to continue dealing with Kakrekt, though. Now . . . whatever we do there, we'll have to do it and get out as quickly as possible. If there's a chance of the creators returning, humans will not go near Battleground again. Maybe, if there are results from the research someday, we'll be able to present the mission as a qualified success. But not yet. The best we'll be able to say for some time to come is that it wasn't a complete failure. And your part . . ."

Hanna looked back at the river. She was not going to meet his eyes.

"They'll tell me," he said, and there was genuine sadness there, "that you didn't really play a large part in what success we can claim. They'll tell me you just did your job."

Neither of them moved for some seconds that felt like years. Finally Hanna did get up. She was preoccupied with thoughts of captivity, the varieties of it. She meant to walk away from Jameson without another word, not for the first time but maybe for the last.

He said behind her, "Are you sure you ought to be alone? I could come with you—"

"I won't be alone." She turned to face him, to speak after all. It was a large room. She seemed to be looking at him across the space of light-years again. "Thera and Mickey are there. And Gabriel. I want Gabriel to go through my program and then I want him working for Contact. He'd be the perfect liaison for a group of displaced exiles on Nova. I trust you have no objection? I can have that reward, at least? And he's going to live with me until he's ready to move on. I'm not even going to ask if you object to that."

She turned once more, and was gone.

Chapter III

THE DOMICILE HAD TRANSPARENT walls and its highest levels seemed to float in a bower of trees. It spilled down a river bluff and was located next to a great park that bordered, on the opposite edge, half an hour's walk away, Starr Jameson's property. The place had been purchased by Province Koroth at considerable expense, justified by the argument that many D'neerans would like to see Earth for themselves but did not go because there were no telepath-friendly accommodations. Evidently the price Hanna must pay for a home of her own was to become an innkeeper. If it meant the company of D'neerans, she was all for it. None seemed inclined to come immediately, however. It would take time for D'neerans to get used to the idea.

Mickey learned where the doors were, and the words to open them, at once. Gabriel programmed the doors to respond to a particular sequence of barks, and the Dog learned how to open them almost as quickly as Mickey. The Cat just sat by the wall wherever it chose and said *Meow* until someone came and picked it up and put it out. Sun and moonlight poured in from all sides; in the daytime it was seldom necessary to use artificial light.

Even so, Hanna spent much of her time outdoors, and did much of her work there, conversing, analyzing, posing questions to her students and answering more while she ran after Mickey and the Dog and went after the Cat when its transmitter said it had gotten too far away. She once delivered part of a lecture on F'thalian dual-brain communication while halfway up a tree, attempting to coax the Cat out of it. Adair Evanomen was stunned by the expense of the mobile holo unit that accompanied her, but was afraid to deny it. She was easier to get along with than he had expected, and she never went over his head—but she might.

This in spite of the fact that she rarely saw Starr Jameson. He survived A.S. again—alone—and resumed an old pattern of sporadic, short-lived affairs. After each, however, he came to see Hanna, each time asking, essentially, *Now?* She saw the loneliness that echoed hers (though no one else did) and her answer eventually changed from *No* to *Maybe next year or the year after that,* so perhaps his hope was justified. And she never did take off the ring.

She was known, among the few people who paid attention, for her choice of venue for seminars covering Battleground. For these sessions Gabriel, until he left Earth for Nova, was not a pupil but stood beside her. She conducted them at Admin, indoors, in tiny windowless rooms that felt unbearably confining. Her students consequently did not devote much attention to Battleground. Hanna said that was all right. The small population on Nova could not reproduce and soon would die out, and the civilization on Battleground, she told them, was not going to last long enough to warrant attention.

But at irregular intervals, she went to see Kwoort where he lay on the edge of life, the shell of his body retained for undisclosed reasons even though the researchers on Nova had specimens enough. *What do you do there,* she was asked, and answered: *I talk to a ghost.*

But the ghost was not Kwoort's, as people supposed—except that once, and only once, she said: *I read the papers, the ones you kept in that sack, the only memory you could count on keeping. I read what you needed to write down.*

Mostly, though, she looked at her life at these times; she acknowledged that she remained the Polity's tool; and the ghost she talked to was her own.

this is not the life we wanted, one of them said.
it's what we have. it's not bad
can we change it
no we can't
do we want to
i don't know
i don't either
any more

RM Meluch
The Tour of the Merrimack

"This is grand old-fashioned space opera, so toss your disbelief out the nearest airlock and dive in."
—*Publishers Weekly* (starred review)

THE MYRIAD	978-0-7564-0320-1
WOLF STAR	978-0-7564-0383-6
THE SAGITTARIUS COMMAND	978-0-7564-0490-1
STRENGTH AND HONOR	978-0-7564-0578-6
THE NINTH CIRCLE	978-0-7564-0764-3

*Available October and November 2013
in brand new two-in-one omnibus editions!*

Tour of the Merrimack: Volume One
(The Myriad & Wolf Star)
978-0-7564-0954-8

Tour of the Merrimack: Volume Two
(The Sagittarius Command & Strength and Honor)
978-0-7564-0955-5

To Order Call: 1-800-788-6262
www.dawbooks.com

DAW 48

S. Andrew Swann
The Apotheosis Trilogy

It's been nearly two hundred years since the collapse of the Confederacy, the last government to claim humanity's colonies. So when signals come in revealing lost human colonies that could shift the power balance, the race is on between the Caliphate ships and a small team of scientists and mercenaries. But what awaits them all is a threat far beyond the scope of any human government.

PROPHETS
978-0-7564-0541-0

HERETICS
978-0-7564-0613-4

MESSIAH
978-0-7564-0657-8

To Order Call: 1-800-788-6262
www.dawbooks.com

DAW 161

Tanya Huff
The *Confederation* Novels

"As a heroine, Kerr shines. She is cut from the same mold
as Ellen Ripley of the Aliens films. Like her heroine,
Huff delivers the goods." —*SF Weekly*

A CONFEDERATION OF VALOR
Omnibus Edition
(*Valor's Choice, The Better Part of Valor*)
978-0-7564-0399-7

THE HEART OF VALOR
978-0-7564-0481-9

VALOR'S TRIAL
978-0-7564-0557-1

THE TRUTH OF VALOR
978-0-7564-0684-4

To Order Call: 1-800-788-6262
www.dawbooks.com

CJ Cherryh
The Foreigner Novels

"Serious space opera at its very best by one of the leading
SF writers in the field today." —*Publishers Weekly*

"Her world building, aliens, and suspense rank among
the strongest in the whole SF field. May those
strengths be sustained indefinitely, or at least
until the end of *Foreigner*." —*Booklist*

To Order Call: 1-800-788-6262

www.dawbooks.com